C000063578

SPECIAL OPS SHIFTERS: DALLAS FORCE

THE COMPLETE SERIES COLLECTION

MEG RIPLEY

SHIFTER NATION

Copyright © 2020 by Meg Ripley
www.redlilypublishing.com

All rights reserved. Printed in the United States of America. No part of this book may be used or reproduced in any manner whatsoever without written permission except in the case of brief quotations embodied in critical articles or reviews.

This book is a work of fiction. Names, characters, businesses, organizations, places, events and incidents either are the product of the author's imagination or are used fictitiously. Any resemblance to actual persons, living or dead, events, or locales is entirely coincidental.

Disclaimer

This book is intended for readers age 18 and over. It contains mature situations and language that may be objectionable to some readers.

CONTENTS

RESCUED BY THE SOLDIER BEAR

SPECIAL OPS SHIFTERS: DALLAS FORCE

1

ASH LEANED FORWARD OVER THE BATHROOM SINK, TRYING TO get a better look at the gray hairs that were slowly making themselves known at his temples. The light was dim and yellow, making it difficult, and he gave up with a sweep of his hand. He considered a shave but decided against it, then grabbed a coat and headed downstairs.

"Where are you off to today?" Old Jim was a well-known resident in this part of Fairbanks, and even though Ash had only been living there for a few months, he was starting to think of the old geezer as one of his good friends. Jim sat in a chair in the corner of the small lobby of the apartment building, which served as nothing more than a place to pick up mail and maybe harass the landlord about a frozen pipe. The elderly man seemed to take incredible delight in seeing the comings and goings of his neighbors, and Ash couldn't help but indulge him.

"Just going to look at another property," he replied as he shrugged into his green Berne work coat. He was never a man who minded the frigid weather, but it seemed a necessity if he was going to spend the rest of his life in a place like Alaska.

Jim squinted, making his narrow eyes little more than slits. "Ain't you already done that?"

Ash laughed. "Yes, and more times than I'd like to admit. Probably more times than my real estate agent would like to admit, too."

"Might as well just settle down right here in Fairbanks. We've got it all, you know. No need to go anywhere else." He made a grand gesture with a wrinkled hand to indicate the entire city, as though it was Jim's to offer. "Many a man has made himself rich here, you know."

"So I've heard." Ash swiped a hand over his face to hide his amused smile. Jim claimed to be an ancestor of E.T. Barnette, who founded Fairbanks in 1901. Perhaps because of the DNA he felt he shared with such an important man, Jim took it upon his shoulders to educate everyone who happened to come within speaking distance. And he usually didn't stop at just one rendition. Ash had heard the stories about a hundred times already, and his friendliness and patience could only go so far. "I think I need something a little further outside the city, though. I'm heading out to look at a big ranch today."

Jim nodded slowly, his gray mustache twitching as he muddled over his next words. "You know, I had a ranch once."

Oh, no, Ash thought. *Here he goes again.* If he would've allowed him to keep rambling, he'd be late. "I'll have to catch up with you about that later, Jim. I don't want to be late, and you know how it is traveling around here." Ash waved goodbye as he trotted out the door to his truck.

An hour later, he was standing at the end of a driveway looking at an impressive log cabin. The mountains in the distance gave a stark but gorgeous contrast to the flat land of the parcel, where the ground was brilliant green with the beginnings of a crop. Ash wished he knew enough to recognize what it was, but at the moment, it simply looked like a verdant carpet that stretched off into the distance toward a massive metal building.

"It's currently being operated as a very successful cattle ranch," explained Mr. Larson, pushing back his sport coat to tuck his thumbs into the front pocket of his jeans. He was dressed like many of the professionals Ash had met during his time in Alaska, who wore button-down shirts, ties, and sport coats over their jeans and boots. "I think it's just what you're looking for. Natural water source, flat land, highway access—and you know how important that can be in this area if you don't own your own plane. Note the equipment shed right over there. It comes complete with everything you need since the owners are retiring and moving to the city. All your tractors and mowers and everything else!"

Ash felt a deep wrinkle forming between his eyebrows. The place was beautiful; there was no doubt about it. It felt more right than the other properties he'd looked at before, but it was still missing something. "Yeah... I don't know."

"Of course you don't!" Mr. Larson enthused, throwing his hands up in the air. "We've hardly even looked at the place. C'mon." He led the way up to the house, where he fiddled with a lock box for a moment until he could get the door open. "This place is just magnificent. I know when you think of a ranch, you're picturing some bare-bones, barely livable tin shack. But clearly, the Alaskan wilderness has far more to offer than that! Check out this beautiful double-sided fireplace that serves both the living room and the kitchen with this open floor plan."

"Yes, it's very nice." Ash turned toward a large window to check out the view, but also to roll his eyes. Mr. Larson had been recommended as one of the best realtors in the area, but he reminded Ash of a sleazy car salesman. "I'm not sure I need a home this big, though. It's just me."

"You never know what your future might hold. A beautiful bride, perhaps? One who would surely appreciate the granite countertops and radiant heating in the floors." He combed his thick mustache with his fingers and waggled his eyebrows.

"Mm. Doubt it." Ash left the realtor in the living room and wandered through the home. He didn't really need to know that it had a separate office area and several bedrooms. The attached storage area for firewood was useful, and it was convenient that most of the furniture and appliances came with the place, but it was too big for just one man.

In all his life, he'd never felt that incessant urge that came from meeting one's mate. While he was still with Delta Force, it didn't matter much. He couldn't exactly worry about settling down while he was busy running down terrorists and rescuing hostages. It was a hard and rough life, one that he enjoyed for the camaraderie and the excitement. There was something special about knowing he was one of the few men the country trusted with those missions, even if they weren't ones that civilians usually heard about on the evening news.

Over twenty years of that life had been enough, though, and Ash knew it was time to slow down. He hadn't anticipated the first few months of his retirement serving as such a poignant reminder of just how alone he was. There was no woman in his life, and certainly no children. He didn't even know any other shifters nearby, and even in the Alaskan wilderness, Ash was forced to keep the secret of who he truly was.

"Well?" Mr. Larson urged as Ash returned to the living room. "Isn't it great? The structure of this home is remarkable and it's very well insulated."

"Mmhm." Ash could appreciate those kinds of facts, and he could even appreciate the vaulted ceiling that really showed off the stone chimney. It was the best place he'd seen yet and the one closest to what he envisioned for his future. Something, though, still wasn't right.

"Okay, you told me you wanted a ranch. So maybe you're not interested in the house, but you'll be spending all your time outdoors anyway, right? Let's go check out the equipment shed. Talk about big boy toys! Have you done any ranching before?" The realtor stepped out the back door and took long, confident strides toward the metal barn.

Ash pursed his lips as he fell into step beside the man. "Can't say that I have. I'll have a lot to learn."

"Good for you, Mr. Cunningham! We need more people like you out here, men who aren't afraid to take their chances working the land. In this day and age, everyone wants to be involved in technology and the internet. But we need people behind the scenes getting things done." He pumped his fist in the air as he slid the door to the equipment shed aside with a loud creak.

The place was impressive, with a concrete floor, full electrical, and all the tractors and equipment a man could possibly need to run a ranch. But Ash felt the reality of what he was wanting to do as he perused the big machines. Sure, even though Mr. Larson had been a little hokey about it, there was something exciting and almost noble about ranch life. But to do it all by himself? To run a place this big when he didn't really know what he was doing? That was asking a lot of himself, but he wasn't a man to turn down a challenge.

"I see that look on your face," Mr. Larson said, leaning against a steel beam. "You're wondering how you're going to do this."

Ash immediately hardened his features.

"It's all right, any man would be out of his mind if he thought he could just dive in and do this. You've got a lot at stake here, and not just money. Come on." He waved Ash to come along with him as he left the back of the shed and led the way up over a small hill. "You've got all their lives in your hands, too," he said as he pointed toward a large cattle barn. The animals milled about within the sturdy fencing, twitching their ears at the sound of the men's voices.

So this was where they kept them all, far back from the road. Ash inhaled the scent and felt his shoulders relax a little. Maybe this was what had been missing when he'd looked at the front of the property where the house was located. It felt like a luxury cabin at a resort from that angle, but *this* was what he'd come here for.

"Now, here's the most important thing you need to know," the realtor said as he headed down toward the fence, bringing Ash's attention back to him. "The owners are retiring, like I said. They want the simple life in the city, where someone else comes and digs them out of their driveway in the winter and they only have to walk around the corner to get their groceries. But they really care about this place, and they want it to go into the right hands. They're willing to stick around and teach you anything you need to know, from operating the tractors so you can grow your own hay, to fixing fencing and birthing calves."

Ash raised an eyebrow, intrigued. "And how much extra is that going to cost me?"

"Just a little bit of time, really," Mr. Larson replied, and for once, he didn't sound like he was trying to get a job as a travel blogger. "This is really important to them. They've spent their entire lives creating this place and they don't want to see it all go to waste."

"I'll think about it," Ash said with a nod.

The realtor heaved a deep sigh. "Look, Mr. Cunningham, I've got to be honest with you. This ranch hasn't been on the market all that long, but I don't think it's going to stay on the market long, either. Now, I know what you're thinking." He held up a hand to stop Ash from arguing with him. "Realtors say that all the time, and you're probably right. But this truly is a great place, and if you ask me, it's a bargain. I've shown you big farms with little houses and little farms with big houses. I've shown you places close to town and far from town, places near the mountains and places near the water. At every single one of them, you just sort of frown and say you'll think about it. I understand you want something perfect, but I'm starting to wonder if you're going to find it." His amber eyes challenged his client.

He could argue with the man and explain that even as great of a place this was, there was still something that didn't quite fit. But Ash didn't feel the need to waste his energy making a stranger understand his reasoning. He just gave a small shrug. "Like I said, I'll think about it."

As he headed back to his rental, Ash chuckled to himself. Mr. Larson might not see a difference between now and all the other times he'd said those words, but this time, it wasn't just his way of being polite. He really was going to think about it.

"Well?" Old Jim demanded as soon as Ash walked back into the building.

"It's a nice place," Ash admitted with a smile. "I just might buy it."

The old man bobbed his head in approval. "Big place?"

"A few hundred acres," he admitted, his lips splitting in a grin he didn't expect. "It's a great ranch. It's got everything I could ever want and more. I think I might buy it."

"When you need yourself a ranch hand, you give me a holler. I need something to do all day besides just sitting here on my rump."

Ash smiled warmly. "I'll keep that in mind, Jim." He

headed up the stairs to his apartment, feeling good about his decision. Sure, it was a big step, but that was what he'd come there for in the first place. He was ready to get away from the wandering life of a serviceman and settle down. The ranch seemed like a world completely of its own, far enough away from everyone else that he could pretend he was the last man on Earth. He hadn't been sure at first, but now he knew it was the right choice.

As he drew his cell from his pocket and prepared to dial Mr. Larson—and to hear the elated and verbose response from the man—it rang. The caller ID flashed 'Restricted' on the screen and Ash frowned at it. No one should've had his number, since he was always careful who he'd given it to. He glared at it another second before answering it harshly. "Yeah?"

"Is this the great Ash Cunningham I'm speaking to?"

Instinctively, Ash began scanning his apartment for the slightest thing out of place. He didn't recognize the voice on the other end of the line. Had someone been watching him? There were a number of terrorist groups that would've liked to see his head on a pike. "Depends on who's asking."

The man laughed casually. His voice was gravelly and slow, like he had all the time in the world. "The Special Ops Shifter Force. My name's Flint Myers."

"All right." He wasn't going to allow this strange caller

to lead him into offering any information, not even his own name. "What do you want?"

"I take it you've heard of us?"

A shiver of energy thrilled up Ash's spine. Of course he'd heard of the SOS Force. They were an elite group of shifters, all of them trained as Special Ops soldiers. They'd taken the task of handling unusual missions involving shifters of all kinds, all across the U.S. At first, Ash hadn't been completely certain they'd existed. It sounded like too much of an urban legend, the kind of thing someone made up because it sounded cool or they were trying to come up with a new television show. But another man Ash had served with on Delta Force had told him the team had come and solved a dispute in his home clan's territory. "Maybe. Not sure if you're real, though."

"Oh, we're fucking real alright. And the fact that you and plenty of others *have* heard of us," he said pointedly, "is exactly why we need you."

"Need me for what? I'm just a rancher." It was at least about to be true, even if it wasn't true yet.

"Right." Another laugh came through the phone as the connection crackled slightly. "Listen, buddy, I know you're way more than that. And I also know why you wouldn't want to discuss it over the phone with someone you don't know from Adam. That's cool. I just need you to come to Dallas and interview. We're recruiting."

Ash's blood thumped loudly in his throat. *A job? With*

the SOS Force? Was this actually someone trying to recruit him for the most specialized, secretive organization outside of the military? It was hard to tell, but then again, how would anyone know? He could call his buddy from Delta, maybe. "Dallas is a long way from here," he finally answered.

"Yeah, I know. You should be used to traveling a lot, though, and that's not going to change once you're on the Force. We need more people, and we need them to be people like you. You'll get a plane ticket in the mail and it'll have all the information for the meeting as well. See you there, brother." The man hung up, leaving only silence in his wake.

Ash's face was hard as he stared at the phone. He tossed the device on the couch and paced the room, suddenly realizing just how small and confining this damned apartment was. There'd been plenty of small or uncomfortable sleeping arrangements while he was serving in the Army, and he hadn't even blinked when he saw the tiny room that was barely big enough for a couch and a TV stand. He laughed to himself as he realized the irony of living in a tiny place in the middle of such big land. But the humor was quickly lost on him as he felt the need to get outside and be in the wilderness alone. The polar bear inside him craved the need to run free; to break through the confines of his human skin.

He took a deep breath and tried to calm himself. Damn

it. If he'd already bought a ranch, or even just a cabin with some acreage, he'd have been able to satisfy that deep urge to let go. But he was stuck there for the moment, and he was going to have to deal with it just like any other human in the city would've had to. Ash grabbed his coat and headed back downstairs, determined to walk until he managed to clear his head and stifle his inner bear.

"Where are you running off to in such an almighty hurry?" Old Jim questioned before Ash's foot hit the bottom step. "You sound like a wild animal galloping down those stairs!

If he'd only known how right he was. "Just got some thinking to do. Might go get some coffee." He had a perfectly good coffee pot upstairs; one that brewed up a drink far better than the watered-down mud he was used to drinking overseas, but it sounded like a good excuse.

"I'll go with you." The old man barely moved most of the day, but he seemed spry enough as he launched himself out of his chair and grabbed a grubby jacket from the back of it. "I know I could use some coffee."

Ash's mouth clenched against argumentative words. "All right."

The cool spring air was inviting and fresh, and it instantly forced Ash to let go of a little of the tension that had been building inside his body. He inhaled it deeply and let it go, falling into step beside Jim.

"Tell me about it," the old man demanded.

"About what?"

Jim gave a hoot of laughter. "You young'uns think you can keep something a secret just by not saying it out loud, but I'm here to tell you that's not true! Something's weighing heavily on your mind. Go on and spit it out. Might make you feel better."

Ash squinted into the wind as they headed down the sidewalk. What could it hurt? "I told you I was going to buy the ranch."

"Right. So what's the matter with that? Money? Can't help you much there. I never had more money to put in my pocket than what everyone else wanted to take out of it."

"It's not that." Ash hadn't been like many of the other soldiers he'd known, who took the chance on every leave to blow their paychecks down to the last cent. It was tempting, since he never knew if he'd live to see the next day, but he'd always had dreams of doing something big with his funds in the future. "See, I was planning to buy the ranch as my retirement project. I may have retired from the Delta Force, but I know I can't just sit around and watch TV all day. I like to be busy. I need something to do. A cattle ranch sounded like the perfect thing." He realized after saying it that Old Jim might take offense to the part about sitting around all day.

But the man simply nodded as he ran his hands through his scruffy beard. "Sure. It's nice to have a plan."

Ash sighed. It *was* nice to have a plan, but a single

phone call had thrown the entire thing up in the air. He just couldn't decide if he should catch it or not. "But then I got a call about a job offer. It's down south."

"As in Juneau?"

"As in *Dallas*."

"Oh." Jim tucked his hands in his pockets. "That's quite a commute."

Ash snickered, despite the serious nature of his decision. "Yeah, a bit more of one than I'm willing to make. So now I have to decide if I should take the job or buy the ranch."

"I see. That is quite a crossroads. You think you'll like this job?"

"I don't know," Ash admitted. "It'll be a lot like the life I just retired from, I think. It's kind of a dream job, if I were still looking for work."

"You're buying a ranch. That's work," Jim pointed out.

"But it's different work," Ash countered.

"It's more committed work, I reckon. You buy a ranch and have a herd of cattle, and you can't ever leave. You don't get vacations and you don't get to sleep in. You get out there every day and you do what needs to be done. A job? Well, now. That's a bit different."

Ash looked at the old man, who kept his gaze stoically forward. He'd struck Ash as just a simple guy with little to offer to society. Maybe he just hadn't had the chance to offer what he had to anyone while he was sitting in the same spot all day. "That's a good way of looking at it."

A grin split Old Jim's gray beard. "I think so."

By chance, since Ash had left the apartment building and turned in a random direction, they happened on a small café. "Come on, Jim. Let's get some coffee. My treat." He held the door open for the old man, knowing he was going to miss him.

2

LANE SHOOK THE WATER FROM HER SCALES AS SHE LICKED HER lips. It'd been a good day for hunting, and even if the penguins and seals were a bit fatty, at least she had plenty to eat despite the chilly climate. She moved across the rocks near the sea, her long body easily accommodating the rough terrain. If someone happened by and saw a dragon moving along the shore of Antarctica, there was no telling what they'd think.

But that's exactly why we're here, Lane reflected. She and her flight had relocated from the burning hot Arizona desert to the frozen expanse of Antarctica decades ago, when it was clear they could no longer avoid the rapidly expanding urban sprawl that threatened their territory. Lane had resisted the move, at first. She'd enjoyed the heat, and she couldn't imagine what it would be like to live in a place so cold and barren that even humans didn't want to be there.

But it'd quickly become clear to her that this new place was just a snowy version of a desert. It looked empty, but not if you were paying attention. The sea around them was particularly full of life, offering a wide array of animals to snack on, and for the days when she didn't feel like a swim, she could always snag a petrel or two out of the air.

Lane slipped behind an icy boulder and squeezed her body through the small entrance to the cavern that was now their home, the rocks brushing the last of the water from her scales. The entrance was a long and twisted tunnel with a low ceiling, and she shifted to make her passage easier. Her brilliant red scales rippled and disappeared, replaced by smooth porcelain skin. Her clawed feet, which she relied on so much when hunting, became hands and feet as normal as anyone else's, her fingers slender. She whisked her strawberry blonde hair over her shoulder as she made her way into the main area of their home, where the others were waiting for her.

"How was the hunting today?" asked Edi. "I thought about going out myself, but these old bones don't like getting out in the cold these days." She rubbed her shoulder under her dark hair, which was streaked thoroughly with gray now.

"I would've brought something back for you if I'd known you weren't getting out. You should've said something," Lane admonished. She worried for the older dragons in their flight. Survival wasn't always easy there, even if it was possible, and age could only make things more difficult. "I'll go back out and grab something."

"I've got it," offered Liam, running a hand through his shaggy hair as he got up and headed toward the tunnel.

Lane settled down next to Edi and they leaned their shoulders together as they stared at the fire the older woman had built in the center of the cave floor. Their shelter was underground and close to a natural geothermal vent, keeping it much warmer than the surface. In the back, a waterfall dripped into a clear pool that made their own little shoreline. It was pleasant and cozy there, even when the worst storms raged overhead.

"Is he gone?" Edi asked after a moment.

Lane glanced over her shoulder, seeing that Liam was no longer visible. "I think so, why?"

"And the others?"

"I think they're still out hunting," Lane confirmed. Their clan was small compared to the legends of what it had once been when old Edi was still a young dragon, but their numbers were large enough that even in the winding maze of the caverns, they weren't usually alone. "Why?"

"I want to ask you something, but I know it's going to embarrass you."

Lane's cheeks colored before she even knew the question. She'd always blushed easily, and she blamed it on the red tendencies of her hair. "I don't think there's much that everyone else doesn't already know," she reminded her elder. "And if you're going to ask me if I cleaned under my claws and between my teeth after I ate, then the answer is yes."

But Edi shook her head. "Not that, dear. But something just as important. More important."

"Go on." It wasn't like Edi to be cryptic. With the license of her age, she was often bold to the point of being brazen.

Her dark eyes were intense as she stared into Lane's. "How do you feel about Liam?"

"Liam?" Lane glanced over her shoulder again as if the man might suddenly appear. "What do you mean?"

Edi sighed. "I mean, dear, that I hate to see you without a mate. Much of the move here from Arizona was my idea, and I thought at the time that the most important thing was to keep us all safe. But now we're just existing, not really living. I'd like to see you have a little excitement in your life, more than just hunting. Maybe even children."

Lane blinked. "Are you talking about finding a mate?"

"Of course, dear."

Turning to stare into the flames once again, Lane concentrated on the way the heat of them felt against her skin. "It's a nice sentiment, Edi, but that's not going to happen. I've spent plenty of time with every member of this clan, and I would've felt it by now if one of them were my fated."

"Are you sure? You and Liam do get along well," the older woman urged.

"We do, but that doesn't mean we're meant for each other. Edi, I paid attention when you told me all those stories about falling in love and what it felt like. The idea of feeling so passionately for someone that you can't even control yourself is immensely appealing, but it's just a fantasy story at this point. Unless I go flying off to find some other clan, there's no chance of it happening." Lane spoke firmly. She loved Edi, but she wouldn't be goaded into this.

"But aren't you lonely?" Edi pressed.

"Yes," Lane replied, exasperated. "In that way, I suppose I am. It'd be nice to have someone to share a bed with at night; someone to have at my side, no matter what. But I've also got you and the rest of the flight. Why should I bother worrying about it when I already have so much?"

Edi raised a thin eyebrow. "It sounds to me like you're protesting too much."

"Oh, stop," Lane scoffed gently. The old woman could be irritating, but Lane loved her beyond measure. "Look, I know you're trying to help me, but I really don't need any help, Edi. I'm fine just the way I am, and I don't intend to change my position on this. Now if you'll excuse me, I have a few things to do." She rose from her place by the fire, skirting the clear pool and the waterfall.

She didn't really have anything to do at all, but it

seemed easier to pretend like everything was all right than to address the real issue. She was lonely. Most of the day, it was easy to forget about. Lane was busy hunting or spending time with the rest of her people, and that made it all right. But in the long, dark hours of the night, she wondered what it'd be like to have someone wrap his arms around her and hold her tight, to whisper of his love in her ear, and for each of their inner forms to crave the other, even when they were only a room's width apart. It was a fantasy, but it was a nice one.

A crash from the tunnel turned her around before she reached her chamber. It was Liam, still in dragon form, despite the narrow entry. He panted and roared as he came shooting into the cavern, bright blood dripping down his pale blue scales. "Get out! Get out now!"

"What's wrong?" Lane demanded, running toward him, her heart thundering in her chest. "How did you get hurt?"

"They've found us. They're coming in the air. We've got to go!" His eyes rolled with panic.

Edi was on her feet now as well. "Who, Liam? Who's found us?"

"I don't know. The military, I guess. Helicopters and boats, guns. They've already taken down Amy and Brandy! Shot them right out of the air."

Bile rose in Lane's throat as she envisioned the incident and she pressed her hand to her lips. "I don't understand... how..."

"It doesn't really matter *how*," Edi said wisely. "Or who. They're here, and they're clearly not our friends. Liam, did they see you come in here?"

"I'm not sure, but they're everywhere."

The older woman nodded. "All right, then. Let's take the back exit and hope for the best. Liam, you'd better shift. You're lucky you didn't get your ass stuck in the tunnel already, and it's even narrower at the back."

Any other time, he'd have given her hell right back, but there wasn't time. He shifted on the fly, his wings folding down into his back, the spines at the back of his head disappearing into his tousled hair. He moved on four legs and then on two as the trio wound around behind the waterfall.

Lane felt a pang of longing as they passed the split-off areas of the cavern that had served essentially as bedrooms for them all these years. They were primitive dwellings, to be sure, but this was their home. She'd felt this pain once already when they'd left the States, and now, she had to feel it again. It wasn't fair.

"Do you think we can take them?" she asked as they squeezed into a small tunnel. There were numerous passages through there, but they knew all the most important ones by heart. "I mean, we can't just let them chase us away."

"There are too many of them," Liam asserted.

But Lane felt the heat of her fire in her chest, and it

raged as she thought about the enemy taking down her loved ones. "They'd burn just like anything else."

"They've got firepower, too, but the kind that reaches a lot further," he reminded her. "Let's just go."

The ground lifted as the tunnel rose to the surface, and Lane's heart lifted with it until it was up in her throat, practically choking her. The sunlight was too much when they burst through the surface, and it brought tears to her eyes. Maybe they could've gotten away if they were in human form. Maybe the soldiers who were invading their home would've believed they were just innocent scientists and not dragons. Maybe they could have even gone back for those who'd been captured.

But she felt the thump of the helicopter blades even before she saw them, and she heard the roar of engines and gunfire surrounding her. The sounds fueled her feet as she ran through the snow and slipped on the ice. Her instinct was to shift and take wing, to get the hell out of there as fast as possible, and shiver at the back of her neck wasn't due to the cold.

"Oh!"

Lane turned at the sound. Edi had gone down. The old woman waved her on. "Go! Just go!"

"Not without you!" Lane admonished. She put one hand under Edi's arm and tugged. "Just a little further. Then we can duck down into one of the other caves, and—"

Something slammed into Lane's back. She hit the snow with a thump, the frozen crystals smacking against her skin. She'd somehow lost Edi's arm, but when she commanded her fingers to reach out for the old woman, they refused to cooperate. Lane's tongue was thick and it refused to make any words, even though she was screaming inside. Light disappeared from the edges of her vision, as though the sun was swiftly retreating from the sky and out into space. Her entire world went black.

———

A WARM HAND HELD HERS. Lane funneled all her attention to that sensation, taking comfort in the knowledge that someone was with her. Every muscle in her body ached; even her face hurt when she tried to speak.

"Hush, now," Edi said in smooth tones. "You'll be all right."

"What happened?" Lane risked opening her eyes, feeling immediate relief when she saw she was in her chamber. She was home. Everything was all right.

"Well, I'm still trying to figure that out. It's best right now to just lie still and wake up slowly. You'll be right as rain soon enough." Edi's face hovered over hers, a fake smile plastered on it.

"Don't bullshit me. Ow." Lane tried to lift her head, but it felt like it was full of rocks. "Were we attacked?"

"Yes, essentially. They got you with some sort of tran-quilizer. I'm guessing it's the same stuff they got Amy and Brandy with, too."

"What about you?" Lane's heart raced. She was at home, but the enemy must still be nearby. She could hear odd, metallic noises that weren't the normal moans and groans of their cavern.

"I'm too old for them to worry about."

It hurt like hell and her muscles fought her every step of the way, but Lane forced herself to sit up. Sure enough, she was in her chamber. Edi was there next to her, looking healthy except for a scratch on her arm. On the other side of the room, Amy and Brandy lay inert on the floor in their human forms.

Her stomach roiled as she turned her head to find the source of that awful racket. Men in uniforms of snow camouflage were busy building something over the entrance to the room, where the cavern was slightly narrower. "Good god, they're closing us in!"

"Turning it into some sort of prison, I'd say," Edi whispered. "The best thing we can do right now is to sit still, gather our strength, and try to figure out what's happening."

"But we can't..." Lane wanted to argue; to rally Edi, Brandy, and Amy and convince them all to fight back right now. Whatever those men had shot her with, though, was taking its toll. She couldn't even argue or stand up, much less do something as foolish as running past men with guns strapped to their sides. "Fine, but just for now. Are they all right?" She glanced at the women on the floor.

"My guess is that they were shot with the same stuff you were."

"Liam? The others?"

Edi laid a hand on Lane's shoulder and pushed her slowly back down to the ground. "I saw them take him past here, and I think we can assume he's in the same situation we are."

"That doesn't make me feel much better since I'm not sure what that situation is."

"I know, dear. I know. And I'm sorry."

"What are you sorry for?" Lane whispered as a tear leaked from the corner of her eye and ran down toward her hairline.

Edi pressed her lips together. "I can't stop thinking about it, so I might as well tell you. I'd seen some activity over near that old science camp last week. I didn't think much about it, because we know there have been people coming and going from that area for years and they've always left us alone. Now I wish I'd said something, because I'm sure it has something to do with this invasion." She was crying now, too, her soft face creased around the eyes as she sniffled.

Yes, Edi should've said something. The younger dragons could've gone to investigate, and if they'd known humans were in the area, they would've taken extra precautions. But Lane knew Edi wasn't getting any younger, and her mind didn't quite work the way it used to. She also knew that every single one of them had grown more and more lax the longer they stayed there and the longer the humans left them alone. They acted as though there weren't any threats, and clearly, that wasn't true.

"It wasn't your fault," she reassured her. "It's all right."

"I see you're awake!" boomed a voice.

Lane sat up and then immediately laid back down, overwhelmed by nausea. It didn't matter since the speaker strode across the room and stood over her, his white lab coat swinging around his legs. Several armed men were gathered around him and moved in unison, never letting the man get more than a step away.

"Sir, I'm not sure you should be so close to them," one of them offered.

"Hush, now. These are my test subjects, and we're all going to have to get used to working in close quarters. Well, as close as this big old cave can get." He laughed heartily, and several of the soldiers offered obligatory chuckles as well.

"Who the hell are you?" Edi asked. "And what are you doing in our home?"

The man laughed again. "I'm Dr. Brian Blake, and this isn't your home any longer. The U.S. Army has contracted me to find out exactly what you are, how you work, and what we might be able to do with you. Fortunately, it looks like the first part of our experiment has worked well, which was to see if we could tranquilize creatures stronger than ourselves without killing them."

"Listen, we're not just some animals you can poke and prod in a lab," Lane countered. She knew her argument meant little, considering she was just lying on the floor trying not to puke, but she hated this man.

With his gray hair and kindly smile, he looked like a friendly family physician. But there was a dark glitter in his eyes that told her otherwise. "Oh, but you are! I mean, you're not even human!" He laughed again.

Lane failed to see the humor. "How would you even know?" They'd shot her while in her human form, and she doubted she'd have shifted while she was sedated.

His smile was a hard one. "You've already proven it to me by waking up. That dose we gave you would've killed any normal woman. And since you're one of the first to come to, I can assume you're also one of the strongest." The doctor turned to his entourage. "Get her into the mobile lab. She's going to be a fun one."

Edi was shoved out of the way as two armed men dragged Lane to her feet and hauled her out of the cave. More men were busy widening the entrance to the cavern and she was dragged past them, outside, and into a large metal shipping container that had been turned into a workstation for the doctor's evil plans.

Lane was too weak to fight as they tossed her onto a hard bed. Heavy straps pinched her skin as the men tightened them down, almost keeping her from breathing. "What are you doing, assholes?" she growled. It wasn't fair. If they hadn't gotten her with that sedative, she could've shifted and torn every single one of them to pieces. She took a little joy in envisioning their blood covering all the white sanitary surfaces in the room.

Dr. Blake wasn't perturbed by her name calling. He whistled to himself as he fiddled with some equipment set up on a table off to the side, and when he turned to her, he gleefully tapped a yellowish liquid in a hypodermic needle. "Just a little something to get us started on the road to figuring out this metamorphosis thing you creatures do."

She tried to flinch away as he approached her with the needle, but there was nothing she could do. The straps held her too tightly, and her body was too weak. "Don't do this," she begged. It had to have been a nightmare. It couldn't possibly have been real. And yet she felt the pinch of the needle as it pierced her skin.

Lane howled as the drug flowed through her body. She could feel it funnel through her veins and it burned like acid as it washed over her cells. Her muscles convulsed uncontrollably, shaking the bed. A high-pitched noise filled her ears, and she wondered what it was for a moment before she realized it was her. Lane was no longer in charge of her own body.

Her skin split and formed scales, but instead of rising to the surface and remaining there, they sank back down into her flesh. Each one felt like a hot coal being pressed into her body. She felt her back rip open where her wings usually emerged, but they stayed tightly curled inside while her blood turned the sheets a dark red.

"Well, well. This is interesting." Dr. Blake had set up a video camera and was writing notes rapidly on a clipboard.

"Stop!" Lane screamed. "Stop this!" She'd always been the one to decide when to shift. She'd always been in ultimate control. She gritted her teeth and tried to regain her jurisdiction over her body, but it was no use. She was stuck in a mid-shift state, and there was no getting out of it.

"Tell me what you're feeling," Dr. Blake said, stepping up near her head.

Lane glared at him before turning to the side and retching, the contents of her stomach splashing onto his pristine lab coat.

He sneered his disgust as he stepped back. "Well, that answers that."

The light fixture overhead moved in and out of focus as Lane's body completely gave up. She succumbed to the darkness for lack of any better option, because at least it didn't hurt as bad as this. Lane spared a thought for Edi and the others, praying they wouldn't have to experience this. The last thing she heard was the sound of her blood dripping onto the hard floor.

3

ASH SLOWED HIS RENTAL CAR AND DOUBLE-CHECKED THE address. The building he'd pulled up in front of didn't look like much. This entire neighborhood seemed to be composed of low, adjoined buildings that huddled together. Right between an antique store and a children's used clothing shop sat a squat white building with a ratty For Sale sign posted in the window. Three steps led up to a tiny covered porch, but that was about the extent of the charm. To the left was a battered garage door.

"Here goes nothing." The package that had arrived shortly after the mysterious phone call contained not only the plane ticket, rental car information, and the time and address for the meeting, but a garage door opener as well. Ash pushed the button, surprised when the rickety door actually rolled up.

He pulled through, his instincts telling him to remain on the lookout. Just because someone called and claimed to be with the elite SOS Force didn't mean this was a safe or smart thing to do. He was in a strange city where he didn't know anyone, and whoever had contacted him knew who he was and what kind of skills he had. It was either going to be the start of something really exciting or a dangerous situation.

The building was dark inside with just a few yellow lights exposing the concrete walls. Ash slowly pulled forward as the garage door rattled back down behind him. Like an explosion of daylight, overhead LEDs flicked on to the right. They showed him into a nice parking garage, complete with an epoxied floor. He pulled into a space and got out. A few other cars were already there, but there were no signs or people to tell him where to go next. He took his chance on a small door at the end of the row of parking spaces.

He found himself in a hallway that smelled of fresh paint and new carpet. He prepared himself for the worst as he moved down it, bracing himself when he opened the door at the end.

A man with dark hair and a serious look on his face sat at the end of a glossy conference table. His dark eyes met Ash's, studious and wary.

"Are you the one who called me?" Ash asked.

"I was about to ask you the same thing," the man responded. "I got a call myself."

Ash glanced around the room. It was just the two of them. "Where's everyone else? There are plenty of cars out there." He thumbed over his shoulder to indicate the direction he'd just come from.

The dark-haired man shook his head and leaned forward on the table. "Don't let all the drywall fool you. These buildings are much bigger than they look from the outside. There's a lot more space here than you've seen if you've just come from the garage."

"Sounds like you know something I don't." Ash gripped the back of a chair, but he wasn't ready to sit. He preferred to be at the ready.

"Only because I've flown over this city more times than I can count. I think it'd be easier for me to find an address from the air than from the street." He hesitated only a fraction of a second before extending his hand. "The name's Max, by the way."

"Ash." He gripped the man's hand and immediately sensed there was an animal lurking inside him. *Another shifter*, he noted. *Interesting.*

"I see I'm just in time for the introductions," drawled a voice from behind them.

Ash and Max both turned to find a tall cowboy standing in the doorway. He smiled at them through his short beard as he bobbed his Stetson in their direction. "Name's Vance."

"Are you able to tell us why we're here?" Ash challenged.

The cowboy advanced into the room and stopped across the table from Ash. "Can't say myself, but that guy on the phone said it was something about a job."

"Yeah, that's what he said, but this isn't like any other job interview I've been to." Granted, Ash hadn't needed to look for a job for a long time, given his military career. He couldn't help but be wary of the situation.

The three of them turned expectantly as yet another man entered the room. His short hair had a faint red tint to it, and he adjusted his laptop bag as he looked at the men gathered there. He tucked his phone into his pocket as he poked his head in the room. "I guess this must be the right place?"

Ash shrugged. "As far as we know."

"It's the only logical conclusion, anyway. Name's Jack."

The rest of them murmured their introductions as the man sat down.

When yet another man entered the room, Ash was ready to start the process all over again. This guy had shaggy hair and a stubbly beard, but his piercing eyes quickly scanned everyone in the room. "Good. You managed to find the place. I guess that's one test down."

Ash immediately recognized his voice. "You're the one who called me."

The man shrugged. "Someone had to do it, and I got stuck with the short straw. But yeah. Here's the deal. We need you. I'm not going to beat around the bush or ask you a bunch of stupid human resource questions to see if you're worthy. We already know you have the qualifications we need." He pointed to Max. "Night Stalker and current helicopter pilot for Luxury Air Tours." His finger swung around to Jack. "Grey Fox and techie who changes jobs more often than he changes his underwear because all the big tech companies keep luring you out of your current contracts."

Jack looked slightly embarrassed but acknowledged this with a nod of his head.

Next, the man pointed to Vance. "Green Beret, which doesn't take much explanation."

Ash stiffened when the finger swung his direction.

"Only recently retired from the Delta Force, where you took out more terrorists than the civilians were even aware existed."

"Flint, you were supposed to wait for us!"

Three other men filtered into the room, looking much more authoritative than Flint. "I apologize for the behavior of my associate," said the one who appeared to be the leader. "I'm Dr. Drake Sheridan. You've already met Flint, and this is Hudson and Garrison. As you know by now, depending on just how coherent Flint's been, we're the Special Ops Shifter Force. We're shifters and have served in Special Ops units, just like you. We've been operating out of D.C. for the last few years, dealing with various issues among shifters that their local conclaves aren't capable of handling. It's been a successful operation to date, but there aren't enough of us to take care of everything. That's where you come in."

"And what makes you think we'd even be interested?" Max challenged.

"You're here, aren't you?" Flint replied as he flopped into a chair. He pulled a folding knife out of his pocket and began to spin it between his fingers.

"Hard to resist seeing what this is all about after getting a mysterious phone call and an even more intriguing package in the mail," Vance drawled.

"Curiosity killed the cat?" Flint asked, one eyebrow up.

"Stop," Drake growled.

Ash watched the interaction between them, fascinated by the dynamic between the four men. He could sense that same animal force inside each of them, just as he had with Max, Jack, and Vance. But there were clearly some major differences among those in the room, and it would be interesting to see how it all worked out.

"I'm not so sure about this," he hedged. "I was just about to put a down payment on a ranch up in Alaska and retire to the quiet life."

"And I've already got a big operation I'm taking care of. My life is pretty full," Vance agreed.

Drake folded his hands on the table. "If it's not you, then it's someone else, but we think you four are the best candidates to get our Dallas unit started. We'll work in conjunction with you, especially at first while you're learning the ropes. It won't be the same as your military experience, I can tell you that. And yes, it's a time commitment. It's something you have to be sure of. But there are shifters all over this country who need your help. We know you can give it to them."

"Tell me some more about this building," Jack said, holding his phone in the air. "I can't get even the tiniest bit of a signal."

The man Drake had indicated as Hudson smiled. "That's the way we like it. We can't risk anyone interfering with our communications system here. There's too much top-secret information. I'll be going over all that in detail with you later as part of your training."

"We have quite a bit of that set up, actually," Drake said. "Hudson here runs Taylor Communications, and he's been in charge of all our technology. He'll go over all our systems with you. Garrison handles all of our engineering issues, and it was his construction company that took this old building and turned it into what it is now."

"Don't worry," Garrison said with a smile, "I left the outside that way on purpose."

"I'll be doing complete physicals on each of you to make sure you're in top shape for your missions," Drake continued, "and Flint has, I'm sure, put together a rousing presentation about all the weapons available to you."

Flint grinned.

Ash's brain was working quickly, trying to keep track of it all. Drake the doctor. Garrison the engineer. Flint the weapons specialist. Hudson the tech guy. Okay. Simple enough. But then there were the other three men who he would now be working with. Who were they all, really? Could this actually work? Was he making the right decision by giving up the idea of his ranch?

"The first step is to get the telepathic link between the four of you established," Garrison said. "You'll need as much time as possible to get used to being in each other's heads, just like a regular clan or pack. I'll show you to the living quarters at the back of the building where you can rest up from traveling, and then I'll be back to get you later tonight."

As Ash followed him through a door, he wondered just what the hell he'd gotten himself into.

———

DRAKE SEEMED to be the one in charge of the SOS Force, and Hudson was obviously the comm specialist. But it was Garrison who had taken charge when they stood in a field in the middle of nowhere several hours later. He'd offered no explanation of what was about to happen or how it would work on the trip out there when he'd loaded them into a van and left the city proper.

The stars were brilliant overhead as the newcomers watched each other and the original SOS Force members carefully. Someone had prepared wood for a fire in a small ring in the center. Garrison arranged Ash, Max, Jack, and Vance around it. "Just as any other group of shifters is able to speak to each other inside their minds, it makes sense for the Force to do so as well. It still only works when you're in your animal forms, so you can have your privacy when you need it."

"Just how do you propose to do that?" Jack questioned. "Somehow, I imagined we'd be taken to a lab and have chips implanted in our brains or something."

Garrison gave him a dark look. "I'm afraid it's more primitive than that. This is an ancient ceremony for my people, one that's been handed down through the genera-tions. We are few and far between, and much of our knowl-edge of magic has been lost over the years. This particular spell is a simple and yet very effective one."

Ash pursed his lips as he listened. He looked up at the big sky overhead and once again thought about that ranch he'd been about to buy. Part of him regretted getting on that plane and going down there, but maybe the universe had other plans for him. Why else would he have gotten the phone call from Flint right after he'd decided to buy the place? He could still hear Old Jim's words echoing in his head, telling him to take the chance while he can. This was it. He was committed.

Garrison had produced a knife and held it reverently in his hand. The blade curved backward and the handle curved in the opposite direction. "Your blood must flow into each other. You must cut each wrist to expose yourselves to your new brethren." He handed the knife to Max.

The chopper pilot did as he was told and then handed the blade to Ash. He hefted the knife in his hand, realizing the handle was made of a giant claw. There was only a moment to contemplate this before he made the requisite cuts and then passed it on.

"Shift so that your new brothers can see your true forms. Then you must touch your wounds so that the blood flows through each of you."

Drowning out the rest of the crowd around him, Ash tapped into his true identity. The polar bear inside him had been anxious to come out for several days now, impatient with the preparations for leaving Alaska and all the travel time. He no longer had to be cooped up, though. Ash let out a breath as his face elongated into a white muzzle and a dark nose. His ears rounded and softened as they changed position on his head, and his spine cracked slightly as it stretched to accommodate the rest of his animal form. The pale starlight illuminated his fur, making him feel conspicuous.

When he was finished, Ash looked around. Where Max had stood only a moment ago, a massive tiger now paced. Jack had melted into a fox with an intelligent face. Vance the cowboy was now Vance the cougar, and Flint's cat joke now made sense.

But the biggest difference Ash noted was that Garrison was no longer stalking around the outside of their circle on two legs. He, too, had changed, but into a creature that Ash had to blink before he recognized. Deep green scales shimmered in the night, leathery wings hung down from his back, and huge spikes protruded from the back of his head. He was a dragon.

The massive reptile stepped inside their circle. His chest puffed out and everything froze for a moment before his head shot forward. As he parted his lips, a fireball escaped, igniting the wood that had been arranged in the center. He stepped back when it was done as though it'd been the simplest task in the world. "Touch wounds," he reminded the inductees.

Blood dripped darkly down Ash's fur as he extended one paw toward Max and the other toward Vance. They crowded closer together to account for Jack's smaller form. Already, Ash swore he could feel something going on inside him.

Garrison stood nearby, speaking in a rasping language

that Ash couldn't identify. The sounds had a lilting cadence that made Ash think of the origins of the universe. He repeated them and then translated them to English. "Our blood becomes one, flowing within each other. Bonded as brothers, our nexus strong."

But Ash didn't need the interpretation to know something significant had changed inside him. He could feel his two selves, just as he always had. His polar bear and his human had lived in a state of acceptance of each other, even when they fought for space. But now, those two creatures weren't alone in his head. He felt the presence of the others, even before he heard Max.

Holy hell.

Ha! It actually worked! That was Jack, for sure. Ash instantly understood he was the skeptic of the bunch; the one who wasn't just uncertain about the new people, but about everything.

That'll be convenient. Even in cougar form, Vance's Texan accent was evident.

"The ceremony is complete," Garrison intoned. "Even when you break the blood bond of your wounds, you'll still be connected to each other." He officially ended the ceremony by shifting back to his human self, his emerald wings folding into his body as his back shortened and straightened.

"We found out last time that it's an exhausting process, so we've brought food," Drake announced. "Let's eat."

A large array of food had been laid out on several picnic tables not far from the fire. Ash's stomach growled, and he wondered how he hadn't noticed them before. But he'd been preoccupied with whatever the hell was going on there, something he was still trying to figure out.

The new and the old members of the SOS Force sat together. Ash expected more explanations about rules and training, but the atmosphere was much more relaxed than it'd been back at their new headquarters. They spoke of their time in the service and adjustment to life afterwards, something Ash had hardly even gotten a chance to do before he'd been beckoned there. Still, as he piled his plate high, he had a good feeling about this. He was going to get along with these men. Maybe it was the blood bond created by Garrison's dragon magic; he couldn't be certain.

When Flint offered to show them a new flamethrower he'd designed, Drake touched Ash's elbow to keep him back from the crowd. "There's something I'd like to talk to you about."

"What's that?" Ash wiped the grease from the fried chicken on his napkin and stepped into the shadows with the doctor.

"We've already got a mission for you."

Ash tipped his head back. "Me? I thought we were a team. And I thought there was supposed to be all this training first."

"Yes, you're right on both counts. But as I said, we've got

a lot of calls coming in. We have to filter them out and decide which ones to take on, and that often means we have to split up as well. Some of them really aren't that bad, but every now and then, we get one that gives me a bad gut feeling. It's the kind of thing we need to investigate right away, and the rest of the training and the lectures can wait until later. If you take this mission, you'll still be able to reach us for consultation and backup."

Ash shifted his weight, watching the man carefully. "Tell me about it."

Drake cleared his throat. "It's an unusual one. We typically only handle calls from within the U.S. We're talking things like both intra-clan and inter-clan disputes that also involve drug or weapons trafficking and issues where the conclave isn't strong enough to interfere. This call comes all the way from Antarctica, though."

"You're kidding me, right?" Ash had traveled widely in his time with Delta Force, but never to a place like that.

"I'm not. A killer whale pod has been spotting some very strange activity. They're in the region regularly, since it's near their hunting grounds. We don't know a lot of details, but we're talking about a sudden increase in military presence." Drake's jaw clenched with concern.

Ash didn't understand. "I don't see what that has to do with shifters."

"The whales have also been spotting dragons."

Running a hand through his hair, Ash sighed. "If you'd

said that to me an hour ago, I would've laughed at you. I didn't even know there were still dragons around."

A shadow detached itself from the tree line and joined them, his form resolving itself into that of Garrison. "For a long time, I thought I was the only one left until I found my mate. She and I have been spending all our free time searching for evidence of more dragons in the world, but we wouldn't have expected to find them in Antarctica."

"No offense, but why don't you go?"

Garrison huffed a sigh of frustration. "Because Maren —my mate—would be desperate to come with me. She's pregnant, and even if I could convince her to stay here, I don't think I should be that far from her."

Drake smiled at his comrade before turning back to Ash. "You've got experience in cold climates, and you're also the one who's most recently out of the military. We know your counter-terrorism skills will help out on this mission as well. If the U.S. Armed Forces *and* the dragons are down there, then we need someone who can not only handle the cold, but who can be extremely discreet. We trust you with this, Ash."

It'd already been a big decision to go there, and Ash had committed to that decision by going through the ancient ceremony that established their psychic link. There was no point in backing out now, even if the mission before him sounded like something out of a late-night science fiction movie. "When do I leave?"

4
_____

ASH HELD TIGHTLY TO THE RUSTY RAILING OF THE OLD fishing boat as it bumped up against the rocky shore, grateful the ride was over with. He'd dressed appropriately for the trip and the cold didn't bother him, but the rough passage through wild waters had been more than nauseating.

"You're sure this is the right place?" the captain asked, coming up behind him as the deckhands scurried about. The man had a thick accent, but he spoke English well. "There's nothing here, not even one of the science stations."

"That's all right." Ash had checked and rechecked the location, thanks to the stunning ability of the cell phone Hudson had given him. The lion shifter had assured him he'd never lose signal as long as he could see the sky, and so far, the promise had been a truthful one. "I know where I'm going."

The captain shrugged and gestured toward the shore, where giant white-blue humps of snow and ice showed just beyond the rocks. "I know I said no return passage, but I don't feel right about leaving you here. You explorers always think you can use your smarts to navigate the land, but one man on his own can't survive in a place like this. I'll take you back right now, no extra charge."

But Ash shook his head. It'd been a long and arduous trip to get there. Antarctica wasn't the sort of place that boasted commercial airports and a Starbucks on every corner. Even though there were cruise lines he could've taken, Ash preferred to take the route that required the least amount of attention and paperwork, a method that Drake had approved of. He wasn't about to turn back now, and no matter how the mission went, he wouldn't be looking forward to those rocky seas on the return trip. "That's kind of you, but I'll be fine. I promise."

"Very well." The captain threw his hands in the air as though he thought he was throwing Ash's life away. "Oskar will take you in the dinghy."

Ash pressed the envelope of cash into the captain's hands, who accepted it gravely before he headed back to the bridge.

Oskar said nothing as he guided the dinghy to the shore, and he merely gave him a salute before he turned the tiny boat around and headed back for the rusty hulk that had brought them there in the first place.

Ash stood on the shore and watched the boat slip away, waiting until it'd nearly pulled out of sight before he turned and surveyed the new land. He'd been in blazing hot deserts, dripping wet jungles, and hard foreign cities, but never had he seen a place quite like this. Even Alaska, with as much of a reputation as it had for being wild and untamed, was a luxury vacation by comparison. There was nothing for miles and miles except snow and ice. A vicious wind whipped around him, seeking a weakness in his parka and other protective gear.

The chill and loneliness of the place reminded him of what he'd been planning to do with his life right now. The growing season had just started up near Fairbanks. If he had that farm, he'd be working with that couple who wanted to retire to the city, learning what kind of hay to grow for the cattle, how to keep them from escaping the fence, and which heifers to breed to which bulls. Once more he questioned joining the Force.

Cunningham, you're just not ready to let go of your youth, he chided himself as he trudged along, the snow crunching under his boots. The terrain there was rough and rugged, not flat and pristine like what he'd seen on documentaries. *You felt old when you retired, and you realized how much of your life had been given to the government. But now what are you doing? Giving it to some private group who might or might not be any better. Good job, soldier.*

A sound caught his ear and stopped him from his inner grumbling. He instinctively ducked behind a large boulder, now grateful for the rugged topography he'd just been whining about. But he knew that sound was an engine, and that wasn't good for a place where there weren't supposed to be any people. Like the captain had said, he wasn't even near any of the scientific camps.

Fortunately, Ash was in the perfect place to disguise himself. He morphed, still crouched behind the boulder. So what if polar bears weren't native to Antarctica? He would at least blend in with the landscape, and whomever he was after probably wasn't paying much attention to the wildlife.

On all fours with silent paws, Ash continued his journey. An LMTV bumped along in the distance down a smoother portion of the land. The camouflage paint on its sides was old and faded; no one had bothered to convert it to the snow camo that would've made more sense there. Its growling engine made it obvious, anyway. Whatever mission was being run there either wasn't enough of a priority to get funding or they simply weren't concerned about being noticed.

Ash used the lay of the land to his benefit, sticking to the snowy areas that would hide his presence the best as he followed the general direction of the LMTV. He stilled when he heard a plane in the distance, but it was too far away to spot him. He ambled around boulders and through valleys, wondering what the hell someone could want with this place.

Eventually, Ash stepped out onto what could only be a road. His paw slid too easily across it, and he took several steps back. Another LMTV—or possibly the same one he'd seen earlier—came barreling back from the other direction, its tires outfitted in sharp studs. Ash studied the vehicle carefully, but the canvas covered bed wasn't giving away any secrets.

The road wound around low foothills until it reached the wide mouth of a cave. Busted rock, dirt, and bits of debris had been blown out all over the snow, indicating the cave hadn't always been there. Warm wind blew forth from it and drips of water sprinkled down over the entrance. Ash narrowed his eyes as he surveyed the area. Several other vehicles had been parked in the snow nearby and he watched as one soldier shared a cigarette with another near the entrance. These men were outfitted in white and gray snow camo.

He didn't like the look of this. His mind immediately flashed back to some of the quick deployments he'd been on in the Middle East. The first men to go in were always equipped properly with the right color of camo, wearing their DCUs to make the first foray into enemy territory. But there wasn't always time to get the backup units updated to accommodate the new battleground, and he'd seen plenty of green camouflage vehicles in the middle of the desert where there was hardly any vegetation to blend in with.

Did something like that happen there, where a unit had gone in for the first strike and left everyone else to filter in afterwards once it was considered a safe zone? If that were the case, then there was a lot more going on there in this remote region than he ever would've imagined.

Ash desperately wanted to investigate, but they weren't likely to let him through the front gate, no matter what form he was in. Keeping his bear configuration for the moment, he gave the Army encampment a wide berth as he explored the territory. The more he knew about the land, the better prepared he'd be, no matter what happened next. It seemed that all the soldiers were concentrated near that large cave opening. Ash knew from his experience with extremist groups that there was always a backdoor. No one ever left themselves just one exit, and there had to be another way in.

He paused and took a deep breath, tapping into the most primitive areas of his animal instincts. Ash rarely had a chance in his life to truly become the animal that lived beneath his skin. He'd shifted when he'd found himself alone in a remote area, when he had the chance to open up and just be wild for a moment. But there was so much more to his polar bear self than he'd ever allowed to come out and play. Ash rounded the makeshift military station, understanding the lay of the land in a way that only a beast could do.

There it was! He knew it the same way he knew which end was up. The ice there, about half a mile from the cave entrance, was much thinner than it was everywhere else. He could sense the hollowness underneath, like the sheet of ice had formed over a secondary tunnel. It was still thick enough to support his weight as his wide paws explored the area. Still pulling on that subconscious knowledge, Ash lifted his front end and brought it crashing back down on the ice. He pounded on it the way his wild cousins did, with a tenacity and determination that told him he had every right to get to whatever was on the other side.

He was rewarded when the ice cracked and then split straight down the middle. But he'd put too much of his weight on it, and as the glazed chunks fell, so did he. Ash scrambled for his footing, his claws reaching for the snow around him. He was falling too fast. His weight dragged him down before he could do anything about it. When the whiteness of the snow darkened into earth as he fell further, he managed to decelerate just enough. He hit something hard as a shower of dirt covered him.

Ash's body was in shock, and his brain wanted to be, too. But his training had taken over now, knowing he was in a dangerous situation. He scanned the area he'd fallen into, waiting for soldiers to fall in on him. But the small, underground cave was silent for the most part.

He could hear evidence of human activity further down the tunnel. None of it sounded urgent. He'd learned to understand the difference even when the enemy wasn't speaking the same language. Somehow, no one had seen or heard his clumsy entrance.

Ash picked himself up and scanned the sloped tunnel he'd just come through. It was steep, but not so much so that it couldn't be used to make his escape. He'd keep it in mind once he figured out just what the hell was happening down there.

He contemplated shifting back but decided to keep his furry white coat on for now as he ambled through the narrow tunnel. It widened as he moved through it, and the sound of voices drifted nearer. His heart thundered, but he tuned out the sound as he listened.

When he rounded a corner, Ash flinched. These underground hollows had likely been created by ancient volcanic activity or ice melt, but they certainly hadn't been rigged with brilliant LED lighting the way they were now. The smaller chambers that shot off from the main structure in either direction had been partitioned off with crude metal bars drilled into the rock. One of those drills seemed to still be in use, by the sound of things.

As odd as it all was, Ash was most taken aback by what he saw behind those bars: dragons, just as Drake had mentioned. Not just one or two, but dozens. They lay on the cold hard ground inside the improvised prison cells.

Some of them moaned in pain and clutched at their bodies, their own claws making deep marks in their flesh. Others were caught mid-shift, blood pouring from their backs as their wings tried to decide if they should be in or out. The skin on their fingers had ripped apart to allow their claws to spring forward.

They weren't all so unfortunate, but that didn't mean they were better off. A massive dragon to the left pounded against the bars that held him back. His pale blue scales were bruised from slamming himself into the metal so many times and his eyes rolled crazily in his head.

Ash kept to the right, watchful of the uniformed men who occupied the cavern further away, where he assumed they were closer to the main entrance he'd initially seen. They paid no attention to the thrashing dragon as they worked on setting up equipment and creating more barriers.

Something moved to his right, grabbing his attention. Ash swiveled his head, watching the shadows. The prison cells—because Ash was now convinced that was what they were—weren't lit nearly as well as the central part of the cavity. He retreated a step as a human woman crawled toward him.

She appeared just in the edge of the light. Her light red hair had been braided over her shoulder, but the loose strands made a net of knots around the plait. Her blue eyes were exhausted and slightly sunken into her face, confused as she stared at him through the bars.

It was clear to Ash that she'd been through a lot, but this woman enthralled him in a way he didn't expect. He dared to move a little closer, sniffing carefully. The air was clogged with the scent of unwashed bodies and a sharp medicinal odor. Was she a human or another shifter? Was she even a dragon, or did she hide some other beast inside her? He couldn't tell, and it bothered him.

Whomever she was, the woman glanced aside at the soldiers before reaching her hand through the bars. Ash stood a short distance from her, unmoving as the tips of her fingers barely touched his fur. She couldn't hurt him, no matter who she was. The bars would keep her back, as evidenced by the blue dragon who'd been unable to break them. But Ash wasn't concerned about getting attacked by her. There was something else about this woman that kept his paws rooted to the ground, his dark eyes entranced by hers.

"Get a tranquilizer in him, will you? I can't think with all that racket!" barked a voice.

Ash jolted, recognizing that something was about to change. He backed away from the woman and further into the darkness from which he'd come as a soldier approached, fiddling with a tranq gun.

The trooper paused in front of the cage that held the

blue dragon. "You like to cause a lot of fucking trouble, don't you?" he questioned.

The dragon's only response was to lash out, pushing his clawed feet through the bars in an effort to swipe at the uniformed man.

The soldier laughed. "Good luck, you scaly asshole. These bars aren't going anywhere, and neither are you. Now you'll shut the hell up and let us get some work done." He aimed and fired, watching with glee as the dart sank into the animal's hide. The dragon continued to thrash for a moment before he began losing his momentum, his clawed hand curling in on itself as he sank to the cold floor and closed his eyes. "That's what I thought," the soldier mumbled to the inert body.

Ash had pressed himself against the wall, but he was prepared to spring to action if the soldier looked his way. Fortunately, the man turned on his heel and returned to where he'd come from. When he was gone, Ash dared to peek around the corner at the woman once more. She'd retreated from the bars, a dim shadow. He hesitated a moment before turning and retreating to the sloping tunnel through which he'd found this horrid place.

It was a hell of a climb, and he had to make the choice of heaving his heavy bear body up through the tunnel or sacrificing the strength of his limbs and the sharpness of his claws if he morphed back into a human. Overall, this whole continent seemed better suited to his bear form, and so he kept it, even as he reemerged into daylight and headed away from the compound.

Anyone there? he dared to ask in his head. He'd hardly used the telepathic link Garrison had helped them establish, and at first, he hadn't been entirely certain he would. But he was part of a team again, and Drake had stressed repeatedly that he should report in as often as possible.

Jack speaking, came the fox's voice in his head. *How are things going down there on the bottom of the world?*

I guess that depends on your opinion. Ash dared to glance over his shoulder. There was no sight of the encampment from there, but still he could sense it as though he had a natural radar. *I found the place I was sent here to find, but it's not good.* He did his best to describe it, though the images had been disturbing.

Wow. That's wild. What's the next step in your plan?

Ash wasn't used to the way the Force was arranged. As far as he was concerned, there was no need to share much detail with Jack. The guy wasn't his commanding officer, or anything. But at the moment, he was the only link Ash had with headquarters. And Ash understood that some missions simply couldn't be completed alone. *No one saw me, but if anyone discovers my break in the ice, they'll know that someone either got in or out. That means they're guaranteed to ramp up security and I won't be able to get back in as easily. And even if I do slip in the back entrance a second time, I know I can't take them all down by myself. I need to get more information and see what I'm really up against, and I may need some serious backup.*

Jack was quiet long enough that Ash wondered if he was still there. *I have some strings I may be able to pull to get you in,* he finally replied. *You said this is some sort of scientific mission?*

As far as I can tell, Ash confirmed.

Let me check with one of my connections. I'll see what I can do.

Thanks.

It only made Ash feel minimally better to know he wasn't the only one working on this problem. He had no idea what Jack had in mind, but he hoped it worked. Something had to be done, that was for sure.

Ash shambled on for another couple of miles before the tiny shack came into view. It barely stood out against the wilderness, the same color as the mountain it crouched against, and was nearly covered with snow. No one had bothered to lock up the abandoned science station before they left, and he only had to contend with the weight of the snow against the door to get inside.

All the equipment and tools had been packed out, leaving behind a ragged bunk with a threadbare sleeping bag and a coffee pot that wouldn't work without the generator that was no longer sitting outside. Still, the dilapidated station was a damn sight for sore eyes; much better than the conditions those dragons were being held in. At least he was free to come and go as he pleased.

Shivering as he resumed his human form, Ash threw himself down on the creaky bunk. Night was falling, and there was nothing for him to do now but wait. He could feel the long hours stretch out before him, a vast amount of time in which he could do nothing to help those dragons. He closed his eyes and saw them clearly. Whatever was being done to them was most definitely torture. They were thin and pitiful, and it was obvious from the bars that they hadn't volunteered for this research. They all deserved freedom, and it bothered Ash that he would have to fight against the Army—the very military that he'd given his life to—in order to rescue them.

But what bothered him even more was the effect that woman had on him.

Even now, miles away from the prison, he could feel the brush of her fingers on his fur. His bear roiled inside him at the thought of her, demanding to know why he'd left her there. Those bright blue eyes held so much.

Ash had cared greatly about the men and women who were suffering around the world at the hands of poor government or extremist influences. He'd always acknowledged that change needed to happen, but it'd long since stopped affecting him. A man gets desensitized after seeing starving children and beaten women over and over again.

Even in the midst of a war zone, Ash had slept well because he'd known he had a full day's work ahead of him.

This was different. He tossed and turned, reminding himself continuously that he'd be an idiot to march back over there and take that entire base down single handedly. He'd only get himself killed, and that part, he could live with.

But what would happen to *her*?

You don't even know her name, he scolded himself as he tossed and turned. *Start thinking with your other head, soldier.*

He couldn't, though. His bear kept looping thoughts of the enchanting beauty through his mind all night long.

5

"DID YOU SEE THAT?" LANE'S THROAT FELT TIGHT AS SHE retreated to the back corner of her chamber, the place that had once been so comforting to her. But this was no longer a natural cave that served as a bedroom. Those soldiers had converted it into a jail, and the only time they brought her out was to push needles into her. Then, they stood back while they observed the results.

Right now, though, the only thing on her mind was the mysterious beast that had been on the other side of the bars just a few moments ago.

"See what?" came Edi's voice. She'd aged considerably since the attack, but Lane no longer knew how long ago that was. She'd completely lost track of time.

"That... bear," Lane stuttered. The words didn't sound

right on her lips. "There was a polar bear in here just a minute ago."

Edi, who'd been sleeping in the back corner, lifted her hand and patted Lane's cheek. "Sometimes the drugs make us see things, dear. Don't forget that. We have to stay as grounded as possible and we both know there aren't any polar bears here." She dropped her hand as though it were far too heavy for her to hold up any longer.

Lane gently placed the older woman's hand back on the blanket. "I know that. But this was completely different. It stood right there on the other side of the bars, and the way it watched everyone and everything was incredible, like it knew what was going on. I even touched it; I couldn't have imagined that." She stared at her fingertips as she recalled the way his fur had felt against her skin.

"You could've," Edi replied drowsily. "I've dreamt countless times that this was all over with; that we were back to the way we used to live and the bars were gone. And I swore it was real. But then I'd always wake up and nothing had changed. We should just get used to it."

Lane gritted her teeth. She hated when the old woman began to lose faith. She had her moments when she rallied, but it was always the worst when Edi gave up. It made Lane want to give up, too, and she knew the others felt the same. "We can't do that," Lane scolded. "I know everything looks bleak right now, but it can't stay like this forever."

"Can't it?"

Visions of spending the rest of their years languishing in that cell came rushing to Lane's mind, and not for the first time. It'd been more than difficult to handle these soldiers on their territory, changing their home into both a prison and some sort of lab. The bars were incredibly strong, and though the dragons had tried numerous times, none of them had been able to escape so far. Every day, the scientists came and took at least one from their flight away to experiment on them. Lane had endured the injections and the side effects from them so many times that she was becoming numb to the way her body reacted, fluctuating between forms. The one saving Grace was that they hardly ever took Edi anymore. Even the stupid soldiers knew the old woman wasn't up for being a guinea pig.

Exhausted and confused, Lane moved back to the front of the chamber. She peered through the bars at where the polar bear had been. The earth was packed hard, and there was no evidence that his wide paws had been there, but it was all too real. It couldn't have just been in her mind.

"I saw it, too," came a grumpy voice from the other side of the hall-like tunnel that ran between the chambers.

Lane lifted her head, shocked to see that Liam was still awake. "Are you sure?"

He lay on the floor of his enclosure, his long muzzle pressed against the bars. Speech was an effort for him, and he took a deep breath every few words. "Yes. It was before they... got me. Again. Bastards."

"So you don't think it was all in my head?" It'd been harder and harder to determine reality from some fictional world ever since these men had invaded their home. Even the nightmares she often experienced were more tempting than what she would inevitably wake up to. It made her wonder how everyone else was experiencing this captivity, too.

"No," Liam panted. "I saw him. I smelled him. He was there and he... looked me in the eye. Besides, I haven't been... seeing things."

Lane nodded her understanding, even though Liam wasn't looking at her at the moment. "I wonder if they're injecting you with something different than what they're giving me." Liam had been in his dragon form for weeks now, as far as she could tell. It was taxing on any shifter to remain in one form for too long, and she could only imagine that it was doubly hard to remain a dragon. His temper often got the better of him, as evidenced by the bruised and missing scales all down his hide from thrashing against the bars.

"I don't know. They don't exactly like to talk to me." Liam let out a giggly laugh, unlike any sound he would've emitted in their former lives as simple shifters who'd come to this remote area to escape humans. His head rolled on the floor as his tongue flicked over his sharp teeth. "They won't even accept my invitation to dinner!" He snickered again.

"You're just stoned on sedatives," Lane said, more to explain his odd behavior to herself than to remind him. He knew, and she couldn't blame him if he wanted to forget. Liam had been an interesting test subject for the scientists, but in a different way than Lane was.

"He's not wrong, though." This came from Brandy. She and Amy had been put in the same cell with Lane and Edi, presumably because they were all women. She dragged herself forward to lean against the bar next to Lane. "I know you still think we have a chance of getting out of here, but we're far outnumbered and outgunned. Those G.I. Joes might be soft and squishy inside and no match for dragon teeth, but it changes the game completely when they've got all their guns and drugs."

Lane scowled. She knew her friend was right, and this wasn't the first time they'd gone through their situation, looking for holes they could take advantage of. Even so, she didn't like to think everyone else around her had just submitted to these assholes. "There's got to be a way, and I'm determined to find it."

Brandy lay a hand over Lane's, her dark hair falling in tangled mats over her shoulder. "That's noble of you, but I'm not sure it's worth it. You'll only get yourself killed if you fight back against them."

Ignoring her, Lane continued to brainstorm. "I still think our priority should be to figure out *why* they're holding us here."

Brandy's lips tightened as she gestured to the series of injection sites on her arm, some of which were beginning to scar over. "Isn't it obvious? They think we're just big scaly lab rats."

Lane rubbed her own arm, remembering too easily the way those needles felt when they sank into her flesh. "But that still doesn't explain why. What good would it do?"

"What does it matter?" Brandy retorted, letting out a huff of exasperation. "For all we know, they think we hold the cure for cancer or the secret to eternal youth." She paused, one clawed and oozing finger tapping her chin. "Actually, that last one could be a possibility, considering how long we live compared to them and how we age. But anyway, I don't see what their motives have to do with finding a way out of here."

"I don't know for sure, but I think it's stupid of us to just give up." Lane put her chin in the air, feeling a sense of defiance and determination that was hard to come by these days. "I'm going to figure this out, and I've got more than enough time to do it in." She retreated to the dark corner near the back where she spent most of her time.

"I'm sorry." Brandy followed her and sank down next to her once again, putting a thin arm around Lane's shoulders. "I guess there's nothing wrong with getting as much information as possible. It's just hard to feel like there's any hope most days."

"Don't I know it." Lane tipped her head onto Brandy's

shoulder, grateful that even if they didn't have their lives and their freedom, they at least had each other. "You're pretty. Maybe you can seduce one of them."

Brandy laughed at the notion, the noise echoing against the high ceiling. "Right. I have a pretty good feeling they're not interested in us that way, and even if they were, I think I'd just vomit."

"That can be fun, too," Lane pointed out, remembering the disgusting look on the doctor's face when he'd done his first test on her.

Her friend tightened her arm. "We'll keep our eyes and ears open at least, okay?"

It was all she was going to get for now, and she couldn't really ask for more. Lane nodded and closed her eyes, a bright vision of that big white bear flashing before her eyes. "It's at least a start."

———

"LANE!"

Lane opened her eyes. Her head ached, as it always did these days, but she was awake in a moment when she understood the urgency of Brandy's voice. "What is it? What's wrong?"

"It's Edi." Brandy was crouched over the old woman's pallet, one hand on her shoulder. "She's not breathing right. I think she's really sick."

Lane was at her side in an instant, but she felt helpless. Even though scientists and doctors surrounded them, she knew they wouldn't be willing to help. "What's wrong, Edi? What can we do for you?"

The old woman moaned, but she didn't speak or open her eyes.

The two younger women exchanged glances over her inert form. "I don't like this," Lane said, a furrow growing deeper between her brows. "I'm not even sure what to do."

Brandy glanced around the room and then darted across it. She tore off a strip off her shirt and dunked it in the water pail they were all expected to share. The water was never as clean as what they'd been able to get from the waterfall before the soldiers had come along, but Brandy was careful not to spill the liquid, treating it as though it were the most precious material on Earth. "Maybe this will help. She feels too hot, even for one of us."

Lane laid a hand on Edi's forehead and instantly understood what Brandy was trying to say. Dragon shifters usually kept a higher internal temperature than normal humans, thanks to the furnace that naturally burned in their chests. She reached out for the rag. "It's worth a try."

The two of them took turns bathing the old woman, constantly checking the temperature of her skin to see if their efforts were helping. Lane wondered what would happen if this was something Edi couldn't make it through. She highly doubted the soldiers would allow them to properly take care of their dead, and she wouldn't even put it past them to take the body and use it for their own scientific exploration. She shuddered at the thought, feeling guilty for even thinking that way, but it was a very real possibility. "Hang in there, Edi. We're here for you."

A noise from the hall caught her attention, and she turned just in time to see a scientist standing on the other side of the bars. He was dressed in a long white lab coat like Dr. Blake wore, but this definitely wasn't Dr. Blake. His hair had been cropped short, sporting a bit of gray at his temples which indicated his age. An array of armed soldiers flanked him as he studied the dragons in the chamber. "That one," he said, pointing at Lane.

"You sure? She's a frisky one."

The man in the lab coat nodded. "I'm sure you're more than capable of handling her."

The soldier who'd tried to argue with him puffed up his chest and tightened his grip on his weapon. "Of course, sir."

"I want her in the mobile lab outside."

"But we've got a new one set up right down here—"

"Do you make a habit of arguing with your superiors?" the newcomer demanded, his deep voice threatening.

He'd instantly cowed the soldier. "No, sir. Sorry, sir."

The man in the lab coat whisked away while the soldiers unlocked the bars, swinging out a small section so they could step inside and grab Lane. She knew better than to fight by now, unless she wanted a new array of bruises to join the ones already trying to heal on her arms and legs, and she stumbled along with them as they pulled her out of the chamber and locked it.

She gritted her teeth as she allowed them to guide her down the tunnel toward the front of the cavern. The soldiers had not only widened the passageway and installed blinding lights all over the place, they'd also taken a section of the main cavern near the waterfall and turned it into a large lab. They'd literally constructed a box within the cavern, a space that Lane imagined made them feel like they were still part of civilization.

Dr. Blake operated out of that lab now, but the soldiers did as they were told and marched her outside. She had only a minute to enjoy the sunshine and brisk wind on her face—improperly dressed as she was—before they shoved her inside the cargo container where she'd lost so much blood on that first day. Someone had cleaned it all up now, though she could still smell the fear of everyone else who'd gone in there and suffered at the hands of these horrid humans.

"Leave her here," the new doctor commanded. "You can go."

"But, sir!" The argumentative soldier gestured wildly at Lane. "That's crazy!"

"They didn't send me here because I'm a pussy, Nelson.

Now get the fuck out of my lab!" The doctor pointed at the door.

The underlings scrambled out, the door making a thick thump behind them.

Lane was now close enough to the new man that she could see the ID badge clipped to his lab coat. "They're right, Dr. Cunningham," she said as he rummaged around for whatever instruments he needed. "It's not smart of you to be in here with me alone."

His back was to her, and he carried such a relaxed posture, it was clear he wasn't threatened. "And why's that?"

She couldn't resist the opportunity to tell him just what she thought of him and the rest of the bastards who'd infiltrated her life. "Because any of us would gladly take the chance to rip into your skin and chunk your flesh out piece by piece."

"I'm sure you're right," he replied as he turned around, his dark eyes meeting hers calmly.

Her breath caught in her throat as she stared into them, her tongue working against the backs of her teeth. She fought the urge to shift, but only because she thought it would satisfy him to think that he could scare her or manipulate her. But there was something about him that was so incredibly familiar... Those eyes...

She cleared her throat. "I haven't seen you here before. What sort of trouble did you get in for someone to send you out here?"

Dr. Cunningham pressed a cold disc against her chest. She hadn't even realized he was holding it until that moment. "You underestimate me. There's a lot to learn here, and I'm here to do just that."

She swallowed again, unable to rid herself of the tightness at her throat. Her dragon whipped around inside her, but not with the urge to attack him. "Then maybe you can tell me exactly what it is you're here to learn."

He lifted the stethoscope from her chest and picked up a blood pressure cuff. His hands were gentle but efficient as he wrapped it around her arm. "I think that's obvious."

Lane gave a snort of derisive laughter. "Really? It's obvious to you why the United States government would want to imprison and torture a group of people who just want to be left alone?" She dared to look up into his eyes and then looked away again. The depths of them were too much, and they told her things that were far too uncomfortable to contemplate.

"People?" he questioned quietly as he tightened the cuff. "Is that what you call yourselves? Seems to me like there's something completely different going on here."

The wave of rage overtook her so quickly, Lane hardly even knew what she was doing. She shoved against the doctor with every bit of strength that hadn't been drained from her body by bleeding and constant shifting and starvation. He toppled backwards into a rack of test tubes, several of which fell and shattered on the floor.

"Yes, people! And we have a right to live peacefully instead of being attacked by assholes like you!" She launched herself off the table and marched straight up to him, unafraid of what he might do. Let them kill her. If she could take a few of them out in the process and improve the odds for the rest of the dragons, then it'd be worth it. "If I wanted to, I could slit your throat and bleed you dry so fast, you wouldn't even have a chance to blink."

She might've thrown him off balance physically, but the doctor was unruffled by her efforts. He put his palms on the table that held the test tube rack and straightened, the effort pushing his body against hers as his gaze bored into her. "Yes, you could. If you wanted to."

"Is that a dare?" Her wings pulsed against the underside of her skin. They couldn't have done her much good in that tiny space, but her true, complete form longed to come out for the first time since the attack. She felt the pain of her claws threatening to emerge from her fingertips, ready to shred his skin into ribbons.

"No," Dr. Cunningham replied quietly. "I think you know as well as I do that both you and the others are much better off if you keep your heads down and cooperate. That's exactly why you've been doing it all along, too. Now I suggest you get back on that table and let me finish up before I have to call those buffoons back in here to sedate you."

Lane could feel the heat of his skin against hers, but it

was subtle. He had a completely different feel to him than either the humans or dragons, and it aroused her curiosity in a way she couldn't explain. So did his calm and patient manner with her. Dr. Cunningham had been quick to snap at the soldier he'd been bossing around, and it would've made sense for him to treat her at least as poorly, if not more so. Dr. Blake acted like the dragons were nothing more than animals, often ignoring the fact that they even knew English. Why should he even give her a second chance?

She could easily do just as she'd said and slit his throat, but she found herself backing up toward the exam table and sitting on the end of it once again. Lane told herself it was because she didn't want to risk any revenge by the doctors or his henchmen on her people for her actions. She clenched her jaw as she kept her head turned away from him while he finished getting her vitals.

"Hold still," he cautioned as he approached with the needle.

Lane felt her body instinctively tighten, but she forced it to relax. The injections always hurt worse when her muscles were taut, and it was purely self-preservation that made her let go. Or was it? She was already behaving differently around him than she did around the other humans.

Her stomach churned in anticipation. Lane expected the burning heat of the drug to sear through her veins, but it only caused a slight chill. Her skin didn't erupt in scales, and she didn't feel the creak of her bones as they were caught somewhere between species.

She swiveled her head to look at him. "What did you just give me?"

"Has anyone ever told you before?" he asked calmly, not rising to the bait of her ire.

"No," she admitted, "but I can tell this is different."

"It's just a bit of saline solution. You're dehydrated. It should make you feel better." He capped the needle and tossed it into the sharps container.

Lane studied the injection site, disbelieving. "Why would you give a shit about that?"

"Doesn't it make sense to keep our subjects alive?" He picked up a clipboard and scribbled something on it.

She wanted to keep arguing with him just for the sake of doing so, but her mind had shot back to what she'd left in her chamber. "In that case, my friend is very sick," she said quietly. "She needs help."

Dr. Cunningham set the clipboard down and folded his arms in front of his chest. "What kind of sick?"

"A fever maybe. She's burning up and she doesn't want to wake up." Her heart ached as she thought of Edi. As she told the new doctor about her old friend, she wondered if she'd regret it. Dr. Cunningham had just said he wanted to keep them all alive, but what if he was just saying that to keep her from killing him? And what if a sick dragon who was hardly used for the experiments anyway wasn't worth keeping alive in their eyes?

But the doctor nodded slowly, his brow creasing. He scratched his chin. "I'll see what I can do."

"Thank you." The words felt wrong on her tongue. She couldn't possibly be polite to these bastards, and yet here she was begging for help and groveling as soon as he gave her even the slightest reason to hope.

His hand closed on her elbow to help her down from the table. "Time for you to go back." He escorted her only as far as the door where the lackeys with guns were waiting. "Take her back and bring the old woman here," he commanded. They did as they were told without argument this time.

Lane was stunned as she went along with them, hardly even registering the walk back into the cavern and to her chamber. She was jolted out of her distant thoughts as the soldiers put their hands on Edi and Brandy tried to fight them off.

"Leave her alone or I'll separate your skin from the rest of your body," she snarled.

Lane put a hand on her shoulder and gently pushed her back. "It's all right. She's going to get help." She kept Brandy at bay while Edi was lifted onto a gurney and trundled off down the passageway.

"Are you nuts?" Brandy exploded. "There's no telling what they're going to do to her! We'll be lucky if we even see her again!" Her blue eyes were electric with rage and a shimmer of scales erupted on her arm without any prompting by strange drugs.

"I promise, it's all right. Or at least, it's better than it has been. There's a different doctor here now."

"Instead of Dr. Blake?" Brandy asked breathlessly.

Lane shook her head. "I'm not sure. I didn't even think to ask him. I just know that he's new, and he's different."

Brandy wasn't buying it and she glared at Lane curiously. "What kind of *different*? Does this mean you decided to seduce someone instead?"

"Of course not," Lane said firmly. "It's nothing like that. But he gave me a shot of saline instead of anything else, and he was talking about how important it is to keep us alive."

"I see," Brandy said with a roll of her eyes. "This is— what do they call it?—Stockholm Syndrome. You're not seeing them as the bad guys anymore. Just take a gander across the way there at Liam and maybe that'll remind you what side you're supposed to be on."

"No, no. It's not like that, either. I'm not saying he's a good guy. He can't be. But I don't get the same feeling from him as I do the others. Don't give me that look. I know how it sounds. I do. Just trust me on this. He said he's going to help Edi."

Brandy gathered her dark hair and twisted it into a knot at the nape of her neck as she paced the chamber. "All I can say is that I hope you're right. We're living in some pretty fucked up circumstances right now, and I don't have any good solution to it." She flopped down in the corner, pulled her knees up to her chest, and wrapped her arms around them.

Lane moved to comfort her just as Brandy had done for her, but she couldn't get Dr. Cunningham off her mind. There was a chance he was just buying time and buttering the dragons up so they'd be more cooperative, and then he could turn around and show his superiors just how talented he was at taming wild beasts. It could be that he simply hadn't worked around shifters before, as most humans hadn't, and he'd change once he understood.

Maybe, just maybe, he was genuinely a decent person. Maybe he would be the factor that would change the dragons' chances of survival. She could easily feel his hand on her arm, a memory that had been tattooed into her brain. Whoever this man was, she hoped she was right about him.

6

Ash's heart sat like a stone in his chest as he waited for the meeting to start. He was grateful to Jack for not only having the right connections to get him in there, but for having the right talent to alter his credentials in the system so Ash could pass himself off as a doctor. He'd been through a basic amount of training as a medic in order to offer help to fallen fellow soldiers, so he certainly knew more than simple first aid, but he definitely didn't qualify for his new position.

And even though it benefited him to get on the inside and see what was going on, Ash was incredibly disturbed. His first visit there had been troubling enough when he'd seen all those dragons in pain. But he was finding that the more time he spent there, the more appalled he was.

"All right." Dr. Blake sat down with a mug of coffee in his hand, smiling around the room as though this was a routine meeting at some small-town hospital back in the States. "I guess it's time we got started. I think you've all met Dr. Cunningham."

The rest of the team nodded their acknowledgement. Though Ash and Dr. Blake were the "official" doctors, the Army had assigned an entire scientific team to this location. Ash had seen them gathering and analyzing data from the dragons, staring through microscopes, and swapping petri dishes. He noted that none of the soldiers had been invited to the meeting. Clearly, Dr. Blake didn't see them as anything more than grunts.

"I know some of you have already asked me why Dr. Cunningham has been brought in," Dr. Blake continued. "There was plenty of work here for the rest of us, and so I have to wonder that myself. Dr. Cunningham, perhaps you can fill me in on exactly why I'm no longer good enough for my own job." He was smiling, but there was ice in his voice colder than the weather outside.

Ash smiled back. He might not have been a doctor, but he knew how this game worked. Dr. Blake felt threatened by his presence; he wouldn't have been someone Ash could've counted on as an ally even if he didn't know that Ash was truly a polar bear. Folding his hands on the table in front of him, he replied, "Oh, I assure you it's nothing like that at all! There's no plan to take you off this project. Rather, the government just wants to see it move along a little faster."

"And why would your presence here help that?" Dr. Blake asked baldly. "As far as I saw, you don't have any better medical credentials than I do."

Ash shook his head. "No, I don't. But what I do have is experience. I'm not at liberty to explain all the details, but I think I can safely say that I've worked with shifters before."

This shook Dr. Blake enough to wipe that fake smile off his face. "You have? But I thought this was the first shifter experiment we've had!"

"Like I said, I'm not at liberty to explain all the details," Ash repeated. Pretending to have classified information could be just as valuable as actually having it. "But the president believes I can move this process along a little faster and help us get some real results. I've had a chance to look through some of the records, although I admit that's been slowed down a lot by the fact that we're not doing anything digitally for security reasons. At this point, I think it would be helpful if we just talk about what's been going on here, where we're at, and what sort of timelines we think we can expect from here on out."

Dr. Blake didn't appreciate having the meeting taken over, but a young woman across the table who'd been staring at Ash with doe eyes was eager to speak up. "Personally, I think we're making significant progress in that we've been able to get some of them to shift permanently into their reptilian state."

"Permanently?" Ash questioned, his stomach turning as he imagined what it'd be like to be stuck in one form or another.

She lifted one shoulder. "Permanently, at least so far. Obviously, it's not going to help us as much if we have to keep giving them continuous injections to keep them in that state. The fewer interactions we have with them the better, but we're still waiting to see how long the effects of the drug will last. Subject 245 has remained in his reptilian state for over two weeks now."

"I see," Ash replied quietly, trying not to react too much. The idea wasn't one he liked to entertain. "What other conclusions can we draw?"

A young man next to her with thick glasses and messy hair spoke up. "Even if we manage to keep them in their reptilian state, I don't see how we can ever possibly use them."

"What do you mean?" *Use* them?

The nerd shrugged. "I mean, how you can you truly utilize a weapon you can't control? Sure, we've been able to keep them as dragons—at least for the time being—but that's about the extent of our progress. Take Subject 245 for example. Yes, he's a dragon. No, he doesn't show any signs of reverting. But he's also completely unmanageable. We have to tranquilize him several times a day just to keep him from killing himself, and even then we're not able to completely sedate him. We didn't have that problem when he was in his human form, which leads me to believe that his resistance to current medication has something to do with what form he's currently in."

Ash felt a chill sweep over his body like a wave. Their goal was to weaponize the dragons. These scientists not only knew that shifters existed—something that was foreboding for any shifter, regardless of species—but they were planning to exploit them. In his mind's eye, Ash could see all the possible scenarios the government thought they were going to get out of it. Ruthless killing machines who could be sent to dangerous territories with the simple command to kill on sight? That sounded just like something they'd do.

He cleared his throat and fiddled with his pen. "I see. While I wasn't here to take over, I was asked to see how everything was going and assess if any sort of improvements were needed. The first thing I suggest is altering the way we're taking care of our patients. They're thin and dehydrated, to say the least. One older subject that I took care of yesterday appeared to be at death's door. These creatures aren't going to be of any use to anyone if they're dead."

Dr. Blake flung his hand carelessly in the air. "Who

cares? Even if the government doesn't use them as their latest weapon, we owe it to the scientific community to see just what they're capable of. Besides that, we know they're just going to get killed in battle, anyway. There's not much point in worrying about them."

"I think there is," Ash argued. "In the studies that I conducted, the subjects did much better when they were kept in decent conditions. That means we need to do a better job of feeding them and finding a way to keep them from getting so listless. Maybe some vitamin and saline injections, too."

Dr. Blake pounded his fist on the table. "This isn't the humane society, Cunningham. We're not here to make them happy so someone will want to adopt them. We're talking about dangerous animals; ones who'd just as soon bite our heads off! What you're proposing is ridiculous and a waste of time."

Ash forced another smile onto this face. He knew that he was just as capable of ripping Dr. Blake limb from limb as the dragons were, but it'd have to wait. "I'm wasting time?" he asked. "Is that why they sent me here to speed up this experiment and get the fucking show on the road? You might not know anything about my work, Dr. Blake, but the U.S. Army most certainly does, and they wouldn't have spent the money getting me down here if I wasn't worth it."

"What you said makes total sense," enthused the young woman. Ash realized he might have to actually learn their names at some point, depending on how long he was stuck there. "The drugs might be having a different effect on the dragons if they're not in good health. It shouldn't take all that much more effort to give them a better life while they're here." The other scientists nodded and murmured in agreement.

"Ridiculous," Dr. Blake repeated, more subdued this time now that it was clear everyone was against him. "The next thing I know, you'll be sending them on a spa cruise to thank them for their troubles!"

Ash didn't want to anger the man, but only because he wasn't ready to show his hand just yet. "All I ask right now, doc, is that you give it a chance. See if it makes things go a little more smoothly. It's just an idea."

Dr. Blake lifted his chin and puckered his mouth. He knew he was being cajoled like a petulant child, but he didn't seem to mind. "Have it your way, but I'll be keeping a sharp eye on the results."

"Thank you."

The rest of the meeting flew by in a blur of various statistics and ideas. Ash tried to pay attention, but he couldn't stop thinking about what was truly happening there. If the government had its way, the skies over enemy territory would soon be filled with fire breathing dragons.

———

HE WAS STILL THINKING HARD as he swept through the cavern an hour later, his lab coat flying out to either side of him. His assigned bodyguard rushed to keep up, and he managed to get the argumentative soldier moved somewhere else. The last thing Ash needed right now was to be unnecessarily questioned.

What he did need was to find a way to get the dragons on his side, especially since they would start feeling much better soon if he had anything to do with it. There were still some kinks to work out, and he knew he'd be spending a lot of time reporting in later that evening, but he'd find a way to make this work.

"That one," he barked. This time, he stuck around as the soldiers got her out of the cell. It was the same woman who'd shoved him into the lab table just a couple of days ago. She'd combed her hair out with her fingers. There was more confidence to her step and a pugnacious upturn of her nose as she walked along next to him and headed toward the mobile lab.

Ash could feel his eyes on her as he waited for the door to close behind them after one last uncertain look from the soldiers.

"I don't know what you're doing, and I know for the most part I don't like it, but I do want to say thank you for making Edi feel better," the dragon told him quietly, apparently just as aware as he was that someone could be listening in. "She was able to get some food down today and her fever seems to be gone."

"Good," Ash replied genuinely. It'd broken his heart to see the old woman moaning on his exam table the previous day. He hadn't known for sure what was wrong with her, but some anti-inflammatories, a saline IV, and a hot bowl of soup could make anyone feel better, at least a little. A good dose of IV glutathione hadn't hurt, either. "Hopefully it was just a virus of some sort."

She glared at him doubtfully. "How would she get a virus in a place like this? It was probably something Dr. Blake did to her." She swept her gaze away from him, staring angrily into the corner of the lab instead.

Ash sighed. There was a chance she was right. He hadn't had a chance to dig through all the records yet. Blake and the rest of the team had been keeping extensive notes, and once he'd understood what their mission was, he hadn't worried too much about the details. "I suppose it's possible."

He picked up his clipboard, noting that it only had her subject number at the top. "What's your name?"

Her head spun fast as she turned to look at him again. "What?"

"Your name," he repeated, trying to be patient. But he knew he was on a time limit.

"Why do you want to know?" She narrowed her eyes.

He stepped closer and set the clipboard on the exam table. "Because I'm here to help you."

"Ha!" Her bark of laughter was too loud, and it made Ash glance toward the door. "I'll believe that as soon as all this ice melts and we find ourselves on a tropical beach."

"I'm serious," he insisted. Damn it. He could've gone to any of the dragons to explain his situation. Well, almost any of them. The angry blue dragon wouldn't have been the best candidate. But there were plenty of others he could've tried to talk to. He needed them to understand what he was there to do and how they could help both him and themselves. "I'm not with the military, at least not anymore, and I'm here to help you and the rest of the dragons."

She was silent for a breath as she studied his face, her azure eyes drifting down his nose, along his jawline, and back up to his salt and pepper hair. He felt her scrutiny like a physical presence, as though she'd reached out and touched him with her fingers. Ash felt himself leaning slightly closer, wishing that she would.

"I don't believe you," she finally said.

Ash rubbed his hand over his eyes. "All right. Then at least tell me why not." There had to be some way to reason with her.

The dragon shook her head. "Nobody else knows we're here. Up until your buddies showed up, we'd been living alone for decades. And it doesn't make sense that someone would come swooping in here to rescue us if they don't know we exist."

"Okay. Fair enough. Let me try this again." He couldn't reveal that he was with the Special Ops Shifter Force, not unless it was absolutely necessary. That secret was new enough to him, and with her living in Antarctica for so long, he doubted she'd heard of them anyway. "You're a shifter. There are other types of shifters in the world, right?"

She nodded slowly, her forehead creasing. "Right."

"I'm one of them."

Her eyes were a magnet for his own. She stared into his soul, and yet he couldn't look away. His bear was going wild inside him. He didn't understand why. This nameless woman made both his brain and his body do strange things. It was difficult to think around her, and his former commanding officers would've been disappointed in his lack of eloquence.

"You're telling me you're a shifter," she said slowly. Ash noted the slightest change in her eyes, but it was clear she was still skeptical. "I think you've been inhaling too many fumes here in this little laboratory. Or you've been working too hard. You need to take a vacation."

Ash sighed. "It's not like that. I can't give you all the details right now. I don't even have them all, and I certainly don't have much time. If I keep you in here for too long and you're not howling in pain, then Blake and the others are going to start wondering what's going on."

She waved her hand at the door where they both knew the soldiers were waiting on the other side. "Would you prefer I start screaming? I've never thought of myself as an actress, but I suppose I can try." Her voice dripped with sarcasm.

"All I'm asking you to do right now is to believe me. I want you to understand that I'm not the enemy. There's nothing I want more right now than to see you and the rest of the dragons released from here safe and sound." He spoke quietly, his face only inches from hers. He could feel the distance between them, down to the very millimeter.

She hopped off the lab table, increasing the distance and pulling her face away from his. "That's a lovely thought, but I'm afraid it's not realistic."

"You're just a difficult woman, aren't you?" The words had come out of his mouth unbidden, and he instantly wished he could take them back. He sounded like such an ass, and the only thing he wanted was to help. It wasn't even about the SOS Force anymore, except for the fact that he would need their assistance to make this happen.

"Just realistic," she corrected him. "And if you're a shifter like you say you are, then why don't they have you locked up, too?"

Ash realized that although he'd given her that piece of

information as his way of proving his identity, he'd actually given her a weapon. This dragon could turn him in to Dr. Blake, and then he'd be a test subject right along with them. It was too late, though. "They don't know," he ground out.

She inspected him as though she were looking for some physical evidence of what he'd said. "And I don't know, either."

"Fine." Ash was only barely in control of his own body, maintaining just enough command to keep himself from pinning her against the wall and inhaling her scent. What he was about to do was difficult and dangerous, but he didn't see any other option. He wondered only briefly what Drake and the others would think if they could see him as he yanked back the sleeve of his lab coat.

A shiver rippled up his spine, across his shoulders, and down his arm, where he let it expand. He clenched his jaw against a low moan as a patch of white fur erupted from his forearm.

The woman stared at it. Her fingers twitched, and he was instantly reminded of the way she'd touched him only a few days ago. That seemed like an eternity ago now, and Ash couldn't explain why he longed for her to do exactly that.

"I'm a shifter," he repeated huskily.

"I suppose that's true enough. It doesn't prove that you're actually here to help, though." She turned away from him again.

He felt his shoulders slump in defeat. "I suppose not."

She gestured at the various medical equipment around the lab. "Is that all? Or are you going to shoot me up with something?"

Ash felt like the evil wizard who'd been vanquished from the castle. This woman was simply impossible, and he wasn't sure she would ever believe him. "No. I'm not here to do that."

"Right. I'll just be on my way then." She headed for the door.

Ash was instantly behind her, knowing it would give everything away if she just marched out of the lab by herself. She glanced up at him as he took her elbow, but for once, they understood each other. She spoke just as he reached for the knob.

"It's Lane, by the way."

"What?"

"My name. It's Lane."

When she was gone, Ash took a moment to forge the records for her visit to the lab, lest Blake have any more reason to question who he was and why he was there. It was difficult to even come up with reasonable numbers on his own in the wake of her presence. This woman had such an effect on him that it made Ash wonder if he'd even be able to complete this mission. After flicking back to look at the previous records so that he could make a decent forgery, he grabbed a parka and headed outside.

A scowl towards the guards at the perimeter allowed him to leave without question, and Ash headed into the wilderness. He didn't have any specific direction in mind. He only knew that he needed to get away from this awful place for a moment and figure out how he was going to take the dragons with him, with or without Lane's help.

7

It was late. The dragons who were able to sleep were snoozing away, and even the night guard of soldiers was lax. They relied on the bars to keep the dragons at bay.

Lane listened to the sounds of heavy breathing around her, noting the sound of someone weeping further on down the cavern. She wished she could reach out to whoever was still awake and grieving over their situation, but it would only call attention from the guards.

Instead, she flopped angrily on her uncomfortable pallet. It would've almost been easier if Dr. Cunningham had been the villain she'd pegged him for. Then it wouldn't matter how undeniably attractive he was or that he'd helped Edi. The way he affected her would simply be a product of the various chemicals constantly being pumped into her immune system, but that was a difficult excuse to use when he hadn't done anything of the sort. She huffed as she writhed on the hard floor.

"Are you sick, child?" Edi's muffled voice asked in the darkness.

"Only in my mind, I think," Lane replied quietly. "I can't seem to shut my brain off."

"Sometimes it helps to talk about it."

Lane nodded, but then she stopped. "I'm sorry. I don't mean to burden you. You need your rest."

The dark form of the older woman moved, sitting up next to Lane. "I can sleep all day if I want to, dear. Lay it on me."

Taking a deep breath, Lane hesitated as she thought of all the other dragons around them. If anyone woke up, they could hear the awful secret she was about to reveal. But they were her flight, her people. They'd known her for decades, and the only reason they didn't already know what was going on with her was because they'd been separated and assigned numbers.

"It's about the new doctor. He's different," she began.

"I can agree with that. I wasn't sure what to expect when they brought me to him. I thought they might put me out of my misery, so to speak. But he was very gentle, and he made me feel a lot better. I'm not sure how much of a benefit that is, considering I'm still here, but I'll take what I can get."

Lane smiled, even though she knew Edi couldn't see it.

"I'm glad he was able to help you. I worried so much that I'd made the wrong decision when I told him you were ill. But I could tell right away there was something different about him."

"Maybe the government decided to send in someone with morals."

She couldn't help but let out a snicker of laughter at that. "That's a possibility, but there's much more to him than what we can see on the surface."

"Oh? Then maybe you should stop beating around the bush and just tell me what's going on."

Lane lowered her voice to the barest whisper. "He's not part of the scientific team. I don't even know if Dr. Cunningham is his real name, but he told me today that he's here to help us. I tried to argue with him about that because I just couldn't believe it was possibly true. But then he told me he's a shifter."

Edi sucked in a breath. "One of us?"

"Not exactly. He's a polar bear. And I wasn't even sure I believed him, but he showed me. *He's* the polar bear I saw here in the cavern just a little bit before he arrived as a new scientist. I mean, he didn't say that, and I was too shocked to ask him, but it makes sense." She shivered as she recalled the image of that bear just on the other side of the bars and the way his fur had felt under her hand. When Dr. Cunningham had shown her the same fur bursting from his skin, it'd been all she could do not to touch it.

The old woman's cool hand touched her own. "If that's true, then maybe there's hope after all."

"I know. I just don't understand why a polar bear would be interested in saving a group of dragons. It doesn't make sense, and that bothers me."

"Maybe we shouldn't look a gift horse in the mouth. If he says he's here to help, and he's the only chance we have at a friend, then I don't think it would be wise to turn him away. Did he have a plan?"

Lane shook her head. "I don't think so. He was rather vague, and he seemed more interested in convincing me he was a shifter than anything else."

"I see." Edi was silent for a moment. "I suppose we should spread the word to make sure no one kills him before he can get us out of here. Liam over there has already taken out a couple of soldiers, and Dr. Blake won't even take him out of his chamber anymore."

"Do you think it's wise?" Lane questioned. "I mean, what if he can't save us after all? That's going to be very disappointing for everyone."

"True enough, but hope is a powerful thing. Sometimes people can achieve things they wouldn't have otherwise simply because they *believe* they can. We won't make any grand announcement. It just needs to be a whisper passed among us. We can do that."

"Right. Okay." Lane nodded, forcing herself to acknowledge Edi's good sense. "There's one other thing that bothers me, though."

"Yes?"

"He's a polar bear, and I'm a dragon, but..."

"Go on, dear."

The words were hard to push out of her throat, even though they'd been lurking in the back of her mind ever since Dr. Cunningham had shown up. "I think I'm fated to him. No one has ever made me feel like that. I get this unbelievable urge to let my dragon out, and yet I want to remain human so that I can interact with him. I want to be near him, even though it drives me crazy. All the signs are there, but how can I possibly be attracted to a *bear* of all creatures?"

"And why not?" Edi questioned as she wrapped a comforting arm around Lane's shoulders. "We always think of our mates as being just like ourselves and the rest of our flight. I admit it's convenient when things work out that way, but we don't get to tell the universe what we want. So he's a polar bear. If he makes you feel things, then that's all that really matters."

"You really think so? I was afraid you'd be disappointed in me." The older woman had talked to Lane numerous times about settling down and finding the right person, and though recent events had shoved those ideas temporarily aside, they weren't avoidable forever.

Edi gave a soft chuckle, the noise vibrating through her

chest. "Disappointed in you? My dear, you're one of the strongest women I know. Even when you were a child, you never let anyone boss you around. Your sense of determination has often been one of your strongest qualities, and it's always been a comfort to me to know that you can get through anything the world throws at you. I can't be anything but happy as long as I know your heart's happy."

Lane hugged the old woman, suddenly feeling sleep drag her eyelids downward. "I needed that."

The very next morning, the two of them set about the task they'd assigned themselves. Lane whispered to Brandy, and Edi had a long conversation with Amy in the opposite corner of the chamber later that day. Without even speaking, they'd decided that it would be too much if all the dragons were seen conferring with one another. When the guards took their lunch break, Lane managed to whisper across the hall to Liam.

"This would be a lot easier if we could all just shift and speak telepathically," she grumbled to Edi later on that night.

"I wonder if the scientists know that," the old woman mused. "Hopefully, we won't be around long enough to see them tackle that subject."

Through their various states of dragon and human, word spread among the flight. Lane didn't know if it was her own optimism making her see things, but she could swear she saw a new sense of confidence and expectation in her own people. Their eyes were brighter and they ate with more appetite than she'd seen in a while. They cooperated with guards when they were taken off to see Dr. Cunningham, and they always returned with more energy than they'd left with.

There was a change in the soldiers and the scientific team, as well. More food and fresher water were offered on a regular basis. The goons weren't as rough and rude as they handled their test subjects. It was obvious to Lane that Dr. Blake was still administering his experimental drugs, since every now and then she'd hear moans of pain and catch the scent of blood. It wasn't an ideal situation, by any means, but even the smallest improvement felt like a big change.

Unfortunately, it seemed the other change was that Dr. Cunningham was rarely seen in the cavern. Lane caught a glimpse of him here and there as he conferred with the other scientists about the dragons in the other chambers, but he stayed well away from her.

"Don't be so downhearted about it," Edi whispered one night. "If you know what the relationship is between the two of you, then it's quite likely he does as well. His position here is risky enough. No reason to make it any more complicated."

Lane only hoped she was right.

A week later, Dr. Cunningham appeared outside her chamber with a man on either side of him. One of them was tall and broad, with styled hair and dark blue eyes that made him look like he should be on a television soap opera. The other man had dark hair and green eyes, his figure too well-muscled to belong to a scientist. Lane narrowed her eyes as she looked at them. All three wore lab coats to denote their positions as doctors, but she instantly knew the one with green eyes was absolutely not a human.

"Subject 438, I need you to come with me," Dr. Cunningham said quietly. He hadn't even brought any soldiers with him.

Lane knew that was her, and she knew by now that she could trust Dr. Cunningham, but she sensed a change in the air that made nervous energy crackle around her stomach. Something was happening.

The four of them made their way toward the cavern entrance, but Dr. Blake stepped out of his lab and stopped them. "What's this, Cunningham? I wasn't informed!"

Dr. Cunningham lifted an eyebrow. "You didn't get the memo? My associates have been brought in to evaluate the experiment and decide if the government is going to continue funding this experiment."

"I most certainly did not!" Blake spluttered. "I suggest you get that thing back in her cage and come to my office. I'm going to get this sorted out once and for all. I send all my reports up the chain and there's no reason for anyone to come all the way down here just to make sure I do my job!"

"With all due respect, we've got work to do." Cunningham resumed his walk toward the exit.

Blake wasn't taking no for an answer. "Let me remind you that I'm the commanding officer of this base! You have no right to waltz around here like you're in charge!"

Cunningham sighed. "Gentlemen, if you'd like to take the test subject to the lab I'll be with you momentarily. I can personally guarantee your safety now that I've achieved complete control over this creature."

His words pissed her off in a way she could hardly put into words, but it wasn't as though Lane had a chance to do so anyway. The two big men swept her on down the tunnel as Dr. Cunningham remained behind to deal with Blake.

"We don't have a lot of time," said the dark-haired man when they reached the mobile lab Cunningham used, "so I hope you don't have a lot of questions.

"I have one I'd like to start with," Lane asserted. She didn't know these men, but she could only assume they were on her side if Cunningham was. "You're one of us, aren't you?"

He nodded and put out his hand. "Garrison Stokes."

She took it, pleasantly surprised at the thrill of dragon energy that shot through her body when she did so. It was the same feeling she got when she was around anyone else in her flight, a sense of family and ancient remembrance, like visiting a long-lost cousin. It instantly made her feel better about everything. "But how?" she stammered. "I... I thought we were the only ones..."

"Like I said, very little time for questions. If all goes as planned, we can talk about it all later. Right now, you need to understand the plan."

Lane nodded. "I'm listening."

"Dr. Drake Sheridan," said the other man, shaking her hand as well. "Just a boring old bear. I'm afraid we have even less time than we'd originally estimated now that Dr. Blake is throwing a fit. He doesn't strike me as the kind of man who's just going to step aside and let us do whatever we want, unfortunately." He turned from her and began fiddling with the various test tubes on a nearby table.

"Ash has already been working on building you and your people back up," Garrison began explaining.

It took Lane a moment to understand who he was talking about, but she soon understood that was Dr. Cunningham's first name. "Yes. I swear I see a difference."

"As you should," Drake offered. "Antioxidants, anti-inflammatories, vitamins, and saline are much healthier than whatever shit this is." He frowned at a test tube full of brown liquid.

"Unfortunately," Garrison added, "Dr. Blake has been continuing his experimentation, so not everyone has been able to recover. That's why we're here."

"I'm getting rid of every bit of nastiness, both out of this lab and the one in the cave," Drake said, making a disgusted face at several more beakers and tubes. "It's easy enough to do it here where Ash has been working, but it'll be a little more difficult to get into Blake's lab."

"What can I do to help?" Lane offered.

At least this was a question they didn't seem to mind, and Garrison was quick to answer. "We mostly need you for communication at the moment. In order for this to be a success, we need to have all the dragons behind us."

"Not a problem," she assured him. "I've already told them that Dr. Cunningham is on our side, and I think they've been very receptive to it."

"Good. As soon as we get the rest of our team down here, we're going to come in fast. The doors on those chambers will blow. The soldiers will be taken out. My biggest concern is that I don't want any of your flight to be fighting against the wrong people."

"We know these people well at this point. They've been keeping us here for a long time, and I think we can handle targeting the right ones." Now excitement joined the hope sizzling inside her.

"We're not asking you to do that," Garrison corrected. "We're just trying to get you healthy enough to escape for the time being."

Since he was a fellow dragon, Lane was already thinking of him as a brother. She reached out and laid her hand on his arm. "But you *should* be asking us to do that, or at least let us. What we've been through is horrid. I have no doubt that some of us will be grateful just to get away, but I have no doubt it'd be therapeutic to help take these bastards out."

Garrison hesitated for only a moment before he nodded. "All right. I'm not going to turn down having as many people as possible on our side. There will be a boat docked on the nearest shore when this all goes down. That's where everyone needs to be heading when they're done."

"Understood."

"Good. Now with what time we have left, I need you to tell me everything you know about this place. The more information we have, the better chance we've got of pulling this off."

Lane immediately began speaking, telling them everything she could think of about the structure of the cavern, the lay of the land above, and the schedules of the scientists and soldiers. It felt like a dream. She'd been reluctant to put her faith in Dr. Cunningham, but maybe it was all going to work out after all.

———

THE NEXT DAY, though, that no longer seemed like the case. Dr. Blake strode confidently up and down the center passage of the cavern, examining the occupants of the chambers and dictating notes to one of his groveling assistants. "Just look at them, Hopkins. That Cunningham asshole thought he could swoop in here and take over my entire project with his whining about humane treatment and health. These things are weapons! I don't give a shit if they live or die, as long as they get me my next promotion!" He laughed loudly, a sound that filled the chambers.

"Yes, sir," Hopkins replied nervously.

"The first thing we're going to do now that Dr. Humane Society is gone is get these dragons back on the same regimen I originally wanted for them. There's no reason to pamper them so much when all I really care about is how the drugs are affecting them. Once we can nail down the right formula, we can start worrying about how it affects their health."

"But sir, Cunningham mentioned he had some of them completely tamed. I looked through his research files, and he didn't make any note of how he'd done it. I don't know if it was the drugs or just some special bond he had with them. How do we plan on proceeding with that part of the process?" Beads of sweat stood out on Hopkins' forehead, despite the cool air.

Lane turned toward the wall to hide her smile. No doubt, Hopkins and the other assistants and soldiers had gotten used to the seeming domestication of the dragons, and none of them were interested in having to worry about whether or not they'd literally get their heads bitten off.

"Again, that's something that can wait until later," Blake

retorted impatiently. "Let's not waste any more time. Let's start with this one, Cunningham's little pet. I think she could use a good dose of DH709, don't you?"

"Yes, sir. Right away, sir." Hopkins gestured for the soldiers to retrieve Lane from her cage.

She went with them willingly. It disturbed her that Cunningham and the others were gone, and Blake's confidence in regaining control of the facility couldn't be a good sign. Had they been killed? Or had Blake just been able to pull some strings with the Pentagon to have them ousted? Either way, she knew the drugs Cunningham had worked so hard to develop were long gone.

But they didn't lead her on down the passage toward either one of the labs. A soldier gleefully twisted her arms behind her back, causing her knees to crumple underneath her as Hopkins stabbed her in the arm. He wasn't very good with a needle, and she felt it tear through her blood vessels. Lane gasped in shock as she felt that old, familiar burn. Her eyes widened and she turned to her chamber, hoping to communicate somehow to her fellow dragons to let them know they weren't out of the woods yet.

Her body writhed uncontrollably in the grip of the soldier. "Should I put her back, boss?"

"No, not yet. Let's see what happens. This is my latest formula, one that even Cunningham didn't know about. With a little bit of luck, I'll be calling General Thompson within the week to tell him we're on the right track." Dr. Blake grinned as he watched Lane flail in pain.

Her lungs stopped working as her back twisted. She was shifting, but it had to be the most painful transition she'd ever been through. Her wings felt like razors as they burst from her back, knocking one of the soldiers aside in a shower of blood. Each of her scales were like blunt spears being stabbed through her skin. Loud cracks sounded from her spine as it stretched and twisted to accommodate her other body. Blood darkened the crimson of her scales as she lashed out with her newly clawed hands, reaching for the doctor.

He backed away. "Finally! A complete transition on this one! I think we can call this a success!"

But his workers didn't seem nearly as excited about it as he was. The soldiers could no longer keep a hold of her as her tail and wings thrashed through the air, and Hopkins had pressed himself against the farthest wall.

"Stop being babies and sedate her, you idiots," Blake barked.

"I didn't bring it," Hopkins murmured, cowering behind his clipboard.

"You what?" Blake's face paled as he turned to the dragon who squirmed and twisted on the floor.

Lane's instincts were taking over just as her body was. All the logic and reasoning of her human side was gone. She knew only who the enemy was, and it was her job to tear him apart. "I know what you've done to my people," she rasped. "You deserve a punishment that's ten times worse."

Blake turned on his heels and ran.

Lane didn't quite have control of her body. She dragged herself across the floor, her back legs refusing to work and her wings flapping uselessly. Every cell buzzed and vibrated, alive but not listening. Her mouth watered as she craved her revenge, and she was determined to get it.

Thunder rolled through the cavern. Lane paused in her efforts, feeling dirt and rocks rain down on her from above. This was it! She knew it in her gut. Whatever had happened to Cunningham and the others, they'd come back, just as they said they would.

She turned for her chamber. "You've got to get out," she growled. But she knew from experience that even dragons weren't strong enough to get those bars open. How was this going to work into Garrison's plan? How were they possibly going to get out of there? Gunfire raged near the entrance, and what soldiers were left in the cavern streamed toward it.

The back entrance, however, the one the soldiers had deemed too small to worry over, suddenly became flooded with animals. To her amazement, a wolf came trotting casually into the passageway, a pack of explosives on his back. He was joined by a large red fox who was equally burdened. The wolf paused only long enough to shift, his neck cracking as he took on the figure of a man.

" I need my damn hands!" The former wolf whipped off his pack and began setting charges near the base of the bars.

The fox, too, had changed into a human, although he slightly retained some of the coloring in his hair. "Stand back," he said to the women in the chamber as he assisted the wolf.

A familiar polar bear followed them, a dark grizzly at his side. As Lane watched the great white creature, she no longer knew if her inability to move was because of the drug Blake had injected her with or because of her close proximity to Ash, each of them in their animal forms. The pull was strong, but they had more important matters to take care of.

Whatever was happening outside, it must not have been going well for the soldiers. They came surging back into the cavern for shelter just as the first charge exploded. It rocked the cavern and filled the air with dust. As it cleared, Lane saw Brandy emerge through the broken bars. She'd shifted and let out a roar as she flew through the tunnel. Amy and Edi came after her, somewhat more slowly, but not any less resolute. Lane could feel them in her minds now, a refreshing sensation that she hadn't experienced in ages.

A massive green dragon was at her side. "What's

wrong?" Garrison asked in the scratchy voice of his reptilian form. "Why can't you move?"

"It's the drugs," she explained. "Blake had more of them."

"I'll get you out of here."

"No." She put out one hand to stop him. "It's getting better and I'll be fine soon. Get the others."

He gave her an uncertain look before heading off to tear down any bars that remained after the explosives.

The soldiers that had come back into the cavern were faced with the reality that it was no longer a safe place for them. They were met with the onslaught of two angry bears with an appetite and a cohort of dragons with a taste for revenge. Lane felt rage flood through her veins, adrenaline draining the rest of the drugs from her system. She shoved her back legs from the floor, testing out her muscles and snapping her teeth. This was the moment they'd all been waiting for, and she'd be damned if she was going to stand aside and watch it happen.

She fell into line alongside Ash and Drake, pulling yet more energy from his presence. He was glorious and terrifying, his roar deep and threatening. His brilliantly white teeth had matched the pale tones of his coat only a few minutes ago, but both were now soaked with the blood of his enemies. They fought together, her claws ripping and his teeth tearing. He instinctively knew when she was about to send her flames shooting out to attack, and he took a cautious step back to stay out of the path of the flames before diving back into catch anyone who'd managed to survive it.

As they made their way toward the front entrance, Lane was grateful for the fact that the soldiers had widened the tunnel. The tiny slit in the rock that had barely allowed the dragons to get through in their natural forms was now large enough for several of them to shoot through on the wing, keeping their advantage over those on the ground. She rejoiced as her people darted out into the sunlight.

Lane was about to follow them when she saw movement to her left near the laboratory that'd been built near the waterfall. She could charge outside toward freedom, but her gut feeling told her to pursue it. She left Ash's side as she hurtled toward the lab.

He let out a bellow of protest and she turned to see the concerned look on Ash's face. "Get my people out of here!" she called. "I'll be out in a minute!"

Unable to reply so easily in his bear form, Ash gave a reluctant nod and a grunt of acceptance before checking the last of the chambers and leaving the cavern.

Lane slid quietly up next to the lab door. She could hear the heartbeat of her prey thundering inside, and there was no doubt in her mind who it belonged to. Dr. Blake was hiding in there, the coward! One quick shove with her shoulder and the door was open. The thick scent of rubbing alcohol attacked her nostrils and the bright lights burned her eyes. But the gunfire from outside had ceased and the blasts from the explosives were no longer necessary. Everything was silent.

"Agh!" came a cry from behind a cabinet as Dr. Blake shot out. Blood and dirt stained his lab coat, and more blood trickled from his nose, but he was strong enough to charge at her with a pistol in his hand. "Take that, you disgusting reptile!"

His efforts at bravery made Lane want to laugh. She dove forward, dodging to the right to avoid the pistol. He wasn't quick enough. Her clawed hands pushed into his soft body and sent him reeling backwards, his bullets flying uselessly up into the ceiling. Glass shattered around them as they fell to the floor together.

"You're a monster," Dr. Blake screamed underneath her. "You're a filthy, bloodthirsty monster!"

Her tail whipped back and forth with impatience. "Really? We were living here peacefully until you came along and tried to turn us into weapons. You wanted to fill the skies with us, using us to kill your enemies and do the dirty work for you. You tortured us. Tell me who the real monster is."

"Fuck you," he snarled. "You're just a dirty animal, and you'll never be anything more than that!"

"Fine with me." Lane reared back and then plunged forward, snapping her teeth around his neck until she felt the satisfying crunch of breaking bones.

8

"It's all ready," Garrison said as he joined the others on the shore, the fox and the wolf at his heels. "We can literally blow this popsicle stand, and it's a good thing. It's not very steady right now."

Drake crossed his arms in front of his chest. "That sound would stop anyone from doing too much investigation. The Army knows enough about what happened here, as far as I'm concerned. Flip the switch."

"Wait. Lane's still in there." Ash's heart pounded in his chest. He'd killed his share of the enemy, and there had been a certain amount of satisfaction in that. Even more thrilling had been watching Lane transform not just from a human to a dragon but from a captured creature to a fearsome predator.

"She didn't come out with you?" Jack questioned.

He shook his head. "No, she said there was something else she needed to take care of." Ash wanted to kick himself for ever letting her get separated from the rest of them. The scientific unit had altered the cavern quite a bit already to accommodate their equipment, and then the explosives the Force had set to eliminate the bars from the cells had only weakened the natural structure further. What if the cavern collapsed before they pulled the trigger?

Garrison glanced at his watch. "We don't have much time. I'm sure someone got out a distress call, and we'll have company before you know it.

Ash sure as hell wasn't going to leave her there. He'd gone to Antarctica because that was the site of his mission, but it'd quickly become apparent to him that he was there for so much more. He was destined to go to this remote place, and he was destined to meet Lane. "Is everyone else accounted for?"

Jack checked the list. "Seems to be."

"Then I'm going in." Before anyone could tell him otherwise, Ash took off. He'd morphed back to his human shape once he'd come out of the foray and he no longer needed his bear body to fight off the enemy. But wide paws and a thick coat were better suited for this wild land, and he shifted on the fly.

Be careful, Ash. It was Jack, speaking in his head. *The electricity in that place is pretty wonky, and we've got the explosives rigged through it. If there's a spark in the wrong place or a sudden pulse of energy, the whole thing could blow without us triggering it. Drake says you should come back.*

Not until I know Lane is safe.

Fortunately, Jack was smart enough not to continue arguing with him. Ash was willing to take his chances. It was his own life he was sacrificing if he went into the cavern and it fell in on him. He was all right with that, but he definitely wasn't okay with the idea of leaving Lane behind.

He'd been too busy to really wrap his head around it, but Ash knew in the very depths of his soul that Lane wasn't simply a gorgeous woman, a fierce dragon or just part of his rescue mission. She was the one he was supposed to be with. At this point in his life, he'd assumed he wasn't even going to find that special person, and he most certainly hadn't thought he'd find her in the form of a dragon shifter, but he had. Now he just had to get her out safely before it was too late.

The ground rumbled beneath his paws, sending shots of adrenaline straight into his heart. *What happened?* he commanded.

Jack was still in his fox form and able to reply. *Nothing from our end.*

Shit. That didn't make it any better. He had to get to her. Ash hurtled forward, forcing his tired muscles to keep moving.

He was just nearing the entrance when a great red beast

came shooting out of the cavern. She shot a triumphant burst of flames into the sky as she spread her wings in the air. A fireball erupted from the mouth of the cavern as clods of dirt and ice rocketed skyward. Ash skidded to a stop, keeping his focus on Lane as she shot overhead. She was out. She was safe. And she was spectacular.

———

THE NEXT HOUR was a blur as he and the rest of the Force that had come to assist made sure everyone was on the boat. Drake had used his contact with the killer whale pod, a group of fishermen who were more than happy to help rescue the dragons they'd been spotting from the sea. Ash fell easily into the role of caretaker, ensuring that everyone had food, comfort, and medical care.

It was as he came up from the cabin where the elderly and injured had been stowed that he found Lane leaning against the rusty rails of the fishing boat. The wind had teased a strand of her hair from the inside of her parka, making it whip around her face as she watched the great chunk of ice recede.

"You okay?" he asked quietly as he came up behind her. Ash wanted to reach out and run his hands down her body; not just because of the demands of his inner bear, but he wanted to make sure she was still in one piece.

She nodded. "I'm fine. It's just strange to be out here.

I've lived in those caverns for a long time. I saw my home turned into a prison, and now I've seen it blown to smithereens."

"We had to do that," Ash explained quietly. "Someone from the government is going to come along and start poking around. It's best they know as little as possible."

"Oh, I understand. But that doesn't make it any less strange." She rolled her hands along the railing, still looking off into the distance.

"Lane, I know we didn't exactly start off on the right foot. I want to apologize for anything I might've done to make you uncomfortable. It was a tough situation for all of us, and—"

"No." She turned to him then. Lane's eyes were the color of shadowed ice, but there was much more warmth in them. "If either one of us needs to apologize, it's me. I misjudged you when you walked in there with your military ID and your lab coat. I knew there was something different about you, but I'd been so scared and helpless for so long that I couldn't imagine that anyone would truly be there to save us. And I owe you my thanks, too. We're finally free again."

Those last words should've been joyous, but Ash could hear the sadness in them. "Where will you go?" With special licensing arranged by the Force, the fishing boat could get them all the way back to the U.S. From there, the original D.C. unit of the Force would head to their homes and the new unit would reconvene in Dallas. The dragons were free, but they no longer had their home to return to.

"I don't know yet. I'll have to talk to everyone else. We moved to Antarctica because we wanted to be away from people. I still feel that way, and I think the rest do, too, but I'm not sure where that will take us. I don't think I could handle returning to the desert right now."

Ash felt the words bubbling up through his body, not simply a product of his mind and tongue, but of his heart. "Come back to Dallas with me."

Her brow creased. "What?"

"Lane, there's something between us. I know it, and I think you know it, too. Every time I'm near you, I don't know what to do with myself. Even back there, when we were taking down that entire military base, I couldn't keep my mind off you. I find myself wanting to be a bear so I can protect you but longing to be a human so that I might talk to you... or maybe even touch you. I know this is bold of me, and if you're not interested, then it's going to be one hell of a long ride back to the States, but I'm falling in love with you, Lane." There. He'd said it. It wasn't even everything, but it at least summed up the thoughts that'd been spinning around in his mind ever since he'd literally stumbled into that cavern full of dragons.

She blinked at him and then smiled. "You are?"

Lane sounded so astonished that Ash wasn't sure what to think at first. Everything between them thus far had been so uncertain when it came down to what they'd expressed and shown on the surface, but he couldn't deny what his bear had told him. It didn't matter what form he was in; he needed to be near her. That had to mean something. "Yes."

A note of laughter escaped her lips as she put a hand against his chest. "You don't know how happy I am to hear that."

His own throat laughed in reply. "Really?"

"God, yes. I've been driving myself crazy wondering what this was all about and how we could possibly mean that much to each other. I'd always thought that if I found someone it would be another dragon like me." Tears shone in her eyes, and she blinked them away quickly. "I guess it doesn't have to make sense as long as it works for us, though. Right?"

"Right." Ash bent forward to kiss her, his body working without any thought. He didn't need any. He just needed to know that he had her there in his arms and that they had a chance of being together. Their circumstances had already been impossible, so if they were able to overcome them, then they could get through anything.

"Your nose is cold," he said with a smile when they broke apart. His own body was filled with heat from the velvety touch of her lips, and Ash knew he could've stood out on the deck with her all day. But he was concerned about her after all she'd been through, and the gray cloud to the west indicated a storm was coming in. "I suppose I'd better get you below deck."

Their hands naturally clutched each other as they made their way down.

Drake met them below. He looked tired but pleased when he saw his new comrade. "You did an excellent job on this mission, Ash. Everyone's going to be fine. I've got them put up for the evening because I think they all need to get plenty of rest. The captain said there are still a few cabins left if you'd like to claim one." He gestured toward the prow.

"Thanks." Ash moved along, Lane trailing behind him with their fingers woven together until he found an empty cabin. It wasn't much, with a simple bunk built into the wall and a few drawers underneath it. A lamp on the wall and a heater below it completed the amenities.

"It's not exactly a luxury cruise, but it looks like the cabins are filling up quickly. Why don't you go ahead and take this one?" Ash gestured for her to step inside the room.

She did so, pulling back the hood of her parka as she sat down on the edge of the bunk. "What about you?"

"Ah, don't worry about me. I can find some place. Besides, I'm a polar bear, remember? I can go catch an iceberg drifting by and bunk down there."

"And I've been sleeping in an old cave for the last few decades. I don't need this."

Ash stood there in the doorway, admiring the strength and stubbornness of this woman. She was a difficult one, and certainly not like anyone else he'd ever met, but he liked that about her. Lane challenged him in new ways. "You deserve it."

Her eyes were steady on his. "At least come and sit for a minute."

He obliged willingly, especially since he hadn't wanted to leave her in the first place. Ash closed the door behind him, cutting off the general murmur of a ship full of dragons, whales, and several other creatures who'd all just survived a harrowing experience. "You say that, but I wonder if it means the same thing to you as it does to me."

"Oh?" Lane's eyes were a challenge.

"Well, you're talking to a man who believes he's just found the woman he's destined to be with. And even under the bulk of a borrowed parka, he knows just how beautiful she is. He knows how her body curves and how her heartbeat feels through her skin." Ash touched her hand, once again feeling that electric jolt that pleased him so much.

"I know I am," she said with a smile, threading her fingers through his and leaning close. "And you're talking to a woman who's not only been alone for a very long time, but who's had her knight in shining armor come help rescue her and her people. She's incredibly grateful."

Their lips met and Ash explored the neat rows of teeth that could turn into weapons at any moment. Their tongues danced together, getting to know each other without words. Ash pulled back just enough to trail more kisses down her jawline. "I wouldn't want gratitude to be your motivation here."

"What about something more?" she tempted. "What about the fact that I tried so hard to hate you and found it absolutely impossible."

His hands made quick work of the snaps and zipper of her parka. It was suddenly growing incredibly hot in the cabin. Ash didn't know if it was his own heat or hers, but the two of them could make a lot of it when he felt the curve of her body through her sweater. Ash pulled her into his lap as he pushed her coat off her and to the floor. "I want to see you," he mumbled against her throat as he tugged at her clothing.

"Do you really think this is the place?" she asked. But Lane's head was tipped back, her eyes closed, her fingers buried in his hair. They ran down to the back of his neck and around to the front of his chest, moving of their own volition to rid him of his coat. Her fingers were sweet and cool against his heated skin, giving no indication of just who and what she was underneath.

"I can't think of any place better," he replied huskily as he dared to touch the curve of her breast. Damn, she was hot. His bear was going crazy, demanding that he get what he needed, but for once, Ash wasn't interested in listening. He wanted this to last as long as was possible. He peeled off her sweater and her jeans, her boots hitting the floor with two dull thuds. It was all moving too fast, yet he didn't want to stop it.

He was rewarded when he had her laid out on the bed, her skin glowing in the warm light from the lamp. The delicate collar bone, the swell of her breasts, the way her waist tucked in underneath them. Everything about her was unreal, and his hands shook as they reached for the waistband of his jeans.

"Let me," she said, a pleading note in her voice. She stripped him with painful slowness and delicacy, her hands skimming each new part of his body as it was revealed.

Ash swallowed as his skin touched hers, his hardness demanding against her heat and softness. "You don't know what you do to me, Lane."

"Yes, I do," she said with a laugh. "I absolutely know." She moved her legs to accommodate him and he plunged inside, gasping at the exquisite sensation of being inside her. They had no reason to know each other well, given that their interactions had been within the confines of that torture chamber they'd just left behind. And yet the two of them moved in sync, her hips lifting and pulsing in time to his, their bodies creating a symphony of movement.

"Lane," he breathed, tasting her name on his tongue as he touched his lips to her skin, focusing on the pulse that fluttered beneath it.

"Ash." It wasn't a question, and she drew out the single

syllable into something luscious and enticing.

He'd never felt so at home before, even out there in the middle of the ocean. Ash closed his eyes, his muscles tensing. He wasn't going to be able to remain in control for long. "I really do love you, Lane." He spoke the words not only to reassure her, but because he needed to hear them out loud to know this was all real. It wasn't just a lucid dream from too many nights in the desert, and it wasn't some vague promise of a good life once his work with the military was done. He'd thought he understood his life's work as he'd taken down terrorists, but all that was just what he had to do to get here.

"I love you, too." Her breath choked into a gasp as she fell into convulsions around him. Her thighs gripped hard against his legs, her nails sinking into his back.

Ash let go, plummeting into her for all he was worth. He buried his moans in the nape of her neck, wanting to keep their pleasure between the two of them.

When he lay next to her, feeling the way her body fit against his, even when they were locked together by nature's demand, the real world started to trickle back into Ash's mind. Some of it could wait, like discussing all the final details with Drake and the others. They had a long ride back to friendly territory, but there were some decisions that had to be made. As much as he wanted to preserve this gentle stillness between them, it couldn't last forever.

"You never answered me," he said softly, uncertain if she was awake or not.

She was, but her voice held sleep in it as she rolled toward him. The bunk was only made for one person, and it was tight with the two of them in it together, but Ash would gladly sacrifice a little room as long as he got to lay there with his arm around her. "Answered you about what?"

"Dallas." The word sounded big and heavy coming out of his mouth, filling the room. It was easier to admit his love and passion for her—both verbally and physically—then to force her to decide what she was going to do with the rest of her life. "I know it's a lot to think about, but I don't want to be away from you."

"Oh." She was quiet then, and Ash thought she might've drifted off, but then she sucked in a breath. "I don't know what's going to happen to the rest of my flight."

"Drake assured me we can find temporary accommodations for them until they decide what they want to do." Was she determined to stay near her family? He couldn't blame her, although he hadn't been a part of a clan for a long time. "I'm sorry. I just want you near me."

"Don't apologize." She turned the rest of the way in the bed so that her head was tucked up under his chin. Lane's arms circled him, holding him close. "I'll come to Dallas."

His bear relaxed into utter bliss, and Ash fell into a deep and dreamless sleep.

9

LANE GASPED, FLYING TO A SITTING POSITION IN BED. SHE clutched at her chest, feeling the rapid thunder of her heart. "What is that?" she whispered aloud into the dark, terrified by the noise that sounded just outside.

Ash touched her arm with a sleepy hand, his head still buried in the pillow. "It's just a car alarm. Nothing to be worried about."

"Oh. Right." She slowed her breath as she tucked herself back under the covers. She'd been in Dallas with Ash for an entire week now, and still she couldn't get used to the noise of the place. He'd done a lot of explaining on the fishing boat, wanting to make sure she understood he was part of this Force and that he didn't even have a place of his own to stay at in Dallas, other than the living space that'd been built into their headquarters.

Lane had nodded her understanding, and at the time, it'd been easy to think it would be fine. She'd lived in some of the harshest environments in the world, and before they'd moved down to Antarctica, she'd had some experience living among humans. She could handle that, especially if it meant having Ash at her side.

But the noise and busyness of the place grated against her very bones. She lay awake, listening to the car alarm beep into the night until someone finally shut it off. The relative silence that filled the air after that was a relief, but as she watched sunlight creep into their little apartment, the noises started up again. People were up and moving, doors opening and closing, dogs barking, cars buzzing by with their stereos bumping and buses zooming down the street with their horns going.

Lane felt like she was constantly shaking inside. She slipped out from under Ash's arm and the covers and padded into the small kitchen. Everything had changed so much since the last time she'd lived this way, but at least she understood the coffee pot. The last thing she needed was more caffeine, but it offered a warm comfort she found in so few other places.

"You're up early again today," Ash said with a smile when he came into the living room an hour later. He planted a kiss on her forehead and poured himself a cup of coffee. "I've got a text from Drake, so I'm going into the office today. The Force wanted me to go through some training, but that mission to Antarctica interfered with that a bit."

She forced a smile to her face. Lane loved Ash. She truly did, and even trying to live there in Dallas hadn't changed that. Her heart lifted when he walked into the room, and when he took her into his arms, it was easy to believe that everything would be all right. "I guess the training never stops for a man like you, does it?"

"Not really, but I don't mind." He sat down across from her at the tiny table. "I figure there's always more I can learn, and it keeps me all the more prepared for the next mission."

Ash was so lively, so full of energy, so happy there. The contrast between the way he felt and the way she did was a heavy burden on her heart.

"So, what are you up to today?" he asked innocently.

"Maren is coming over for a little bit." The female dragon was Garrison's mate, and she'd met them in Dallas as soon as they'd arrived. She was more than eager to get to know yet another dragon and explained to Lane that it was now her goal to find all the dragons in the world she could and let them know they weren't alone.

"Good." His voice and his smile were genuine. "I'm glad you've got someone else to talk to. I know I'm gone a lot, and I'll be leaving for longer periods of time when I start getting regular missions. You've already got your flight, but Maren will be a great friend to you."

"She's very sweet." Lane could see why Garrison was so smitten with her, and she was surprisingly easy to talk to.

Ash knocked back the rest of his coffee. "I've got to jump in the shower and get going."

He left twenty minutes later, and Maren showed up at the door midmorning. Her jet-black hair and bright blue eyes were becoming a familiar and welcome sight for Lane, as was the gentle rounding of her belly where she and Garrison's dragonling was growing. "Good morning," she chirped. "Do you want to step around the corner with me for some coffee?"

Lane felt a familiar burning sensation on the backs of her eyes. It was one that was getting harder and harder to fight off, even though she knew she should be happy. "Actually, I'd rather stay here if you don't mind. I do have coffee, though."

"Of course." Maren stepped into the apartment and set her purse on the side table. "I don't mean to brag, but I have to say Garrison and his team did a decent job of fixing this place up. He sent me some pictures before they started, and it was hardly anything but concrete. So cold and unwelcoming! A little small, maybe, but he wanted to make sure there was plenty of room for anyone on the new unit of the Force who needed a place to stay."

"It's nice," Lane said as she poured them each a mug.

"But?" Maren raised a dark eyebrow as she reached for the creamer.

Lane sighed. "But nothing. It's a nice place. It's the perfect size for the two of us." She carried her mug to that same small table where she and Ash had been sipping their coffee not too long ago. Already, she was tired of looking at the same wood grain over and over.

"There's something bothering you," Maren said softly. "If it's something I can help with, then I'd love to. I know it can't be easy for you to come to a place like this."

Her seeming ability to read Lane's mind touched her deeply, but it also opened the floodgate of tears. Lane turned her face away, not wanting her new friend to see her looking so miserable. "No, it's not easy at all. It's miserable. Don't get me wrong. Garrison really did a great job building this place. But I feel like the whole world lives right here with us. There's all this commotion around me all the time, but I feel like I'm stuck in one spot."

"Oh, Lane. I'm so sorry you feel that way. If it's a matter of getting out a little more, then we can arrange that. I can come by more often. And I've gotten your flight settled into a nice big house out in the country. We can visit them anytime."

It was a nice idea, but it didn't reduce the hopeless feeling that'd become lodged in Lane's chest. "But I can't just keep relying on you to cart me around. It's not fair to you, and besides that, you and Garrison will want to get back home soon before the baby is born."

Maren pursed her lips, her arctic blue eyes searching

the air for a better solution. "I suppose that's true. Have you told Ash how you feel about all this?"

Lane shook her head. "I can't. He's so damn happy! That should make *me* happy if we're really supposed to be together. The man practically jumps out of bed every morning and whistles all the way to work, but I just sit here feeling sorry for myself. I don't understand what's wrong with me, but there must be something. Otherwise, why would I be the only one having such a hard time adjusting?" She snagged a paper napkin and dabbed at her face, ashamed that she'd broken down like this.

Her friend was silent for a long time as she ran her fingertip around the rim of her mug. "Has Garrison ever said anything about how the two of us met?"

"I don't think so."

She tipped her head back. "He was part of the SOS Force, just like he is now. Former military, lots of different and very worldly experiences under his belt. He came out to Lake Tahoe on a mission, and he found me. The local residents had me pegged as a lake monster, some mythical creature that couldn't possibly be real. But he soon discovered that I was real, and that I was just as feral as you'd expect any other lake monster to be."

Lane dried her eyes enough to study the other woman. With her pearl stud earrings, gently waved hair, and designer shoes, she certainly didn't look like a savage. "That's hard to believe."

"Oh, believe it! I'd had a little exposure to humans, but I was trying so hard to stay away from them and their culture. I didn't think anything modern could possibly be good. And I was pretty overwhelmed when I came to D.C. to be with Garrison. I wasn't sure I'd made the right decision, not because of him, but because of everyone else."

"You seem to have adjusted well." Lane twisted the napkin in her hands. "I keep telling myself that I'll adjust, too. I've always thought of myself as a pretty strong person, and I was just so confident that I could do this."

"You can," Maren insisted, "but you have to give yourself some time. It's not easy, and it's not something that's going to happen overnight. But you also don't have to do it alone. I'm going to be here for at least another week, and even when I'm gone, you've got your flight and you've got Ash. Hell, you've got the whole SOS Force at your back. It might be hard to believe, especially from someone like Flint, but they're really just one big blended family. Give yourself a chance. Just push yourself a little bit each day instead of expecting it all to fall in place at once."

"You really think that'll work?" Lane sniffed. She felt like such a fool. There were millions of other people in the world who could handle this, and there was no reason she shouldn't be able to do this same.

"I do. I have every bit of confidence in you, and I know that Ash does, too. It's not always easy, and that's okay." Maren let out a short laugh. "Trust me, I've thought more than once about what life is going to be like once this baby comes. Little ones don't always know how to control their shifting, and the last thing I want is for my child to end up on the cover of the tabloids because he or she sprouted a tail in the middle of a playground."

Lane couldn't help but smile. "Fair enough. At least I don't have to worry about that."

"And don't underestimate Ash. Really. I don't know him all that well yet, but he never would've been asked to be part of the Force if he wasn't a good man. They're not just looking for military skill. Let him know how you feel and he'll help you."

When Maren left to take care of some other errands, Lane spent the rest of the day trying to convince herself that the other dragon was right. There was no reason to worry, and there was no reason to think that she had to get it all figured out at once. It would be all right. It had to be.

Ash swept in the door that evening smelling of the outdoors, his dark eyes lit up with excitement as he scooped her into his arms and kissed her. Lane gladly fell into his embrace, relishing the way his hands appreciated her flesh.

"That's quite a hello," she purred against his chest.

"What can I say? I missed you." Ash pushed back to hold her at arm's length. "You know, I think about you all day. It doesn't matter how busy they keep me; I just want to be home with you. And now that I am, let me take you out to dinner. Someplace nice."

"What's the occasion?" she asked nervously.

He swept his hand over her backside and back up around her hips as he pulled her close once again. "Do I need a special occasion? Maybe I just want to celebrate being with you." He pecked another kiss on her bottom lip. "Let me just go get cleaned up."

Lane glanced down at her clothes and touched her hair. She felt so inadequate. Was she even good enough for a man like him? The deepest parts of her mind chided her for being so self-conscious, but she shoved them aside again.

Being a typical man, polar bear or not, Ash didn't take long to wash his face, change his clothes, and comb his hair. He came out from the bedroom and wrapped his arms around her from behind. "What's wrong, love? You feel tense."

She recalled her conversation with Maren. The other dragon was right. She should be able to confide in her mate. "I'm just a little nervous. I'm not used to the crowds."

"You don't have to worry about that," he soothed as he nuzzled her neck. "I'll be right there with you. It'll be fine."

But it wasn't. She could handle stepping out of their apartment and down a hall to the other side of the building where his car was parked. But her stomach lurched inside her as soon as he pulled through the overhead door and out into traffic. It felt like everyone else in Dallas had left work at the same time and was rushing to get somewhere. Her muscles stiffened as she flinched every time a car changed lanes next to them.

"Just relax, baby. I know there's a lot of traffic right now, but I'm used to it." True enough, Ash was confident and capable behind the wheel. He wasn't fazed in the least when a truck pulled out in front of him or a car swooped to the right without using a turn signal.

When they arrived at the restaurant, Lane thought it was all over with. She'd gotten past the worst part, and now all she had to do was sit down with her mate and enjoy some good food. There was no need to panic about what the drive home would be like just yet, because worrying wouldn't make any difference.

But as soon as Ash opened the wide entry door to the restaurant, Lane froze. It was packed with people, every one of them dressed to the nines and looking elegant. She swore they paused with their drinks and forkfuls of salmon in the air to stare at her, to assess her, to see the animal that she was under the surface.

Ash's hand was on the small of her back. "What's wrong?"

"I—I can't do this." She turned away from his touch, but the sidewalk was no more comforting. Other patrons were trying to get into the restaurant, and the torrent of traffic was far too close. She felt the hardness of the concrete under her feet as she made her way back toward the car.

Ash was at her side again in a second. "Lane, wait! What's going on? Talk to me."

She turned to him, seeking comfort in those dark eyes. "I just can't do this. There are so many people."

"That's all right. We'll just go home and order in." But there was disappointment in his eyes, maybe even hurt, as he guided her back to the car and opened the door for her.

Lane's throat was tight as she tried not to cry on the ride back home. "I'm sorry. It's just that things weren't like this when I lived in Arizona. It was kind of a remote place, and as soon as the population started increasing, we decided to leave. Everything was at a slower pace back then."

He put a hand on her thigh. "I'm sure that's true. Everyone is always in a hurry these days."

Lane was quiet for the rest of the ride home and said little after Ash picked up some sandwiches from around the corner. He held her close while they sat on the couch and watched TV together afterwards, something that she'd originally thought would be a good way to help her study modern life, but that now just seemed like a big tease. The characters had their challenges, sure, but none of them were practically aliens coming to live in a new world.

Every now and then, Ash would pull in a deep breath and pause, like he was about to say something, but then he'd let it go without a word passing his lips. Each time,

Lane felt her muscles harden and her breath stopped as she waited for what was about to come. When it didn't, she found that she didn't feel any better about it.

That night as they lay in bed, Ash fell asleep quickly. Lane listened to the sound of his breathing, measuring it against her own. They were so compatible in so many ways. They'd each felt that deep and burning urge for one another; that magnetism that the universe had conferred on them. They may have been a bear and dragon, but they were both animals and people who needed each other in the deepest and most primal ways possible. She'd felt her body and soul react to him, and she'd known that he felt the same.

But was it possible that they'd only tricked themselves into believing that because of the extenuating circumstances? Could it be that when she knew she was in danger and he believed he could save her, they'd created a relationship out of that instead of the truth? It wasn't unheard of. If that were the case, Lane wasn't sure they'd make it in Dallas.

Slowly, she sat up in bed and looked down at her mate. She'd disappointed him. Lane had seen that written all over his face when they'd left the restaurant. He was trying so hard to make this happen. Ash enjoyed this life in Dallas. He had a purpose in his job with the Force. He left the house smiling and returned the same way. This was the life he wanted.

Lane knew she was dragging him down. She didn't want to hold him back. He was a good and talented man, and he deserved so much more than some sobbing, miserable woman who couldn't handle being around other people in the middle of a city of over a million people.

Slipping carefully from the bed, Lane found a duffel bag in the closet. She hadn't had the chance to take her few possessions with her from the cavern, and she hadn't accumulated very many since she'd arrived in Dallas. Her clothes and hairbrush easily fit in the bag, and she waited to zip it until she'd left the bedroom, lest she wake him.

Lane didn't know exactly where she was going. She simply knew she had to get out of there. Making her way quietly out of the building, she tensed her shoulders against the night and didn't look back.

10

ASH'S MIND WAS WORKING BEFORE HE WAS EVEN COMPLETELY awake. His mind had been heavy ever since Lane had reacted that way at dinner the night before. He'd been watching those uneasy feelings build inside her ever since they'd gone back to Dallas. He'd told himself that it wasn't that bad and she'd be fine once she had a chance to get used to it.

But as evidenced last night, it wasn't getting any better. Numerous times, he'd thought about asking her. He wanted her to open up to him and let him know what she was actually feeling. But if Lane wasn't ready for that, he didn't want to push her. She'd already been through so much.

And that made his mind immediately throw back to everything that had happened in Antarctica. There, Lane had been strong and tough and stubborn. She'd told Ash just what she thought about him, and she didn't hesitate to exact her own very personal revenge on the man who'd been so terrible to her and her flight. Ash was proud of her for that, and it was one of many things that had made him fall all the more in love with her.

She was a different person in Dallas; he could live with that. Ash knew he'd love her, no matter what. But she wasn't happy, and he wanted to change that. It was time to finally tell her what he'd been thinking about for the last several days. He rolled over to wake her.

But Lane was already gone. The blankets on her side of the bed were pulled up and carefully straightened, just as she always left them. He swung his legs off the side of the mattress and poked his head out into the living room, expecting to find her sitting there with a mug of coffee as she usually was. Lane hadn't been sleeping well and she was almost always out of bed before him.

But the living room was dark. The coffee pot was cold and empty, as though it hadn't been used at all that day. Panic spread through his chest as he pulled on his clothes, his mind running through numerous scenarios. Ash had made a lot of enemies in his days with Delta Force. Had some terrorist organization managed to track him down, deciding to exact revenge on him by kidnapping Lane? Or did Dr. Blake get a hold of someone in the Pentagon before his ultimate takedown and find a way to get his retribution from beyond the grave?

His phone rang and he looked at it hopefully, sure that it would be Lane. But it was Drake. "Hey."

"Hey, I know it's early, and I know I said I wanted you to go through another week of training, but I've got a mission for you that simply can't wait."

"It's going to have to," Ash interrupted before he could say any more. "Lane's missing."

The other end of the line was quiet for a second. "Are you sure?"

"Yeah." Ash had just discovered the missing duffel bag and the empty drawers where her clothing had been. "I'm sure. She packed up and left."

"Did you two have a fight or something?"

"No." Things had been tense, but they didn't argue. "This means she must've left of her own will, but I still don't like it. She doesn't know much about modern living, Drake. She could really get herself in trouble."

"I'm already on my way to headquarters. I'll be there in a few minutes. We'll get the others and we'll find her, Ash. I can promise you that."

"Appreciate your help." He couldn't get to the conference room fast enough. Ash knew he was working with a team of experienced and talented people, but he still felt the rush of alarm that they may not be able to find her. Lane didn't have a cell phone yet, even though he'd offered her one. She had no credit or debit cards, considering those weren't exactly necessary when living in an icy wilderness on the bottom of the world. She didn't have any of the modern conveniences that would help them track her down.

A short time later, everyone who was available from the Force units had crowded into the conference room. Max, Jack, Vance, Drake, and Garrison had joined him, and the sense of urgency filled the room.

Garrison looked concerned. "I've sent Maren to check in with the rest of her flight. I didn't want to alarm them, but that seems like the first place we need to eliminate."

"And it's not all that far away," Vance pointed out. "Most people having domestic problems run back home."

"We're not having domestic problems," Ash growled.

The cowboy put his hands in the air. "Didn't mean to offend you. I just thought that might be what we're looking at."

"It's sensible, and given how long Lane had been living in Antarctica, I don't know where else she'd go." Drake leaned forward and put his elbows on the table. "But if we end up ruling that out, I'd like to have our backup plan ready to go.

Flint had joined them on a screen, his cabin in the Colorado mountains serving as a cozy backdrop. "I can help you with tracking, but only if she stayed on the ground. I've got a good nose, but I can't exactly follow her through the sky."

"Flint has a good point," Garrison acknowledged. "We can assume that if she's not right here in the city, she must've shifted and flown somewhere. It only makes sense for a dragon."

Ash didn't like any of this. They were attacking this like any other mission. That was good in a way because he knew they were taking this just as seriously as he was. But it made it feel less personal, and he was too concerned about her to be able to step back and give it the same kind of distance the others were.

"We might not be completely out of luck if she's flying," Hudson said. He'd joined them via videophone as well, although the signal always went through private and extremely secure channels which he'd created himself. "A dragon flying through the sky isn't likely to go unnoticed, especially if she's going over heavily populated areas. I can use my equipment to check all the police and emergency frequencies to see if anything has been reported."

Ash's gut twisted. Hudson ran a major communications company, and from what Ash had been told, there was much more going on with it than the general public saw when they went to buy a new cell phone. That made Hudson more than capable of doing exactly what he said he was going to do, but Ash didn't like the idea of Lane being reported in like some UFO. God only knew what people might try to do to her if they thought she was a monster trying to eat their livestock!

Garrison's phone buzzed and he checked it. "That's Maren. She's with the rest of the dragons and none of them have seen her."

"Shit." Ash had been holding on to that hope. Hell, he could've gone out to their house himself to figure it out, and he would've if Drake hadn't encouraged him to sit still and let them all use their resources.

Drake noticed the look on his face. "We'll find her, Ash."

"Right."

———

EVEN THROUGH HEADPHONES, the chopper blades thumped in Ash's ears. He scanned the ground as Max's helicopter swooped into Arizona, even though he couldn't see anything. The mountains below looked like a brown wrinkled blanket that someone had thrown down carelessly. "I should've known she'd head out here. She mentioned they'd lived this way before they'd moved down to Antarctica."

"Don't blame yourself. Women are unpredictable at best," he grumbled.

Ash gave him a sideways glance. "That sounds like the voice of experience."

"You could say that. I've decided I'm much better off just minding my own business and keeping this chopper in the air. Now then, where exactly did Hudson say she was spotted?"

He'd already consulted the map about a hundred times, wishing for something that sounded familiar. But Lane hadn't offered up much information about her past. "Someone spotted her over the Fort Apache Reservation, heading west. I highly doubt she's considering Phoenix, so our best guess is somewhere in Tonto National Forest."

"Did the rest of her flight tell you where they used to live?"

Ash sighed. "Yeah, but they said a resort cropped up right nearby and that's when they decided to move. I doubt she'd go anywhere near people, given what Maren told me." He could kick himself a hundred times over for not realizing just how bad things had been for Lane. Yes, he'd known she wasn't completely happy. But the miserable portrait Maren painted was heartbreaking. He'd never forgive himself if he'd found his true love once and then let her go.

Max glanced at him. "Don't keep that depressing look on your face or else she'll never want to come back," he cracked.

Ash knew he was joking around, but it was hard to find the humor in anything when Lane was out there some-where. She might've lived in this area before, but it was much more populated than it'd been half a century ago. Plus, she'd had the rest of her family with her. "I'll work on it," he groused.

"I'm going to head down lower," Max informed him. "We should be able to do a decent survey of the area from the chopper, which will be a lot faster than trying to cover all this ground on foot. We can start by looking for any likely place for her to make camp."

"Probably some sort of cave, based on what Edi told me." The old woman had agreed to meet with him just before they'd taken off, but even knowing what their flight had done in the past didn't give them any guarantee that they'd be able to find her again.

They swept through the canyons and gulches, zooming around and over mountains. Ash could feel his eyes getting tired as the sun began to set, and he realized just what a big space they had to sift through in order to find her. It was an impossible task, yet he wasn't ready to give up.

Max, however, had other plans as he turned away from the mountains and toward the highway. "It's getting dark and that's not going to do us any good."

Ash understood the logic of his words, but it didn't stop his inner bear from wanting to roar with rage. He couldn't just give up on her, not now. "If you need to rest, I understand. Just drop me off somewhere and I'll keep looking."

The pilot shook his dark heard. "Trust me, Ash. I'm all about being the Lone Ranger and doing things by myself, but you've been through all the same training with the rest of the Force that I have. We might not be on active duty anymore, but we're still expected to follow certain rules. We have to be smart about this. There's no point in looking when it's dark. We'll miss too much."

Ash sagged against the seat. "Yeah. And you can probably only fly for so long."

"Is that a challenge? I can fly this baby from here to the end of the Earth. But once again, it's not going to do us a damn bit of good if we can't see anything. I'll find a place to land and we'll get some food and rest. Send a message to HQ while I get this bird on the ground."

Begrudgingly, Ash did as he was told. He waited patiently while Max searched for a safe place to land near a small mountain town, and then he waited even longer while the chopper blades slowed. It was a fast way to travel, but it felt terribly inconvenient at the moment.

They trudged into town. Most of the dusty sidewalks had already been rolled up for the night, but the vintage neon over a small diner proclaimed it to be open all night. The scent of greasy burgers drifted out through the door as a man in a wrinkled suit came through and held it open for the two shifters.

"Thanks," Max said as he caught the door and led the way inside.

It was too bright in the small space, and the checked floor and red upholstery made Ash's eyes cross. His stomach lurched with hunger now that the heavy scents from the kitchen reminded him just how long it had been since he'd eaten. He plunked into a booth at the far end of the diner across from Max.

Their waitress was an older woman in a button-up dress that was far too short for her. "What can I get you boys?"

Ash didn't even have the energy to look at the menu.

"Just some burgers and sodas," Max answered for him.

"You want the special?"

"Sure. That's fine." Max watched as the woman disappeared through the swinging door into the kitchen. "It'll be all right, Ash. It really will."

He straightened, knowing he wasn't behaving like someone who served with the Delta Force. "You know, I've been through some hellacious stuff. The movies don't hold a candle to the things I've seen in person. But this bothers me far more than I ever thought it would."

"We'll just have to be patient. I know that's hard, but we're doing everything we can. So are the rest of the guys. I'm sure as we speak, Hudson and Jack are analyzing the cell phone records of everyone in the state."

The waitress returned and plunked their food down in front of them. "Just holler if you need anything else!"

Ash ate in silence. He didn't want to admit it, but the food in this little greasy spoon was actually pretty good. He focused on it in an effort to keep himself from dwelling too much on Lane. It was impossible, though. Ash laughed at himself as he thought about the kind of restaurant he'd tried to take her to versus a place like this. She'd probably have been perfectly at home there. If he ever found her, he'd tell her exactly what he wanted out of life.

The door swung open and admitted a scruffy looking man in khaki shorts and a t-shirt. He carried an olive drab duffle bag that looked reminiscent of something Ash would've had in the military, and he let it fall to the floor with a thump as he perched on a stool at the counter.

"Hey, Frank!" the waitress said warmly as she came out from the back. "You want the usual?"

He bobbed his shaggy head, running a hand through his tangled beard. "Sure, but I wish you had something a little harder to go with it."

The waitress paused as she was about to turn toward the kitchen. "What's wrong? Cops trying to kick you out of the park again?"

"Naw, that would be easy compared to what I've just been through."

All thoughts of his order set aside for the moment, the waitress leaned down on her side of the counter. Her heavy eyebrows drew together in concern. "That can't be good."

Frank swallowed and rubbed his hands nervously on his thighs. "I was looking for a place to bed down for the night. It's getting harder and harder since they've put so many official campsites throughout the national parks these days. Tourists always wanna call the cops on me just 'cause I'm not using a big ol' RV or some fancy tent."

"Right." She nodded, urging him to continue.

"So I started working my way a little bit further up into the mountains. I thought hell, I oughta just go make my own little campsite all to myself. I even found a nice cave, way off the beaten path, and I knew I wouldn't need to worry about running into anyone. It was big enough that there weren't any snakes trying to hang out in there, so I untied my bedroll."

"And?"

Frank put his head on the counter for a moment before he lifted it again slowly. "I swear to God, Alice. I saw a dragon."

A prickle of energy spread from the back of Ash's neck down his back. He couldn't help but listen to the man's testimony, given that it was such a small, quiet diner. He shot to his feet and came to sit next to Frank. "What do you mean, you saw a dragon?" He sensed Max right behind him.

Frank looked from one man to the other. "Aw, go on with you. There's usually nobody here at night but Alice, and the last thing I need is for someone to put me on the internet as some crazy guy. I'm really just trying to live a true life out in what's left of the great wilderness, you know. No need to make fun of me."

"We're not," Max assured him. "And I promise we're not putting anything on the internet."

Frank squinted one eye at them and then turned to the waitress. "You know these fellas?"

She gave him a helpless shrug. "Can't say that I do. They just came in here tonight. No trouble from them, though."

"Well, all right. I guess you heard everything I was saying anyway. I had just laid out my bedroll, and I had a beautiful view of the park down beneath me. I heard something further back in the cave, but I wasn't too worried about it. I'm not afraid of animals. And then it charged. It came thundering out of the darkness, roaring at me! Fire came out of its mouth. Just about shit myself!"

"Then what?" Ash pressed.

"Well, I left! That creature sure as hell wanted me out of there, and I sure as hell wasn't going to stick around and argue with it. Didn't even grab my bedroll. I don't think I've run that fast since I was a kid, and I managed to catch a ride back into town. I think I might stick to civilization for a little while."

"Where was this?" Ash gritted his teeth to keep his body in check. He knew Lane was out there somewhere, and this could only be her.

"Near Mazatzal Peak," Frank explained. "On the south side."

"Thank you." Ash shoved his hand in his pocket,

pulling out a wad of bills. He pressed some of them into his hand. "That should cover the cost of your bedroll. And here, for dinner." He gave the rest to the waitress, barely giving her a moment to take them from his hand before he was heading for the door.

"There's over a hundred bucks here!" Frank protested.

"Then get a really nice one! C'mon, Max. Let's go!" Just before the door swung shut behind them, Ash heard the waitress speak to the other diner.

"Don't look a good tipper in the mouth, Frank."

"We could still wait for morning, you know," Max said evenly as they trotted away from the restaurant toward where they'd left the chopper. "Better chance of finding this cave, even if we do think we know the general location."

"We could, but then we also risk her not being there." Ash had his phone out, studying maps as they went. "If he came to the diner right after he got into town, then he probably wasn't out there any more than a couple of hours ago. Lane had bedded down for the night, and if she's already chased off an intruder, she might not stay any longer than she has to."

"You're the boss," Max replied. "Well, for right now."

They climbed into the helicopter and headed west. Ash felt hope and fear mixing heavily inside him. He might have a chance of finding Lane, but they also might drive her off as soon as she realized it was them. What if she didn't even *want* to see him again? Maren had explained how upset Lane was over city living, but that didn't mean there weren't other issues.

"That could be the one," Max said as they swooped around Mazatzal Peak. "It's big, and it's in the right area. How do you want to go about this? There's not exactly a helipad in front of it."

"Just find someplace to set me down and I'll make my way up to it."

The rough terrain didn't make things easy, but Ash had jumped out of a chopper or two before. He zipped down a fast rope to a small bit of trail that he hoped would get him far enough to get to the cave. Ash signaled to Max, and the thump of the chopper faded off into the distance.

The stars stood out brilliantly against the mountains as Ash gave his eyes a moment to adjust. He considered shifting, but he knew his polar bear would be too wide and bulky for some of the narrow paths he'd be moving along. He felt each scuff of sand under his feet and every scrape of the unforgiving flora as he moved through this elevated desert land. Every now and then, he paused to listen.

This was the kind of place that humans were advised to stay far away from at night, especially if they weren't experienced on the trail. But Ash didn't need any special trail markers to tell him he was going in the right direction. He could sense Lane now, in the same way that any animal could sense where to go for water and food. But that only made sense considering he needed her in the same way that those other elements were needed for survival. She was a part of him, and he couldn't bear the idea of living without her.

Slowly, picking his way along a narrow and dangerous path, Ash approached the cave. His heart lurched in anticipation, and all of his training seemed to be forgotten. He was moving too fast and too loud, but he didn't care, as long as he got to her.

The trail ended in a steep wall of rock just over his head. Ash took two steps back, prepared to launch himself up it, when a curvy silhouette blocked out the stars overhead. "What are you doing here?"

"I'm here for you, Lane. Let me come up so we can talk." His lungs were stiff and inflexible as he waited to get over this last obstacle to get to her. It wasn't even the rocks that kept them separated now, simply her willingness to allow him in again.

She stood for an eternity with one hand on her hip staring down at him before she finally moved away from the edge. "All right."

Ash hurled himself over the wall, but he stayed near the edge. He didn't want to risk chasing her off, and there was no doubt Lane could move more easily through this terrain than he could. "Lane," he breathed, unsure of where to begin. "I've missed you so much."

She was facing away from him, still a dark shape in the night. "It only made sense for me to return to where my people came from," she explained quietly. "You should've just let me go."

He ran a hand through his hair in frustration. His bear was displeased at the idea and longed to get out. "Why would I do that?"

"Because I want you to be happy, Ash. You deserve that. I wasn't happy in Dallas." Lane sat down on the opposite end of the small ledge in front of the cave, curling her knees up to her chest and wrapping her arms around them.

"I know you weren't, and I'm sorry for that. I only wished I realized earlier just how miserable you were. All you had to do was tell me." He felt desperate, every cell of his body trying to reach out toward her.

"How could I do that when you were so happy?" she asked. "You were practically whistling the days away, and all I did was disappoint you when I couldn't handle it."

Ash dared to go sit beside her, leaving a small amount of space between them. "Lane, the only reason I was happy in Dallas was because I was with *you*. Living in the city and being part of the Force isn't actually what I had planned for this point in my life. It was bearable because I'd finally found my mate."

A hint of a smile curved the corner of her mouth and the starlight was brilliant enough for him to see it. She danced around his proclamation for her. "What did you have in mind, then?"

He let one leg dangle off the edge. "I had retired from

the military and was just about to buy a big ranch in Alaska. The only thing that stopped me was a phone call from Flint asking me to join the Force." It seemed like a lifetime ago already; so much had changed since then.

"Flint?"

"The scruffy one that likes knives," he reminded her. The Force had immediately accepted Lane as Ash's mate, and that had automatically cleared her for being in on the secret.

"Right."

"Anyway, the timing of that call made me realize I needed to take the opportunity while I had it. As soon as I committed myself to a cattle ranch, I wouldn't be able to go off on missions anymore." He paused for a moment, feeling like he was two different people rolled into one. "And while I'm still not sure I made the right choice as far as a career, I do know I made the right choice because it helped me find you."

Lane touched the back of his hand. He rolled it over so that he might hold it properly. "So, you don't actually want to live in the city?"

He let out a short laugh. "No," he replied. "I really don't. As a matter of fact, just before you left, I was thinking about asking you if you'd come back to Alaska with me. I hesitated because I didn't know how you'd feel about ranch life, and I didn't want to risk driving you away."

She wrapped her fingers tighter around his. "Sounds like both of us need to be a little better at communicating."

"So, what do you think?" He held his breath, hoping like hell she'd say yes.

"A big ranch in the middle of nowhere? With you? Sounds like a dream come true to me." She was in his arms, then. Ash opened his mouth, relishing the feeling of her lips and tongue as though he'd starved for the last few days. And indeed he had. In the short amount of time they'd been apart, Ash knew he wasn't the same again.

She kissed him back, her fingers clinging to his shirt. Lane pulled away and buried her face in his chest. "I feel so foolish for running off."

"I'm a fool for not speaking up. But I'd live anywhere in the world, Lane, as long as you were there. I love you."

She pulled in a deep breath that made her body shake against his. "I love you, too."

11

THE TRUCK BUMPED ALONG THE OLD ROAD AND LANE SET THE window down to suck in the late summer air. There was something special about living up there in Alaska. The air, the soil, everything just seemed so much cleaner, untainted by the progress of man. She turned off the highway and onto the side road that'd become so familiar to her over the last few months. What had been wild and new was now so familiar, she felt she'd memorized every branch on every tree, and she loved each one of them.

Turning over the cattle gate that marked the beginning of their driveway, Lane smiled at the sight of big round bales of hay in the field on the right. The dried grass had been neatly rolled into giant pillows of pale brown, a beautiful contrast to the bright green of the grass that still grew around them.

In the field to the left, cattle munched lazily on the grass that was allowed to grow long for their benefit. Lane slowed down to admire their deep shaggy coats and big eyes.

She pulled up in front of the small barn closest to the house just as a massive piece of machinery pulled up alongside her. Ash shut off the engine and jumped down. "Saw you coming up the driveway. Do you need any help with the groceries?" He pulled open the passenger door.

"You don't have to do that. Looks like you're busy enough," Lane replied, but her mate already had his arms full of bags.

"I am, but I like it. I'm happy to say I baled that entire field myself. Mr. Jenkins said I'd get the hang of it quickly, and he wasn't wrong. The next big challenge will be calving in the fall." He smiled at the thought of that challenge as he pushed his way into the front door of the house.

"And what about the Force?" she asked as they walked through the living room toward the kitchen. "You haven't said much about it since you officially retired." She'd felt bad when he told her he wouldn't remain a part of the outfit because she'd been afraid he was doing it only for her sake.

But Ash seemed more than happy to live the country life he'd originally set out for. "I've got a conference call later. They seem fine with keeping me on as a consultant. It works for me, since I can still help out without ever having to leave you and the farm."

"I have to admit, ranch life looks good on you." She dropped a kiss on his cheek before setting her bags on the counter.

"And you. It looks like these little trips to town are getting easier. I'm glad." Ash washed his hands before he began to help unload the bags.

"It really is. I think I can even dare to say I enjoyed it this time." Lane had loved the solitude of the ranch as soon as they'd relocated to Alaska. Ash had been pleased to find the ranch he wanted was still available, and the only people they usually saw were Mr. and Mrs. Jenkins. That was enough at first, and then she began venturing into town along with Ash when they needed to pick up supplies. The fact that she was doing it on her own now meant so much to her.

He set down a can of soup and touched her cheek. "It means the world to me to see you happy. You're always beautiful, but you're positively radiant when you smile."

Lane could feel the air sizzling with energy between them. They worked closely together on the ranch, yet she never tired of seeing him. They still had that same bond that had been built back in Antarctica, and she could tell what he was thinking, even when he didn't say it out loud. "Oh?" she asked with a challenge in her eyes. "And just what are you going to do about it?"

His hands were on her hips, then, boosting her easily onto the countertop. She spread her legs to let him step closer to her as his lips reached up to meet her own, but she squealed a little when she felt his hands reach up her shirt. "Ash, right here in the middle of the kitchen?"

He diverted his attention from her lips to her collar bone, where he planted cool kisses along the collar of her shirt. "Why not? There's no one here to see. In fact, we could go right outside in the middle of the pasture if we wanted to."

She laughed at his tawdry suggestion, but she felt a bolt of energy shoot through her at the idea. That might be something for them to try later. "Here is good."

"Mmm, I thought so." Ash parted the buttons of her shirt, dropping his kisses from her neckline to her breasts, teasing one nipple out from the confines of her bra in order to pull it into the moist heat of his mouth and suckle it gently.

Lane let out a sigh of satisfaction. He knew her body so well. "You shouldn't tease me like that," she warned as she felt her core igniting.

He moved to the other breast, giving it equal and thorough attention that only increased the fire in her blood. "Who says I'm teasing? I fully intend to make good on this promise."

She clung to him, both to keep his lips in contact with

her flesh and to keep herself from falling over. "I'll hold you to that," she breathed.

"I certainly hope you do, since it means you have to uphold your part of the bargain as well." His fingers moved along the waistband of her jeans, sending brilliant sparks to her skin as he undid the button.

"Don't look at me. I wasn't the one who started this."

Ash didn't reply as he slipped her jeans down off her hips, leaving her sitting in her bra and panties on the kitchen counter, her nipples still exposed and wet. His eyes were dark as his hands moved up her inner thighs, the lightest touch encouraging her to spread her legs further apart. He moved aside the thin fabric of her panties and latched his mouth to her most sensitive place.

Lane moaned. He seemed to love doing this to her, and while it'd made her feel incredibly self-conscious at first, she'd easily learned to love it. She wrapped her legs around his head as his tongue worked her flesh, flicking and pulsing in all the right ways. Her own hips moved in time to his ministrations as she laid back on the counter, opening herself up to him completely.

His moan of pleasure reverberated against her, and Lane gasped as she felt her muscles tighten. She took her breasts into her own hands, flicking her nipples with her thumbs as she closed her eyes and focused on the delight of his mouth against her heated center. Everything was building inside her, winding around itself and through her body until she was forced to let it go with a cry that echoed up to the vaulted ceiling.

Ash kissed the inside of her thigh. "I could do that all day," he growled. The animalistic desire in his eyes increased as he took in the sight of her hands on the orbs above her bra.

She let go in order to push herself to a sitting position once again. "But then I won't have a chance to return the favor," she argued as she began sliding off the counter.

He caught her by the waist before her feet touched the floor. "No. I think I've got other plans for you." Ash eased out of his clothes as his eyes savored her naked body, and Lane relished the sight of his bulky muscles. A smattering of salt and pepper hair across his strong chest trickled down to a trail between his abs and then further down, to show her just what he had waiting for her. He was hard and ready to go, and Lane felt her own tongue flick out to touch the corner of her lips in anticipation.

Unclothed, he stepped forward and slid her off the counter, settling her straight onto his manhood. She was already slick and ready, craving the fullness of him inside of her, but still she drew in a breath as they fit together.

"You all right?" he murmured against her neck.

"God, yeah." He had her braced against the counter as he moved inside her, the tension of her muscles rewinding that tightly coiled spring that she'd already let go of once. The softness of his chest hair and the hardness of his muscles against her breasts only increased the potency of what they were doing.

Lane bit her lip as she felt him thicken inside her. Knowing he was just as turned on as she was only pushed her further, and she cried out. He pulsed rapidly against her as he brought himself to the final peak and exploded, growling his satisfaction as his teeth scraped gently against her shoulder. They breathed heavily and held each other tightly as they recovered before Ash finally lowered her slowly to the floor.

He pressed a kiss to her cheek. "You're one hell of a woman. And we've made one hell of a mess."

Lane looked over her shoulder. She hadn't realized that in the throes of their passion, she'd knocked over several of the grocery bags. Cans and boxes were scattered over the counter, and a few of them had fallen to the floor. She shrugged and smiled. "I think it was worth it, don't you?"

"Absolutely."

How had she ever risked letting him go? A man who loved her, who took care of her and protected her, who was patient with her as she learned the tasks of the ranch—and who knew how to drive her to the heights of ecstasy over and over again. That wasn't an easy thing to find. And she was content knowing she'd never have to live without him again.

THE END

PROTECTED BY THE SOLDIER TIGER

SPECIAL OPS SHIFTERS: DALLAS FORCE

1

———

THE THUMP OF THE BLADES OVERHEAD WAS BOTH A COMFORT and a stressor as Max Jennings swooped the chopper over the dark desert. There was too much input through his headphones and the instruments in front of him. They seemed to cancel each other out; he couldn't hear what the base was telling him to do.

But that was all right. He knew what his mission was, whether he agreed with it or not. Max knew this mission was a futile one, and that was precisely why they'd chosen him for it. As a Night Stalker, he was one of the most talented helicopter pilots the U.S. Army had on hand. They knew he could cut low and fast over the dangerous sands of Iraq, deploying the soldiers that were needed for the mission.

He just had to wonder if the soldiers in the back of the bird had any idea what they were getting into.

The situation was a critical one. Max had to get them in and get himself out before the enemy forces had any clue what was happening. Max adjusted the throttle and control stick. "We've got a strong crosswind," he said through the headset. "We've got to do this as quickly as possible."

There were several noises of affirmation from the back.

Pulling the chopper into a hover, he gave the sign that they'd reached their destination and were ready to go. The open side of the craft gave easy access for the men as they leaped out into the darkness. Max watched them go, sliding down the line and disappearing into the vast space beneath him. It could've been a few feet or a mile; only the instrument panel would tell him the truth. Max dusted the display with his thumb. Everything there was so goddamn dusty all the time! But he still couldn't read the numbers behind it. He rubbed harder, but the digits only blurred.

Panic bloomed in his chest. "Something's wrong. Abort!"

But it was too late. The cargo area was empty, and he was alone in the sky. Max reached for the switches that would fire up the spotlight. He had to find them and get them back! But that would only kill him, and there was nothing he could do. He'd dropped them off to their deaths. They wouldn't be coming back home. Theirs would be the faces that all of America would see on the nightly news in several weeks. Max wouldn't see it, stuck in the hellhole of the world as he was, but he would know. He was the one who'd gotten them killed.

The gasp that filled the room startled Max until he realized it was coming from his own throat. He launched himself away from his pillow and, just as quickly, turned around to punch it.

Another fucking dream, he thought. *Will they ever end?* He grabbed his phone to check the time. *5 a.m. Great.*

He fell back into bed, his pillow giving a soft whiff of protest, and tried to close his eyes.

But the images were still there. It didn't matter that he was awake now. Max could reason with himself all he wanted, explaining that they were just old memories twisted by his dream-state into even worse visions. He rolled onto his side, frustrated.

The truth was they hadn't been so dissimilar. Max had flown on numerous missions during his time with the Army, and they blurred together. It wasn't a surprise, considering they were always quick assignments completed in the dark over strange places, and they were all of the utmost importance. His schedule was rarely ever explained to him ahead of time. His commanding officers expected him to hop up and do whatever he was asked, whenever he was asked. Max had flown missions on Thanksgiving, sending heavy fire into enemy territory. He'd worked many Christmases, which always carried a special sense of loneliness, even when he was surrounded by his comrades. It was one hell of a way to live.

And now, even safe in his apartment at the Special Ops Shifters headquarters in Dallas, far from the war of his past and everything he'd experienced there, he knew he was still living with it.

There was no way he was going to sleep now. His eyes refused to shut without replaying those old scenes again, and his limbs twitched with the need to do something useful. He shoved himself up and out of bed, yanking on a t-shirt and a pair of shorts. Within a few minutes, he was outside and on the sidewalk.

Dallas was quiet for a big city, especially at this time of night. Anyone sane had long since gone home, locked the door, and shut the curtains. But Max had always known he was a bit different, and this place was a playground compared to where he'd worked overseas. The worse he might run into was a drunk who hadn't managed to stagger back to his house earlier. Max knew he could easily outrun or outfight anyone who wanted to give him hell. The problem was that he longed for the chance.

His feet hit the concrete hard as he watched the sun rise over the city he'd come to know as his home. Max knew he needed far more sleep than he was getting, but rooting himself in the reality of this place was much more helpful than tossing and turning in his bed. He focused on the way the darkness shifted, melting away from the buildings and streets it'd claimed during the night in favor of the sun, which shimmered in triumph on the glass windows of various office and apartment buildings. The sun captured them from top to bottom, warming the roofs before sliding down to the cold concrete of the sidewalks and ushering the occupants from their beds.

He pushed himself harder. If he was going to be out there, then he was going to get in one hell of a workout. That was one consolation of insomnia, and he was determined to take advantage of it. It also helped ease his inner tiger, which demanded to come out far more than was reasonable for city life.

Once he'd returned home and showered, Max headed to work at Luxury Air Tours. He tried to head straight out to the hanger to start his pre-flight check, but a heavyset man intercepted him before he could make it.

"There he is! And bright and early this morning, too!" George Stephenson was more round than anything else, and Max liked to joke to himself that the man rolled instead of walked. But he was the one who'd started up this business, and his signature was on Max's paychecks. "I wanted to talk to you about your flight logs last week."

Damn it. "Yeah, I'll get them finished." But his boss was

waving him into the office, and he had no choice but to follow.

George sighed as he closed the door behind them. "Max, you're one of the best pilots we've got. No, I take that back. You're *the* best pilot we've got, and I think you know that. But you can't just get by on talent alone. There's a protocol to contend with here, and that includes filling out your flight logs and not pissing off the clientele."

So that was what this was *really* about. George didn't usually say much if the flight logs weren't perfect. He was the one who set up the tours in the first place, so he knew exactly where all the choppers were going and at what time. Max slumped down in the ripped chair in front of George's desk. Luxury Air Tours might be all about the amenities for their clients, but not for themselves. "All right. Who was it this time?"

"Biff and Muffy Burns." His thick eyebrows raised as he looked up at Max, like a father reproaching his errant son.

Shit. "Yeah, I guess that's a big one, huh?"

"A big one? Considering how much business they send our way and how many connections they have? Hell, Max. I'd hardly have a company here at all if it weren't for their money and the fact that they spend it like water."

George's tirade continued, but Max wasn't listening anymore. He looked through the large window on the side of the office that looked directly into the hangar. The machines were bright, beautiful, and agile, things of art and style made to appeal to the wealthy. A gust of wind from the wrong direction would send them tumbling. Max always felt that something was missing when he looked at these particular helicopters: guns.

It was impossible not to compare his current life with his former one. There were still choppers, but they were completely different. Even the people who piloted them weren't like the Night Stalkers he'd known when he was actively serving. Some of them were just yuppies who wanted their pilot's license because they thought it sounded cool and ended up with a job. One guy had been a chopper pilot for a news program on the East Coast before transferring there. His coworkers weren't bad people, but they had a different mannerism about them. They didn't take things as seriously as he and the rest of the 160th did.

And then there were the passengers. If anything had changed the most, it was them. Max was used to carting around highly trained men and women who knew their duty and were willing to give their lives for it. They faced disaster right alongside him. Sometimes, they had to do things they never would've done if they'd been stateside, but it was different when you were on a mission.

Now, he was carting around the rich and famous who wanted to see what their new hotel complex looked like from the air. He was taking honeymooners out over the city because George had created special packages in the hopes that they'd come back and pay for another tour. Once, he'd even picked a guy up because his limo was stuck in traffic, and he "just didn't want to deal with it anymore." And of course, there were people like Biff and Muffy Burns, the richest, snobbiest, biggest wastes of space he could have ever imagined.

"Max? Are you even listening to me? This is serious stuff this time."

He blinked, once again back in the chair in front of George's desk. "Yeah. Sorry."

"Look, I know you're not great when it comes to customer service. But you've got to get your head in the game, both for your sake and mine. I have to officially write this one up, considering how many I've let go on the wayside. Sound reasonable?"

"Sure." Max knew he should be glad he could use his skills in his post-military life, but sometimes he thought it only made things more difficult. The tourism business was a shallow one compared to the old days.

"And do us both a favor and keep your nose clean for a while, huh? I don't want to have to do this again. Here's your schedule for today. I'm sorry that it's filled with more of the patrons you hate, but remember, we wouldn't be in business if it weren't for them." He slid a printout across the desk.

Max took it, barely glancing at it as he headed out into the hangar.

———

Max swooped the chopper through the sky over Dallas. The city seemed to be made for viewing from the air, surrounded as it was by lakes. Even the corporate hotshots who owned the skyscrapers downtown had gone to the trouble of giving the buildings different colored lights to make them stand out. There was so much to see, whether it was day or night.

But the couple that was riding along with him didn't seem to notice. They were too busy sucking face to be awestruck by the beauty below them.

"On your left is the world's largest potato chip, bigger than any building in Texas. We like to do things big around here." Max waited for them to break their liplock and search for the fictional tourist trap, but they didn't reply at all. The only thing he heard through the mic was the smacking of their lips and moaning as they groped each other.

He grimaced. He'd have to decontaminate the chopper at the end of the night at this rate. With a sigh, he buzzed around the city and waited for their time to run out. The newlyweds had booked a night over Dallas with Luxury Air Tours, taking advantage of the package offered along with their hotel. Max was tempted to do something really stupid and pull some maneuvers that would get him fired just so he could get the satisfaction of hearing them scream, but damn it if he didn't need this job.

And damn it if it didn't remind him of the past. Max was a good chopper pilot, otherwise he never would've been accepted into the Night Stalkers. His military record included plenty of metals and ribbons for the missions he'd carried out successfully. There were some of them he couldn't even tell anyone about, since they were still classified. Not that he had anyone he felt like sharing them with, anyway.

For a moment, Max was no longer hanging in the sky over Dallas. He was over the desert, keeping the bird steady as soldiers slipped down the fast rope to their duty. There was sand in his eyes and in his hair and everywhere else, and as soon as he found the chance to shower, he'd just be full of sand again. The sun was too bright and the air was too hot, even for his inner tiger sensibilities. Bullets pinged the sides of the chopper, missing him by only a few inches.

He sucked in a deep breath and was back in Texas again. A place that was safe, or at least a place that was supposed to be. But Max hadn't been able to bring himself to trust anyone since his honorable discharge. There was too much going on in his head, and it was easier to just fly into the air and pretend none of it had never happened.

An hour later, when the kissing couple had been dropped off at the helipad and had thanked him with flushed faces, even though they hadn't seen a damn thing, Max got in his car and headed home. He wove through Friday night traffic the same way he buzzed through the air, feeling that the cars around him were too close. He didn't trust them to follow the rules of the road, and he pressed the gas pedal a little harder until he pulled into the garage.

"Good, you're here!" Vance said as Max entered the common living area at the headquarters of the Special Ops Shifter Force's Dallas unit. "I was just about to call you and tell you about your new mission."

"Can't it wait until I've had a shower?" Max grumbled. He felt tired and dirty, and the mere memories of his time overseas made him feel like he was covered in sand all over again.

"Not really. Let's go to the conference room." Vance turned and headed down the hallway, expecting him to follow.

Max stared longingly at the door to his left that led to his little apartment. The original SOS Force was stationed in D.C., but they'd recently started a Dallas unit, and Max had been recruited to be a part of it. Since living quarters were provided for those who needed them, it'd been easy for Max to let his slummy little place on the wrong side of town go. Besides, if he was working both for Luxury Air Tours and for the Force, it made for a little less driving to stay at HQ.

Reluctantly, he joined the others in the conference

room. "All right. What's the latest emergency?" he asked as he flopped down into a chair.

Jack, the resident intelligence officer—and a fox when humans weren't looking—tapped a tablet on the table in front of him. "I just finished up a call with Hudson. We've got an unusual task in front of us."

"And?" Max pressed. He just wanted to get this over with. He felt restless and cagey, and it was easy to imagine how his cousins who lived in the zoos must feel.

Vance leaned back in his seat. "You're wound up tonight."

Max heaved an impatient sigh. "It's just not a good night for me. I'd like to wrap this up sooner than later if you don't mind."

Jack looked up from his tablet. "You could say we have a private client. There's a rather affluent shifter in Fort Worth who's a major witness in an investigation being conducted by the local conclave. I guess there have already been some incidents that have made her believe her life may be in danger until this trial is over. We've been asked to protect her."

Max scowled. "So now we're just really well-trained babysitters?"

"Think of it as a bodyguard mission, man. She lives in a penthouse apartment with a helipad on the roof, so that'll make it really easy for you to chauffeur her around to work, her appointments, and the court hearings," Jack continued. "The rest of the time, we can take turns guarding her."

"Right. Okay. No different than what I do all day anyway: hauling around rich-ass folks who think a normal car isn't good enough for them. Just give me the info and let me know when I'm supposed to pick her up."

Jack consulted the tablet and gave him the address. "Tomorrow afternoon, actually. The name's Sabrina Barrett."

Max's vision turned black around the edges, and his tiger surged as he focused solely on Jack. "Sabrina Barrett?" he said hoarsely. It could be a coincidence. Surely, there was more than one Sabrina Barrett on the planet. And the one he'd known hadn't been such a rich bitch as to need a helicopter to take her out on errands. He swallowed the thickness that was building in his throat. "What, uh, what does she do for a living?"

Jack frowned at the tablet. "Says here she's some hotshot cosmetic surgeon."

Shit. Shit shit shit. If the client had been some financial advisor or movie star or something, he'd have felt a lot better. But it seemed clear he wasn't going to be able to escape his past the way he'd wanted to.

"You all right?" Vance drawled.

"Yeah. I'm fine." Max pushed himself out of the chair, his body feeling too heavy. "Just tired. I'd better get some rest if I'm going to fly tomorrow. We done here?"

"Sure. Go ahead."

He stumbled down the hallway, running his hand through his dark hair and wondering how he was going to manage this. It was one thing to play air cabbie for some snob.

It was a completely different thing to do for the woman he'd practically left at the altar.

2

"ALL RIGHT, EVERYONE. ALMOST DONE HERE. I'VE JUST GOT to get this closed up, and then we'll be good to go." Sabrina Barrett's fingers moved almost automatically as she carefully stitched up the incision. She remembered a time when she'd had to work much harder to make the stitches even and perfect, reducing the amount of scarring that would be left behind. Of course, it was much easier thanks to finer needles and the right fibers.

She'd spent the last few hours lost in the world of surgery, and the hours before that had been consumed with other patients. Now that her shift was nearly over, she could feel the ache in her feet and lower back from standing on hard linoleum all day. Sabrina shoved the pain down a bit longer. It was nothing a little yoga wouldn't fix later.

Twisting the forceps to create the final knot that would fix everything in place, Sabrina set her instruments on the waiting tray and stepped back from the table. "That's a wrap. You guys have been great. Thanks again."

She sighed to herself as she stepped out of the OR to clean up. She could feel eyes on her, even there at work. The operation had been consuming enough to help distract her, but now it was impossible. He was there again.

She began to peel off her gloves. It'd been a long day, and she was eager for it to be over. What'd made it even longer was the fact that she didn't find much satisfaction in the work she'd just completed. Although Sabrina knew she'd done an excellent job with the rhinoplasty, it had felt empty. So what if another Hollywood housewife (the Dallas version, anyway) would have a tiny new nose to show all her friends at brunch in a few months over mimosas? So what if that same spoiled woman would give Sabrina's contact information to all her friends who wanted implants, lifts, tucks, and complete remodels of their faces and bodies? Sabrina was good at her job, but her heart just wasn't in it.

As Sabrina left the surgery wing, she could feel his presence once again. He was closing in on her as she made her way down the hall, skirting past orderlies trying to get their patients to the right places. Sabrina sensed his eyes like a physical presence on her back, pressing against her spine. She instinctively walked faster, trying to keep her body from breaking into a full run.

Not for the first time, she allowed herself a short vision of what it would be like to show her other form in the middle of this busy hospital. With the sterile white walls and floor, no one would expect to see a wild animal pounding down the hallways, mouth open and brilliant teeth showing. She could practically feel her paws as they pounded the floor and hear the screams of the staff as they backed away from the massive tiger. Sabrina's muscles longed for the freedom of her big cat, the ease of movement, the pure instinct that could go unchecked.

But that would have to wait. Dr. Sabrina Barrett was, after all, one of the most prominent surgeons in Dallas, even in the whole state of Texas. She'd had her name in medical journals across the country, and she knew the hospital administration was watching her closely. Sabrina was the rising star they were counting on to attract all the business they could ever want. It wasn't necessarily a burden she enjoyed.

"Heading home?" asked a familiar voice as she passed the recovery ward.

Sabrina turned to find Dr. Lance McCarthy smiling at her. He was a tall and handsome man with dark hair that never seemed to get tousled by a surgery cap. With his sparkling smile, Lance looked more like a doctor from a soap opera than a respected surgeon. He joined her as she strode down the hallway.

"No, I've got one more meeting first. Then I'll pop back here and check on the day's patients. After that, I think I'll be heading home." Now the stare that she'd been able to feel on her back all day had been shifted toward Dr. McCarthy. The other surgeon was no threat to her, but it amused Sabrina to think he was being watched so closely now.

"You know, the nurses and the orderlies can take care of your patients for you. This is one of the nicest hospitals in the state, and the patients expect the utmost care. Everyone who works here knows that and they're willing to give it to them." Lance flashed that toothpaste commercial smile at her once again.

Sabrina turned slightly to the side so he wouldn't see her rolling her eyes. Yes, he was right. The nurses and other support staff at the hospital were amazing, but that didn't mean she shouldn't come back and personally check on her patients. "I like to see them with my own eyes instead of relying on whatever someone bothered to write in their chart. All people are fallible, even us."

"Even with that expert stitching you've perfected?" Dr. McCarthy asked with a raised eyebrow. "Everyone's talking about it. You're creating quite the ripple in the cosmetic surgery field."

"That's not why I did it." Sabrina didn't want the fame

that came with her innovations, but she was pretty sure most of the other people in her field didn't understand that.

"You're making people jealous, whether you want to or not. Someone's even circulating a rumor that you took a sewing class to improve your work." Lance laughed as they got on the elevator.

Sabrina watched the doors close, smiling at the man further down the hall who'd lose sight of her now. It was a small concession for her, since it meant she'd be stuck in the elevator with Lance for several floors, but she'd have to take what she could get. "I did, actually."

"Wait. What?" Dr. McCarthy put his hand on the elevator wall near Sabrina's shoulder and leaned too close. "You seriously sat down with a bunch of old ladies and took a sewing class?"

"They weren't a bunch of old ladies, and it was an embroidery class. There were people of all ages there, and they know an awful lot. I think it would benefit everyone to do something like that." There was no point in denying the rumor because it was true and nothing to be ashamed of.

"So what? Now you can make a doily when you're done with surgery?"

"Actually, Lance, it means I've honed my technique to reduce scarring and recovery time, not to mention how it affects the look of the overall surgery. You could benefit from it yourself, if you think you could handle a bunch of women telling you what to do." She scowled at him as she slid away.

He was unaffected. "I think I could. I like strong women, and you're one of them, Dr. Barrett. The two of us would make one hell of a couple. I can see it now—"

"Before you get lost in fantasy land, I'm not interested," she interrupted. "I don't have time to get involved with anyone."

Lance moved close once again, his finger touching the underside of her chin. "That's all right. It doesn't have to be a relationship, per se. After all, we're both adults. We both know what we want."

Was it the movement of the elevator that was suddenly making her nauseous? Sabrina didn't think so. She pushed her hand against his chest before he could be any more forward. "You should really stop embarrassing yourself now while we don't have an audience. I'm not about to continue this discussion in the weekly meeting."

The elevator dinged and opened its doors, letting in a rush of fresh air that Sabrina hadn't realized she'd needed until she felt it. She charged through, slowing her steps when she saw the stairwell door open in her peripheral vision. So he'd found her on this floor, too. There was no getting away from either one of these guys.

"You know, you've been single long enough." Lance was off the elevator right after her, still at her shoulder. "I think it's time you gave someone else a chance."

"Like I said, not interested." She kept walking.

"And why not? I'm successful. I'm good looking. These rich people pay me far too much money, just like you. I think we've got more in common than you think, and you should give me a chance."

Sabrina stopped in her tracks and closed her eyes. There were too many emotions roiling around inside her right now. She wasn't in the operating room, so she could let them all out if she wanted to. But that wasn't the time or the place, no matter how much Lance deserved it. It didn't help that she could still feel the other man's eyes on her, watching them from a distance. When she opened her eyes, Lance was still standing there, looking confused.

"You don't get to tell me what to do, Lance. I don't know what makes you think otherwise, and I don't know what your obsession with me is all about. I suggest you get over both of them, and fast."

"Look, I'm just concerned about you." Dr. McCarthy ran his hand down her arm. "You were in a pretty serious relationship from what I understand. It's not good for a person to go through a bad breakup and then just remain single forever. You've got to get back on that horse."

"And I suppose that horse is you?"

One side of his mouth quirked up, and he moved into her personal space once again. "I'm willing if you are."

Her jaw hurt from gritting her teeth together so much in the last five minutes. How dare he give her advice like that? This was the man who'd been caught with every nurse on their floor. And how dare he bring up Max when she'd fought so hard to forget about him? Yes, Sabrina had thought she'd found the love of her life. Yes, she'd thought it was something that would last forever, and she hadn't hesitated to tell everyone just how great their bond was. She'd imagined it was unbreakable, and she wanted the whole world to know about it.

But she'd been wrong, and she didn't need this jackass to remind her. "I'm sick of you, Lance McCarthy. I'm sick of the way you think you can just order people around the way you do in the OR. I don't want to hear any more of your bullshit, and I'm not going to put up with it. Stay the hell away from me from now on unless there's a patient we need to discuss."

"Hey, hey. Easy now. You don't have to get upset. Let's get through this meeting, and then we can go out and have a drink. How about that?"

"Why don't you shove that drink up your ass!" She felt heat flush her cheeks and spread through her veins as she fought not to shift. Talk about not the time or the place! Granted, getting attacked by a tiger on the fifth floor of a hospital would undoubtedly make an impression on the man, and Sabrina could easily imagine the look of shock on his face if she had the chance to swipe at him with her paw, but that would have to remain a fantasy. "I'm tired of all the fake people I meet in this line of work. You and most of the other surgeons I know are just out to make a quick buck and then get a quick fuck when you're done. You don't care about your patients unless they're some strange case that's going to get your name in a medical journal." She felt her eyes flash.

His eyes widened and he took a step back. "H-hey, I'm sorry. I didn't mean to piss you off like that. I was just trying to be nice. I'll see you tomorrow." He trotted down the hallway toward the conference room.

Sabrina followed at a more leisurely pace. She should've taken pride in eviscerating him like that, but knowing Lance, he'd be over it in less than a day and then start hitting on a nurse or some unsuspecting volunteer. He was a piece of shit, and there were plenty of others like him.

Entering the conference room, the din of small talk met her ears. Sabrina helped herself to a bottle of water and sat, ignoring Dr. McCarthy as he seated himself quietly at the other end of the table. She listened as they ran through the events of the week, what would be coming up the next week, and upcoming changes to the computer system. The entire time, Sabrina could feel his eyes on her. He was just outside, finding some way to casually hang out in the hallway without being seen. If anyone had noticed, they hadn't said anything to her about it yet.

But he finally caught up to her in the elevator when it was time to leave, casually pushing the button to close the doors early before he turned to her. "That was quite the trick you tried to pull," he said quietly. "You know I'm not supposed to let you out of my sight."

"Sorry, Russell. I know you're just trying to do your job, and I'm not making it any easier on you." Sabrina sighed as she leaned against the elevator wall and lifted one foot. She'd bought new insoles, but her feet were still killing her after being on them all day. "I just don't see why the conclave had to send you in the first place. I'm fine."

"That's what everyone thinks until the day they aren't," he warned. The elevator let them off at the parking garage, and he stayed immediately by her side as they crossed the concrete floor.

Sabrina begrudged him having to follow her around like this. It made her feel like a little girl who wasn't old enough to cross the street by herself. But at least his presence was completely different than Lance's. Russell was like an overprotective older brother, and she knew he'd never hit on her. He was too professional. Granted, he was an attractive man. Tall and dark, with evidence of his inner black bear showing through occasionally, he was a completely different sort of handsome than Lance was. "But seriously, don't you think someone would've already come after me if they were going to? Why bother waiting around and giving me that much more time to give my testimony? It's kind of silly."

He sighed as he opened the passenger door of her car and waved her inside. "The conclave doesn't think it's silly."

Frowning at the open door, she turned on her heel and went around to the driver's side. It was her car, after all. "Then, I guess I should run for a position the next time elections come around."

Russell sighed as he slid into the passenger seat. "You're going to get me in so much trouble."

"It's my car, after all. I might be stuck letting you follow me around like some stalker all day long, but I don't have to add you to my insurance." She fired up the engine and allowed herself a smile. Poor Russell. She probably would've been a lot nicer if she hadn't just dealt with Lance for the millionth time.

"Okay, Sabrina. I get it. You don't like having me around. You don't think you need me, and maybe you even think you're more than capable of protecting yourself. But the fact is that you witnessed a murder, and the suspects don't exactly have the best reputation. You're important not just to the medical community, but to the local shifters, too."

She glanced sideways to give him a dirty look just before she pulled out of the parking garage. He was right. A shifter's physiology was different from a normal human's, so it was essential for them to have a few experts in the field when someone needed medical care. Hell, if it hadn't been for the way her people needed her, she'd never have been at that medical convention where she'd gotten herself into so much trouble in the first place. "It's not fair of you to bring that up."

He spread his hands in the air innocently. "I'm just being honest. And while I'm at it, I have to say you did a pretty good job of telling that asshole doctor off. He was driving me crazy. Guys like him shouldn't be allowed to harass women that way."

Sabrina smiled. She'd gotten close to Russell fairly quickly in the week or so since he'd been assigned to act as her bodyguard. She liked him, although she hadn't imagined she'd ever feel anything but resentment for someone who babysat her all day. "I don't think 'allowed' is the right term, but he gets away with it because he's rich, talented, and good-looking. I'm sure some women are even flattered by him. For me, I'd rather he just fall down the elevator shaft."

Russell laughed, an unusual noise from him. "Just make sure you haven't ditched me in the break room if you manage to make that happen. I want to see it." He fell silent suddenly, tapping his knee as he glanced out the window.

"What is it?" she demanded. Maybe it was just because they were both shifters, but Sabrina had learned to read his body language like a book.

"Something I don't think you're going to like."

She turned onto the highway and gunned the accelerator to fit in with the flow of traffic. "Might as well just tell me now and get it over with."

He nodded. "The conclave is hiring a professional unit to watch over you."

Her eyebrows drew together as she tried to understand what he was saying. "A professional unit? What does that mean?"

"People with special skills who do this for a living, not just some big dumb guy like me who happened to fall into the right position with the conclave."

"You're not dumb. In fact, you're quite smart to know I wouldn't like this news. How do I get out of it?" She could easily envision not just one person following her around discreetly, but an entire entourage swarming around her. That might be how the movie stars lived, but it wasn't her.

"You don't. This is a direct order, and it's already been taken care of. Don will be standing guard outside your apartment tonight and I'll be at work with you tomorrow as usual, but after work, the new guys take over."

Sabrina rolled her eyes. "This is really getting out of hand, you know?"

"It's a big case, and you're a big deal. The conclave doesn't want to take any risks. But soon enough, it'll all be over with and you can go back to your normal life. Hopefully." The last part he muttered under his breath, but Sabrina still heard him.

And she knew what he meant. Depending on how the trial went, she might never have a normal life again.

3

"YOU SURE ABOUT THIS?" VANCE ASKED, EYEING HIM sideways as they lounged in the common area at their headquarters. The cowboy had chosen not to live in one of the provided apartments since he already had a ranch outside of town, but just like everyone else, he spent a lot of time there.

"Yeah. Why?" Max turned away from the window to glare at him.

The cougar shrugged. "Oh, just a hunch, considering you haven't stopped pacing for the last hour or so." He grinned from his place on the couch, where he lounged casually.

That was easy enough for him to do, considering this woman they'd been put in charge of protecting wasn't his ex-fiancée. "I'm fine. I'm just antsy because I don't have anything left to do. I was already down at the hangar this morning to clean up my chopper, and I've made out my flight plan. Turns out, I can go straight from the roof of the hospital to the roof of her apartment building." He wouldn't say it out loud, but it'd galled him to see that Sabrina was living in a place like Sandoval Terrace. That showed him more than anything just what a hotshot she'd become since the two of them had split. It was the sort of ritzy apartment building she'd have made fun of only a few years ago, and now she was living on the top floor.

"All right," Vance drawled. "If you say so."

"What's that supposed to mean?" Max curled his fists at his sides. The other men of the Force were supposed to be his comrades now, but that didn't mean he could give one of them a busted lip, right?

He put his hands in the air in self-defense. "Hey, I'm just saying you seem like you're having a hard time with this. You've been acting weirder than normal ever since we got the job. I know the local conclave wanted us at least in part because of your piloting skills, but if it's not going to work, then we can make other arrangements."

"We don't need other arrangements," Max growled. How dare Vance question him like this! "I'm just ready to get this show on the road."

Jack whipped off his headphones and shut his laptop. "Look, either fight or don't fight. But I'm tired of listening to the arguing, either way. I'm trying to get some work done."

Max pressed his lips together. He wanted to turn his anger on Jack as well, but the fact that both of them were getting irritated told him something. He was lashing out again. It wasn't the first time, and it was difficult to control. Maybe it was because he'd spent so many years with someone telling him what to do, or perhaps it was just because he had a stubborn streak a mile wide, but he didn't like anyone questioning him. "I'm just eager to get this show on the road."

"Or in the air, rather," Jack joked. "I spoke with the president of the conclave, who was able to confirm there haven't been any suspicious activities since they started protecting Dr. Barrett. They just want to be extra careful since she's the prime witness to this murder. The trial is in a week, so we'll be back to our regular style of assignments after that, I imagine. In the meantime, I've worked up a rotating schedule."

Max practically jumped when his phone pinged, Vance's phone echoing the noise across the room. He checked the screen to find a message from Jack. "You really like being organized, don't you?"

Jack didn't bother taking it as an insult. "It helps, especially in this line of work. Anyway, that agenda should sync up with what Dr. Barrett has going on for the week. There will be a lot of downtime, just hanging out at the hospital or her place, but hopefully, it won't be more exciting than that."

"Oh, I don't know," Vance countered with a smile. "I reckon I could use some excitement. I don't have a lot going on at the ranch right now, and I wouldn't mind taking down an enemy shifter here and there."

Max only replied with a snort. He *knew* there'd be plenty of excitement, but not in the way Vance pictured. Sabrina had always been an incredibly talented woman, and not just with a scalpel. She had a way of letting the troubles of the world slide right off her back like they didn't matter. He'd thought it was a sign of strength, but he'd come to learn during his relationship with her that it just meant she was incredibly cold. He couldn't imagine anyone who fit in better with the clients she was now serving as one of the top cosmetic surgeons in the area.

"Whatever happens, I'm sure we can all be professional about it." Max grabbed his jacket from the back of the sofa and headed out. "I'll see you guys tomorrow."

The others called a goodbye after him, but he wasn't paying attention. Max was too busy brooding to himself. He knew he shouldn't give two shits what Sabrina Barrett was doing these days. It shouldn't matter if she was rich and famous or just a nobody doctor in a small town outside of Dallas. The two of them were through, and he'd made that more than evident when he'd moved out in the middle of the night. He was a professional, as he'd just reminded himself a minute ago, and he could show her that he could be just as cold.

It was a beautiful day, or it would've been if he'd been able to focus on it as he whirled over the city. He waited a moment for an air ambulance to clear the launchpad before he descended. His stomach lurched, and he wished he could blame it on the movement of the craft. But Max could sleep through a crash landing at this point. It was definitely not the chopper.

Leaving the rotor going to save time, Max sent a message to the number he'd been given and waited. He was there. He was doing his job. No one could fault him for that.

The rooftop door opened, and she emerged. He knew it was her, even from a distance. The white lab coat was obviously a dead giveaway, but it was more than that. It was the way she'd pulled her dark hair away from her face in a doubled-over ponytail, the deep chestnut strands glistening in the late afternoon sun. It was her tortoiseshell glasses that she insisted on wearing when she worked because she felt she could see better through them than with contacts. It was the sexy way she walked when no one was looking.

But her steps faltered as she and her guard approached the helicopter. She put up a hand as she squinted against the buffeting winds created by the spinning blades. Disdain dripped from her, but the guard didn't seem to notice. He stepped forward and reached inside the aircraft to shake Max's hand. "I'm Russell. President Whiteside asked me to tell you to call him with any issues. Dr. Barrett is to be kept under surveillance at all times.

Max eyed the guard. Who was he to tell him how to do his job? He knew what the hell he was there for. But he let it go for now. The hard part was yet to come. "Will do."

"Great." Russell helped Sabrina into the helicopter and stepped back. Max noted that even though he'd been relieved of duty, the man didn't leave the rooftop. He was waiting to see them off.

Max instantly felt a surge of something take over his body as he wondered what this man's relationship was to Sabrina. Was this her new mate? Had she gone on and found someone else as she discovered a new career for herself? If she had, then why the hell wasn't that guy going to keep her safe?

But he kept all his questions to himself as he ascended and adjusted his heading.

It was Sabrina who finally broke the silence. Her hands were folded in her lap, and she watched the buildings below them with far more interest than the usual tourists he had with him. "It's strange to be flying with you again."

"Yeah. I guess when the conclave asked us to do this, they didn't bother to ask if there was any personal history. Is it going to be problem?" He could hear the bite in his words, only somewhat reduced by the mic and headphones.

"No. I know you're a good pilot."

So that was it? She didn't feel safe with him because she knew he'd protect her at all costs, but simply because he was a good pilot? Because of the training he'd received through the Army? It was almost insulting.

He shook his head and concentrated on flying. He was getting too deep in his head again, a bad habit that had formed over the years he'd been out of the service. It was difficult to control, but he needed to work harder on it. He had to.

"I guess you must be doing well for yourself," Sabrina said, looking around at the inside of the cockpit. "You know, I never did sit down and memorize the insides of these things, but this looks like a nice one."

He shrugged. "Not as well as you've done, apparently. I'm surprised you didn't already have some private chauffeur and security guard."

She turned to look at him thoroughly for the first time since she'd gotten in the chopper, and Max felt his inner tiger lashing out at all the intense feelings it brought. "What's that supposed to mean?"

He shoved his tiger down. His wild instincts had been incredibly helpful when it came to fighting the enemy overseas, but he'd found his human side was more helpful when it came to his current life: that, and a healthy dose of sarcastic wit. "Come on. Your name pops up in about a million search results now that you've made it big."

Sabrina made a face. "You Googled me?"

He lifted one shoulder, realizing how lame that must've sounded. "It's a standard procedure if I'm going to be working with a new client. So yeah, I know about all the work you've done and how much attention it's gotten you. And money. They don't let just anyone live at Sandoval Terrace, much less on one of the top floors. I guess that little place on Easley Street would be way too far beneath you now."

She folded her arms across her chest, and Max could swear she was leaning away from him even within the confines of the seatbelt. "What exactly did you expect? That I'd just sit around in the same old place?"

"I don't know, but definitely not that you'd live in one of the most bougie buildings in the city." It just wasn't her. He easily remembered the way she used to spruce up their crappy little place. Sabrina would get so excited about something like a pair of new curtains or a coat of paint, and she'd go on and on about how much money they were saving compared to some of their friends.

"I live there because it's a nice place and I like it. I don't have to justify that to you." Her scowl was a familiar one.

That was just fine with him. Let her be on the defensive. Let her be mad. It made it that much easier for him to ignore the way his body was reacting. Max had gotten decent at keeping his tiger in check these days, but all that progress went flying out the window in Sabrina's presence. What was it about her that made him lose control like that?

Even now, he could feel a shiver down his spine where his fur was threatening to explode. He gripped the controls until his knuckles turned white to stave off his claws. For just a moment, he considered letting a tooth or two come through just to release some of the pressure, but it was a short trip from there to the fully-fledged beast. He was a talented pilot, but he couldn't do this without his human form.

"Yeah," he finally responded. "Almost there." He did his best to concentrate on navigation, on the skyline, even the overly familiar thud of the blades overhead. Instead, he was keenly aware of the curves of her body. Simply being in her presence was overwhelming.

Fortunately, a helicopter ride across the city was much faster than fighting traffic would've been, and they arrived at Sandoval Terrace in no time. Max tried to keep himself trained on the matter at hand as he settled down onto the generous roof. This landing wasn't going to be as quick as the one at the hospital since he had to shut everything down entirely. That was going to take some time.

Sabrina unbuckled herself. "I guess I'll just see you tomorrow on the way to work?"

"No. I'm staying here."

"What?" Her glasses had slipped ever-so-slightly, and she shoved them firmly back up her nose. "I really don't think that's necessary. Nothing has happened."

"So far," he reminded her. "It's an order, Sabrina. Just give the rotors a few minutes. Then we can go inside."

She shot him another dirty look but remained where she was. That was something he could always count on when it came to Sabrina: she was a rule follower. Not that there weren't times she stood up and demanded the rules be changed, but Max had never seen her go against someone solely for the sake of doing so.

Finally, when the chopper was shut down and secured, he escorted her inside the building. Max held his tongue as the rooftop door led them to an elevator that was nicer than any house he'd ever lived in. He merely lifted an eyebrow when he saw her unlock her apartment door with her fingerprint. But he couldn't contain himself any longer when they stepped inside, and he let out a low whistle. "Even swankier than I imagined."

She set her bag down on a side table and let a breath out through her lips. "It's not swanky. It's just nice. I wanted someplace comfortable to come home to in the evenings, and there's nothing wrong with that. Shit. There I go justifying myself to you again. If this is how things are going to go all night, then I can't wait for morning to come."

A twinge of guilt made him turn away from her. Max strode through the house, checking the windows and the fire escape. Everything was immaculately clean. The thick trim in every room was reminiscent of a more ornate architectural style that would've been popular over a hundred years ago, and the thick rugs squished gently under his feet. He had to admit the place had a cozy, comfortable feeling, even though it seemed a bit grandiose. Still, there was one thing about it he didn't like. "The security measures here are pretty minimal, considering how much money you probably paid for this place."

"What are you talking about?" She'd stepped into the laundry room for a moment and reemerged in a fitted button-down shirt, wide-legged dress trousers, and pumps. Sabrina was gorgeous in a powerful way that he'd always found hard to resist.

That made it difficult for him to remember exactly what it was he'd been trying to tell her. "The window locks are pretty minimal, for one thing."

"Do you really think someone is going to climb all the way up here? I doubt I even need locks on the windows."

She might have been right, but Max wasn't going to give in just yet. "Then there's that lock on your front door. A fingerprint is fancy and sounds very difficult to get past, but anyone with a little hacking skills could pop it open in an instant. Or just take an ax to it, that works."

Sabrina rolled her eyes. "It's fine, okay. It's all just fine. And if you're so concerned about it, then at least you're here to make sure someone doesn't put suction cups on their feet to walk up the side of the building and that there aren't any crazy ax murderers breaking down the door. Now, I'm hungry."

He followed her into the kitchen. Most of the place was an open floor plan, which meant the kitchen was simply one large corner of the apartment. The granite countertops and stainless-steel appliances were just as clean as the rest of the place. "Do you actually cook?"

"In case you don't recall," she said as she grabbed a takeout menu off the fridge, "I'm a pretty darn good cook. But these days, I'm too tired to. I'm thinking barbecue." She waved the menu in his direction.

Max felt the urge to be difficult again, but he took a deep breath and set it aside. It wasn't Sabrina's fault the Force had been hired to protect her. If she was going to at least be kind enough to think of him when it came to dinner, then he could lay off being such an asshole. Maybe. "Yeah. Barbecue is fine." It was going to be a long night.

"I'M GOING TO BED," SABRINA SAID A COUPLE OF HOURS LATER after the dishes had been cleared away, and she'd mostly gotten over Max's rather rude treatment of the delivery driver. She shifted from one sore foot to the other. Don and Russell had been standing guard outside her door, but Max hadn't shown any signs of leaving her apartment. "What are your plans for the night?"

He answered exactly the way she was hoping he wouldn't, and even included a rather mischievous grin with it. "My orders are to stay right here."

"As in, *here* here?" she asked, pointing to the floor. "I don't even know if there are any sheets on the guest bed. I'll have to look in the linen closet."

"Don't worry about that," he assured her. "I'm not here for a slumber party. I'm here to guard you. I'll be right here on the couch, staying awake and listening for anyone who isn't fooled by your fancy electronic lock."

"Somehow, I'm not sure that makes me feel any safer." She turned around and marched off to her bedroom, shutting the door firmly behind her and then sinking back against it.

Why? Of all the people the conclave could've hired to watch over her, why did it have to be Max? Sabrina had managed to avoid him ever since they'd broken up. Granted, that wasn't difficult. Max wasn't the sort of guy who attended medical conventions or frequented local parties among the wealthy, and she wasn't the sort to hang out with a bunch of soldiers going out for drinks. That was one of the problems they'd had, after all. They were just two completely different people.

Still, as she slipped out of her heels, she couldn't help but wonder why Max should show up in her life right now. What was the universe trying to tell her? Sabrina was all about science and technology, but she also felt there were times when you couldn't ignore the signs right in front of you. If this meant she was supposed to take Lance McCarthy's word that it was time to move on, then she'd have to move on to a different city.

Sabrina went into the master bath and stripped off her clothes, dropping them into the hamper. Usually, she didn't even bother to shut her bedroom door, much less the bathroom door. This time, knowing it was the only thing that separated her from Max, she not only shut it, but locked it.

She stepped eagerly into the warm shower and stood under the water for a long moment, letting it run down her body. She and Max used to do everything together, even bathe. It shouldn't have been difficult to have him in the next room. He might be a bit crude, but he wasn't going to come barging in on her just to get a peek at something he'd already seen.

Watching the water swirl down the drain, she wished she could think of anything else besides the tiger sitting on her sofa. She went through the familiar motions of washing her hair and body, scrubbing away the day. It was a ritual that always left her feeling refreshed and ready to slip between the sheets, but Max's presence only made her restless. Her legs craved a long walk or even a run, and her muscles twitched irritably at knowing she was supposed to go to bed soon. The fact that her feet were killing her after being on them all day didn't seem to matter in the slightest.

Toweled off and moisturized, Sabrina wrapped a soft robe around herself before going back into the bedroom. She stared at the door for a moment as a reminder that she was absolutely not in the same room with Max before she pulled back the covers and slipped into bed. With a flick of the switch on her bedside lamp, the room was enveloped in darkness.

Darkness that allowed every memory, feeling, and worry to come simmering to the surface.

Sabrina was just finishing up her residency when she'd met Max. She could still see the way he'd looked when she'd been called out to work on an injured shifter. Even back then, when no human hospital would've let her work unsupervised, the shifter community had relied on her. The jackass had injured himself in a bar fight. Even bloody and bedraggled, he'd been handsome. No, it was more than that. He'd excited the animal inside her. It was the one thing Sabrina had held onto over the next few years with Max, even when they didn't get along all that well. Her tiger responded to him, and she'd known he was different than any other man she'd met.

Stop it, she told herself, rolling onto her right side and forcing her eyes shut. *It's time to sleep.*

Her body might've thought so, and she could tell herself that, but the back of her mind didn't agree. It churned with thoughts of Max, running through all the conversations they'd already had, analyzing every tiny piece. What did that look mean? Why was he acting so protective and yet like such an asshole? What had she said wrong? Why did she think she'd said anything wrong at all? Maybe it was entirely him.

Frustrated, she flung the covers off and let the cool air of the ceiling fan wash over her. Eventually, she pulled them back on again. She rolled over onto her back, her stomach, and each of her sides. Nothing was working. Insomnia wasn't a completely unusual experience for Sabrina. No matter how tired she was from work, there'd always been times here and there when she couldn't sleep. She'd learned a long time ago that the best therapy was to get up out of bed and find something else to do. Sabrina would clean the house, throw in a load of laundry, or study up on something she'd been interested in. Before long, her eyes would get heavy and she'd be ready to try sleeping once again.

Done with fighting with herself, Sabrina chucked the covers off once again and launched herself out of bed. She marched to the bedroom door and then stopped in her tracks. Max was on the other side of that door. She couldn't just go out there wearing nothing. Even if she tossed on a robe, she wasn't sure she'd feel comfortable with him seeing her like that. Damn it. She was trapped in her own room.

Still, Sabrina needed something to do, and she put her robe back on just for good measure. She went back to the bed and kneeled next to it, pulling out the plastic tote that was now her memory box. Her baby photos and trophies from high school had been stashed elsewhere. This was the time capsule of her adulthood, of all the time she'd had ever since she'd moved out of her parents' place. Setting the lid aside, Sabrina dug through the more recent editions and down into the past of a few years ago until she found the stratum that indicated her life with Max.

Maybe it was all stuff she shouldn't be dwelling on, but she'd been unable to stop thinking about him anyway. Sabrina knew there was a good reason the two of them weren't together, and she needed that reminder. This would put her in the right frame of mind to deal with Max as a professional she had to work with and not her ex.

The first was an invitation to a graduation party. Sabrina ran her hand over the embossed letters, remembering the red dress she'd worn for Maria's big day. It was of a much more daring cut than she usually allowed herself, but she'd been feeling bold. If she was honest with herself, she was even more rebellious because Max had refused to come with her. The two of them were new to each other, and she'd been excited to show him off to her friends.

Max hadn't wanted anything to do with it, and he'd been almost rude about it when he'd turned her down. Out of spite, she'd put on the sexiest thing she owned and went out anyway.

"Wow, Sabrina! You look amazing! I thought this was supposed to be my party, but I think you're about to take center stage." Maria handed her a red cup full of something strong.

"Oh, don't be silly." But Sabrina enjoyed the compliment.

She spent most of her time in a lab or the library, and no one really talked to her like that. "But do tell me if there are any good-looking guys here tonight."

Maria cocked a dark eyebrow. "I thought you were with that Army guy. What's his name?"

Sabrina flicked a hand in the air, watching the way the colored lights sparkled in her jewelry. "Max? Well, we'll see about that."

"That's not like you."

"What do you mean?" Sabrina frowned at her friend.

"You just don't seem like the kind to love 'em and leave 'em," Maria replied with a shrug.

But it wasn't fair that everyone always expected so much from her just because that was what she always delivered. Just because she was a good person didn't mean she didn't want to have a little fun now and then. Sabrina flicked her hair behind her shoulder. "I'm a grown woman, and I don't need to depend on a guy like Max to have fun tonight. And if I'm honest, he said he didn't want to come."

"Oh." Now it was Maria's turn to frown. "Why? Did he have other plans?"

Thinking about it only made it even more of a sore point. "It doesn't matter. He didn't want to be here, but I am. So I'm not going to worry about it. Now let's celebrate all that hard work you did in school and the hard work you're about to do at that law firm!"

But try as she might, Sabrina just couldn't get into the party.

She saw other couples pairing off to dance or snuggle, and she wished she was one of them. Her friends were there for her, but she really only wanted to be with Max. The real kicker was when Maria's hot cousin Rob came over to talk to her. He got her another drink. He asked her to dance. He flirted. But he just wasn't the same. Rob didn't create that animalistic urge inside her, the one that made her feel like she was so much more than a regular woman.

When she got home later that evening and found a text message from him, apologizing and even hoping that she still had a great time, she knew she only wanted to be with Max.

SABRINA GROWLED her disgust as she pitched the invitation back into the box. That wasn't what she was looking for. She needed something that would remind her of exactly why they *weren't* together, not why they should be. Max was simply irresistible. It didn't matter if she was considering his dark eyes and hard body, or the way he made her feel.

Ah, that was the problem. It had always been about the way Max made her feel. Love was pure emotion, but a successful relationship had to be based on more than that. She needed logic, order, and sensibility. Sabrina knew she couldn't possibly find that with a man like Max Jennings, and the proof of it was somewhere in this box.

She flicked past several receipts and movie ticket stubs

until her fingers found a photograph. In the day and age of digital photography, a real picture was a pretty rare thing. Sabrina couldn't remember the last time she'd had one printed out, and the photo she held in her hand could've very well been it.

The two of them were grinning at the camera, their smiles so cheesy it looked painful. Light and love were in their eyes, not to mention excitement and hope for the future.

"WHERE ARE WE GOING?" Sabrina asked from her seat in the helicopter. Max had just recently taken a job with Luxury Air Tours. She knew he was a capable pilot, so she wasn't worried about that. But she didn't want him to get into trouble.

As he always did, he sensed her tension and laid his hand on her thigh. "Just relax and enjoy the ride. Mr. Stephenson knows I have the chopper out for the day."

That only assuaged her worry a little. Max was a wonderful guy in many ways, but he also liked to push the envelope any time he got the chance. Sometimes that made him fun, and other times, it just made her concerned. "All right. If you say so."

Max laughed and shook his head. "You're so uptight sometimes, Sabrina. I know that makes you a good surgeon, but you can't be Dr. Barrett all the time."

"I'm not!" she protested. "I do lots of other things, too."

"Such as?" he challenged.

"Well, I..." She trailed off when the only things she'd done recently included reading medical journals, doing research online related to the latest trends in cosmetic surgery, and volunteering at an underfunded clinic. "Oh! I had lunch with Melanie and Astrid the other day."

"Doesn't count since they're also in the medical field," he replied with a grin.

She scowled playfully at him. "It does, too."

"Did you talk about anything remotely related to medicine, patients, anatomy, surgery, or health insurance?"

"Maybe." Sabrina could see the ocean coming into view on the horizon. It wasn't a complete surprise, considering how long they'd been flying, but it made her sit up and look around a little more. "Okay, really. Where are we going?"

"You'll just have to wait and see, kitten."

She wasn't a patient woman, and she knew that about herself. He knew it, too, and he enjoyed torturing her that way. But when he added 'kitten' to the end of any sentence, it made everything better, no matter what was happening.

Sabrina watched her surroundings, looking for something familiar. Stretches of sand mingled with the blue-green of the ocean, like Earth's natural tie-dye. It was beautiful, but she still didn't understand why they were there.

Not until Max swooped lower and massive letters appeared in the sand. 'Sabrina, Will You Marry Me?' had been carefully written below them, but they blurred and almost disappeared as tears filled her eyes.

"Max! How did you do this?"

He grinned. "I don't think that's the most important question right now." He was holding out a tiny black box. The ring's impressive blue diamond was flanked with alternating blue and white ones down the sides of the band. "Don't look so surprised. I pay attention."

"You really do," she said. It hadn't been anything they'd discussed, just something she'd mentioned in passing when they'd seen a jewelry commercial on television. The usual white diamond engagement rings from chain stores were what everyone else had, and she didn't like to follow trends. "Yes, Max. Absolutely yes."

Carefully keeping control of the chopper, he managed to extract the ring from the box and slip it on her finger. It felt cold and solid, a perfect reminder of what was about to happen.

SABRINA PUT her thumb over Max's face and focused on herself. There were elements of the girl in the photo that were still the same as what she saw in the mirror now. It wasn't as though she'd aged considerably. But the Sabrina who existed when that photo was taken seemed to exist in a completely different lifetime, or even a different dimension. She most definitely wasn't the same now.

She slid her finger aside and studied Max. He wasn't the same either, especially if she only went off the photo. In it, she could see the light and happy side of him. But Sabrina knew he very rarely let that out to play back in those days, and she had a good feeling it was still the same.

Laying the photo gently back in the box and feeling angry with herself for finding all the wrong memories, Sabrina picked up a piece of cardstock wrinkled with glue from all the magazine photos that'd been cut out and pasted on it. This was her mini vision board for her wedding, something she'd pieced together out of bridal magazines as she dreamed of the day she and Max would get married. There was the picture of a model wearing the gown she'd picked out. It seemed simple enough, a V-neck sheath that dropped to the floor. But the elegance was in the details, and the bodice was covered with the tiniest white beads, the pattern dripping down into the skirt. A picture up in the corner showed the white lilies and pale orange roses she wanted in her bouquet. Another image showed the shoes she'd hoped for, even though she knew she'd pass up something as expensive as Louboutins and grab something from the local department store. She'd included a photo of Malaquite Beach where he'd proposed, hoping for a seaside ceremony. The bridesmaid and flower girl dresses, the table decorations, her jewelry, the cake, it was all there together. That piece of paper made it look so easy to throw a wedding together.

But that wedding had never happened.

There were no physical mementos to remind her of how things had gone down over the last couple of months of their relationship. Sabrina needed only to close her eyes to remember how it all felt. She'd been incredibly busy with her work at the hospital. The administration was becoming aware of her talent and wanted to use her as much as possible to keep their ratings high. She'd been glad to accommodate them, considering it also meant more money in her pocket and better chances for promotions.

"Jesus Christ, Sabrina. Are you ever going to get a day off?" Max was still up when she got home. A couple of empty beer bottles indicated how he'd been spending his time while he'd waited.

"Why are you still up? You should've gone to bed hours ago." She knew he had to get up early and get to work.

"Not like I sleep well, anyway," he grumbled. "But we're not talking about me right now. I think it's about time you told your boss to give you at least a day or two to sit down and breathe for a second."

Sabrina sighed. "It just doesn't always work that way, Max. You knew when we got together that my career was going to take up a lot of my time."

"Yeah, but not all your time. At least tell me you've got some time on the weekend." He stood up and chucked his bottles in the recycling bin. Max wasn't drunk, just angry.

"Of course, I...Oh. Actually, I've got that dinner I'm supposed to go to for the American Society of Plastic Surgeons. Why don't

you come with me? We can make it a date!" She rarely got the chance to show her fiancé off to her coworkers, and it'd be fun.

But he frowned. "I don't want to go to some stuffy dinner."

"It's not like it's black-tie," she countered. "It'll be fun. I promise."

"I'm busy." It was late, and he should've been on his way to bed, but he plopped back down in front of the television instead.

Sabrina crossed her arms. "I didn't even tell you what time it starts yet."

"Doesn't matter. I'm busy." He wasn't even looking at her now, a sure indicator that he was upset. Not that she didn't already know.

"Fine. You complain about me being busy, but you don't want to go to the slightest effort to spend time with me when I try to make it work. I'm going to bed." Sabrina stormed off to bed, angry that he'd always put her in situations like this. Why should she have to be the one making accommodations for their relationship all the time? Shouldn't both of them be making compromises? She twisted the sparkling ring on her finger, wondering just what she was getting herself into for the rest of her life. The wedding was only a few months away.

By the time she woke in the morning, she'd gotten over her irritation with his lousy attitude. It was true that she'd been working a lot, and maybe that wasn't fair to him. There were only so many hours in a day, and their work shifts rarely correlated, but that didn't mean she couldn't make a few more efforts to do something he wanted. Max didn't want to be toted around *like a little dog in a purse to all her events, and she could under-stand that.*

But the bed beside her was empty. Sabrina frowned. If he'd spent all night on the couch, then he was committed to this argu-ment. She decided she'd be the one to step up and say she was sorry and headed out into the living room.

But Max wasn't there. It was too early for him to have left for work, and an instinctive panic spread inside her. Sabrina raced back to the bedroom and saw what she hadn't noticed before. His side of the dresser was empty. Flinging open the closet doors and the dresser drawers only told her more of the same story. Max was gone.

He'd left her. He'd actually left her, without a word. After all the time they'd spent together, after the bond their tigers shared, he'd decided that one little argument was enough to call the whole thing off. Sabrina sank to the floor next to the bed, soaking the sheets with her tears.

THE MEMORY BROUGHT a tear to her eye, and she wiped it away. This wasn't fair. She'd worked so hard to try to get past him, and now there he was in her apartment. Worse, he was being *paid* to be near her, serving as her bodyguard. Somehow, he must've thought that translated to also being allowed to criticize her life and her home as much as he wanted. He was selfish and arrogant, and that hadn't changed a bit.

So how could she still feel the way she did, even after all this time? He'd hurt her—deeply. Sabrina had nearly put her career in jeopardy after he'd left her, since she'd spent all her time in bed or with her head in the fridge. It hadn't made things any better in the long run, but it'd made her feel better in the moment.

Stop being such a baby, Sabrina, she scolded herself. *Dwelling on the past isn't going to do anything to help your future. Go to bed.* She reached for the lid to the memory box, ready to slide it back into the dark recesses under her bed.

5

MAX WIGGLED HIS TOES ON THE PLUSH RUG. EVERYTHING about this apartment was cushy and luxurious, and it was driving him crazy. There was no rational reason for it, but as far as he was concerned, there didn't need to be. Sabrina was just getting to him.

He'd seen the look on her face when she'd emerged on the rooftop, and he'd sensed the hesitation in her body before she'd boarded the chopper. She didn't want him to be a part of this mission any more than he wanted to be. It was an awkward situation they'd been put in. It was just too bad she wasn't being more cooperative about dealing with it.

They'd eaten dinner at the breakfast bar in the kitchen, sitting two feet apart and hardly speaking. She hadn't even given him the chance to chip in for his portion of the meal, paying for it ahead of time to show off just how much money she'd been making. As if he hadn't already been able to tell how loaded she was.

His phone buzzed in his pocket. Max liked to keep the ringer off when he could so he wouldn't have to hear the noise.

It was Vance. "Hey. Just thought I'd check in and see how things were going."

Max was immediately suspicious. Had Sabrina called and complained about him already? No, that was ridiculous. It wasn't as though just anyone could track down the phone numbers for the Force. Even her conclave probably wouldn't have given her that information. "Just fine."

"No problem making the transition from the conclave guard?"

"No." Max had wondered exactly who the guy who'd been assigned to her was, his tiger's jealousy rippling just under the surface. He'd noticed the warmth and affection with which the guy had looked at her, but he'd restrained himself enough not to pursue that conversation yet.

"Good. And her place is secure?"

"As secure as it can be," Max scoffed. "You know, I haven't looked up real estate listings for luxury apartments like this one, but if I did, I'm sure I'd find they cost enough to warrant coming with their own bodyguards. And you should see the windows in this place. With just a flip of a latch, they're open."

Vance didn't say anything for a moment. "You sure you're all right with taking this job?"

Was he sure? Of course not. But he wasn't about to admit that. Max had learned a long time ago that ignoring his weaknesses was often the easiest way to deal with them, even if it wasn't the best way.

No, he wasn't sure he could stand being around Sabrina like this. No matter how comfortable her expensive couch was, there was no way he could actually sit still for more than a few minutes because his tiger was raging and roiling inside him, demanding to come out. It didn't matter that the only person there to see that was Sabrina, and she'd long ago learned how to shut off those instinctive feelings.

He'd wondered about that with her. A long time ago, Sabrina told him she'd wept almost every night when she came home from working her residency. That was before she'd found her passion in cosmetic surgery and was still learning the in's and out's of cutting people open for a living. She'd watched people die. She'd seen them suffer as they awaited treatment and answers. When the patients were under anesthesia and didn't know what was happening, Sabrina had witnessed their loved ones anxiously waiting. She'd claimed it'd been a heavy burden on her.

But that wasn't the Sabrina he knew, the one who could brush off all the touchy-feely stuff because it was getting in the way of getting the job done. The Sabrina he knew was stone-cold in the operating room, not thinking about anything other than the instruments in her hands and the vitals of the person on the table. She'd carried it over into her personal life, too. If her tiger had responded to his presence when they'd seen each other again on that rooftop, she'd given no signal. Sabrina was the ultimate ice queen.

"Yeah, of course. I'm fine." He'd nearly forgotten that Vance was still hanging on the other end of the line, concerned about whether or not he could do the job. "You don't need to check up on me, man."

"I'm not. It's just that this is a different mission than the ones we're used to getting. I reckon it's important that we do a good job since the local conclave has hired us. We don't want to piss them off since our relationship with them could be vital to our operations."

He sounded more like some pompous executive than a simple rancher. "It's good to know you trust me with this," he replied, his voice dripping with sarcasm.

"It's not that, Max. You were acting pretty fucking weird this morning, so my concern is both for the job and you."

Max appreciated the thought, but he didn't need someone worrying over him. It was only going to make his moodiness worse. "Thanks, but no thanks."

Vance sighed. "All right. If you say everything is fine, then I'll take your word for it. Just promise you'll call if anything changes or there are any emergencies. I'll be meeting you tomorrow morning at the hospital to take over for the day.

Have fun spending all day with Dr. Distance. "All right. See you then." He hung up, not wanting to risk hearing any more of Vance's worries. Everything was fine. He would get through this, and then he and Sabrina could go their separate ways again.

Feeling restless, he pushed himself up off the couch and patrolled the perimeter of the apartment. Opposite the front door, he paused and looked out the wide, sliding glass doors that led out onto a long patio. The view from there was stellar. Max was used to seeing the city from the ground when he went for his early morning jogs or from overhead when he was at work. This was completely different. The skyscrapers downtown were illuminated for the evening in bold shades of blues, greens, and yellows, but they were far enough away that the light pollution didn't reach Sandoval Terrace. Thunderclouds rolled in, darker than even the charcoal skies they obscured. Brilliant forks of lightning traced across the urban vista, searching for some connection.

Max instantly related to them. For years, he'd been drifting through the sky, looking for something to tether him down. Any time he thought he'd finally found it, he immediately began pulling back. He wanted to be grounded but not trapped. It was a very fine balance, and for a while, he thought he'd found it with Sabrina.

Unbidden, he pictured her the way he used to see her. Not the upper-class surgeon she was now, requiring private transportation and a hired guard everywhere she went, and not even the angry and distant woman she'd been when he'd decided to leave. No, this was the younger and happier Sabrina, the one who still knew how to have fun. The one who could distract him from all the hell inside his brain, the one whose feline sensuality could pull him to the bedroom with little more than a glance from under her lashes or a quirk from the corner of her mouth. He found her incredibly attractive, and when they slipped between the sheets together, he'd practically worshipped her body. But she was also smart, funny, and so unbelievably strong.

How had it all come to this?

Running a hand through his hair, Max turned away from the window and moved through the darkened kitchen. Sure, he'd already given the place a once-over to analyze it for any weak points. It was such an automatic habit for him, no matter where he was, that he didn't know how to turn it off. He even did it at headquarters, even though Garrison from the D.C. Force had designed and renovated the place to make sure it was up to standards. But god damn, Army life had fucked him up good.

As Max turned back toward the front of the apartment, he spotted a line of light limning the bottom of Sabrina's bedroom door. His heart froze as he stared at it for a long moment, listening for any evidence of an intruder. She'd gone to bed long ago. Anything could be happening on the other side of that door. Had he let her down already?

His body surged to life, barely in control as he charged across the floor. In the fleeting moment it took him to get to her door, he was back in Iraq. Someone's life was on the line. He had to fix things. There had been blood, so much blood.

The knob was cold against the palm of his hand for a split second as he shoved it open with his shoulder. It shuddered on its hinges as it slammed back against the bedroom wall. Spotting Sabrina on the floor next to the bed, and his heart squeezed in panic. It was too late.

But just as quickly as terror had overtaken him, Max realized he was utterly wrong. Sabrina was, indeed, on the floor. But she wasn't dead, dying, or even bleeding or bruised. She was wrapped in a plush cream robe that did little to hide her curves—and even less to hide the smooth muscles of her thigh as she pushed something underneath the bed.

She was on her feet in an instant, pulling her robe tighter in front of her chest and tugging the bottom of it down to cover as much leg as possible. "Max! What the hell are you doing?"

He swallowed, taking in the sight of her standing there next to the big bed. Her deep brown hair was down for a change, the dark waves hanging damp past her shoulders. She'd never been the kind of woman who needed a lot of makeup, and she wore none now, yet her smooth cheeks and heavily lashed eyes didn't need it. Max cleared his throat, forcing his gaze to remain on her eyes. "I saw your light on, and it's late. I thought something was wrong."

"I just can't sleep, okay?" She glanced severely at him through her glasses. "Just because you were told to stay here all night doesn't mean anything about my life has changed."

He'd been so worried, and now he privately chastised himself for doing so. "No, of course not. You wouldn't dare go even an inch out of your way if it was for anyone else, would you?"

Sabrina's left eye narrowed more than the right one as she fixed her gaze on him. "And just what is *that* supposed to mean?"

"As if you didn't know." While just a few minutes ago, he'd been reminiscing on how loving and warm she could be, Sabrina had reminded him of why they weren't together anymore. He knew precisely why he'd left, and even why he hadn't bothered to tell her before he packed his shit and slipped out the door.

"No, I can't say that I do. What I do know is that you're here in *my* apartment, and all of a sudden, you think you can dissect my life like some high school science project. Oh, and there's plenty of extra credit for anything that somehow doesn't meet your standards." She took a step closer to him, her hands gesticulating wildly as she spoke. "I happen to notice, though, that what disturbs you the most is the fact that I'm actually doing well for myself!"

"Maybe you're right," he growled. "Maybe it does bother me to see just how far you've come, considering I know it's only happened because you're so cold-hearted and calculating. You bought this douchy apartment on the blood of innocent people."

Her voice was quiet when she responded, her eyes glistening. "What the fuck did you just say to me?"

"You heard me." Damn it. He was being an ass and he knew it. Sometimes it was too easy for Max to get tied up in his thoughts; he lived in his head more than he wanted to admit. But eventually, he caught up to himself and realized what was going on. Unfortunately, it was too late to back out now.

"I bought this place with the income I've earned from performing my job. And we're not talking about innocent children from families who can't afford surgeries. We're talking about wealthy men who want their wives to look like they're twenty again, and the wives that are shallow enough to agree with it. We're talking about people who can't be satisfied with the looks they were born with and feel the need to rearrange their face into someone else's to meet some random socially accepted standard."

Her bare feet punctuated her words as she stepped forward. Max had been thinking of her as nothing more than a frigid woman, but in that moment, he was heavily reminded of the tiger she truly was. Sabrina stalked him from across the bedroom as her strong legs moved slowly and deliberately, her feet setting down heel-to-toe, her stare unwavering.

"So yeah," she continued. "If you want to say I have the creature comforts in my life because I took advantage of people, then fine. I took advantage of people who were more than eager to throw their money at me. It might not be the work I want to do, and you might not be able to see what it's going to get me in the long run, but the way I see it, that's none of your fucking business!" Light flared in her eyes as all her fury was directed straight at him.

He snarled. All that anger might be for him, but it wasn't making him want to turn away. His inner beast was responding now that she was showing hers, and all the frustration and resentment he'd been dwelling on was shifting. "What's your end goal here? Where the hell could you go from here, when you've already got a job at the nicest hospital in the state and an apartment better than ninety-nine percent of people around these parts can afford?"

Sabrina shook her head and pursed her lips. Her tongue poked the inside of her cheek, and Max could tell she was debating whether or not to continue this argument. She was only a foot or so away from him, which forced her to look up as she spoke. "You really don't know?"

"That's what I'm saying." He clenched his fists at his sides to fight off doing something rash, but it certainly wouldn't be violent. That bed of hers with the covers cast aside was so damn close.

"I don't have to tell you, you know. The two of us are through, and there's no reason to justify myself to you." Her feet hadn't moved again as she stood poised for whatever may come, and yet Max could swear she'd come even closer.

"I know."

"You think I'm shallow because I want the fame of being a top surgeon. I do want that fame, and I can't help that money happens to come with it. But the *only* reason I'm taking these jobs is so that I can have enough leverage to create the space and funding for those who fucking *need* it. I want to get back to helping veterans who need reconstructive surgery after being wounded and children who've been sick or injured. If you can't understand that, then call up whoever it is you work for and tell them to send in someone else." She lifted her chin defiantly, daring him with every cell of her body.

Fuck. He'd been such an asshole. He'd been so caught up in himself that he hadn't bothered—or maybe hadn't allowed himself—to think about who she was as a whole. Sabrina could be who she needed to be in the moment, but that one temper tantrum or unwillingness to deal with him wasn't the sum of her parts. She was daring him, but she had no idea just what she was daring him to do.

His hands moved swiftly, latching onto her hips and

pulling her close as he pressed his lips to hers. Sabrina was stiff in his arms, frozen from surprise. But her tiger was dominant now, and it soon melted in his palms. Sabrina became soft and pliant in his grasp as her lips explored his. Max felt their animals stalking around each other, sniffing, inspecting, wondering. He lifted his hand from her hip and moved it to the curve of her lower back, pressing her harder against him, wanting her to feel exactly what she was doing to him.

But that was when she retreated inward again. Max could feel her tiger moving away, defensive, almost scared. At the same time, Sabrina put her hand on his chest and pushed herself away, her lips ruddy from their short but intense liplock. She held them just barely apart as though she were breathless, her eyes wide. Her intense look was enough to make him want to yank her back against him and relive that moment over and over again. But it was gone, and no matter how much of a dick he could sometimes be, he wouldn't push her that far. She was fully human again, having locked her creature away where it couldn't influence her any longer.

Sabrina made a small sound in her throat as she retreated another step, still facing him. She gestured nervously at the bed. "I think, um, I think it's time I got to bed. I've got to work in the morning."

Max glanced once again at the bed. It was one of those tall numbers, the kind most people would need a boost to get up on. The fluffy down comforter was sheathed in a cream duvet cover the same shade as her bathrobe, but it was pulled back to reveal smooth sheets of a deep burgundy. The dark stain on the four-poster bed completed the picture, making it look so incredibly luxurious and inviting.

But he'd understood that she most definitely wasn't inviting him to bed. He backed toward the door, which still stood open. "Right. Early morning. I'll just be right out here."

She nodded. "Thank you for checking on me."

It was the slightest fissure in that austere façade she'd so carefully constructed. It was tempting, making Max want to pick at it like a fresh scab. He'd pushed things far enough, though. "Sure. I'll be out here if you need anything." He continued to back out of the room, feeling foolish when he realized he must have looked like some groveling servant who's not allowed to turn away from the queen, and shut the door.

Once he was out of her sight, he spun around and headed straight back for the couch. "If you need anything?" Max echoed to himself in a whisper as he flung himself on the cushions. "Yeah, I think we both know what 'anything' meant." He'd botched this all to hell, but in retrospect, he didn't know how he would've changed his actions. Sabrina did things to him. She made him act crazy, and he wasn't entirely sure if it were a good crazy or a bad crazy.

The one thing he did know was that it was damn hard to have merely a door separating them. Had she taken off her robe, exposing the creamy curves of her skin, fresh from the shower, before slipping between those sheets? It was too easy to imagine her there under the covers, the swell of her breasts barely hidden beneath the comforter, her hair splayed out against the paleness of the pillow.

Max adjusted his straining pants and took his cell out of his pocket to dial Vance. He couldn't be the one to stay there with Sabrina. It wasn't right, and he was too dangerous. He'd just have to get over himself and explain his past to the cougar. Vance would understand, and he was bound to find out eventually anyway. The three Force members of the Dallas unit were too close to each other not to.

He flipped the screen off before hitting send when he realized that meant someone else would be there with Sabrina. Someone else would be sitting on that sofa, envisioning the naked woman on the other side of the bedroom door.

Nope, he told himself. *That's not happening.* He put his phone away and tried his best to get comfortable.

6

Sabrina slowly opened her eyes as her mind vaguely searched for the cause of that annoying noise. It had invaded her dreams, which were cloudy images at best. She'd fallen into a deep sleep born of exhaustion and a desire for retreat from the world. It made her mind feel muddy and her body feel heavy, but at least some sleep was better than none.

Coming further into consciousness, she realized the annoying noise was her alarm. She flung her arm through the dark toward the nightstand until she found her phone, sliding her finger across the screen to silence the damn thing. Sabrina took a deep breath and did the first thing she did every morning. She blinked a few times as she tried to remember what day it was and what she had going on that day. It was her way of centering herself and preparing for what was to come, whether it was surgery or meetings or both.

Her breath left her lungs when she remembered not only what the day was, but who was waiting for her on the other side of the bedroom door. She squinted at it as though it were the enemy. Unfortunately, she knew that wasn't the case. She couldn't completely say that Max was the enemy, either. It was the two of them together and the uncontrollable chemical fire they created when they got together.

Sabrina rubbed her eyes and pushed her way out of bed. That was fine. If she could identify the problem, then that meant she could solve it. That was exactly what she was going to do. Sure, they'd each lost control of themselves for a minute, for one minute full of passion and desire and all the raw things that'd been affecting them. They'd gotten it out of their systems. That didn't mean anything between them had changed.

She dressed self-consciously, choosing one of the most conservative tops she owned and a pair of slacks that she'd never thought was all that flattering. There was no point in provoking things any further. Maybe she wasn't giving Max enough credit that he couldn't control himself. After all, he'd taken it as gospel when she'd stopped things between them last night.

A ripple of heat surged in the lowest pit of her abdomen and spread over her body as she recalled that kiss. It shouldn't have affected her so much. It wasn't as though they'd gone tumbling into bed together. But the way his hands had wrapped possessively around her body—not to mention the hardness in his jeans—told Sabrina that he would've been happy to do just that. It was no great stretch of the imagination to visualize exactly what they would've done. In her mind's eye, she could feel his deft hand slipping the soft fabric of her robe aside, cupping her exposed breast as he continued to claim her mouth. Max had always been an incredibly passionate tiger, and a generous one, too. Sabrina knew he'd have made sure she got every bit of pleasure she could stand before he took his own. She also knew it was an ego boost for him to know he'd thoroughly satisfied her, but that was one aspect of his arrogance she could handle.

"Stop," she muttered as she slipped into her shoes and headed to the bathroom to put her hair up in a braided bun. "You're an educated woman who people entrust with their lives every day. Surely you can handle an awkward situation like this."

A few minutes later, she breezed out of her bedroom and barely gave Max a glance on her way to the kitchen for some coffee. Sabrina always had it pre-programmed and ready to go the night before so she could enjoy the smell of fresh brew as soon as she got up in the morning. "There's plenty of coffee if you want some." It was only good manners to offer; it wasn't as though she were serving it up for him.

"Yeah. Thanks." He took a mug from the rack.

It irritated her that he looked so at home there, as though he already knew every square inch of the apartment. Then again, maybe he did, considering he'd probably stayed up all night. His clothes were wrinkled, his dark hair rumpled. Stubble dotted his strong jawline. But for all the exhaustion he might've felt from staying up all night to work his shift as a bodyguard, she could still feel his eyes observing her.

"Bagels and cream cheese, oatmeal, cereal... help yourself." She grabbed an everything bagel, something she'd taken a recent liking to. There was something about a savory breakfast that was so much more satisfying than a sweet one. After covering the bagel in cream cheese, she parked herself at the breakfast bar where she could look through the patio doors.

Max moved through the kitchen behind her. Sabrina didn't turn around to see if he needed any help or find out what he was doing. She didn't need to. She could sense him in the most indescribable, primal way. The nerves on her back reacted to every move he made, sending a picture of the movement behind her to her brain. It was like painting a picture without being able to see it. Sabrina had to smile to herself a little over that one. If she'd ever brought up such a thing in one of the many medical conventions she attended for humans, she'd be laughed right out of the business. It wasn't logical or reasonable. The shifter community, on the other hand, would know exactly what she was talking about.

He was next to her on the other barstool a few minutes later with a full mug of black coffee and a bowl of blueberry oatmeal. She tightened her jaw as she waited for him to bring up last night, to question her, even to tease her about the way she'd reacted to him.

Fortunately, he decided to go a different route to start the day. "I suppose if I'm going to be guarding you, I ought to know what it is I'm guarding you from. The only thing I've been told is that you're a key witness in some trial. Can you tell me about that?"

Good. He'd decided to be just as professional as she had. A small part of her, the one she often shoved to the back of her mind and told to stay put, was a little disappointed. Too bad. "Yes, I think I can do that. I was attending a medical conference for the shifter community. We'd organized at a shifter-run hotel on the outskirts of town, nothing fancy, with the idea of staying off anyone's radar."

"We?" he asked, poking a blueberry with his spoon.

"Yeah. I've been trying to set up a better system for shifter medical care. As it is, the clans just call in whomever they happen to know, and treatment takes place in a kitchen or bathroom at best. It's not right, and we deserve more. The challenge is that we can't be open about it." She frowned at her bagel, calling back to mind all the trouble she had just getting representatives from all the local clans and packs to come together and at least start talking about it. Of course, that meant she also needed other doctors and nurses to be on board, and they had to be ones that were safe to talk to about such things. "It's been much more of a project than I'd anticipated, and it hasn't been easy to do all that on top of my normal work, but I think it's something worth doing."

"Okay, so you were at a conference. And?" he prodded.

"Oh. Sorry." She focused on the smooth lines of the cream cheese. How had she slipped into such normal conversation with him? If anything, she should be angry at him for agreeing to take this job when he must've known she was the witness. No, wait. Those weren't the thoughts she was supposed to be having right now. She was cool. "Anyway, there were a lot of different representatives from different groups, shifters from all over the place. I was trying to sleep because I had to get back to work the next morning, but I couldn't because everyone was getting so wild. For some reason, the hotel management didn't make any complaints. But the guests in the room below me were thumping their bass so hard it made my bed vibrate."

Max snickered. She ignored him.

"My room was right by the stairs, so I skipped the elevator and headed down there to tell them to turn it down. But when I opened the door to the stairwell, a man lay at the bottom covered in blood. A wolf stood over him with blood all over his fur. He looked up at me." She paused, remembering that night. Her brain screamed at her to run down the stairs and help the man, but her instincts told her to run away as fast as she could before she became the next victim. The wolf had been massive, his amber eyes intense.

"So the wolf is the killer," Max concluded. "Sounds pretty straightforward to me."

"Unfortunately, no. The man killed was Isaac Rutledge. He is—was—the Alpha of a local bear clan, and a very well-respected member of the shifter community. I have no idea who the wolf was, but I've heard that he's from a pack that's taken up issue with Isaac's clan."

"What kind of issue?" Max had finished his breakfast and got up to rinse his bowl in the sink.

Sabrina shrugged. "Something about them having rival companies that were getting into each other's territories. Nothing that I would think validates a murder."

Max let out a harsh laugh. "You'd be surprised what groups will fight over and the extent they'll go to in order to make their points. I've done a lot of work like that lately, and I have a feeling there'll only be more."

This brought up a point that somehow hadn't occurred to Sabrina thus far. "So who, exactly, is it you work for? I thought it was some sort of high-end security company, but you make it sound otherwise. And the last I knew, you were working for Luxury Air Tours."

"I didn't get fired, if that's what you're thinking. George might not always like my attitude, but he needs a pilot who's not afraid to go out in iffy weather. The biggest threat is always the passengers, anyway." He leaned casually against the breakfast bar, the edge of a tattoo peeking out from under the sleeve of his t-shirt. "More recently, though, I've been recruited for an elite team of Special Ops Forces vets who all just so happen to be shifters. When the clans and the conclaves can't handle their business, they call us."

"Sounds like a good job for you." Max had never been completely satisfied with giving air tours, she knew. But a second position that relied on his Army skills just as much as the first one sounded right up his alley.

"Mostly, yes." He took a long and thoughtful sip of his coffee as he turned his head slightly to look out the window. It made him look like an advertisement for whiskey or beard oil.

Sabrina waited, thinking he might continue. When he didn't, she asked, "Mostly?"

His shoulder twitched in a partial shrug. "It's not always easy doing something that reminds me of the service."

She didn't ask for anything more after that. When the two of them had gotten together, he'd told her about his military experience with a distance that indicated he didn't want to talk about it in detail. She'd seen the medals he earned, but she didn't ask how he'd gotten them. She never asked about how many people he might've killed or what it was like living among people from such different cultures, though she was secretly curious. Occasionally, when the moment was just right, Max would open up and share one of his experiences with her. Afterward, he would sink into a sullen silence that told her his mind was still on the subject. She'd always skirted carefully around the issue, not wanting to upset something that had to be so difficult for him. "I see."

He slugged back the last of his coffee and waved off her solemn comment. "Don't worry about it. It's fine. And it's a good job that I couldn't get anywhere else. It's even gotten me a better place to live. Nothing like this, of course..."

Oh, here they went again, with him ragging on her just because she had a nice place. It wasn't like she wore designer clothes or drove an extravagant car. She shot him a look.

He put up his hands in a defensive gesture as he returned to the sink to rinse out his coffee cup. "Hey, I'm just saying it's not like this. They'd have been crazy to make it this nice, since it's just a group of bachelors living there."

Well, that was another question answered, even though she hadn't thought to ask it. Sabrina hadn't bothered to look for a wedding ring or ask about a spouse or girlfriend. She'd just assumed everything about him had stayed the same, as though her memory of him were the only reality possible. How could she be so selfish to imagine his life hadn't changed, especially when hers had so much? "Well, I'm glad it's been good."

Perhaps he sensed that she needed to change the subject. "So about this trial. What makes you or the conclave think the wolf is after you?"

They'd lost track of that conversation, hadn't they? It was proof of exactly what she'd experienced with Max previously. They spoke to each other like the ebb and flow of the tide, moving back and forth in whatever direction the current took them, and they always ended up right back where they belonged. It was part of what had let her know they belonged together, another aspect of the bond that told her their tigers were fated.

She polished off her bagel and licked a spot of cream cheese off her finger. "I obviously reported what I saw to Isaac's clan and to the conclave. I knew I'd be called on to testify should it come down to it, but I didn't think much more of it than that. Then the death threats started showing up."

His eyes changed, flashing yellow. "Death threats?"

Sabrina shook her head as she put her plate in the dishwasher. "Yeah. I reported it because it felt like I should, but I didn't think much of it. The conclave thought enough of it that they assigned me a guard and then you guys. I wish they hadn't. It's been awkward having someone following me around at work all the time, taking note of my every move and listening in on every conversation. The only time I've been able to get away is when I'm in the operating room, and even then, I sometimes wonder if they've replaced one of my surgical techs with an extra set of eyes."

Max seemed oblivious to her concerns about being constantly on display. "Exactly how were these death threats delivered?"

She sighed. She didn't really want to go into it, but she had a feeling there wouldn't be any way around it. "A phone call here. A mysterious note there."

"And have there been any more of them since the conclave assigned you a guard?" He was no longer leaning against the counter, but standing at attention, poised to jump into action.

"Just one or two, but they seem to have stopped now. As a matter of fact, you'd think the conclave would've just left me with the guards they had on hand if no one was actively threatening my life anymore." She wasn't concerned about it, especially since no one had actually made an attempt on her life.

Clearly, Max didn't feel the same way. He came around the breakfast bar toward her, and when he put his hands on her arms, it was only to emphasize what he was saying. "If anything happens, I want you to tell me right away. A weird phone call, a text message from a new number, a note, someone following you that you don't recognize. Anything."

"Max, I don't think you get it. This whole bodyguard business is just the conclave taking extra precautions. The case has been blown out of proportion because Isaac was such a prominent guy. If people lose their faith in the conclave president to protect our people, then he might lose out on the next election." The conclaves assembled every five years to choose their new leaders, and the politics of shifter life were just as involved as those in the human world.

He backed off a bit, but he still didn't look convinced. "Who is the president right now?"

"Whiteside. Harris Whiteside." Sabrina hadn't known much about him at first, but she'd involved him in the idea of a shifter hospital. Now because of the trial, she'd had even more contact with him. He seemed like a nice guy, but the look in Max's face made her uncomfortable. "Why?"

"Nothing, really."

"Do you know him or something?"

"No. I'm just naturally suspicious. Anyone who's involved in this, as far as I'm concerned, is guilty until proven innocent." Max took another step backward and began tapping his fingers on the counter.

"All right. I've already got them making a far bigger deal out of it than need be. I don't need you to do the same thing."

He gave her a smile and a careless shrug. "Too bad. Max Jennings is on the case now."

"The only thing you need to be worrying about is getting to work. Let me just brush my teeth and I'll be ready to go." The very last thing she needed was Max getting any more involved in this than he already was. Wasn't it enough that he'd be taking her to and from work every day and lurking around her place at night? Wasn't it enough that she had to deal with all her feelings, past and present? Apparently not. The sooner this trial got over with, the better.

A short time later, as they flew back toward the hospital, Sabrina knew she had to say something. What had happened between them was a mistake. She'd known it at the time, and that was why she'd pulled back, but it was crazy to tease herself by even entertaining the idea of the two of them again. It would just open her up to getting her heart broken again. "Max."

"Yeah?" He flew so easily, his hands and feet moving of their own accord. It made him look like even he was along for the ride.

"I want to talk to you about last night. It was a mistake. A big one." He didn't respond right away, so she continued. "I've got a lot going on with my career and my other projects, and I don't need to mess that up. Or mess up your life, either."

His hands had tensed on the controls, his knuckles white. "I'm not sure why you think you need to say this now."

She huffed out an impatient sigh. Max never liked talking about anything that made him uncomfortable. "I'm just trying to be practical, and I think we should be on the same page before either one of us gets the wrong idea."

The chopper was plenty noisy, but the silence that came through her headset was difficult to listen to. "And what, exactly," he finally said, "makes it the wrong idea?"

"How could it not be? I mean, what do you think is going to happen when this job of yours is over and you're not assigned to me? Are you just going to fly off into the night without saying a word like you did the last time?" All the pain and rage she'd felt before came bubbling to the surface, spilling over without any way of stopping it. "Why should I be expected to open myself up to that when it hurt so bad last time? Why would anything be different now?"

His jaw was tight, his brows drawn down. "I guess it wouldn't be."

"All right then. I'm glad we understand each other." Her body was tense, every muscle fighting the urge to move. She hated to be confined, just sitting there waiting for the ride to be over. Sabrina liked to be productive, especially when she was irritated. She tapped her foot against the floor.

Max said nothing further for the rest of the ride. She should be glad he was letting the subject drop instead of arguing with her any further, but she wasn't. She wanted him to launch into a speech about why they should be together and how much he needed her; how his inner animal couldn't possibly live without her. She'd reject him, because it was the only practical thing to do, but that didn't mean it wouldn't be nice to hear.

As they neared, a man stood waiting on the roof of the hospital. Sabrina didn't know him, but given that Max didn't voice any concerns, she had to assume he was another member of the Force. His belt buckle winked in the sun over his bootcut jeans, and he held his Stetson on his head with one hand to keep the downdraft from taking it. He smiled and gave a nod and then stepped up to open the door of the helicopter and let Sabrina out. "I'm Vance Morris. I'll be working with you today."

She shook his hand, which was rough and callused. "Sabrina Barrett. Nice to meet you."

He leaned toward the pilot. "Everything go all right last night? Anything I need to know about?"

Max just scowled at him and grunted.

Vance seemed to take this in stride. He nodded again and escorted Sabrina inside the building.

When they'd gotten to the surgery floor, Sabrina gestured toward one of the restrooms. "Excuse me for just a minute."

"Of course."

The fluorescent lights weren't flattering as she braced herself against the sink and leaned forward to look in the mirror, focusing on her own eyes as she tried to look inside herself and figure out just what the hell was going on. She'd overreacted when she'd finally told him what she'd been thinking, and the words had been an unstoppable flood from her mouth. It was no surprise that he was pissed, even though he wasn't entirely in the right, either. She just needed to get through this week and the trial, and then life would return to normal. Of course, that meant she had to put up with Max for that time.

She sighed, her breath creating a momentary cloud on the glass. "That man makes you crazy, Sabrina."

7

MAX SAT ON THE COUCH BACK AT HEADQUARTERS, FLICKING A ball into the air and catching it repeatedly. He leaned his head back and stared at the ceiling, catching the ball purely by instinct as his mind whirred. He should've gotten some sleep after he'd dropped Sabrina off at the hospital. There was no reason not to, considering Vance was taking care of her for the day. His instinctive response to see her going into another man's care had made him unreasonably jealous, but Vance was a shit ton more professional than he was. It would be fine.

The sound of a throat clearing pulled him out of his thought cloud of misery. He caught the ball and looked up to find Jack glaring at him. "Something I can help you with?"

Jack closed his laptop. "I was going to ask you the same thing. You've been acting like a zoo animal all day."

Max resented the comparison, even though he made it himself from time to time. "No, just a circus one."

"What does that mean?"

He felt he had to perform when Sabrina was around. He didn't know how to be himself, and that was complicated even more by the fact that Sabrina always managed to bring out his true self. It was like the façade he'd put up to deal with life got mixed in with who he really was, and he didn't know how to untangle them. "Nothing," he replied.

Jack cast him a look that said he didn't believe him. "If you say so."

"I don't know why everyone around here is suddenly so determined to psychoanalyze me," Max retorted. "So I'm feeling a little restless. Is that such a surprise for a tiger shifter?"

"No, I guess not. But you're more restless than usual. I don't think I've seen you sit still in several days. If there's something with this witness, then maybe we should talk about it." In some ways, Jack was every bit the tech freak, constantly carrying around a laptop or other gadget. He spent long hours video chatting with Hudson back in D.C. about current technology and ways to improve their computer systems. Given the men's backgrounds in intelligence and communications, that made perfect sense. But

Jack wasn't a skinny little nerd. The brawny fox shifter was always working out with the rest of his comrades in the gym downstairs, and the only giveaway to his true passion at those times was the tattoo in binary code on his arm.

Max knew he could trust Jack as a fellow soldier, and he reminded himself that they were all on the same team. "You're right. There is something we should talk about."

Jack quirked an eyebrow and waited.

"We know that Sabrina—Dr. Barrett—is a key witness in a murder trial." He scooted forward so that he sat on the edge of the couch. "She told me an Alpha bear was killed, and she was the one who saw a wolf standing over his body."

"I'm not sure if she's supposed to talk about the trial..." His eyes narrowed in concern.

Max waved it off. "We've known each other for a long time. Anyway, that's not the point. My point is that she started receiving death threats as soon as she was identified as a witness. That's why the conclave appointed her a guard and then ended up hiring us."

"Right."

"But there's something about it I just don't like. Why would a wolf kill a bear? Sabrina mentioned the bear—Isaac something—was an important guy and that the wolf pack and the bear clan had some sort of beef with each other. I just don't see what the two of them would be arguing about."

He'd been unable to stop thinking about it ever since Sabrina had told him the situation. That is, except for those excruciating minutes when she'd decided to go over all the details about why a simple kiss was some big, life-changing mistake. Then, he'd been more than able to forget about it.

Jack rubbed his face. "There could be any number of reasons, Max. You've been on these missions with us, and you know how territorial clans can get. One guy looks at someone's sister the wrong way, or one clan claims the right to run their business in a certain area, and everyone goes nuts. We're all just animals inside, after all."

Max shook his head. To him, for whatever reason, it just didn't seem as simple as that. "There's got to be something we can do, some way to investigate this."

"I'm pretty sure President Whiteside hired us as goons with guns. He doesn't care about our detective skills. Not that I don't have them, of course." He cracked a slight smile. The small amount of hubris he'd just allowed himself was more than deserved, based on what Max had heard about his military career.

"I know, but if we're already in the mix, then there's no reason we can't go a little further. I want to know more about the clans and specific people involved. Sabrina isn't worried about any of it, but I am. I think it'd be helpful if we had some sort of database of all the shifters we know about."

The intelligence officer shifted in his seat. "Actually, that's something Hudson and I have been working on."

"Really? Fuckin'-A! How do we access it?" He was dying to get his hands on some information about the other shifters around there. Though he'd been living in the Dallas area for several years, he'd never bothered to join a local clan or get too involved in the community. Now, he was desperate to know who this Isaac guy was, why he'd been so important, and why someone might've killed him.

"Well," Jack said, tipping his head to the side, "it's all still very preliminary. Most of what Hudson and I have put in the system involves those we've already had dealings with. I've been doing what I can to expand the directory, but it isn't as though there's some other list I can pull from. The feds have plenty of information on people when it comes to driver's licenses, social security numbers, and prison records, but as I'm sure you can imagine, there's nothing out there that mentions whether or not a person can morph into an animal."

"Fair enough." Max tapped his chin, thinking. "Can we at least check into this guy who was killed? I think she said his name was Isaac Rutledge."

Jack reopened his laptop and began tapping away, but he glanced up at Max. "Just how familiar are you with the witness, anyway?"

Max stiffened. He'd gotten comfortable and said too much. That was something he preferred to avoid at all costs. But where, exactly, had it gotten him? The only things he had going on in life were his two jobs. He no longer had a fiancé, and it wasn't as though living at head-quarters meant much to him.

"Fine, I'll be honest. Dr. Barrett and I used to date. Actually, we were engaged. We broke up a while ago, and it was messy." He let out a breath he hadn't realized he'd been holding. It didn't sound like such a big deal when he said it out loud.

"Did you tell anyone else about this?" Jack asked quietly.

"No. I didn't want to be taken off the job or anything. It's not like it's a big deal." Or at least, it shouldn't have been. With all the training and experience Max had under his belt, he should've been able to handle this as though he were working for any other client. That fact that he hadn't been didn't need to be a topic of discussion.

"If you say so. I did manage to find Isaac Rutledge in the system." He turned around his laptop.

Max was grateful for not being pushed any further. Jack probably had no idea just how difficult it'd been to admit even the most basic facts. He sat next to the techie and took the laptop. "Let's see what we've got here. Isaac Rutledge. Alpha of a black bear clan based out of Nacogdoches, ascending to that position after the previous Alpha died without any children and thus any obvious choice for the next leader. He was a medical lawyer, so that at least explains why he was working with Sabrina to open that shifter hospital."

"A shifter hospital? That's not something I've heard of yet."

"Something Sabrina hopes to bring about so we get better medical treatment without having to scrounge up the closest person with a needle and thread. It's great that Isaac was in on that, and from what Sabrina told me, he was a great guy. But I don't see anything here that's going to help me dig into the case."

Jack shrugged. "Like I said, it's still pretty basic. Even what we have on Mr. Rutledge is only there because President Whiteside agreed to give us some information to add to the database."

"Did he provide info on anyone else? Like the rest of his clan members? Or the wolf that they suspect?" Max's specialty hadn't involved tracking down terrorists or gathering intelligence, but he was convinced there was something he could sink his claws into.

"I'll see what I can find without a name. Eventually, I'd like to build up such a good system that we can cross-reference almost anything. We're far from that right now." Jack took the laptop back and rattled away at the keyboard.

Max glanced at the computer suspiciously. "So, does this mean all the members of the Force are in that database?"

"Yes, but the information is limited. There's basic information that you could find almost anywhere, like the fact that we were in the military and what city we currently live in. But there's nothing saying we're actually in the Force. Hudson has taken a lot of precautions to make sure our systems are secure, and I've confirmed it myself, but I'm still edgy about it. Here." He turned the computer around. "This is one of the guards who was assigned to Sabrina before we were brought in."

Max recognized him immediately. He'd been with Sabrina when he'd picked her up from work the previous day. He'd taken an instant disliking to the man because of how friendly the two seemed with each other, but now it was time to dig down and apply a little more logic and reasoning to the picture. "Let's see. Russell Barclay. Part of the same black bear clan and operating as a guard. Interesting. I wonder if he was supposed to be guarding his Alpha on the night Isaac Rutledge died. I'd be keen to know what their clan dynamics are."

"That's not anything we'd have in here, or at least not yet. I think the more we put in, the better, and that might very well include things like that as we come to know them. For now, that's all I've got for you."

"Yeah, all *you* have." Max handed the laptop back once again, and then he was on his feet. He always thought a little better when he was moving.

"Why do I have a feeling Vance isn't going to like what

you're thinking?" Jack asked as he shut down the computer and set it aside.

"Hey, no one said he was the leader of our unit."

"Dr. Sheridan, then?" Jack referenced the head of the D.C. unit and founder of the Special Ops Shifter Force.

Max sighed. "Either way, you're right. No one's going to like what I'm thinking. As you pointed out, we weren't hired to figure this out, only to keep Sabrina safe. But I'm not sure I can do that."

"And is that because you have, shall we say, a certain attachment to our charge? Or are you just trying to be a modern-day Sherlock Holmes?" Jack grinned.

"I'd rather not say," Max admitted. "But I might see if I can track down this Russell character and find out what he can tell me about the victim. It's at least a start."

Jack waved a hand of defeat in the air. "Fine, but don't come running to me when Vance finds out."

Everyone had looked to the cougar as the leader of the Dallas Force. At first, Max had thought it would be Ash, a polar bear who'd been sent out on the very first assignment of their unit. But that mission had been all he wanted of this life, and they only saw him now and then when he served as a remote consultant. Regardless, Vance didn't seem like the type of guy who would get all that angry. The man had an easy smile and a relaxed attitude that Max hadn't seen break yet. "Don't worry about Vance or me.

Hell, I might not even get the chance to talk to the guy before the trial. It's just a thought."

"You certainly don't have time to talk to him now, considering you're supposed to be leaving to pick up Dr. Barrett right now." Jack pointed at the clock on the wall.

"Shit." Max grabbed his things and darted out the door.

He took advantage of the short flight to center himself. It'd felt surprisingly good to let Jack in on his secret about his relationship with Sabrina, even though he'd managed not to give away too many details. But whatever the two of them had been in the past, Sabrina—no, Dr. Barrett—had made it more than clear she wasn't about to go down that road once again. She'd frozen over just as she had in the past, and he should've expected it. That was all right. He could do the same.

Max told himself the only reason his heart was thudding in his ears when he landed was from the excitement of flying, even though he knew better. Vance was waiting with her on top of the hospital, and Max knew he'd owe the man an apology for being rude that morning. But later. It could wait.

He watched Sabrina get into the helicopter, unable to stop himself from thinking how natural she looked riding along next to him. Most of the clients he served at Luxury Air Tours were awkward, unsure of whether they should stand up straight or bend over as they headed to their seats. They'd put out their hands to steady themselves, yet be afraid they'd touch something that would crash the aircraft, their fingers shaking when they reached for the buckles to secure themselves. Sabrina could've been scrubbed in for surgery with how calm she was.

"I'm not going straight home tonight," she explained without preamble. "I've got a meeting with the hospital board over at the Baxter Executive Building."

This had his attention right away. He was prepared to have a night similar to the previous one—minus that kiss— and he was immediately suspicious of Sabrina going anywhere but home. It opened her up to too many dangers, and his protective feline instinct was quickly getting the better of him. "Why are they meeting there instead of at the hospital?"

She gave him only a quick glance before returning her gaze to the windshield. "The board room is being remodeled."

"Right." It was a simple enough explanation, but he still didn't like it. Maybe all this business was getting to his head, but he was certain that something fishy was going on. "And why do you have to meet with the board? Are you in trouble or something?"

"Of course not!" Her glare was longer now, and she straightened the collar of her lab coat assertively as if to make up for the insult. "I'm trying to get them to open up a new wing, and they require a lot of presentations, figures, and plain old buttering up."

"You? A kiss ass? Never!" Max quipped.

She punched him playfully on the arm, but her chin was stuck out in defiance. "I'm just doing what I've got to do."

"What's this new hospital wing all about? I thought you were trying to open an entirely new hospital for people like us."

"I am."

He waited impatiently for her to go on, but she didn't. Apparently, she was still just as miffed over their little argument that morning as he was. "So, what's this one for?"

"Reconstructive surgery," she admitted quietly. "I truly do miss what I used to do when I first started. There are plenty of plastic surgeons who will give people new boobs and butts, but I want this to be something completely different. If I can get the board to work with me, I might even be able to set up a fund so that those who aren't able to pay can still find a way to get the surgery they need."

It was an admirable goal, but there was just something about her that made him want to play devil's advocate. "Wouldn't it be easier to just lower the price of medical care and surgery in the first place?"

"That's what everyone who's not in the medical field thinks, and it's not as simple as it sounds," she scoffed. "The equipment that's needed isn't something you can just go buy off the shelf at a discount store. We're talking specialized tools that only get sold to specialized surgeons. Not to mention running the building, all the various machines involved in diagnostics like MRIs, microsurgery, robot-assisted surgery—"

"Don't sign me up for that one."

"It's actually really safe and very accurate. Anyway, there are a lot of costs that doctors, surgeons, and hospitals just can't make go away. Surgery is going to be expensive no matter what, which is why I want to set up this wing and this charity. People will get the help they need without having to worry about it." She opened her mouth to say more but then shut it again and looked away.

He thought about pressing the issue once again, but he decided against it. Sabrina was a good person. She'd already told him about her hopes for a shifter hospital. No doubt that would be a massive project that would take years of work. And now she'd just told him about yet another idea to help those in need.

But that was the problem, wasn't it? Sabrina always gave herself, and no matter how much she did, it seemed that she always had more to give. She wanted to help others and didn't pay any attention to what it might cost her. Of course, it always seemed that instead of draining her, it lifted her up.

Max simply wasn't that way. He could only handle being around people for so long, and then he needed some time by himself to recharge. Even once he did, he didn't always have enough of himself left to share with anyone else. That was exactly why he'd left Sabrina, even though he'd never been able to tell her so. He'd known he just wasn't good enough for her. He wasn't good enough for her career, her friends, or her life.

"Sounds like a good cause," he finally said. The conversation between them had died, and that was for the best. Otherwise, he was just going to put his foot in his mouth again.

As he neared the building she'd indicated, Max realized there was a problem. "I wish I'd known there was a change of plans. There's not enough room for me to land on the rooftop."

Sabrina frowned. "Even if you could, I don't know that I'd be able to get in the building from there."

"I'll have to find another place." He zoomed away from the building in search of an alternative. If nothing else, he could take her back to her place and then arrange for a private car—no doubt that would make her late for her meeting, though.

"There's a park just over there," Sabrina said, pointing. "What about that?"

"It'll have to work for now. It's almost dark, so there shouldn't be too many people there, anyway." He was probably going to catch some shit for this later since it wasn't something he was supposed to do, but Max didn't care. The only thing they'd told him to do was fly Sabrina around like some jet setting movie star, and if that involved putting the chopper down on a convenient stretch of grass, then so be it.

He was still justifying this to himself as he walked with her to the building. Sabrina said nothing and seemed preoccupied. It wasn't until they'd reached the conference room where the meeting was supposed to take place that she spoke again.

"You don't need to be in here with me." Sabrina set her bag down on the table and took out several file folders packed with stacks of papers.

"Of course, I do. I'm supposed to stay with you at all times, remember? It's my job." And whether she liked it or not, he was doing his job. Max had noticed there was only one door to serve as both the exit and entrance to the room. This was both good and bad, since it meant no one could get in without him knowing it, yet Sabrina had only one way to leave, should things go unexpectedly.

"I think you can do your job from the hallway." She pointed firmly to the door.

He pulled his attention away from the windows and crossed his arms in front of his chest. "Nope. I'm with you every step of the way."

Sabrina let out a huff of air that sounded an awful lot like her animal form. "This meeting is incredibly important, Max. I don't need you to give me a hard time."

"I'm not." Was he? Maybe at first, but this trial she'd gotten involved in bothered him. If something happened to her while she was shut in this room and he was banished to the hallway, he'd never forgive himself. "Look. I can pull a chair right over here in the corner. I'll be behind you, but you'll never know I'm here."

"Oh, trust me. I'll know," she shot back. "Tell me, Max: have you ever done a job like this before?"

He narrowed his eyes. Sabrina was going to find some way to rationalize this all out so that she won the argument. She'd done it to him plenty of other times. He didn't usually mind that much, but her life was literally at stake here. "Not exactly. But I think if the United States Army can trust me to take a thirty-eight-billion-dollar helicopter overseas to drop off a section of Special Forces officers, then I think I can handle it."

She pursed her lips and leaned on the table. Her eyes closed. "Fine. You've got me there. I'm not trying to doubt your skill here, Max, but this trial and the whole idea of having a bodyguard is severely interfering with my career. I'm surprised no one has said too much about my new luxury transport, but there's no reason to shove the situation right in the faces of the board members. They don't need to know what's going on in my personal life. If they think I attract danger, they might change their minds about what they're willing to do for me."

That didn't seem fair to him, but he supposed it wasn't fair that any of the shifters had to hide who they really were from the world. "I don't like it."

Sabrina zipped her bag back up and set it on the floor just under the table. "I doubt anyone even knows I'm here besides the board members, and they're all a bunch of old farts who've been working for the hospital forever. They're not interested in anything but how much money it'll cost them to listen to me."

Max poked his head back out into the hallway and looked around. "So, this place is mostly just empty office space for rent?"

"Some floors of the building are leased out long-term, but as far as I know, this floor is by the hour."

"Good. I'll find a place to make myself a little more discreet. But if anything happens, just scream. I'll hear you." His body was fighting him on this decision. Max was trying to be sensible for her sake, and he knew the likelihood of anything happening to her was minimal. But he was having a physical reaction to the idea of leaving her alone in a room with a bunch of strangers and no easy way to get out should someone try to stop her. Every cell in his body was surging toward her, his tiger longing to put himself between her and any potential danger.

But the resolute look on her face told him she wasn't interested in any heroics. "Thank you, I appreciate that. I promise I'll try to keep this as short as possible."

He eyed the stack of files she'd just put on the table. "A whole new wing for the hospital plus the funding to build it and support the patients doesn't sound like a short meeting to me."

"They don't have that much patience, actually. I find that they prefer to have a lot of short meetings instead of fewer meetings that last all night." She straightened the files, ran her hands down the front of her lab coat, and adjusted her glasses.

Max realized she might actually be nervous. "I'm sure you'll do great." He ducked out of the room and around the corner just as he heard someone come off the elevator. Max pressed himself against the wall as he listened, tapping into his big cat's instincts. It was two men, probably older, given the way they walked and the timbre of their voices. They were joking with each other about how poorly they'd done on the golf course the previous weekend. *No one to be concerned about.*

This part of the hall seemed to be unoccupied, and the wall he leaned against was a component of the very conference room where Sabrina's meeting was taking place. It wasn't ideal, but it was a start. He was running out of time to look for a better position as the elevator dinged once again. Max wasn't about to let her stay in there without having his ears trained on her.

He adjusted his back against the wall. This wasn't exactly the worst case of guard duty he'd ever been on. There were plenty of times in his military career that he'd pulled guard, and at least there in that office building, he didn't need to worry about sand in his eyes. If he sat, there was no risk of having a scorpion crawl out from the shadows and sting his ass.

He was suddenly back there, at a small base that'd been established as a way station. He'd landed for the night, exhausted and frustrated with the weather. The transport of new soldiers that'd been due a day ago still hadn't come through, and the men stationed there were feeling the same way. Max could either work a shift or spend all night in the crowded barracks with a bunch of strangers. The closeness to his fellow soldiers was something he'd grown used to, but that didn't mean he enjoyed it.

The chain-link fence behind him dug into his shoulders as he leaned against it, the metal seeking out all the soreness in his muscles. Sand had drifted up around it, making the footing impossibly uncomfortable. Those were minor inconveniences compared to the wind. It drove through the night, whipping up the sand and blasting it like tiny bullets into his skin. Max, like many of the other soldiers stationed anywhere other than home, imitated the locals with a shemagh around his face and neck. The large lightweight scarf helped, but it didn't do anything to keep his eyes safe. The sand stuck in his eyes. If anyone wanted to choose that moment to attack, it'd be a safe bet that he'd never see them coming.

Max came to with a start, finding himself not in the middle of the desert, but in an office building in the southern U.S. just before dinnertime. The fluorescent lighting flickered overhead as he rubbed his eyes, expecting to find clumps of sand in the corners. Damn. He'd slipped again. For a few moments, it seemed as though he were in a different place and time. It was so disorienting to come back that it didn't always feel like a relief.

He focused his attention on the room at his back. He heard the deep timbre of a male voice, followed by the lighter tones of Sabrina. She sounded calm and cool, two words that should've been her name. Everything was fine. Max let out a breath and forced his shoulders to relax. Of course everything was fine. It had been for a while, and it was only his overly suspicious mind that was making it otherwise. Sabrina was right about no one knowing she was there, and there was little chance that anyone would come jumping around the corner to attack her. It'd just been fun to irritate her by making her think he was going to sit in on the meeting.

His nerves twitched when the door finally opened and board members began filtering out. He'd have imagined they'd be eager to get home for dinner, but they ambled just as slowly away from the conference room as they had on their way there. The door was open at least, and he could hear better.

"Dr. Barrett, I'm impressed," said an older, reedy voice.

"You've put together quite the presentation. I was particularly interested in some of the financials."

"Thank you, Dr. Corton." Sabrina's reply carried the breathiness of being pleased and relieved. "Your opinion means a lot to me."

"Of course it does, since my opinion on this will have a lot to do with how the rest of the board votes." He laughed, a gentle wheezing noise. "They're a bunch of kiss-asses, but I do think they have good intentions."

"As do I with this new wing. I truly believe it could make a difference, and not just locally. I didn't have this in my presentation because I knew everyone would be eager to leave, but I think it'd be great to pull some local businesses into this idea. Maybe work with some hotels to arrange lodging for the loved ones of those who come into town for surgery, things like that."

Dr. Corton let out another chuckle. "My dear, you're far too much for just one person. You're an incredibly talented surgeon, but it turns out you have quite the head for business. Not to mention a heart for charity. I'll be looking over the figures and discussing things with the board over the next few meetings. We'll be getting back to you."

"Great. Thank you again."

When the older man had disappeared back down the hallway and Max was fairly certain the room was clear of all the board members, he came around the corner. Even though he would've heard if anything drastic happened, and even though he'd just eavesdropped on her conversation with Dr. Corton, Max still felt incredibly relieved to see her whole and unharmed. "That sounded like it went well."

She was stacking her file folders back into her bag, and she looked up at him and smiled. It was a warm smile that reached her eyes and lit up her face. "It really did. I'm so glad it's over, but I also feel like I'll never sleep again because I'm so excited!"

"Does that mean you'll get the wing?"

"Oh, no. Not necessarily. There's still a lot to go through. But it was a step in the right direction." Sabrina zipped her bag and followed him to the door, turning off the light on the way. "And I'm starving. I don't remember the last thing I ate today."

"Then let's go to dinner." His mouth suggested it before his mind had a chance to catch up. Perhaps his tiger was still thinking about the way her lips had felt the night before: lush, comforting, and warm. He was reminded of how her body had felt pressed against his, how inviting he found her hips and the way her body tucked in around the waist under her ribcage...

"Sounds good to me," Sabrina replied, bringing him back out of her bedroom and into this dull hallway with its gray carpet and standard potted ficus. "I'm tired of takeout. I think I could use a good steak, and I think I might even deserve it." She laughed as they stepped onto the elevator.

"You're happy," he noted. "It's a good look for you." Heat

spread through his body as he stood next to her in the elevator. There they were, once again confined to a small space where there was no option but to be incredibly aware of each other. His eyes measured the distance between them. It would take only a slight movement, lifting his hand from where he leaned on the rail on the back wall, to touch her arm, her back. It could be a friendly gesture, offering his congratulations.

Her sparkling hazel eyes changed as he watched her pupils dilate, and he knew she felt the same things he did. Their human lives and their human bodies got in the way of so many things, but their tigers always knew what was best. Her gaze flicked down to his mouth and lingered there, but then she turned away. "There's a great outdoor place not far from here over on Commerce."

It'd been too much. Max tipped his head back to watch the floor numbers tick by. It was just as well that she could keep her head, since he couldn't. If he'd given in even a fraction to his most primal urges, he'd have had her naked and satisfied before they reached the lobby. He cleared his throat, even if he couldn't clear that rather delightful picture from his mind. "That'll be fine."

It was a short walk back to the helicopter. The sun had set fully now, and the yellow glow of the streetlamps cast sharp circles on the sidewalk before leaving pedestrians to plunge back into darkness. Max watched the shifting light play over Sabrina's hair, sliding over her features and changing them from moment to moment. She was beautiful at any angle. "I heard you mention to that doctor that you wanted to pair up with businesses to get other services for the reconstructive patients of the new wing."

She eyeballed him over her shoulder as they moved off the sidewalk and into the park. "You were listening?"

"It's my job," he reminded her. "I had to keep my ears open for your scream, remember?"

Sabrina made a dismissive sound. "Yes, I did say that. What about it?"

"You should talk to George down at my work. He's all about business and getting as much money as he can out of his wealthy clients, but he knows a little bit of charity can do a lot for his public image. He might be willing to help out with some sort of transportation, or maybe even just a fun helicopter ride for some kid who's been through a tough time."

"You think he'd go for it?" He could hear the eagerness in her voice.

"Probably. Especially if he knew there was a pilot willing to participate."

She paused her pursuit across the short grass of the park and turned to him. It was dark there under the trees, with just enough ambient light to see silhouettes, and she was practically in his arms. "You'd do that?"

Max knew she likely hadn't meant to get so close to him. After all, she was the one who'd made it abundantly clear they couldn't be anything more than a pilot and a surgeon. But his hands automatically reached up to catch her elbows. "Of course I would. It'd be fun." And in that moment, he'd have done absolutely anything she asked of him.

"Max, that is so sweet, and so thoughtful. I just love it. I—"

"Shh." He clenched his grip on her arms and turned his head, listening. "I don't think we're alone."

"It's probably just some homeless person looking for a place to spend the night. They're in the parks a lot."

"No." It was a rational explanation, something Sabrina was exceedingly good at, but what he sensed didn't line up with it. A frisson of energy crackled up his spine as he turned to his right, just in time to see a massive form spring out of the darkness.

Max operated on nothing but pure impulse now. He shoved Sabrina to his left, putting himself between her and the attacker. He launched forward, feeling his body begin to change. His spine lengthened as his hips thrust his top half forward. Max's fingers became shorter and rounder, but they held the deadly weapons of his claws. He unsheathed them just in time to swipe across the lupine face. His back paws dug into the ground, preparing him for the next move. His human eyes hadn't been able to see much, but shifting was like turning on night vision. Max now saw every inch of the park as though it were midday. His tail swished irritably as he rounded on his prey.

The wolf snapped his jaws and lunged to the side, trying to avoid Max's teeth and claws. He wasn't retreating, though. He sprang through the night, his teeth gleaming as they reached for the tiger's neck.

The wolf was big, but Max's feline body was heavier and stronger. He ducked low just as the wolf leapt. When he shoved his body upward again, it was like a midair body slam to the lycan. The wolf rolled to the side but recovered quickly, getting to his feet just in time for Max to bound on top of him. The two rolled through the grass. Max knew he was better equipped to win this fight. The wolf might've had the element of surprise at first, but the only true weapons he had were his teeth. Max had the added advantage of claws.

He sank a full paw of them into the wolf's side, eliciting a yelp. Max pressed harder, holding back to give the shifter a chance to surrender. Instead, the cur used his pain to drive his assault. He went for Max's throat once again.

That was all the information Max needed. He dug in with all his fury as the low, guttural roar of his people welled up in his throat and spread throughout the park. His claws swiped through the thick gray fur and into flesh, repaying the wolf with the exact attack meant to kill him. As the tiger ripped out the soft spot at his enemy's neck, blood sprayed across the grass, peppering Max's fur.

Max turned to see Sabrina standing there behind him. Her arms were still partially extended from catching her balance when he'd shoved her aside. She stared past him to the dead wolf, her eyes wide and her mouth agape.

Slinking off into the deeper shadows, Max kept a sharp eye on her while he licked himself clean. Sabrina needed him, but not in the form of a bloody killer. It'd been a long time since he'd had to do something like this. Adrenaline exhilarated his bloodstream, and what he truly wanted to do was barrel through the park to get it all out of his system. There was no time for that now, and he wouldn't dare leave Sabrina there alone.

When he'd shifted back, his human body felt awkward and useless. He put his hand on her arm, bringing her startled gaze up to his. "You all right?"

She nodded slowly and then gave one firm nod as she closed her mouth. "Of course. Of course I am. I'm fine. Completely fine. But what do we do about him?" Sabrina gestured vaguely toward the wolf's carcass.

"Already on it." Max put in a call to headquarters before jogging to the chopper for a tarp. He wrapped the body and stowed it in the back. "It'll have to ride with us for a bit, but someone will be at your building to take it."

"At *my* place?" She fanned her fingers across her chest. "Do we have to?"

"We can't just leave it here for someone to find," Max reasoned. "He died as a wolf, which means he's going to stay in that form. It would be bad enough to find a dead wolf in an urban park, but even worse to find that he'd been killed violently by some other creature. The whole city would be in an uproar."

"Oh. Right." She followed him back to the aircraft and climbed inside, firmly buckling her belt and keeping her head turned away as he prepared for takeoff.

Max had his hands full already, but he watched her. She was too quiet. "Are you sure you're all right?"

"I said I was," she replied coolly.

"Yes," he agreed, "but it's not easy to see someone die like that."

"I've seen plenty of people die, thank you very much. I suppose you've forgotten that I'm a surgeon?" She lifted her chin, but she still refused to look at him.

"Okay. That's true." But there was still something very wrong. He could feel the tension between them like a force in the air, driving them apart. "Are you upset with me for killing him? I mean, there wasn't any choice. He was there for blood, and he would've killed me first if I'd have given him the chance."

"No." Her bitter reply crackled through the air. "I'm mad at you for not giving me a chance to defend myself."

If he'd been driving a car, he would've slammed on the brakes and pulled over. "What?"

"You heard me."

"I heard some words, but they didn't make much sense.

Pardon me, Dr. Barrett, but I was under the impression that I was hired to do exactly what I just did. Someone threatened you, I took care of it, end of story."

Now Sabrina did turn to look at him, and her eyes shot daggers in the dim glow of the control panel. "You didn't even give me a chance to defend myself! All you did was shove me out of the way. Might as well have said, 'Stand back, little lady. I'll handle this.' I'm a tiger, too. It's insulting!"

He pressed the fingers of his free hand against the bridge of his nose. "Sabrina. You're the most intelligent, logical person I know. In fact, I'd be willing to bet that most people who know you could say that about you. But what you're arguing right now is crazy!"

"It is not," she spat back. "Just because I'm a woman doesn't mean I need some man to jump to my defense like a helpless princess."

"Maybe not necessarily a man, but someone. No one would ask me to operate on someone who needed their appendix out. They'd call you. We each have a role to fulfill, and I think it's pretty clear who should do each one."

"Right. You're saying it's clear that I'm a wimp. So kind of you." Sabrina crossed her arms in front of her chest."

"Sabrina, you didn't even shift!" He felt like a real jerk for pointing it out, but she'd driven him to it. "You just stood there. If you wanted to jump in and do something about it, you certainly had the chance."

"Easy for you to say after you pushed me out of the way." Her shoulders were so tight, they were lifting up near her ears.

Max adjusted the controls aggressively. George would be pissed if he did so much as got a scratch on this chopper, and yet he had a dead body in the back of it. Just a short time ago, he'd have done anything Sabrina asked him to do. Now, he wished he could just drop her off and call someone else in to finish the shift. Technically he could do that, but he wasn't about to be the one to give in. "Right. Nothing ever makes you happy, Sabrina. Nothing is good enough for you. That might serve you well in your career, but it makes real life awfully fucking difficult."

She gasped and opened her mouth for a reply, but for once, she couldn't find one. She worked her lips, opening and closing them a few times until she snapped them shut. The rest of the ride was silent.

Max knew the night would be, too.

8

SABRINA WOKE TO THE SOUND OF HER APARTMENT DOOR opening and closing. Low male voices vibrated through her bedroom door, making her heart thud in her ears. Had someone else come to attack her? Why was this happening all of a sudden when there hadn't been any other threats lately?

But when someone knocked on her door, she figured it probably wasn't anyone who wanted to kill her. Sabrina cleared her throat. "Yes?"

"Jack is here to take over for the day. Thought I'd make the introductions." Max's voice was gruff and clipped. He didn't want to be talking to her any more than she wanted to be talking to him.

"I'll be out in a minute." Feeling sassy, Sabrina considered taking her sweet time getting dressed before coming out of the bedroom. But the faster she complied with Max's wishes, the sooner he'd be out of her apartment. She threw on jeans and a t-shirt as she recalled the night before.

It'd been utterly terrifying to have someone come at them out of the dark, and even more so that it was someone as their animal. For whatever reason, Sabrina had always imagined the death threats she'd received as coming from someone in their bipedal form. But of course, a wolf would be more fully prepared to attack. Max had dispatched him quickly, almost easily. He was right that he'd done his job, but it left her with a cold feeling in her veins that she still couldn't shake. Sabrina glanced in the mirror as she ran a brush through her hair and then opened the bedroom door.

Max was standing at the breakfast bar, a coffee mug in his hand as he spoke in low tones to a tall man with broad shoulders. He straightened when he saw her and gestured to the other man. "Jack, this is Dr. Sabrina Barrett. Sabrina, Jack."

She plastered on a smile and made sure it was directed only at the newcomer. "It's nice to meet you."

"You as well. I'm afraid I don't come with a helicopter like Max here, but I understand you have the day off today." He had a warm hand and a friendly smile, and he was about as much the opposite of Max as you could get.

"I am off work, but I do have some errands to run."

Max rubbed his chin. "I'm not sure that's a good idea after last night. It's best if you just stay here."

She looked past him through the patio doors. "I'm fairly certain you were hired to watch over me, not to keep me prisoner. I have appointments, and I plan to keep them." Sabrina didn't turn to look, but she was aware of the two men exchanging a glance.

"We can handle it," Jack said. "I've brought the company car."

Max's lips were tight, but he looked ready to say something. Instead, he gave them a curt nod and left.

Sabrina let out a sigh of relief as the door closed behind him. She didn't know Jack, and it should be more unnerving to have a stranger in her house than someone she knew, but she was more than ready to get rid of him.

Jack proved to be an amiable bodyguard. He had mastered the art of small talk much more than Max had, making him easier to talk to. As she got ready to head out for the day, Sabrina realized that the man simply didn't carry the same rigidity with him that Max did. It was a nice change.

Nor was he as insistent about hovering over her as he did his job. When she joined Angela in the booth at Grayson's, Jack had taken up a seat in the far corner. She could see him, pulling out his laptop and settling in, and she allowed herself a satisfied smile. At least she wouldn't feel like he was in a hurry to leave, and she could try to enjoy her day off as much as possible.

But that was a bit more challenging when the conversation unavoidably led to Max. "So, I feel like I haven't talked to you at all ever since this whole trial thing came up. How are things going with your newest hired guns?" A distant cousin of Sabrina's, Angela knew all about shifter life.

Sabrina twirled her fork in the air to encompass all the trouble, feels, and uncertainty she felt about the situation. "I think it would be just fine if one of those hired guns didn't happen to be Max."

Angela tipped her chin down and widened her eyes at Sabrina. "Surely you mean some other Max, right?"

"I'm afraid not."

"And I take it that hasn't been going well. Tell me, did you rip him a new one for running off and leaving you hanging like that? I know you've wanted to do that for a long time." Angela sliced into her rare steak, the juices running out onto the plate.

Sabrina sighed. "Sort of."

"Sort of? That doesn't sound like the kind of drama I was hoping for here." She gave Sabrina a sparkling smile to let her know she was kidding.

"I did bring it up a little, but that was only after we kissed in my bedroom."

The sound of Angela's fork hitting the plate caused several other diners to look in their direction. "You what?"

She hated to say it all out loud, but Sabrina needed to get everything off her chest. "It was really random. Max came and picked me up from work the other day. I knew it would be one of the new guys, but I didn't know he would be one of them. I was just so shocked at first that I didn't know much of what to say. But he got to me without even trying. Max has always had this way of looking at me when he knows I'm having a vulnerable moment. It's like he's saying he's on my side and he understands, but then he turns right around and acts like the jackass we all know him to be."

Angela rolled her hand in the air. "Yeah, yeah. Get to the kiss and whatever good stuff comes after that."

"No good stuff. It was just a kiss, and I told him the next morning in no uncertain terms that it was a mistake and that we had no business behaving that way. It's been fire and ice between us ever since. As soon as we get past our anger and start getting along, things become so physically intense. Then things get awkward and we're at each other's throats again." They were certainly at each other's throats right now, and she could only imagine how awful this lunch would be if Max were there instead of Jack. Then again, she always felt safe when he was watching over her. She knew he'd do anything to protect her.

"What's that dreamy look on your face? Do I need to get you a composition book so you can write 'Sabrina Loves Max 4-Ever' all over it?" her friend teased. Angela knew about the bond Sabrina had with Max, the type of fated tie that had drawn them to each other as mates. It was the kind of thing only shifters could understand.

"Absolutely not," Sabrina replied tartly. "I know that Max and I are a poor match, and I don't care what our tigers have to say about it. But it's been a lot harder to be around him than I imagined it would be. I always figured if I happened to run into him somewhere, I'd either chew him out or give him the cold shoulder, move on, and live my life as though it'd never happened. But now he's in my apartment all night, and last night, he actually had to kill someone who tried to attack me."

Angela pushed her plate away this time. "Girl, if you had this much drama to talk about, we should've gone to a place with better wine. What happened?"

She relayed the events in the park as best as she could remember them, although she didn't think the image of that bloodied wolf would leave her mind any time soon. Max had said the Force would try to determine who the attacker was. "I was just so angry with him for treating me like a damsel in distress."

Scratching her temple just under her fringe of short hair, Angela made a face. "I hate to break it to you, but you *were* a damsel in distress. And don't you think you should be thanking him for saving your life? There's no telling what might've happened if he wasn't there."

Sabrina took a sip of iced tea. "I like to think I would've

taken care of myself."

"But *he's* the trained soldier. He's been through all sorts of situations like that, pilot or not." Unable to resist, Angela pulled her plate closer and began eating her lunch again.

"You're not supposed to be on his side, you know." Sabrina slumped a little in her chair. "Maybe I was a bit of a bitch toward him. This whole thing has been incredibly stressful, and I'm ready for the trial to get over with so I can go back to a normal life."

"One without Max?" she challenged. "Or are you going to keep him on your couch for a while like I know you want to?"

Sabrina made a sour face at her friend, but then she laughed. "You're terrible, you know that?"

"Only because I'm right," Angela asserted. "You and Max are crazy about each other. You have some differences to work out, sure, but I don't see how either one of you can actually move on with your lives unless you either work this out or find a way to end it once and for all. You both left everything hanging, and that's a lot of dirty laundry to go through."

"Even if we did, I'm not sure it's worth the effort. He's got a stubborn streak about a mile wide, and he constantly shuts down when he doesn't like how things are going. He criticizes every aspect of my life." She was getting angry all over again just thinking about it.

Angela reached across the table and put her hand on

top of Sabrina's. "He's not the only one who's stubborn, and I happen to know you're more than capable of packing away your feelings until you're ready to deal with them. Take it from a third party who's seen the two of you together before. You have a lot more in common than you think. If you just find a way to talk about it and really let each other inside, you might be surprised."

"When did you become a counselor?" Sabrina joked. But she was genuinely touched by how much Angela cared. She was more interested in the reality of the situation instead of just stirring up more drama. There were plenty of women out there like that, and Sabrina didn't have a use for them.

"Hey, all those high school kids I'm teaching seem to want a lot more from me than how to construct a proper sentence. They might be young, but some of them have some very adult problems." She pushed the bone from her steak aside and started in on a baked potato. "So, now that we've got all that figured out, tell me how things are going with your other projects."

Sabrina realized as she started in on her meeting with Dr. Corton and the other board members just how badly she needed a girls' day. There was something unbelievably refreshing about just talking and hashing everything out. They didn't need to come to any sort of conclusion, necessarily, but she was able to lay everything out on the table.

And she could always expect an honest opinion from Angela.

When they left Grayson's to do some boutique shopping, Sabrina had nearly forgotten that she wasn't alone. It wasn't until Jack just happened to be exiting the restaurant at the same time as they were, giving a very convincing show of being a kind stranger opening the door for her, that she remembered she was under constant surveillance.

The two women headed down the sidewalk on foot, with Jack just a few yards behind them. Sabrina knew that if anything happened, this man would do exactly as Max had done the previous night. But something significant had changed. When the conclave had first assigned her a guard, she'd been actively receiving death threats. The few days without them had made her complacent, but the incident in the park had proven that was a mistake. Sabrina might have a trained Special Ops soldier just a short distance behind her, but she needed to start watching her own back from now on.

9

"I HATE TO EVEN BRING IT UP, BUT DID YOUR COWORKERS GET with the conclave and figure out who that wolf was?" Sabrina was seated in his helicopter once again, finished with a day of work.

Max had wondered if she'd even be willing to accept a ride from him again after the way they'd argued the other night. But Jack and Vance had taken over the job for twenty-four hours, insisting on giving him a break. It'd bothered him far more than he ever imagined it would, and when he should've been finding better ways to occupy himself, he was just trying to resist going to her apartment. In the end, he hoped the time apart would ease the tension between them.

Apparently, it had. "Sort of. They know he's a lone wolf, and not the good kind. He was working as a mercenary doing any work he could get. This time, someone paid him to go after you."

"But we don't know who," Sabrina concluded.

"No, but it would be another interesting piece of evidence in the trial if we could find out." In the time he'd spent away from Sabrina, Max had been working hard to find more pieces of the puzzle. It turned out to be a much harder task than he anticipated.

"It seems like an interesting coincidence that it was a wolf, and not the one I saw in the stairwell that night at the hotel," Sabrina mused. "I have to wonder if—wait. Where are we going?" She peered through the windshield as they headed to the outskirts of town. "This isn't the way to my building."

"It's not," he confirmed. His heart picked up the pace now that she was onto his plan. It was something that had popped in his head as a random idea, but he'd known it to be a good one. Convincing her to agree with him would be a different matter. "I have something in mind."

"Such as?"

He lifted one shoulder. "You'll see when we get there." They buzzed out into the countryside, flying out over farms and fields and tree-lined rivers as the sun started making its way down toward the horizon. By the time he finally landed, setting the chopper down in what was essentially the middle of nowhere, it was nearly dark. "Come on."

She stepped hesitantly out of the chopper, keeping one

hand on the metal hull. "I don't know what we're doing here, but do you really think this is a good idea? I mean, we thought we were alone when that wolf attacked and look where that got us."

"I know, but whoever is after you has probably figured out your schedule." That'd been bothering him quite a bit. Was it someone within the medical community? "This is a completely unscheduled stop."

"And am I allowed to know what we're doing here yet?" She let go of the chopper and took one hesitant step toward him as though she still expected someone to come darting out of the tree line.

Max pulled in a deep breath. This would be a true test of just how much Sabrina doubted him and how much she wanted him to stay out of her life. "Sabrina, you've got a lot going on in your life right now. I don't think there's anything you need more than a good run." His shoulders shuddered as he shifted, feeling the length and strength of his feline body. His sharp teeth poked through his gums, painful only at first. He pushed back when on all fours, stretching his spine all the way to the end of his tail.

"Max." Sabrina cocked a hip. "This is ridiculous."

Tigers or not, the two of them weren't in the same clan. They didn't have the telepathic bond that other shifters shared with their group members when in their animal forms. Any English words he might try to form with his current mouth would come out garbled. Instead, he stalked a small circle around her feet, letting his tail brush against her legs.

"I guess you really mean it, don't you?" She reached down and ruffled the soft fur around his ears.

Max huffed and jerked his head away, but it was worth the laugh that escaped her lungs. He walked a short distance to give her room.

To his satisfaction, Sabrina closed her eyes. She stood motionless for a while, and he knew exactly what she was doing. She hadn't let out her other form in a long time, and it wasn't always easy to recall that command to one's body. Max always started with his back and shoulders; it was the most instinctive to him. It was different for Sabrina. A patch of blackness spread across the skin on her forehead. It split as it reached toward her temples and hairline and wrapped around each of her eyes. Orange coloring bloomed behind it, touched by white near her eyebrows and the curve of her lips. The stripes continued to extend over her body. She melted and molded and changed, losing the form that she wore so much in favor of the one that Max had longed to see. She was more heavily marked than he, with many of her stripes doubled. The fur near her back was the deepest orange that faded slowly to the most brilliant white. Sabrina was the most beautiful tigress Max had ever seen. She stretched her paws experimentally, digging her claws into the earth.

That was when he knew she was ready. He took off,

bounding across the field. Max heard a snort of exasperation, but on his heels, he heard the thuds of her paws. She was coming swiftly after him, closing the distance. He ran harder, moving across the field and toward the trees now. The shadows were deeper there, but he had the advantage of his animal vision.

They darted through the trees and around rocks, sometimes sticking to game trails and other times crashing through the brush. Max took the lead at first, making sure to go slowly enough that Sabrina could keep up with him. But she got the idea, and the next thing he knew, she was passing him. Her lithe body cruised past him easily, and he swore she gave him an amused look as she left him in the dust.

It was a race after that, with the two of them neck-and-neck without any determined finish line. She managed to dash ahead on the long stretch of flat land, but Max's muscular haunches helped him leap faster over fallen logs and rocks.

When darkness had fallen to its full thickness and a deep blue-black expanded overhead, Max turned to trot up a lonely hillside. They were far from anywhere, without so much as a streetlight or a farmhouse in sight. The stars had come out in full force, scattered brilliantly overhead. He sauntered up the hill as he admired the view and caught his breath, soaking in the moment of having one of his own next to him.

But he had to let this body go. As good as it'd felt, there were things he needed to say, and he couldn't do it this way. By the time they reached the top, they'd both returned to the day-to-day form that was accepted in the human world. Max sat and patted the grass next to him. "How was it?"

She brushed her hair out of her face with her hand. The careful ponytails, buns, and braids that Sabrina had mastered in medical school had been undone with the shift. "I have to admit, that was amazing. I thought you were crazy at first, but I really did need that."

"It's nice to have the rest of the world melt away for a while, isn't it?" Max stretched his legs out in front of him. "That's just one of the many difficult things about living in the city. There just aren't enough chances to be ourselves and let go."

Sabrina nodded. "I admit, I was about to get back in the helicopter and just stubbornly wait you out. But I don't remember the last time I got to do something like this. And I hadn't even thought about it since this whole murder case started. It's been absolutely miserable."

Max could hear the thickness in her voice. "Are you all right?"

She sniffled. "I'm just so tired of constantly being followed. It's a huge weight on me whether it's someone assigned to watch over me or some killer springing out of the darkness. I just want to go back to a normal life."

"Has your life really been that normal?"

"Fair enough. Normal for me. Thank you." She gave him a sheepish smile.

He could feel his face soften as he looked at her. It was the same feeling he'd had in all the other good times in their relationship when he realized just how crazy he was about her. Max knew he should stop, but he didn't think he could. "I owe you an apology."

"Max, you don't have to—"

"No, I do. Please, just hear me out. First, I want to apologize for acting like an ass when I got hired for this job. I was surprised, and I didn't know how to feel. I took that out on you, and I shouldn't have done that." Saving Sabrina in the park, knowing their lives were truly in danger and that the threats weren't just some fictional concerns hanging over their heads made a big difference.

"In that case, I should apologize, too. It put both of us in a weird position. I already didn't like having the guards assigned by the conclave following me around, and I definitely wasn't prepared to ride with you to and from work. Not to mention having you spend the night at my house." She laughed softly, letting her shoulder bump slightly against his.

It was the tiniest bit of touch, but he already felt so much closer to her than he had before now that they'd gone for that run together. Being in animal form together could be very bonding for shifters, and that had proven to be true as far as he was concerned. "I also want to apologize for the way I left you. I know you probably don't want to talk about the past, and maybe it would be better if we left all that behind us, but it's been weighing on me. I feel like you should know the truth."

Sabrina squinted up at the stars, and when she spoke, her voice was hushed. "And what is that?"

This was much harder than just saying he was sorry for acting like an ass. This was a much bigger deal. "I had a hard time dealing with how important your career was to you. I didn't like having to share you with the hospital and your patients all the time. Even more, I didn't feel comfortable hanging out with the crowd you did. Everyone was so intelligent and professional. I wasn't their caliber, and I knew I wasn't yours, either."

She turned to look at him now. "Is that why you never came out with me to all those dinners and events? I thought you were just being stubborn. Or that you didn't want to be with me."

He felt that statement in the center of his heart. "I never meant to hurt you. And I did want to hang out with you. But I always felt like everyone else was judging me. I know it's silly and childish. I didn't know how to handle it, and all I ended up doing was pushing you away."

"Oh, Max." Sabrina touched the back of his hand, her gentle fingertips sending sparks of energy up his arm. "I didn't realize. I wish you would've just told me."

"Maybe. But I'm not sure it would've made any difference. You would always have those events to go to, and I'd keep having to say no. It was a cycle I wasn't willing to continue, especially not with having to handle a crowd full of strangers who were all looking at me and wondering why the amazing Dr. Barrett had brought some bum in on her arm. It was just too much."

She was silent for a long time as she leaned back and stared up at the stars. Her voice was low and quiet like a river when she finally spoke. "You know, I wanted to go to medical school to save lives. I wanted to make a difference for people. When I started talking about it, my high school counselor warned me that I'd never have any time to have people in my own life. At the time, I was more than happy about that. I wasn't very popular in high school, anyway, so it seemed like a fitting career. Then, when I got through all my schooling and things started to take off, I was overwhelmed by how big of a social aspect my career involved. My counselor was right in that I don't have a lot of time for my personal life, but there are still all these dinners and fundraisers and events I have to go to just to make sure I keep all the right connections. It's exhausting for me, and I didn't realize I was asking too much of you."

A heavy pressure lifted off of Max's chest, and the difference was so great that it made him laugh.

"What's so funny?"

"Us." Max turned his hand and closed his fingers around Sabrina's. She felt so comfortable, so good. It was hard to understand how the two of them could've been at such odds. "We're old enough that we should have our lives all figured out. We should have our ducks in a row. And yet we're still too obstinate to be honest with each other."

"That's a good point." She settled her head against his shoulder. "So tell me another truth."

"Does there have to be more?" Max let his cheek rest against her soft hair. He could feel his tiger chuffing happily.

Sabrina nodded. "I think there is."

She was right. There was so much he hadn't told her or anyone else. Not even the therapist he'd seen when he came back from war as part of the VA's method of tackling PTSD. It was a nice idea, but it wasn't as simple or as easy as all the psych docs thought. "Have you ever read the book *Slaughterhouse Five*?"

"Sure. Kurt Vonnegut. The one where the guy gets unstuck in time and lives his life out of order." Sabrina allowed his shoulder to support a little more of her weight.

"That's how I feel. Not the getting abducted by aliens part, fortunately. But sometimes I'm not really here. I'm back in a chopper over the desert, dropping men off for their missions that I know are going to lead to their deaths. I'm pulling guard duty at some random outpost. I'm trying to save some child whose been hit by his own people's fire, and then I'm suddenly back at the supermarket or surfing the internet. It's like I'm living two completely different lives at the same time."

Her breath left her lungs in a long hiss. "I'm sorry, Max."

He smiled. "Thank you."

"For what?"

"For not immediately turning around and telling me about all the different options there are to help me with this. For just accepting that it's the way I am, at least in this moment. It'd actually gotten a lot better until about the past week or so." Most of the visions of his past had been limited to his dreams. It was disturbing, but he could deal with it. As soon as Sabrina came back into his life, everything changed.

"So you're telling me I make you crazy?" she giggled.

"Yes," Max confirmed. "And that's exactly why I try so hard to make you crazy."

"What?" Sabrina sat up to look at him.

"Ever since I met you, you've had this hard shell on the outside. You can go through surgeries without getting upset or anxious. You have the same calm attitude whether you're waiting in line at the grocery store or waiting on a promotion at work. You're tough to rattle, and I like a challenge." Here, alone, in the darkness, he could tell her anything. All the truth was going to come out and blend in with the night, and it was an idea he truly relished. They might never be together again, but at least they would both know the truth.

"And you're an asshole!" But Sabrina was laughing, starlight and tears shimmering in her eyes. She flicked her finger underneath them. "I guess I am a bit stoic. I had to be from a pretty young age. Children are terrible little things, picking out the weakest of the bunch and attacking them relentlessly. I realized pretty quickly that if I let them see how much they were bothering me, they'd just do it more. So I taught myself not to cry until I was alone in my room at night where no one could see me."

Max had seen a few photographs of Sabrina as a girl, and he could easily imagine the smaller version of her lifting her chin and stalking off to the other side of the playground. "That's kind of sad."

"Not really. I used it to my advantage when it came to my career. The professors in medical school talk a lot about not getting attached to your patients or letting your emotions rule your head. I already had that part nailed down. It really did help. Until I saw what you did to that wolf in the park."

He started a bit at this, surprised by her admission. "You said you were fine."

"I always say that. But you were right. Seeing that was completely different than someone dying on the table or slowly slipping away from a disease. It was uncomfortable at the least, and I'd already seen Isaac Rutledge right after he'd been killed. I like to think I'm pretty tough, but I guess there are still some things I can't quite handle."

"Seems normal to me." Her hand was still in his, and he squeezed it slightly. "One more truth?"

"Sure."

"I love you, Sabrina. I'm not asking you to say it back, and I'm not trying to rope you into any sort of relationship. I just need you to know, and I need to know it, too." He didn't think he'd like to admit it, but it was as though the more they talked to each other, the better he felt. Max could feel his tiger leaning against hers, their souls blending and melding.

Sabrina reached up and touched his cheek, her fingers drifting down to run along the angle of his jaw. Her eyes were soft and bright as she studied his face, focusing intently on his lips. "Max, I—"

"Don't. Don't say it. Even if you think you mean it. I don't want it to just be a reaction. I want it to be real." And he did want it, more than anything he'd ever wanted in the world. But it had to be freely given and not just taken.

Sabrina nodded solemnly and let her hand fall. But a moment later, her lips were on his. She wasn't telling him, she was showing him. She kissed him fully and passionately, bringing her hands up into his hair and digging her fingernails into his scalp as her tongue danced with his. They could've talked all night long and have never been able to say what they felt as precisely as they could by doing this.

Max pulled her onto his lap, feeling her legs slide down on either side of his hips as their kiss deepened. He let his hands rove over her, feeling her curves. She was soft and comforting in all the right places, unyielding and demanding in the others. Her body was just like her personality, and Max knew this was so much more than a physical relationship.

He moved his lips from her mouth and trailed them down her neck to her collarbone. His fingers worked of their own accord against the buttons of her shirt, longing to remove the modest garments and see the woman he knew was hiding underneath. Her breasts strained the material, and she let out a low moan when he finally freed her from the confines of it. Max wasted no time in reaching for the clasp of her bra, longing to feel the heaviness of her breasts against him.

Sabrina's hands were cool but determined as she found the hem of his shirt and lifted it over his head. His arousal had already been building, but feeling her skin against his was enough to drive him wild. The tiger inside him was desperate, and he could feel Sabrina's beast reacting the same way. Their actions quickened as they shed all the garments that society demanded, leaving a deflated pile of clothing next to them in the grass as they experienced each other fully.

She sank down onto his shaft, her warmth spreading through him like light as she slowly rocked back and forth. Silhouetted against the starry sky, Sabrina was a goddess he gladly worshipped. Max groaned with the satisfaction of simply being there with her like this. He skimmed his palms along the smooth lines of her thighs, the roundness of each hip, and the sweet seduction of her waist before finding her breasts once again. He pulled her down toward him, wrapping his warm lips around a nipple and flicking it with his tongue.

"Oh, Max," she whispered. "I forgot just how good you felt." Her breathing was coming faster, and he could feel the motion reflected in the rest of her body.

He wanted this to last forever. He wanted the entire Earth to stop moving so that he might revel in this moment with her for all eternity. But their bodies had greater demands. He cupped her soft backside, feeling her movement against him as she rode him harder. His hips worked in unison, encouraging the parting and meeting of their bodies that wound a ball of tension inside each of their bodies. When he brought his mouth up to hers and felt the depth in her kiss, her tongue against his, the inside of her body pulsing around him, he knew there could be no more.

His body gave as hers gladly took, their minds and their souls and their physical bodies pulsating against each other. Sabrina's toes curled against his legs as she rode him harder and took what she needed, giving him just as much. Max grunted as he gave her everything he had.

They cuddled up together, naked in the starlight. Max cradled her body against his. Everything about this moment was perfect: the feel of her skin, the scent of her hair, and the deep satisfaction of knowing that at least for one night, he'd been able to do exactly what he needed to do.

"Max?" she asked, her voice vibrating against his neck where she'd buried her face against his chest and shoulder.

"Hmm?" Even the sound of her saying his name was enough to move the earth beneath him.

"I do love you. Whether you like it or not, whether you want to hear it or not, I love you."

It was just like her to say it that way, and he loved her all the more for it.

"I love you, too, kitten."

10

"ARE YOU READY FOR THIS?"

Sabrina turned away from the mirror to find Max standing in her bedroom doorway. He'd insisted on staying in the living room overnight, wanting things to be as professional as possible until the trial was over. The moment they'd shared on that remote hillside had been utterly magical and they both knew they'd have to talk about it again at some point, but for now, it was easier not to get too wrapped up in the possibilities.

"Yeah. I've just got to get my shoes on."

"I don't mean physically ready, although that's important, too." Max glanced at his watch. "I mean inside. I know this case has been difficult for you."

Sabrina crossed the room to her closet for a pair of Chelsea boots. It was strange getting ready for a shifter trial, since they didn't happen in typical courtrooms. Had this been something the humans were in charge of, she'd be putting on her best pantsuit. As it was, she wore a loose flannel shirt and skinny jeans. Max had told her to prepare for a hike. "It has been," she admitted, "but I'm actually kind of excited to get it over with. I won't have to dread it anymore. They'll call me to the stand, I'll describe the wolf I saw in the stairwell, and then it'll be all over with." When she turned away from her closet, Max was right there behind her.

His brow was creased with concern. "That's not necessarily true."

"Why not?" She stepped to the side to get around him.

Max sighed. "Because, Sabrina, you're giving a testimony that could potentially convict a man of murder. Depending on what connections he has or how powerful he may be, you could still be in danger."

Sabrina opened her mouth to argue, but no words came out at first. How had she not thought of that before? Perhaps because she hadn't taken the initial death threats all that seriously, and once the wolf in the park had let her know otherwise, she hadn't wanted to think about it anymore. "I suppose that's possible. I'll deal with it when it comes." She finished slipping her boots on and rose quickly from the bench at the foot of her bed.

Max caught her arm, his fingers gently closing around hers. "Sabrina, please. I know you're good at stuffing everything down inside. I actually kind of admire you for it. I do the same on my good days with PTSD. But there's also reality to consider. You can't just be cavalier about this and risk your life."

She shot him a look, her fear making her angry. "Are you sure you can handle being my protector during this trial? Or do we need to call in someone with a cooler head?"

His face transformed from one of worry to one of displeasure. "I'm fine. And there's no way in hell that anyone is going to be at your side today other than me."

"I don't need you getting all overprotective." Sabrina pulled her arm out of his grasp and headed for the front door. In the back of her mind, she knew she was being unreasonable. But at the moment, she just wanted this all to be over with.

Max's footsteps were heavy as he followed her out to the elevator. "I have reason to believe that this trial might not go the way you imagine."

She shook her head. "It doesn't matter what they do. All I have to do is give my statement."

"That's true to a point, but I think there might be a lot more to this than just some random wolf who wanted to kill Rutledge. I took the liberty of doing some research on the shifters in the area and—"

"You took the liberty?" she repeated testily as she

climbed in the chopper. "Max, you can't just intrude on my life like that. It's not your business."

"It is my business when someone's trying to kill the woman I love." His dark eyes were ablaze as he whipped his head to look at her from the pilot's seat.

It was the first time the word had been mentioned since their tryst on the hillside two nights ago, and it made a lump rise in Sabrina's throat. She hadn't realized she was putting up such walls against him until he said it, and she could feel them slowly sinking back down. But once again, Max was keeping her from shoving away all the emotions that were too hard to deal with. It was time to get back under control. "Okay," she said simply.

"Let me at least tell you the information I came across. There's no reason you shouldn't go in as fully prepared as possible."

"Fine." Sabrina didn't think there was anything Max could tell her that would make a difference, but if he could get it out and then leave her alone, then it would be a worthy sacrifice.

He rattled off some random facts about the shifters involved and their clans while Sabrina watched the ground whisk by. The rest of the ride was silent, and when Max landed in a remote field, Sabrina didn't bother questioning him. She followed him on foot along a narrow path that at times didn't look like a path at all. He seemed to know where he was going, and if he got them lost, then it'd be his fault.

Instead, they arrived on a large clearing in the middle of the woods. A sizeable gathering had already assembled there. President Whiteside was near the opposite edge, chatting with a small cluster of people. Sabrina felt a wave of anxiety turn her skin clammy.

Max put an arm around her waist. "We just need to find a spot along the edge and wait until you're called," he murmured in her ear.

"I'm sorry," she muttered as they settled onto the grass. "I wasn't very nice earlier. This is making me a lot more nervous than it should."

"That's understandable," he soothed, rubbing his warm hand across her back. "Do you hear the stream?"

Sabrina listened intently, filtering out the din of other voices until she found the gentle splashing of water. "Yes. What about it?"

"Concentrate on that. It might make you feel better to ground yourself in something that has nothing to do with the proceedings. I do it sometimes."

She smiled at him. There was something much more comforting she wanted to ground herself in, but now wasn't the time to say it out loud.

The assemblage hushed as President Whiteside stepped to the center of the clearing. "Ladies and gentlemen of the shifter community, it's time to begin." He was a noble-looking man with hair as white as his name, and he stretched out his arms as he waited for complete silence. "Thank you. And I also thank all of you for gathering here today. Let us work together for swift and fair proceedings. As you all know, black bear Isaac Rutledge was killed a few weeks ago. Today we shall investigate the circumstances of his death, as asked by the surviving members of his clan."

Sabrina turned her attention away from both the stream and Max in order to focus on the trial. She listened closely as members of Isaac's clan gave short speeches that not only described what they'd seen at the hotel on that fateful night, but that also honored the former Alpha as a good and caring man. While Isaac's character wasn't being called into question, it was their way of honoring their dead. The gathering approved of this ancient tradition, nodding their agreement in all the right places.

There were no lawyers in attendance. Everyone was given the opportunity not only to speak their minds, but to call others into question. Sabrina fully expected someone to ask her questions before it was officially her turn to speak, but she was startled when it was the very man accused of killing Isaac who did so.

The wolf stepped into the center of the circle and whispers rippled through the crowd. He was an older man, perhaps in his fifties, his skin deeply tanned from his time in the wilds, his hair bleached by both the sun and age. His deep blue eyes skimmed the crowd and he held up his hand. "Please. There is no need to whisper. I already know what you're saying about me and I don't blame you. My name is Hugh Taber, and believe it or not, I was a very good friend of Isaac's."

Another wave of low whispers made its way around the circle.

"Isaac and I had known each other for a long time," he continued when the noise had died down once again, "and there's nothing that pains me more than knowing he's no longer on this earth with us. He was a good man, one who wanted positive change for all shifters in our community. But even with as much work as he did with the conclave, we both knew it was difficult for some to accept that he and I were as close as we were. We often met in secret, choosing to keep the focus on the friendship that we shared instead of what everyone else thought about it."

Sabrina tipped her head. She'd heard of some prejudice amongst the shifters, but she hadn't seen any of it firsthand.

"And while I could stand up here all day and tell you how innocent I am, I choose instead to let someone else do it for me. Dr. Sabrina Barrett, would you please join me?"

Glancing uncertainly at Max, Sabrina stood and stepped forward. She could feel every tendon in her body tighten. If this was the same wolf she'd seen in that stairwell, then she didn't want to be anywhere near him. But she had no choice.

"I'm right here," Max reassured her. He was on his feet, too, but he remained on the edge of the clearing as required by court protocol.

Hugh gazed benevolently at her with those unwavering sapphire eyes as she came to stand before him. "I understand you were the first person to see Isaac after his death."

Sabrina was painfully aware of the distance between herself and this man and how quickly he could close it if he chose to. "I believe so."

"You're not certain?" He folded his hands in front of his chest and bent forward slightly. He was a tall man, and it made him look slightly less intimidating.

Still, Sabrina was on her guard. "I didn't actually see him die, so I can't say."

"Ah." Hugh nodded knowingly. "And since you didn't see him die, you can't say that I was the one who killed him. Correct?"

She didn't like the way he was guiding these questions, and she pursed her lips.

President Whiteside cleared his throat and stepped closer. "Perhaps we should simply let Dr. Barrett tell us what she *did* see." He raised an eyebrow to encourage her.

Sabrina took the cue. "It was getting late and the people in the room below me were getting loud. The management wasn't doing anything about it, so I decided I'd go talk to them myself. The stairs were right there, so I took them instead of the elevator. When I opened the door, I saw Isaac lying at the bottom of the stairs. A large wolf stood over him."

"And what did this wolf look like?" Hugh asked. "Like this?" His jaw bumped out as his ears grew furry and pointed. His shoulders jerked as his other form continued to take over, his knees cracking and bending as he became the exact same wolf Sabrina had seen on that fateful night.

Her throat was so tight, Sabrina could hardly get any air through to her lungs. "Yes," she squeaked out. "That was him."

The wolf eyed her, his eyes the same blue they'd been when he stood before her as a human. His lips curled in a wolfish grin, and he shifted back quickly to the man on trial. "And did you actually see me kill Isaac?"

Sabrina swallowed. She pulled that night to her mind, trying to sort out all the details. These were the images she'd shoved aside as much as possible to save herself from having to deal with them until it was time for the trial, but they came charging back with complete clarity. She could see the wolf standing next to Isaac's body, nudging his ribs with his nose. He stared up at Sabrina for a moment, intent and focused, before disappearing through the side exit. "No."

"Ah. That makes perfect sense," Hugh replied with a smile, "because I didn't."

"Then who did?" someone shouted from the outside of the circle.

"Please," President Whiteside said, holding up one hand for silence, "let's be sure to observe the proper rules."

Sabrina rubbed the back of her neck, thinking. She hadn't been officially dismissed yet, and it felt awkward to stand there in front of everyone, but the question from the crowd had been a valid one. Somehow, she'd managed not to think about it much. She'd done exactly what she did when at work or when she was dealing with something uncomfortable and stuffed it all down. This time, she'd done such a good job that she'd deceived herself into believing her work was done with the simple testimony.

But it hadn't been all that simple. Sabrina glanced across the clearing to Max. He stood at the very outer edge, poised to act if anything should go wrong. He was her protector. He drove her crazy, but sometimes it was in all the good ways. He made her remember that she had to feel things, whether she wanted to or not. And he'd also made sure, even though it irritated her to no end, that she knew everything possible about this trial before she went in.

"The former Alpha died without heirs," she whispered.

"I'm sorry. What was that?" President Whiteside took a step closer. "You'll have to speak up so everyone can hear you."

She wasn't prepared to spout her theories in front of the whole assembly, and she was only just now putting them together. Sabrina met Max's eyes and swore she could feel his thoughts in her mind. "I said the former Alpha died without heirs. The Alpha of Isaac's clan, that is."

The president tipped his silver head slightly. "Yes. And why is that significant?"

"Isaac was voted in as Alpha to replace him, but there were probably others who felt they deserved the position. It could've been someone within his own clan."

Hugh smiled. "I'm afraid even I have to say that's nothing but speculation."

"It makes sense, though. I'd spoken with Isaac earlier that night. We were there to talk about the shifter hospital we wanted to open, but he was distracted. He told me there were issues happening within his clan that he needed to address, and that he would have to get back home soon before things got out of hand. He didn't want to go into any details, but he was worried."

A man stood up on the other side of the clearing. Sabrina immediately recognized Russell. She hadn't expected him to be there. His face was serious as he stepped forward toward her. She'd come to trust him in the few days he'd spent with her, but his sudden appearance made her nervous. "She's right," he announced. "For those of you who don't know, I'm Russell Barclay. I'm in Isaac's clan. I can confirm that we'd been having some problems. Nothing had been right since our former Alpha died and our clan was split on who should be taking over."

President Whiteside was frowning. "Russell, perhaps you could tell us who has taken over the clan now that Mr. Rutledge is no longer with us."

"Ian Saunders," Russell answered. "He'd been angry when Isaac won the vote and took over the clan. He didn't like the way Isaac operated, always wanting to follow the law and keep things peaceful. It was profitable enough for him."

"You lying bastard!" The shout rang out through the clearing as a man came crashing through the brush. "I only wanted what was best for us. It was those bastard wolves who did this. And I happen to know that yet another wolf tried to kill this young lady here before she could give her testimony. To me, there's no question the wolf is the guilty party."

"The one who tried to kill me was a hired mercenary who didn't belong to a pack," Sabrina countered. It was all so obvious now. "And you were there at the hotel that night, too. I remember seeing you argue with Isaac."

Before she could question herself for calling out a man on murder, Ian had shifted. He charged forward, his bear body making the ground shake. He showed his white teeth in a roar and he was coming straight for her.

Sabrina didn't have time to think, but she didn't need to. She let go of her human self and let her tiger take over. She was long and lean and muscular, but Ian outweighed her by a long shot. Sabrina held her ground, her tail twitching. He was coming for her. There was no point in running.

She dodged to the side at the last moment. His weight and his inertia kept him going for a moment before he could stop and turn. She took advantage of the moment and pounced on his back, her claws and teeth sinking into his fur. Ian roared, his lips curling back, and swiped at her uselessly. Sabrina hung on, but he was strong. The bear swung his body to the side, flinging her off.

Sabrina rolled through the dirt and was back on her feet again. Something had taken over, something she hadn't let out in a very long time. This wasn't just hiding her emotions or choosing not to think about things. This was her true tiger soul, the warrior inside her who wouldn't let this bastard win, no matter what. A deep roar emerged from her throat and rattled through the air, telling the bear to bring it on.

He did. Ian had recovered just as quickly, despite the blood that now ran down through his dark fur. She was quicker, but he was stronger. Sabrina was vaguely aware of shouts and chaos that had broken out around them, but she couldn't worry about it now. She had her own fight.

They circled each other as they exchanged blows and searched for the chance to get to the most vulnerable spots on their enemies. Sabrina raked her claws across his face, drawing more blood that dripped from his muzzle. It only infuriated him. When he attacked again, he truly had the advantage of his weight. The bear pinned her to the ground and closed his mouth around her throat. She dug into his underbelly with her back claws. Her front paws smacked uselessly as the world began to go dark.

A blur of deep orange fur sailed through the air. Sabrina thought it might be a dream, because it didn't make sense to her muddled mind. She needed oxygen. But then the bear was gone. She was staring only at a bright blue patch of sky, the treetops dancing in a circle around it. Air rushed back into her lungs, and she gasped with relief.

She rolled over onto her side just in time to see a very familiar tiger finishing off a black bear. Blood stained the paler patches of fur near his belly and legs. Several others had shifted, but they stood back from the fray, waiting.

President Whiteside swam into her vision. His brow was creased as he looked from the bloody scene to Sabrina. "It's over. Everything is all right now."

———

Sabrina, back in her human body, felt exhausted. She leaned heavily against Max where they sat in the shade, wondering if she would ever catch her breath again. Everyone who'd attended the trial had been kept at the clearing while President Whiteside sorted everything out and passed his official conviction on Ian Saunders. He was dead now, but everyone agreed that Ian's actions had proven his involvement in Isaac's death.

Now, President Whiteside walked over to them. "Dr. Barrett, you're free to go. I appreciate your coming here today, and I particularly appreciate everything you did to find the true criminal. It would've been most unfortunate if we'd punished an innocent man."

She gave a weak smile of relief. "I had some help."

Whether he knew what she meant or not, the president turned to Max. "I have to thank you and your team as well. I felt better knowing our star witness was under the care of a neutral party. Not that I didn't trust Russell. In fact, I plan to put in a word with his clan that he'd make a good candidate for their next Alpha. But I still think this was the best option, and I'll be keeping your contact information should we need you in the future."

Max stood, helping Sabrina to her feet before he shook the president's hand. "I appreciate the opportunity."

"I think everything should be under control. You should be safe on your way out. Contact me if you need anything. And Dr. Barrett, I look forward to talking with you further about the possibility of a new hospital."

She'd just been through a terrifying day, but she had to smile. That was the most promising thing she'd heard yet about the specialized medical center. "Thank you, Mr. President."

Sabrina was very aware of Max at her side as they

headed through the woods. "Thank you for what you did today," she said quietly. "You saved my life. Again."

"And I'd do it a thousand times more." He put his hand on the small of her back as they stepped through a narrow passage between two trees. "I'm proud of you, you know. Just a few nights ago, you hardly remembered your inner animal. Today, you tapped into her so quickly, I could hardly keep track of your shift. And you held your own against Ian for longer than most would have. I was trying to get to you sooner, but there was so much disorder as soon as the fight broke out."

She caught his hand in her own. "I hope that's not any sort of apology, especially since I owe you one. I was horrible to you this morning."

"You already apologized for that," he reminded her.

"Yes, but I feel like I need to again. And also to say I'm sorry for not wanting to listen to you about the other shifters involved in the trial. I didn't think it was relevant at the time, and I lashed out. But it was all the information you told me on the ride here that made me realize exactly what had happened. Ian just happened to confirm it."

His fingers tightened around hers. "At least it's all over now."

The helicopter was in sight now. Max would drop her off at her apartment, and then his job was officially over. There was no telling what life would bring them, and it filled her with a sense of longing.

Max must've been feeling it, too. He halted in his tracks and tugged on her hand to swing her around against him. "Sabrina, I meant what I said the other night. I really do love you. I loved you when we were together, and I didn't stop even after I left. I thought I could get over you, but I absolutely can't."

Warmth flooded her body as she sank against his chest. "I love you too, Max. I don't know why we've both tried to fight it so much, but I think it's time we stopped."

"Sounds good to me." He captured her mouth in his and pulled her close. His hands were possessive as they wrapped around her body and skimmed her backside.

Their rendezvous on that lonely nighttime hillside was still fresh on her mind, and her body remembered it as well. She felt her core ignite at the mere thought, and his hardness pressing against her didn't do anything to deter it. "I don't know if I can wait until we get back to the city," she whispered against his lips.

A low growl emitted from his throat as he brought her down to the grassy ground behind the helicopter. They peeled off their clothing, desperately trying to get enough of each other. In another lifetime, Sabrina was vaguely aware of how she would've felt being out there in the wild, stripped naked and tangled up with a man where anyone who might come through could see them. Now, she didn't care. No, it was more than that. It was what she wanted. Her skin soaked up the warmth of the sun and of Max's body, yet the cool breeze filtered it away. She was untamed and free, no longer held down by the constrictions of society and her career.

She ran her hands from the dark stubble on Max's jaw and down into the thick hair on his chest, feeling his heart thunder beneath her palms. She moved her explorations further down to find his rippling abs and strong waist, then skimmed down his thighs as they pressed against her. She closed her hand around his hardness that was waiting for her, feeling the velvety skin and his pulse throbbing underneath it.

He closed his eyes as his hands wrapped around her hips. "Sabrina..." he breathed.

She moved back, pulling herself away from his grip until she could dip her head and take him into her mouth. Sabrina felt tentative at first, knowing this was something she wanted to do, yet uncertain of exactly what he wanted. But he responded with his hands tangling in her hair, his hips pulsing against her, and deep, growling moans issuing from his throat. Knowing he was turned on made heat ripple through her core, exciting her even more.

"Come here." His hands were strong as they pulled her up, moving her around as though she weighed nothing. Sabrina expected him to settle her onto his shaft, ready for the two of them to join once again, but he flung her further so that she straddled his lips.

She braced herself on the grassy ground beneath them

as he gripped her backside and held her against him, working his tongue thoroughly over her most sensitive areas. Over the last week, she'd found so many reasons to miss what the two of them used to have together, but she'd forgotten just how much she missed what he could do to her body. Her legs and arms trembled as he worked her over, the wet heat of his tongue shooting through her nervous system and constricting her lungs.

Finally, when she couldn't take any more, she pushed herself back toward his eager cock, breathing a sigh of bliss and ecstasy as his member sank into her. Sabrina felt her inner tiger rumbling with pleasure as his thrusts picked up speed, bringing them both to their peaks. As the intense pleasure coiled in her belly, her walls clenched around his thickness, making him cry out with his release.

There was no doubt in her mind that they belonged together, not just physically, but in every other way, too. They were fated to each other, both mentally and emotionally.

And she knew she couldn't be complete without him.

11

THE THREAT TO HER LIFE WAS OVER, BUT SABRINA WAS HAPPY she still got to ride to work with Max every day. She glanced over at the pilot with a smile. "What do you think of the new job?"

He smiled, something that happened a lot more often these days. "It's fucking great. I can't believe I never thought to work for an air ambulance company before. It's so much more satisfying than schlepping douchebags around all day. I'm still getting used to the uniform, though. It's a bit bright."

Sabrina looked appreciatively at the red and white jumpsuit he'd exchanged his t-shirt and jeans for. "I happen to like it."

"Good. Then I'll let you take it off of me later." He hesitated for a moment. "I also have to admit this job has been good for my PTSD."

It was something that had always hung over him, something she was still learning to be more understanding about. It was difficult to do when he didn't like talking about it, and she lifted a brow in surprise now. "How's that?"

He lifted one shoulder and let it fall. "There's something about saving people's lives with my skills that makes me feel like I'm making up for everything that happened overseas. I like it."

"I'm glad." Sabrina smiled. She wouldn't push him any further on the subject unless he wanted to talk about it. They were a couple again, and communication was important, but she'd promised herself she'd be more understanding of exactly who he was and what he needed.

Max seemed to have taken on the same ideas when it came to her. He never complained when she had to work late due to various meetings or a surgery that went long. But he was always waiting to hear about her day or just relax with her on the couch when they both finally got home.

"Are you ready for your big day?"

Sabrina smoothed down the skirt of her dress. She wanted to look both professional and stylish. "I think so. I'm excited, but I'm incredibly nervous."

"You don't have anything to worry about. They love

you." Max landed expertly on the roof of the hospital. "You go on ahead while I get this shut down. I'll be there soon."

Half an hour later, Sabrina stood in front of a new set of double doors. A piece of fabric had been draped over the sign for the new ward, and the scent of fresh paint lingered in the air. Dr. Corton and the rest of the board were in attendance, as well as several other doctors and administrators. Even the local news media had shown up. Sabrina didn't have to put on a fake smile for the cameras. This was one of the moments she'd been waiting for.

Dr. Corton cleared his throat, and the small crowd that'd gathered fell into silence. "Ladies and gentlemen, today we're opening a new wing of the hospital. Not only does it boast the most advanced equipment and the most highly trained surgeons, capable of delivering reconstruction surgery for some of the most complicated cases in the world, but also the heart and soul of a caring team. I'm proud to say that this will not be a place where patients have to rely on expensive insurance or draining their savings accounts."

Appreciative applause came from the crowd.

Sabrina scanned the assembly, easily finding Max in the back of the crowd. He didn't want to be standing next to her, beaming for the cameras, but he had his own way of being there for her. Her cheeks warmed as he winked at her.

"And now, I'd like to give the honor of the ribbon-cutting to the person responsible for making this all happen, Dr. Sabrina Barrett." Dr. Corton handed Sabrina a ridiculously huge pair of scissors.

It was silly, but there was no greater honor than taking the shiny gold scissors and snipping the ribbon that'd been stretched across the doors. She was even further surprised, however, when Dr. Corton tugged on the fabric covering the sign. The covering rippled to the floor, revealing her name right there on the wall.

"Ladies and gentlemen," Dr. Corton intoned, "I give you the Barrett Reconstructive Center!"

Sabrina stared at the sign, pressing one hand to her mouth as she fought back tears.

"You deserve it," Dr. Corton said with a wink.

The rest of the day flew by. She not only had the new surgery wing that she so desperately wanted, but Sabrina had officially made her mark in the medical field. When she headed up to the roof at the end of the night, ready to head home, she slowed when she noticed she didn't hear the sound of rotors. She furrowed her brow as she clutched the doorknob, hoping everything was all right.

When she stepped outside, Max was indeed waiting there for her, but he'd changed out of his uniform and into a suit. The air ambulance was there behind him, but he hadn't yet started it up. He leaned against it, but he straightened and came toward her. "There's the woman of the hour."

She beamed. "I'm glad you were there. You strengthen me, even from across a room."

Max pulled her into his arms and pressed a slow kiss to her forehead. "I'm proud of you, Sabrina. You've worked hard for this. Not only did you get the new unit opened, but they broke ground for the shifter hospital yesterday. You're amazing."

Her eyes could focus only on his handsome face and her own galloping heart. "Thank you."

He took her by the hand. "You deserve a nice dinner. Come on." Max led her around the other side of the helicopter, where a table for two waited for them. Gleaming china dishes held lobster and steak, and a bottle of champagne sat in an ice bucket near the taper candles.

"Oh, Max! This is incredible!"

He put an arm around her. "I wanted to take you out someplace nice to celebrate, but I decided there weren't any restaurants around that were good enough for you. Besides, there's something I wanted to talk to you about, and it's sort of a private matter."

She whipped her head to look up at him, but she saw nothing but warmth in his soft brown eyes. "What's that?"

He stepped back and knelt in front of her, producing a small black box from his pocket. His fingers shook ever so slightly as he opened it to reveal a blue diamond solitaire. "Kitten, will you marry me?"

It was a beautiful scene with the table set, a gorgeous

hunk of a tiger asking for her hand, and even a scattering of bright stars that the city lights couldn't drown out, but tears blurred her eyes. They really did have a chance to start all over again. "There's nothing I'd like more."

The ring was cool as he slipped it over her finger, and as they celebrated the beginning of their new life together, he pulled her into a long kiss that made them both forget about the dinner waiting for them.

THE END

FATED TO THE SOLDIER FOX

SPECIAL OPS SHIFTERS: DALLAS FORCE

1

JACK DENTON'S MOTORCYCLE RUMBLED TO A HALT BENEATH him as he pulled through the alley and parked. He ran a hand through his dark hair as he took off his helmet and shook his head. *Leave it up to Winston to pick someplace like this to meet up.* The Basement was one of the seediest bars in Dallas, although that hadn't stopped people from showing up, even on a Wednesday night. Jack watched as two women dressed in short dresses and tall boots held onto each other and giggled on their way down the damp concrete stairs toward the bar's door. Two men followed them, waggling their eyebrows at each other and exchanging a few friendly punches. Jack sighed. It was going to be an interesting night, for sure. His inner fox was on alert, ready for trouble should it arise.

The interior of the bar was just as dim as the alley he'd

parked in, with only enough lights over the counter to make sure the drinks were mixed correctly—mostly. The tables were battered high-tops with mismatched wood, illuminated by old beer signs. Sawdust littered the dark floor, and a flatscreen on the back wall broadcasted a college game, even though no one was paying attention.

Jack paused at the bar. "Guinness, please."

"I've only got that in a bottle, mac." The dim light emphasized the deep scar that ran down the bartender's cheek, and he had an odd hunch to his back that made his shrug look more like a spasm.

"That's fine." He'd trust a bottle over a draft in a shit-hole like that anyway. Taking the last stool at the bar, where he could keep his back to the wall, Jack surveyed the room. The guys he'd followed inside had found the girls they were after, and the four of them now sat at a table near the back, talking and laughing. A scraggly man swayed drunkenly as he attempted a game of darts, but he only succeeded in adding more holes to the walls. Two old men drank in silence off to the right, killing time until The Basement closed and they'd have to find some other place to tie one on. Nowhere did he see the man he was looking for, but that didn't surprise him.

"You waitin' for someone?"

Jack turned to find the bartender watching him, and he quickly looked away again to avoid staring at that grisly scar. "Nah. Just having a beer." He raised his bottle in the air and took a sip.

"I don't think so." The man folded his arms on the dingy oak surface in front of him. "I see all sorts of people come in and out of here. They're all looking for something. Maybe it's sex, maybe it's just a chance to forget the hard times. But you, you're looking for someone."

Squinting, Jack dared to study the man's face more closely. His eyes were the wrong color, as dim and dark as the bar itself, but there was a light behind them he should've recognized right away. All the prosthetics and makeup skills in the world couldn't quite change him completely, though he'd done a damn good job. "Winston?"

"The name's Buzz," he replied with a wink.

"You son of a bitch!" Jack extended his hand to greet his old friend. "When you said you wanted to meet up, I somehow thought I'd get to see your real face. I should've known better."

"I like to make sure I stay in practice." Winston allowed his true voice to come through, an even tenor that befitted the Shakespearean theater more than that dive bar. He was what the movie industry might call a master of disguise. He'd spied on more royalty and government officials than anyone could imagine, and he always got away with it. Winston was remarkably good with prosthetics and optical illusions to make himself look like someone else entirely, and he'd mastered the art of charm and appeal. He was the sort of man that everyone loved, yet no one really knew.

"But you're still working, aren't you? I'd heard you still had some sort of gig after you left the Army." Jack and Winston had worked together closely on the Grey Fox team, gathering intelligence by any means necessary. Those were the good old days, in many respects.

"That's actually what I wanted to talk to you about. Hang on." Winston—or rather, Buzz—made his way to the other end of the bar to serve a couple of cranberry spritzers to the two women, who were waving flirtatiously over their shoulders to the men. He'd slipped right back into the character of the bartender, with his gruff voice and odd stature.

"Only you could go from playing a prince to the Hunchback of Notre Dame in a matter of milliseconds," Jack remarked when his friend returned. "I don't think you have to worry about losing your touch anytime soon."

"I'm hoping you haven't lost your touch, either. You were quite the golden boy back in the day, Jack. I'm sure you haven't forgotten, with all those medals hanging on your wall. That's got to feel pretty good."

Jack frowned into his beer. Winston wasn't entirely wrong. He'd joined the Army right after high school. He'd wanted to go into IT, but his parents' income was too low to pay for tuition out of pocket, yet too high to qualify for most student loans and grants. That problem had been taken care of when a local recruiter showed up at the high school to administer the ASVAB test. Jack had done well enough that the recruiter specifically sought him out to talk about his options, and as soon as he'd dangled that college tuition carrot before him, Jack had been sold.

There was no doubt that Jack had enjoyed his time in the military. He'd found a sort of camaraderie that he hadn't experienced in high school. The training—both physical and mental—was stimulating and inspiriting. He'd been convinced he'd found his true calling in life when he'd begun working on antiterrorism with the department. Before he knew it, he was helping to lock away some of the world's greatest enemies.

"I don't exactly keep them on display," he answered. "It was nice to be acknowledged, but that's not why I did it."

"Oh, of course not." Winston waved a hand in the air. "You did it all because of that sweet, noble heart inside your chest. Blah, blah, blah. You're so boring, Jack."

This was typical Winston, and Jack refused to be offended by it. He knew the game. "All right. Just tell me what you want."

"Who says I want anything? Maybe I just called an old friend to catch up. The world is a lonely place these days, with everyone staring at their phones instead of actually talking to each other. People don't have real relationships anymore, you know." Winston poured himself a shot of whiskey and sipped it.

Jack let out a short laugh. "And if someone has a relationship with *you*, how do they know who they're actually with? I don't think I've seen you look the same way twice."

"Don't flatter me. You'll make my head explode." He took another sip and let out a sigh as it burned. "Tell me what you're up to these days, Jack."

"A little of this, a little of that. I stay busy." The truth was that Jack had been recruited to the Special Ops Shifter Force, an elite group of veteran Special Ops soldiers who also happened to be shifters. Their true animal instincts were a major factor in their successes as they tackled problems that the human world usually didn't know about and the rest of the shifter world wasn't able to handle. It'd been a good transition for him, one that had allowed him to use his natural talent for intelligence as well as belong to a group of men just like himself.

"Well, that's vague." Winston frowned as he poured himself another glass of whiskey. "Does staying busy involve any real work? I have this dreary vision of you sitting behind some desk in a corporate cubicle somewhere, answering tech questions over the phone from housewives who just don't understand how the internet works."

"I'm not just a knob turner," Jack replied. "I know my way around plenty of gadgets, but I've got more of a life going on than that."

"A girl?"

"Not exactly." Life with the SOS Force didn't give him much time for dating, or at least that was what he told himself. He simply didn't have the chance to get out and meet anyone when he was busy taking down the rogues of the shifter community.

Winston stuck out his bottom lip. "Poor little Jackie is all alone? That's sad."

Jack gave him a punch in the arm. "You've always been a pain in the ass, Winston."

"But you love me for it. Seriously, Jack. I think it's about time you settled down." He put his glass on the bar with a gentle thunk and looked his former comrade in the eye. "After you help me out, that is."

"I knew there would be something," Jack admitted. "There's always a catch with you." He said it good-humoredly, though. That was just the way Winston was, and Jack had come to accept it a long time ago.

"I do have that favor to cash in, you know," the bartender reminded him.

"Damn. That must mean this is a doozy." Jack instantly knew what he was talking about. The mission was supposed to be a straightforward one: a simple extraction of an ambassador that would have gone much more smoothly if they could have done it without a show of force. Things had gone sideways, though, and Jack had soon found himself stuck behind military lines. With the small contingent he had with him, their limited weapons, and the surrounding forces, there was little hope of getting stateside again. Winston had shown up as the sheik himself, ordering his troops to stand down and giving his blessing for the ambassador and his entourage—Jack included—to leave.

"You could say that. Just a sec." He skulked back to the other end of the bar, this time to serve a few cheap beers to the older men, taking his time and making Jack wait.

"Before you go into too much detail, you should know that I've already got a job," Jack said. He didn't mind helping an old friend, but he couldn't abandon the Force. They were a small unit, and even if they went on solo missions, they always relied on the others for backup.

"Don't turn me down before you've even heard me out." Winston pushed another bottle of beer at him. "There are plenty of times I could've called in this favor, but I was waiting for something I really needed you for. Something that required your specific skills, not just any old intelligence officer."

Jack finished off the first beer and reached for the second one, suspicious but intrigued. "I might regret it, but I'm listening."

Winston smiled. "I knew you would. I'm working with the Department of Homeland Security now. Still the same sort of stuff, keeping track of all the would-be terrorists and knocking them out as soon as we have enough proof to justify it. You know the drill."

"Sure." That didn't sound any different than what he had done as a Grey Fox, but it was probably a bit safer if it was taking place on their own territory. Missions in the Middle East had a whole different element of danger to them.

"There's one we've been tracking in Illinois. He goes by the name of Ben Jones, but it's just a cover. It's the sort of situation we see all the time these days: he slowly recruits followers, builds his cell around him, brainwashes them into thinking there's some common enemy they all have to fight against to preserve their freedom, even though they all have a lot more freedoms than most people everywhere else in the world... Same old dog and pony show."

"That doesn't sound like anything too extraordinary," Jack commented. He watched as the two women left with the two men.

Winston watched them, too, waiting until they were out the door before he continued. "It's not, except that I have reason to believe this Ben is a shifter."

Jack set his beer down with a thump, the liquid sloshing inside. "You're shitting me. Does the DHS know?" He was more than interested now. Jack took it as a personal offense that anyone should try to harm innocent civilians, no matter what country they were from. Knowing that a shifter was committing such an atrocity—or preparing to—was that much more infuriating.

"I shit you not, and no, they don't know. It's mostly my

own suspicions, but I've seen a lot of animal traffic in the area when we're looking for humans, if you know what I mean. Trouble is, I can't exactly report it to upper management. I'm defying the very laws of our country by keeping this secret from the DHS, but I think you and I can both agree that the very last thing we need is for the government to find out about us." Winston often tended toward theatrics, but at that moment, Jack could tell he was dead serious.

And he couldn't blame him. It was a subject that had come up more than once during his time with the Army. What would happen if the military found out who they really were; if the wrong person happened to stumble upon one of them as they morphed from human to animal and back again? Would they keep them captive for experiments? Rule them as abominations? Ban them from the country they'd been born in? It was all possible, considering everything history had taught them. All shifters, service people or not, had made an unspoken agreement that they would never reveal themselves to the wrong person.

Jack rubbed his thumb down the side of his beer bottle, thinking. "That certainly complicates things."

"It does. Ben Jones, I believe, is not only a shifter himself, but is recruiting others. At this point, we don't know exactly what he's planning. My concern is that it will not only harm innocent people, but expose us." He tapped the bar for emphasis.

Jack rubbed the back of his neck. "I still don't quite see how this involves me."

Winston slapped the dark wood. "Ah, that's the part you really want to know. Of course. The Department of Homeland Security is determined to take this guy down. We're convinced he's a threat, but like I said, we have to have reasonable cause. We can't just barge into someone's home because they were looking up the wrong things on the internet and splatter their guts on the wall. It'll be a scandal. So we have to be incredibly careful. We've got excellent people on the team, but I've convinced my boss that we need one more."

"This is where I come in, I presume?"

"Yes, sir. The department occasionally brings in specialists and consultants, people who have special skills. Your track record with the Army was more than enough for me to convince them you were the man for the job." Winston's eyes, even with those dark contacts, were piercing.

Jack took another swig of his beer and looked around the room. The man who'd been playing darts not long ago was now swaying back and forth in front of the jukebox, dancing drunkenly by himself. He and the others in the bar had no idea that their liberties were threatened on a daily basis because people like Jack were working behind the scenes to take them out. They went to work and spent time with their families and slept in their beds at night without ever being aware of what was actually happening in the world around them. Even those who closely followed the news were only being fed the parts the government wanted them to know. They had no clue how many undercover agents were working on their behalf.

"I'll feel a lot better knowing we've got a shifter on the inside," Winston said when Jack hadn't yet made a reply.

"What do you mean?" Jack narrowed his eyes. He knew he was being coerced, and it wasn't that he really minded considering it was Winston, but he wanted as much information as possible. Jack had learned over the years that it was all right to walk into a trap as long as you *knew* it was a trap. "The DHS already has you. What do you need me for?"

"Oh, I don't know. Your talent? Your skill? All those medals and commendations? You know I'm good behind the scenes, but I've already worked on this case too much. Even with my disguises, it's time to change it up. I've been scouting this one out for a while, and we need to get someone different in there before we make a final move. A shifter is going to handle it a lot better than any human." He tipped his head from side to side, as though considering all the options the future might hold. "And I think a shifter might stand a better chance of getting out again if I'm honest."

Jack let out a long, low breath, not quite a sigh. There

wasn't a whole lot to consider. Someone was out there making threats, potentially planning to harm innocent people, and Jack might be able to stop him. "I've got a few arrangements I'll have to make. I need to get back to you. How much time do I have?"

Winston frowned. "As little as possible, as always. The faster we get this figured out and taken care of, the sooner we can move on to more threats. You know there are always more, man."

"I'm not looking for a full-time gig," Jack reminded him. "If I wanted to dive back into the game like that, I wouldn't have left the Army."

"I know, I know. I'm just saying you never need to be bored." He gave Jack a smile and a wink.

"Is this your regular side job now, slinging beer to the dregs of society? Or will I need to go talk to the head chef at a French restaurant when I need to reach you again?" Jack teased. He knew Winston loved his disguises, and not simply because he'd been able to make a living with them.

"Oui, monsieur," Winston replied in a perfect Parisian accent. "Or perhaps you'll head to the docks to talk to a lowly barge worker about a new position."

"Right." Jack's face split in a grin. "I'll see you around."

JACK WAS the first to arrive in the conference room. He eased into the comfortable leather chair and ran his hand along the grain of the mahogany table. The TV and other equipment the SOS Dallas Force used to communicate with their D.C. unit as well as Ash Cunningham, one of their consultants in Alaska, was all top-of-the-line, provided by Taylor Communications. The conference room was part of the lavish and very secret headquarters that had been remodeled specifically for their needs. While some of the members chose to continue living in their own homes, Jack had opted for the rather nice apartments that had been made a part of the complex as well. Everything he could have possibly needed was there.

It was an opulent lifestyle compared to how he'd lived when he was working overseas. Jack had slept inside tents that were so constantly battered by the wind, they might have blown away at any second. He'd huddled in dark corners to catch a few moments of shuteye before jumping back to his feet to fight the enemy or help a prisoner escape. Even on the rare occasion when he'd managed a night in one of the reinforced tents on a base, he still had to worry about scorpions and other unwelcome critters wriggling into his bed. He'd eaten more MREs than he cared to remember, and he'd sampled some very questionable foreign food that he'd rather not know the actual ingredients of. All in all, he'd left a rough, seat-of-his-pants type of life that was hard to imagine going back to.

"You all right?" asked a low, twangy voice that jerked Jack out of his reverie and back into the present moment. "You look like you found a hole in your pasture fence." Vance was a rancher outside of his work with the Dallas Force, and if Jack hadn't already known, he'd have been able to tell by the dirt around the hems of his black Levi's and the scuffs on his Ariats.

"Yeah, I'm fine. Just thinking."

"Must be some heavy stuff." Vance stepped over to a side table and poured himself a cup of coffee. "Need a little something to give your brain a boost?" he asked, gesturing to the pot.

"No, thanks. I've had enough for the day." And he truly had. He'd slowly sipped a cup as he got ready that morning, and he'd had several more while he brooded over his options. By the time he'd gotten into the conference room, he could already feel the caffeine thrumming through his veins, and it hadn't done a thing to help him with this decision.

Max strode in just then, holding out his travel mug. "I'll gladly take a fill-up," he said with a grin. "It's been one hell of a night. Did you hear about that traffic accident out on 114? I was working it."

Vance shook his head. "I've never seen anyone so happy about a car wreck."

"You're just pissed that no one uses horses for transportation anymore," Max teased. "And it's not that I'm happy about the fact that people were hurt. It's just that working on the air ambulance team has been so much more satisfying. I'm actually doing something rewarding with my life. Luxury Air Tours and all those rich assholes can suck it." Indeed, Max looked much happier than Jack could ever remember seeing him. There was always that grim determination he saw in any shifter's eyes when they were working a mission, but it was like Max's overall life had completely changed in the last few months since he'd reconnected with his mate and found a new civilian job.

"Right," Jack said slowly. "It's all about the job. It doesn't have anything to do with going home and getting to play doctor with Sabrina at the end of the night."

Max swiped a fist in his direction, missing purposely. The gesture carried with it the swift and smooth move-ments of the tiger Max was inside, and the satisfaction in his eyes brought the same reminder. "You can make fun all you want. You're just jealous, and I'm not going to let that ruin my good time." He grinned again as he moved around the table to his seat. "Better than sitting at home in front of a computer every night while beating off to PornHub like you."

Jack laughed. "Whatever you say, man."

"What should either of us be jealous for, anyway?" Vance asked. "I'm as free as a tumbleweed, with only my ranch and this job to tie me down every now and then. I don't need a woman bossing me around."

"You say that, but I've seen you with the ladies," Max remarked. "You want to pretend you're some rough cowboy, but as soon as you see a pretty face, you're running after them. Don't kid a kidder, Vance."

Jack pursed his lips, quickly sinking back into deep thoughts again. He wasn't old by any means, but he wasn't getting any younger, either. His lifestyle had stopped him from really ever settling down, not just in the sense of finding his mate, but in the sense of getting to know himself and other people. His work in the Army had kept him isolated and on the move, and the Dallas Force wasn't much different.

The meeting started as they checked in with the D.C. unit and discussed what missions they had coming up. Jack took mental notes, trying to decide when he should broach the subject. After all, he couldn't just ditch the Force. The Specials Ops shifters were the closest thing he had to a family those days, and disappearing for a while without explanation wasn't going to sit well with them.

"I think that about wraps it up," Max finally announced, tossing back the last of his coffee and standing.

"Actually, there's something else." Jack briefly explained Winston's request for assistance. "It sounds like a pretty big deal, and I think I've got to go."

"Government work," Vance mused. "Sounds risky."

"I know it. But if Winston's right and this little terrorist cult is made up of shifters, then we've got a lot more to worry about than just someone blowing up a federal building. We're talking about recruitment, exposure, all sorts of disasters that we may not be able to handle if we don't get it under control right now." That had been bothering him ever since Winston had mentioned it. How many shifters were being preyed upon by this man? How many of them were willing to follow him because they were desperate for that pack mentality that was a natural inclination for their animal sides?

Max bit his lip. "And it's here in the States?"

Jack nodded. "Right now, the mission's base is in Kentucky. Winston wouldn't give me the actual location of where we'll be headed afterward until I come on board."

Vance glanced at the pilot and back at Jack. "We've got a few things on the list for the week, but it's nothing the two of us can't handle. And Ash did say he might be coming down for a bit, so we know we'll have some backup in the area. I say you do what you feel is right, and we'll find a way to make it work."

The tiger nodded his agreement.

"All right," Jack replied. A heavy feeling had settled in his stomach, but the weight of the decision had been taken off his shoulders. "I guess that's it, then."

2

"LADIES AND GENTLEMEN, AS WE PREPARE TO LAND, PLEASE turn off all electronic devices, stow your items, and buckle your seat belts. The weather in Washington, D.C. is bright and sunny today, and we expect a nice, smooth landing. Thank you."

Erica Brewer closed her book with a sigh and tucked it into the pocket of the seat in front of her. She reached for her seatbelt, only to realize she hadn't bothered unhitching it during the flight in the first place. She'd been too absorbed in her reading to bother, and she flew often enough that peering out the airplane window no longer enthralled her as much as it had before she'd started working for the Department of Homeland Security.

The man next to her rubbed his thighs and bobbed back and forth in his seat. A sheen of sweat stood out on his forehead. "So, where you from?" he asked with a shaking voice.

His fear inundated her brain. Instantly, Erica could feel the sensation of adrenaline in her veins and tightness in her chest. Her own body wasn't actually reacting that way, but her empathic mind was a powerful tool. She sucked in a deep, meditative breath, a defensive tactic she'd learned a long time ago. "I've moved around a lot. I'm not really *from* anywhere."

"Oh, yeah?" The man ran a hand through his hair and left it standing on end. "I'm from Chicago, originally. The nice thing about that town is there's so much there, you never really have to leave. No need to fly anywhere. Want to go to a museum? Got plenty of 'em. In the mood for a foot-ball game? Got a nice big stadium. Of course, you have to be a Bears fan to enjoy that part." He let out a forceful laugh.

"Right." She gave him a smile. The poor guy was clearly terrified of flying. Why did she always get seated next to people like that? She understood that everyone had their fears, but it made her wonder if the universe had put her in the position of comforting strangers. "So, what puts you in the air today?"

"I'm supposed to get a promotion, but that means I have to come out here for training. I wanted to just drive, but there wasn't enough time. I know they say it's a lot safer to fly, with traffic accidents, carjackings, and whatnot." He sucked in a gasping breath. His own attempts to convince himself weren't working well. "I used to think flying was neat. But not after September 11th. I just can't help but look around at everyone else on the plane and wonder why they're here and what they're up to."

"An incident like that isn't very likely," Erica said in her most soothing voice. "That was really unusual. Besides, the government has put a lot of measures in place to keep us all safe. They know what to look for now." She was heavily involved in that part of the government herself, although her work all happened on the ground.

"Sure, they say that." He tugged at the collar of his shirt violently, as if it'd been choking him. "But then I saw this show that said the TSA is all just a front. They don't really keep us safe; they just make us *think* we're safe while they're taking away our liberties and our shoes."

Erica pressed her lips together. She'd heard every argument in the book, but she still believed the Department of Homeland Security was doing everything in its power to keep the U.S. citizens as safe as possible. Nothing was perfect, but she'd certainly worked her own ass off and had taken down quite a few threats. "You know, maybe the best thing is to just distract yourself. I like to bring along a book when I fly and just lose myself in it." She gestured toward the volume she'd just tucked away.

The poor man glanced at the title and then back at her, and now the sweat was dripping down his temples. "Iran?"

he asked shakily. "You're reading about Iran? Aren't they one of our sworn enemies? Don't they threaten this country all the time? I read something the other day about how they have a whole army of computer hackers, and they could take us down with one vicious cyberattack."

He was getting hysterical, beyond the normal fear of takeoff and landing that she usually witnessed. Erica glanced out the window at the swiftly approaching ground. The last thing she needed was for this guy to completely freak out next to her. She was already tired from the mission she'd just finished, and she was getting ready to dive straight into another one with almost no recovery time. No one realized just how hard it was on her to deal with a situation like this. She wasn't like most folks, who could just sit back and ignore it.

Instead, she moved her hand ever so slightly so that it rested on the back of his forearm. With the crowded confines of the airplane, it wasn't all that unusual to touch your neighbor accidentally, so the intentional move wasn't such a stretch. She sent peaceful, happy energy down her arm, through her hand, and into the man's body. In Erica's mind, it was a beautiful blue light with threads of white and gold running through it. This light was something she'd come to use as a tool over the years, and she knew it was a very effective one. "What did you say your name was?"

He hadn't said, but he was too scared to remember that.

"Scott." The plane jumped with turbulence, and his body tensed under her hand.

"Scott, that's right. My name is Erica." She fought back the negative energy that tried so hard to work its way into her own body. Though her eyes were open and she could clearly see the interior of the plane around her, she could see his own flashing thoughts overlaid on the image. He was wondering if she was one of *them,* a terrorist, and he could almost envision her whipping out a tiny knife and taking over the entire aircraft with it. It was beyond probability and even possibility, since there was likely an air marshal on board. But her book about Iran had got him worrying about that on top of his concerns about crashing. Over and over again, he'd imagined the plane crashing into the asphalt, the fuselage ripping to pieces around them, his body being found mixed in with the wreckage. His anxiety was exhausting.

"Everything is going to be all right," she said, forcing his worries aside and pushing her own positive vibes toward him. This didn't always work, depending on how accepting the other person was. Erica didn't even like manipulating people's thoughts this way if she could help it. The process wore her out, and it felt morally wrong. Still, this man needed her. "I can promise you that we're going to touch down on the runway with little more than the bump of the wheels, and the next thing you know, you'll be walking into the airport to buy overpriced souvenirs."

"You think so?" The tension was slowly leaching out of his muscles, but she didn't quite have him yet.

"I know so." Did she really know that? This was something she'd questioned herself many times over. There had been no visions of anything untoward happening. The only images of fire and chaos in her mind had come from the man next to her. Erica sometimes took comfort in knowing she hadn't had any foresight of disaster, but she also knew this was no actual guarantee. For all the power of her mind, she couldn't see everything. Still, it was better to convince this man that everything would be all right.

"Yeah." He nodded, smiling a little at his own foolishness. "You're right. I mean, people fly all the time. They wouldn't keep doing it if it wasn't at least somewhat safe. And hey, the ride is almost over."

Her blue light and the affirmative energy in it had won. She patted Scott's arm right as the plane banked, swooped down toward the runway, and lifted her stomach slightly. She kept her hand in place just in case he needed her again. "That's right. Isn't it funny how our imaginations can run away with us?"

The plane landed with the bump she'd predicted, and the pilot's braking sent them scooting slightly forward in their seats, but they soon taxied to the terminal. The only chaos came from the passengers as they bumped and pushed around each other to retrieve their items from the overhead bins and make their way down the narrow aisles.

———

"I know you'll be putting an official writeup on my desk by tomorrow morning, but initial reports make it sound like everything went well." Randall Holt leaned against her office doorway, a mug of coffee in his hand.

Her eyes hurt from missing sleep, and traveling back to D.C. had made her muscles sore. Yet there she was at her office, first thing in the morning as required. "Of course. I had it all handled without a problem."

"Mmm." Mr. Holt looked down into his mug. "I hope you give a few more details than you did in the last report. I have the distinct impression you're skimming over some important information."

She consciously kept herself guarded as she looked at him. Erica couldn't afford to give anything away, especially not to someone like Mr. Holt. He was her boss, but only because he'd been promoted after Mr. Mitchell had retired. Mitchell had hired her readily and liked her work, and he'd never questioned her as long as she got the results the department wanted. Randall Holt was only looking out for himself, and he didn't trust anyone who wasn't completely in his control. "Why would you say that?"

Randall sneered. "Don't play innocent with me. You think just because you're a woman, you can get away with that kind of shit around here. It's the same in the field for you, too. Mitchell might've bought your 'feminine intuition' crap that always saved the day, but I don't. I want cold, hard facts."

Erica straightened in her desk chair. She'd dealt with her share of sexist jerks in this field, and it was clear to her that things weren't going to get better anytime soon. "Cold, hard facts are fine when it comes to who went where and when. But if you want to know *why* someone acts the way they do, you can't always rely on such things. People are just wild animals inside, really."

Holt's eyes narrowed. He was a short man, and he could never find suits that fit him quite right, nor did he bother to have the pants hemmed. It always made Erica think of a little boy who'd put on his father's Sunday best while he pretended to be an adult. "That's more bullshit. Cold, hard, frigid facts are all I need, and that's what you're going to have to give me if you want to keep working in this field."

She could report him for being sexist. Erica had thought about it many times before. She knew, however, that even if Randall got fired, there would just be another misogynist waiting to take his place. And, just like Mr. Holt wanted in his report, there were no cold, hard facts to really prove he'd said what he did. "Right, sir. Of course."

Thinking he'd won, Randall pushed himself off the doorframe. Erica thought he would turn and go, but he stepped forward and leaned down. He put his hand on the corner of her desk, his fingertips whitening with the pressure. "Women don't belong in this field, and you and I both know it. They don't want you for any of the overseas operations because it's too dangerous. Heaven help the department if one of you wants to go off and have a baby because then you think you deserve all this time off. If I had my way, we'd have a complete remodel of this place."

She met his eyes, putting all her anger and ferocity behind her glare. "I think a complete remodel is *exactly* what we need," she said evenly.

It wasn't what he expected, and he straightened. "I take it that means you're looking for a different job? Maybe a nice secretarial position somewhere?"

"No. It means we'd get a lot more done if all the dicks got out of the way. Now, if you'll excuse me, I have work to do." Pointedly, she turned to her computer and began typing.

Holt sputtered and fumed for a moment before he disappeared.

"You didn't?" Andrea almost choked on her turkey sandwich a few hours later in the breakroom. "Good God, I would've loved to have seen his face."

Erica had worried a little after her confrontation with Mr. Holt. He was her boss, after all. "I did. I've been holding it back for too long with him. He thinks that just because I'm good at my job, there must be something wrong; like if things go smoothly, I must be cheating somehow." In a way, she was. Her psychic abilities certainly gave her an advantage that no one else had. If she was using them to keep people safe, though, it seemed an easy enough thing to justify.

"So, tell me when the grand inquisition is and if I'll be called to trial to testify," Andrea teased.

"I'm guessing there won't be one," Erica replied with a shrug. "Believe me, for about an hour after that, I flinched every time someone walked past my door, convinced someone from HR was on their way to get me. But I didn't hear anything. I figure no news is good news."

"He'd be an idiot to get wrapped up with you in a war like that, considering everything he's said to you," Andrea pointed out. "If you wrote down every incident, you'd have a whole novel to hand over."

"Maybe, but you and I both know this place is a man's world. They think we're delicate little flowers who've tried shoving our way boobs-first into the field just because we don't want to be housewives. It's awful." She stabbed her fork into her baked potato, but it wasn't very satisfying.

"You're telling me. I've made the mistake of referring to myself as Andy so many times that everyone else calls me that, too. Then someone calls my office expecting a man, and they get so baffled when I insist that, yes, I'm Andy." She laughed and shook her head of tight black curls. "Ridiculous."

Erica glanced around at the cafeteria, realizing just how familiar of a scene this was. "You know, when I was high school, I spent a lot of time daydreaming about how great everything would be once I was all grown up and I didn't have to deal with the politics of a small town anymore. It's a shame to find out that isn't true."

Andrea cracked open a Coke. "What do you mean?"

"I mean adult life is just the same as it was back in high school, except we fool ourselves into thinking we're more mature. Holt thinking I'm not capable isn't any different than a football team or robotics league that doesn't want a girl to join their ranks. And look around this room." She gestured widely at the various tables. "It's mostly the exact same groups as there were back then."

Her friend was looking around now, too, understanding what she meant. "There are the preps in their Prada suits, the popular girls wearing all the latest fashions, and even the nerds from IT. Granted, they're not nearly as nerdy as they used to be when I was in school. We've come a long way now that there are better prescription glasses on the market." Andrea waggled her fingers at one of the tech guys.

"See? Like I said."

"Okay, we've got everyone else categorized, but where does that leave us? What table are we sitting at?" Andrea challenged.

Erica tipped her head to one side. "Well, if all things really are equal, then we're the weirdos, the freaks, the misfits."

"I have a hard time imagining that was you." Andrea

dabbed her mouth with a napkin. "You'll have to bring in an old photo of you in black lipstick to prove it."

"No, not a goth," Erica replied with a sardonic smile. In fact, it would've been nice if a difference in style was what had separated her from the other kids her age. She'd tried hard to fit in. That's a difficult enough task for anyone that age who's still trying to figure out who they are, but it's even harder for a girl who's realizing all those strange feelings she has and the odd things going through her head aren't just hormones, but psychic powers. Even now, she still couldn't share her true story there at work. Andrea was a great person, but a secret like that was too much to ask anyone else to keep.

"We moved around a lot when I was a kid," she explained. "We ended up in a lot of small towns because my mom wasn't big on city life. She thought she was doing me a favor because of the kinds of troubles you hear about with metropolitan areas, but she never really understood what it was like for me. I mean, I went to schools where all the other students had practically known each other since they were born. I was an instant outsider, and I'd lived in other places and seen different things. There was no possible way for me to fit in, no matter what I did."

"The guys must have liked you, at least," Andrea pointed out.

Erica shrugged. "A few here and there, but there's something about me that just turns guys away. My dad used to say it's because I'm smart, and they don't like anyone they can't control." She had to laugh at little at that one. "I guess he isn't entirely wrong in that. Even as an adult, guys only like me until I open my mouth and they realize I have a brain."

Andrea gave her a sympathetic look. "I'm sorry, sweetie. That's rough, and even more so because it's true. Around this place, I'm not sure I'd want to date anyway."

Erica waved off her concerns. "Don't mind me. I wasn't trying to make anyone feel sorry for me. I just think the comparison between then and now is interesting. I have a feeling Holt probably didn't fit in any better than I did, and that's why he's always giving me such hell." She glanced around the room once again, thinking about that last remark from Andrea. There were plenty of men working in intelligence, but her coworker was right. There wasn't a single one of them she knew that she'd want to go out with.

"Anyway, on a slightly different note, I'm getting shipped out again in a couple of days. A potential terrorist cell has popped up in Illinois. It should be an interesting operation, considering Winston Anders is involved." She was somewhat grateful to have another assignment so quickly, since it meant that at least someone was taking notice of her, but she also wished she had a little more time to recoup.

Andrea slammed her Coke down. A bit sloshed out onto her fingers, and she licked it off. "You're getting to work with Winston Anders? Girl, now I *know* you've hit the big time in the intelligence world. That man's been everywhere and done everything."

Erica felt her face heat up and decided not to tell Andrea that Winston had specially requested her for this mission. She didn't want to rub it in her friend's face. It was nice to have someone to talk to about work who had the same security clearance she did. Most people could go home and gripe about their customers or their bosses all day long, but as soon as Erica left the building, she had to keep her lips sealed. "It'll be interesting, for sure. I was really excited when I found out I was going to be working with him, but when I went in for my briefing this morning, I was also informed they're bringing in an outside consultant."

"That must mean it's one hell of a big deal," came Andrea's conclusion.

"Maybe, or maybe Randall has told enough people how much he doesn't trust me and Winston's convinced I can't do the job myself. I instantly want to be insulted, but that won't do me much good."

Andrea shrugged. "The one thing I can tell you is that I've never heard a bad word about Winston. Everyone loves him, men and women alike, and the rumors about his skills are everywhere. You'll have a blast."

"Maybe." Erica leaned forward, glancing aside as someone walked to the trash can just to make sure no one was listening. "But if Winston's so great, then why are they bringing in a consultant? Who could possibly be more experienced than him?"

"I guess you'll just have to find out," Andrea replied with a smile.

3

JACK WATCHED THE GROUND DISAPPEAR UNDER THE helicopter. "I have to admit I'm still not sure about this."

"What, working with the government again? I can't say I blame you," Max said with a laugh from the pilot's seat. "You won't catch me letting those assholes boss me around again. I'm happy to keep my work in the private sector from now on."

"Yeah, I get it." Sweat constantly beaded on his skin in this humidity, and Jack wiped his brow. He'd thought a lot before accepting this job, and even once he'd officially taken it, he hadn't been sure. The Army had given him a purpose in life and he'd enjoyed that, but even more so, he'd enjoyed the freedom of the Special Ops Shifter Force. He wasn't sure if this was a good idea, but his urge to keep the country safe from terrorists outweighed all uncertainty. Fortunately, he knew he'd have at least one shifter on his side. "I guess we'll find out soon enough if I've made a mistake."

Max shook his head. "Don't think about it like that. You didn't have much choice."

"Thanks, man." At least there was someone else who understood. He wouldn't have expected it from Max, who'd always been so full of anger and turmoil. The pilot had calmed down a bit over the last few months, though. "Just do me a favor."

"Sure."

"Keep this chopper warmed up to come pull me out if things go wrong." His stomach twisted, and not from the movement of the aircraft. His fox was telling him something. Jack was about to dive into something deep.

"You got it."

A short time later, Max descended the helicopter into a swampy area where thick cypress trees arose from the shallow water. There was a small grassy spot that was slightly drier with a gathering of small cabins. They didn't look like official government buildings, but these were the coordinates they'd been given. "This chopper's too heavy for me to land here safely. I don't want to risk sinking in. Think you're okay for a short jump?"

Jack spent most of his time in front of a computer, but there was nothing like the rush of zipping down a fast rope from a chopper. "Yeah, I can handle it." In fact, he looked forward to it.

The rotors thumped overhead and echoed in his bloodstream as he affixed the rope to an anchor and pulled the door open. He braced himself against the hull, feeling the wind swoop up in his face as the ground swiftly drew closer.

At Max's nod, he let go. It was a short jump, nothing like he'd done when he was still in the service, but the rush of air past him send a thrill of exhilaration through his body. He landed perfectly, bending his knees to absorb the impact. Jack let go of the rope and turned to give Max a thumbs up before stalking toward the cabin.

The place could've just as easily been a wilderness retreat or a scene from a horror flick. Bushy weeds grew up around the foundation, and vines twined themselves around the bowed wooden steps leading up to the porch. The rounded logs that made up the siding had seen better days, but the chinking was still in good condition. It could've been a house that belonged to anyone, except for the small security cameras that'd been mounted within the recesses of the eves. Without looking for them, Jack was sure there were other perimeter sensors in place as well. It wasn't as though he'd tried to make his arrival a secret, considering a chopper had just dropped him off, but it was clear to him that whoever was there was intent on keeping the place secure. His inner fox tensed, watchful and wary.

The porch boards creaked under his weight as he stepped up to the door. Jack knocked twice, paused, and then knocked twice again. The hinges creaked in protest as the door swung open, revealing a tall man with a slim face and brilliant blue eyes. "Jack! I was starting to think you wouldn't show up."

Jack shook his head and stepped inside, the animal that resided within him relaxing considerably. "Hell, I'm not even late, Winston." He gripped the other man's hand firmly, pleased to see his old comrade. As many doubts as he'd had about the mission, Winston had been the tipping point.

"But you're only five minutes early," Winston joked. "Come in and we'll get started. We've got a lot to go over."

Jack grinned, pleased. "Sounds great." He surveyed the open floorplan of the cabin. A small hallway jutted off to the left, probably leading to bedrooms and a bathroom, but the kitchen, dining, and living rooms were all one large area. There was little sign of how the previous occupants might've lived since the place was now filled with various castoff metal desks and battered wooden tables, each covered with computers, equipment, and stacks of files.

This was what he was used to, and Jack instantly felt better about the situation. He stepped past a pile of foreign language dictionaries to follow Winston, ready to get to work. But then the man stepped aside and gestured at a woman seated behind a desk. "Jack, this is Erica. She's quite talented in the field, and she'll be working with us."

She rose from an office chair well-patched with duct tape. Her long dark hair draped down over her shoulders, a sharp contrast to her lucid green eyes. She watched him carefully as she extended her hand. "It's nice to meet you. Winston has told me so much."

His inner fox went mad as he reached toward her, focusing all his control on his hand so he wouldn't crush her in his fingers. She was beautiful, no doubt, but why should he be reacting this way? It was as though every impulse he'd ever felt had come rushing to the forefront of his mind, demanding that he act on them. Jack gritted his teeth and split his lips in what he knew was an awkward grin. "I'm sure he has."

There was something about her that he couldn't quite put his finger on. His vulpine half was utterly captivated; that much was obvious. But he was also on defense. Something was different about this woman, and he was determined to find out exactly what.

He held onto her hand for just a moment longer, trying to deduce if she was a shifter as well. It wasn't always easy to tell, but Jack prided himself on knowing people and how to read them. He searched for some animal inside her, maybe not necessarily a fox like his own inner beast, but something else. Slowly, reluctantly, he let go of her hand. If not a shifter, then what?

"Jack, I'd also like you to meet the head of the CMC, Roger Worth." Winston brought Jack around the back of the room, where a man worked at a large table instead of a desk.

Dressed in a polo and khakis, he didn't look like any of the bigtime government officials Jack had worked with before. His sandy hair was mixed with gray at the temples, and he offered a warm handshake. "Great to meet you, Jack. I've heard a lot about you, and it sounds like you'll be just who we need on this case."

Jack managed to sneak a pointed look at his old comrade. Winston had talked him up just to get him approved for this mission, he was sure, but he didn't know if he should appreciate it or not. "I'll do my best."

"Let me clear a little of this paperwork out of the way and we can get started." When the four of them were seated at the table, Roger turned his computer monitor around for them to see. "This is Ben Jones, or at least that's what he goes by now. From what we can tell, he came to the U.S. in the late nineties. He's currently living in Illinois, running a used car dealership. Ben's record is absolutely immaculate. Not even a traffic ticket."

Jack studied the face on the screen. The photo wasn't a mug shot or a candid image, but a headshot that'd clearly been taken to promote his business. He smiled kindly at the camera, ready to sell a Buick.

"Jones has gone to college and received a bachelor's

degree," Mr. Worth continued. "He hasn't been stockpiling weapons or making any open threats, and as far as we can tell, he's not even in contact with anyone back home in the mountains of the Middle East. The one thing that's odd about him is this particular website." Roger clicked to the next screen.

The website was a standard one, the kind created with a free template for those who didn't know how to code. Jack scanned the screen as quickly as he could, reading Ben's glowing words about fellowship, peace, harmony, and understanding. The man was asking those who wanted to live in such a utopian society to come and see him so he could show them the way. A couple of links to videos were included at the bottom. "Interesting. Sounds more like a cult following than any of the religious extremist stuff we usually find."

"I know," Roger said with a nod. "We have a few other small pieces of evidence that indicate something weird is happening, but nothing that's actually illegal. We've got satellite images of a big compound he's built in the Shawnee Forest about half an hour from his car dealership. Again, no law against that, but it's practically like a small village. More and more people are moving in, too, considering how much traffic we suddenly see on these back-country roads that normally don't have much more than the occasional tractor on them."

Jack tipped back in his chair and folded his fingers

together in front of his stomach. "No offense, but this doesn't really look like anything the DHS would poke their nose into any further."

Winston spoke up now, far more serious than he'd been back at that dive bar. "I've been at the dealership several times, as a few different people, of course. I've inquired about several vehicles and asked him questions about things like financing, where he gets the cars, his family. He comes across incredibly confident and pleasant. He never offers anything unusual when it comes to money, and he hasn't exactly invited me back to his compound to discuss the matter further. He acts like a regular guy, but we know from our satellite imagery that there's more to it than that."

"There's also the fact that the people who do seem to be living in this little village don't leave very often," Erica added. Her voice was smooth, like she was speaking to a wild animal she was trying to tame.

Jack liked it, and once again, he found his fox reacting to her. He blinked and clenched his teeth, forcing himself to focus on her words.

"We've set up some discreet cameras on the nearby roads so that we could more accurately monitor who's going in and out," Erica continued. "Ben leaves every morning, goes to work, and then goes back. That's not unusual, but we've recorded at least fifty people going in and only a select few that actually come back out for supplies or to run errands. It's always the same ones, which means the rest are either forced to stay behind or are brainwashed against leaving."

"Is it possible they're being killed?" Jack asked. It was a terrible notion, since impromptu settlements like this often consisted of families in his experience.

"We don't believe so," Roger said. "They've planted quite a large garden, something much bigger than only a handful of people could possibly need, and someone is taking care of the livestock, too."

Jack rubbed his jaw. Winston had mentioned shifters, and Jack very much wanted to know exactly what evidence had pointed him in that direction, but that would be a conversation for another time. "No offense, Mr. Worth, but all I see here is that we're concerned about someone who's bought a bunch of land and brought in people so they can help him run the farm."

"That's exactly the problem." Erica addressed him instead of Roger, and those viridescent eyes burned straight into him. "We *know* there's something strange going on, but we don't have any definitive evidence. The Department can't just go charging in without the risk of facing some serious backlash. We have to go in and get that evidence, and once we do, we can dismantle this issue before it becomes a true threat."

Jack's eyebrows drew together. "But how do you *know*?" he challenged.

The steadiness in her eyes wavered for only a moment

before she tipped her chin up slightly. "With all due respect, Mr. Denton, I've been working in this field for a long time. I understand you've performed plenty of extraction missions, and you've done your share for this country with your own counterterrorism efforts. An intelligence officer goes through extensive training, but it's the experience of actually doing the work that gives one a sense of people. I don't have concrete proof. That's what we need from you. For right now, I just *know*."

Roger gave a bit of a chuckle. "It might sound odd, Jack. I know your service with the military meant most things were fairly straightforward. It's not always like that with us, and Ms. Brewer has one hell of a reputation for sniffing out the bad guys. Just trust her. I do."

If the man heading up the Counterterrorism Mission Center could accept her feelings about this, then so could Jack. "Okay. So, what's the next step?"

"Direct infiltration," Winston announced. "Spying on them from afar isn't getting us the results we're looking for, so we need someone to get on the inside. We want someone to become part of Ben's little cult or whatever it is and discover what's actually happening."

Jack raised an eyebrow. "Then why would you need me? I thought that was *your* specialty."

His old comrade gave a half-smile. "Yes, but I've already wasted it on all the times that I've been to the dealership. You know I do a killer job with my disguises, but our exposure rules limit me from diving any further into this personally."

"We don't know what kind of security they may have at the compound, beyond a few watchmen here and there," Mr. Worth added. "To keep things as safe as possible, we'd like to send two agents in. We've decided that'll be you and Erica."

Jack tried not to jump up out of his chair and protest. He'd worked with all sorts of people before, and he'd never been one to think a woman wasn't perfectly capable of this job. In fact, some of the women he'd encountered overseas had been the most critical in helping him. But Jack could practically feel the energy between himself and Erica crackling in the air. It was a recipe for disaster, and yet once again, he had no choice but to comply. "When do we leave?" he asked gruffly.

"In two days," Roger replied promptly. "We can spend tomorrow discussing the mission in further detail and packing you up for the trip. In the meantime, we have all the cabins here rented out just for ourselves, so you'll have a place to stay." He picked up a key on the table near the computer and handed it to Jack. "There's a path out the back door. Stick to it, because the land is pretty swampy here and you can ruin a boot without any effort at all. Take a right at the fork and you'll find your place."

"I'll walk with you." Winston was on his feet, and the two men were out the door.

When they were out of earshot of the main cabin, Jack glanced around him. "Do people actually rent this place out? It's pretty primitive."

"Hey, it's got Wi-Fi and cable. What more could you ask for?"

"Maybe some idea of why you think shifters are involved with this Ben guy?" It was frustrating to know that even with the security clearances both he and Winston had, there were still some things they couldn't discuss in front of Mr. Worth. That only made the job more difficult, and it meant Jack had to watch his back even more than he did when working with the SOS Force.

Winston let out a long sigh. "You know, I'm surprised how you reacted to Erica back there."

Jack paused. Had Winston felt that tension between the two of them as well? "What do you mean?" he asked innocently.

He lifted a shoulder. "She told you she just knew there was something suspicious about this Ben guy, and you didn't seem very accepting of that. But it's really no different than what we experience, Jack. I know you're a shifter. I knew it from the moment I met you, just as you must have known about me. Sure, occasionally, we can't quite tell, but you know how it is. I don't think Erica's intuition should be dismissed any more than our own."

Jack nodded. "I see. So you're saying you sensed something about the man?" He was glad to guide the conversation back to the mission instead of focusing on Erica.

"Like I said, I've been there several times. He keeps his animal quiet, though. I can't tell what he is; I just know it's there. And when I've studied the satellite imagery that the DHS has so carefully collected, I'm noticing more than just livestock. No one else pays attention because they're only looking for humans." Winston ducked under a branch that had grown out over the trail. "You're really going to have to watch your back, Jack. I'd much rather go in myself than send someone else to do a job I'm perfectly capable of, but like I said in there, I've already been on the scene too much. You're the only other one I trust with this."

They walked on in silence for a moment while Jack debated saying anything more. Winston was, however, one of the few people he knew he could trust with his life. "What about Erica?"

"What about her?"

He ran his fingers over his lips, concentrating. "She's not a shifter."

"No."

"Doesn't that go against your plans of keeping shifters on shifter business?"

Winston glared at him, the dim light of the darkening woods casting shadows on his face. "There's only so much I can do. She might not be one of us, but I do trust her. She's earned herself quite a reputation, just as you have, and the small amount of time I've spent with her since we arrived has shown me that she's competent and level-headed. I don't think you have a better option."

They arrived at Jack's cabin, and he used his key to unlock the door. The space was much smaller than the one in the main building, but at least the rustic appeal hadn't been tarnished by the presence of computers, desks, paperwork, and government employees. A small kitchenette sat in the far right corner, the queen bed only a few feet from it. Directly in front of the door was a small seating area. The place might've felt claustrophobic if it hadn't been for the vaulted ceiling and the French doors at the back.

"Think it'll do?" Winston asked, one eyebrow raised.

Jack nodded as he dropped his pack on the floor. "I've certainly experienced worse."

His old friend clapped him on the shoulder. "My cabin is just a little further down the way if you decide you want a drink later."

"Thanks. And Winston?"

"Yeah?" The older man turned in the doorway, expectant.

"I appreciate you thinking of me for this mission. I won't thank you for getting me involved, not until we see how it goes, but it's nice to know my work hasn't been completely forgotten." Jack really meant that last part. He'd lived in a world entirely different from most Americans, one they didn't even know about. He'd done things and he'd seen things, and even though he might be hailed as a national hero for his actions, no one would ever know about most of them.

"I wouldn't think of putting any bastard's life on the line but yours," Winston said with a grin. "Get some sleep, Jack. It'll be a long, boring day tomorrow while Roger goes over all the tiniest details you could possibly imagine."

"I will."

But he couldn't. Jack didn't mind sleeping in a strange place. The bed was even pretty comfortable compared to what he'd slept in out in the field. The little cabin was cozy, and he could see it being the perfect place for a young couple looking to escape the rigors of daily life.

For Jack, though, it only left him with his thoughts. He took a quick shower in the small bathroom and tried to sleep. Despite the comfort of the mattress, he tossed and turned. His body and his brain were far too awake. Getting up, he attempted to watch television, but there was nothing on. He felt restless, filled with the need to do something productive. Really, though, he knew there was only one fix.

Jack opened the door at the back of the cabin and stepped out onto a small porch. The deck boards were splintery under his bare feet, and the humid air threatened to suffocate him. Jack tipped his face back to the moon, a waxing gibbous with thick clouds slowly streaming past it. The cicadas sang loudly, filling any parts of the air that weren't already choking with water vapor, and a mosquito squealed in his ear. It was a miserable time to be human.

But not a fox. Jack didn't bother taking any precautions before he let go of his human shell. The others were likely locked away in their cabins this time of night, and if they didn't think they could trust him, they wouldn't have brought him in. His spine rippled as his bones shifted position, his skin tingling as thick red hairs shot out of it in every direction. A thick, luxurious tail extended behind him as his hands and feet curled inward and morphed into black paws. Jack rolled his head to the side as his face extended into a snout, and the sound of the night around him instantly changed as his ears moved up the side of his skull.

God, it felt good to be himself again. Jack enjoyed quite a bit about human life, but there was no greater feeling than the freedom of being a fox. He padded softly off the deck and down onto the swampy ground. His weight was delicately balanced between his paws, meaning he didn't have to worry about sinking in like he did in his other form. His tail provided balance as he moved among the trees, wandering away from the direction Winston had indicated his own cabin lay.

A small noise, so tiny he never would've heard it if his vulpine ears hadn't picked up on it, caught his attention near the root of a tree. Jack paused, listening, watching, waiting. Soon enough, a tiny face poked out of a hole and looked around. It didn't see Jack, still as he was, and it darted out onto the ground. Jack's entire body came to life in the spirit of the hunt as he went after the mouse. His muscles moved without any conscious thought, keeping him light and silent along the forest floor.

The mouse realized it was being pursued and scurried along faster, but Jack already had the advantage. He pounced, his teeth swiping up the tiny body and tossing it down his throat. A fox didn't exactly smile, not the way humans did, but he certainly felt the corners of his mouth pull back as he moved on. This was exactly what he needed. Jack liked people. He liked the feeling of brother-hood that came from working alongside those he trusted most, and he pulled in a certain amount of energy from knowing that the others on the Force always had his back.

There was something incredibly soothing, though, about having time alone. He wasn't the only creature in these swampy woods, not by a long shot, but none of them were like him. Jack moved silently, knowing he could remain completely hidden from the world for a long time if he chose to. This was a therapy he'd employed all during his life, including his time in the Army. It hadn't mattered if he was in basic training or on a top-secret mission overseas, Jack took any opportunity he could to let the other side of himself free. He needed that feeling of wild abandon, of letting himself simply be an animal. There were so many expectations that came along with being a human, and he could only handle them for so long. No one had ever spotted the agile fox darting around the edge of camp here or skirting around an Army base there. There would be only so much time that he could pretend to be a feral creature, though, because civilization needed him.

Stepping out into a clearing, Jack paused as the clouds parted and let the moonlight filter down onto the wet grass and illuminate his fur. He backed up as he realized he'd been so involved in his own pursuit that he'd hardly even realized he was no longer alone. The clearing he currently stood in served as a back yard of sorts for one of the cabins. A lone figure stood on the back porch, her hair lifting in the slight breeze.

Jack studied her, realizing after a moment that it was Erica. She looked completely different from this angle, her arms spread and her hands braced on the railing as she tipped her face toward the moon. Her eyes were closed, her chest rising and falling in long, meditative breaths. Maybe it was just the celestial glow on her face, but she had the beauty of a goddess.

He shifted his paws as she slunk further into the shadows. Even in his animal form and from a distance, Erica did things to him. Saliva dripped from his pointed teeth and his heartbeat quickened. Despite his normal instincts to remain hidden from any potential enemy—and humans were always potential enemies in this form—he found himself fighting the urge to lunge forward, dart across the field onto the porch, and curl up around her feet. It was the most ridiculous notion he'd ever had, whether as a fox or a human, and he mentally chastised himself for it.

Jack was already putting himself in a precarious position by going on this mission. He didn't need the DHS digging into his current job with the SOS Force, because that could potentially lead to his biggest secret being brought out into the open. Even heading into this terrorist's compound meant putting himself and others like him at risk, since it was likely they were dealing with other shifters. How could he possibly explain himself to Erica if the truth came out?

His mind flicked through all the possibilities. He envisioned Erica realizing that Ben Jones or one of his recruits was something other than human. The horror and shock on her face were clear in his mind's eye, and he was already rehearsing how he would de-escalate the situation. Even worse, the next image was Erica catching him mid-shift and understanding that he, too, was one of them. Encounters he would never have coursed through his brain, preparing him for any situation. It was an exhausting state of mind sometimes, but it was one that came naturally for him. Jack told himself that this was exactly why he was so good at his job. He couldn't see the future, but he was constantly preparing for it.

Suddenly, Erica's head tipped forward. She straightened, no longer leaning on the rail as she looked around the clearing. Her green eyes had turned teal in the moonlight as they darted from side to side. "Who's there?" Her voice was barely above a whisper, but Jack heard it loud and clear.

He turned and raced back through the trees toward his cabin. She couldn't possibly have seen him. Even when he'd stepped fully into the clearing, Erica's eyes had been closed. He felt his mind trying to run through scenarios again, visualizing Erica telling him about her odd encounter behind her cabin the night before and how she had the distinct feeling she wasn't alone.

No, he told himself as he paused just before reaching his cabin and shifted back to his human form, just in case anyone had been watching. Erica didn't know him, and from the way she'd spoken to him at their meeting, she didn't really care for him, either. Unless she thought there was a very good reason—like public safety—she wasn't likely to come running to him with her fears.

Jack slipped back into his cabin and locked the door behind him. He took a brief tour of the small building, just to make sure no one had crept inside while he'd been gone. All was secure, and he flung back the sheets before crawling between them.

Though his body felt better from the swift run through the wilderness, he struggled to fall asleep, his thoughts consumed by Erica.

4

"ALL RIGHT. HERE WE GO." JACK GOT BEHIND THE WHEEL AND fired up the ignition.

"Can our first stop be for a decent cup of coffee? The Department always buys the weakest stuff, no matter where they have me working." Erica rubbed her face, the heaviness of sleep still thick behind her eyes. She hadn't slept well for the last two nights. The little cabin resort wasn't exactly a luxury hotel, but it was the type of place that should've been a welcome relief for her. The little winding lane that led back into the woods hadn't been traveled by anyone but the mission team, and the cabins were well spaced out. It was exactly what she'd needed to keep her head clear as she prepared to go into the field.

Something was disturbing her, though. At first, Erica had thought it might be Jack. His presence had inundated her mind, flooding her with flashing images even before she touched his hand. To make things even more frustrating, she didn't understand what any of it meant. Most people were pretty easy to read. Erica could pick up on childhood trauma, abusive relationships, and mental illnesses, and she'd learned to interpret and understand the symptoms fairly early on. Not everyone with a rough past acted out, but they couldn't hide it from her, either.

Jack made her mind feel as though she were suddenly in a small crowd, one that she couldn't parse out and separate to make the thoughts into smaller pieces her mind could handle. Her body reacted to him as well, but that was easy enough to understand. He was tall and well-muscled, his broad shoulders fitting tightly into his t-shirt. The smooth lines of his face and the intensity behind his light brown eyes would've made any woman weak in the knees.

"Didn't sleep well?" he asked as he guided the battered car down the bumpy road.

"Hm? Oh. No, not really." She'd almost gotten lost in her thoughts about him, even though he was right next to her.

"If you're nervous about the mission, I don't think you have any reason to be. This sounds like it'll be a pretty easy operation. We get in, we get the information, and we get out." Jack turned onto the highway.

Erica scowled at him. "For your information, I've been

on plenty of missions before. I don't need your reassurances."

"I'm just trying to be nice," he said with a shrug. "A lot of people get a little tense at the start of something like this. No matter how many times you've gone out, you're always heading into something new."

"I'm fine," she said through gritted teeth, "and I don't need you to mansplain my job to me. The only thing that bothers me about this mission is that I didn't have much time to recover from the last one. That, and I'm working more directly with you than with Winston." She folded her arms across her chest and turned her head to look pointedly out the window. The trees whizzed by, but she wasn't really looking at them anyway. She was too busy fuming.

"What exactly did I do to piss you off?" Jack had been quiet and mild-mannered the previous day as they'd discussed the mission's particulars with Mr. Worth. There was a hard edge to his voice now.

Erica pulled in a deep breath through her nose and let it out through her mouth, but it wasn't slow enough to actually relax her. She had a feeling there never would be any relaxing around this man. "It's not necessarily something you did, I guess, but I have to admit I'm pretty resentful that they would call in a consultant on this mission. I can handle this myself, and I don't need you."

"Clearly, Mr. Worth thinks you do," he pointed out.

"No, I don't! I've worked plenty of missions on my own,

thank you very much. I'm sick and tired of having to deal with men in this line of work who think I'm too delicate to do it. They're all afraid I'm going to have my period or something and not be able to complete the mission. It's fucking ridiculous." All her anger leading up to this was pouring out of her mouth. Erica didn't know how to stop it, and she wasn't sure she wanted to. She'd spent years keeping it all pent up inside, lest anyone should find out how she really felt, and now it seemed like there was no point in trying. It hadn't really gotten her anywhere.

Jack was quiet for long enough that Erica risked glancing at him. He gripped the wheel with his right hand while his left rubbed the back of his neck. Tension filled his face, and she waited for him to explode right back at her. "I'm sorry," he finally said. "It's not fair that anyone should treat you that way. But it isn't as though I was the one doing it. I was asked to come here and help, so I did."

Erica snorted. "The words are nice enough, but I know you don't mean it."

"Excuse me? First, you tell me you're pissed off simply because I happen to be here, and now you're calling me a liar? You don't even know me!" Jack's left hand slapped against the wheel as he adjusted his grip, guiding the car smoothly around a curve despite his anger.

She knew him much better than he realized. True, Erica didn't know how to explain the visions that pounded her head when she was around Jack. Some were easy enough, with a lot of sand and guns and blood, but others were more like a scene from a National Geographic documentary. Even without her psychic powers, she'd seen the doubt in his eyes. He was just like Randall Holt, perturbed over her gut feelings that had served her so well in the past. "I don't need to know you. I saw the way you looked at me when I was trying to explain why we have to go after Jones. You're the type of man—just like almost all of you are— who doesn't believe in anything you can't see with your eyes."

"I see. You've worked with some assholes, and you decide that just because I'm a little skeptical that I'm one, too. What an awesome mission this is going to be." His grip tightened on the wheel now, his knuckles turning white.

Erica sucked in a breath. She didn't know if she felt like crying, screaming, or flinging herself from the moving vehicle. Jack was big physically, taking up far too much space in the moderate sedan Mr. Worth had secured for them. Now that he was angry with her, his already massive psychic presence had grown tenfold. There wasn't a molecule of air or energy that wasn't saturated with him. "Maybe you should just turn around."

He kept the gas pedal steady, with no hint of slowing down or looking for a place to turn. "I don't think so."

"I do," she asserted. "We're clearly not meant to be doing this together. I should've convinced Winston to come with me, or I should've just gone by myself." It would look awfully damn good on her record if she actually got a solo mission. Erica knew that was a rare thing, and even the top-ranked specialists didn't get those opportunities very often. The Department was big on keeping not just the citizens safe, but their employees as well.

"It's not happening." Jack's throat moved quickly, thrumming with his heartbeat.

She was getting him riled up. He was a big man, and the bulge of his arms under the short sleeves of his t-shirt might have intimidated some. Erica didn't sense any threats from him, though, despite his anger. She just needed to push him a little bit further, and then this whole farce would be over with. She'd get reassigned—most likely to the shittiest undertaking DHS could find for her—but she didn't care. "It is. I'm not continuing with you."

"You're not going to continue with anyone else," he growled.

A shiver of electricity flowed through her body and sparked at her pulse points. Her throat tightened and her mouth went dry as she responded to the possessive sound of that statement. The logical part of her brain knew that Jack's protest only meant that he was being stubborn and he wasn't about to let anyone see this mission as a failure before it even started. Her body had other ideas, and she quickly shut it down.

Fine. If arguing with him was only going to make things worse, then she'd use logic as a weapon instead. "Look, there's no way we can possibly make this work. According to everything Mr. Worth has gathered, extremists like to recruit single people who don't have a lot of connections. They don't want families because it's too messy. So he had that whole idea of us coming in as long-time BFFs."

He glanced at her out of the corner of his eye but quickly returned his gaze to the road. "Right."

"We can't pull that off," Erica concluded. "We've only known each other for a couple of days, and we're already at each other's throats."

Jack pointed at the road. "We've got half a day of driving ahead of us. I'd say that's plenty of time to get to know each other and come up with our backstories."

She shook her head. "No way."

His jaw tightened. "Look, you don't trust me. I get that."

"Do you?" she challenged. Erica highly doubted that he understood anything about her. No one did, and she didn't dare try to explain it. It was easier to just avoid people like him, people who gave off waves of emotion and who couldn't possibly accept her for who she really was.

"I can't say that I trust you, either. But—"

Erica wasn't listening anymore. The line of trees through the passenger window disappeared, and in their place, she saw a massive green tractor. As though someone was operating her mind with a penchant for a zoom lens, the machine instantly grew closer. "Slow down."

"I'm going the speed limit."

"Stop!" she screamed. Panic blossomed in her chest.

"I'm just trying to explain—"

"No!" Her foot was pumping the floorboard, instinctively searching for a brake pedal that wasn't there. "Stop the car! Stop the car right now!"

"There's no place to pull over!" he yelled back. "We've been through this!" The sedan topped a hill, and Jack slammed the brakes as soon as they began descending. Their seatbelts strained against them, and the tires squealed as they slowed down just before slamming into the back of a massive John Deere. The tractor chugged along, making its slow march down the road to the next field.

Jack said nothing at first. He concentrated on looking for a safe place to pass the farm vehicle, a flat strip of land where he could see clearly. When they were on their way again without any impediment, he glanced at her. "How did you know about that?"

She'd been waiting for the question. They always came. Sure, most of the time, people didn't really pay any attention, but every now and then, someone realized that things didn't quite add up. Fortunately, Erica was an old hand at making excuses. "I saw the tractor on the previous hill and figured we'd be catching up to it."

"No." His word was firm. "I did plenty of driving while I was in the service, and you learn to keep an eye on everything. You always look as far ahead as possible so you know what you're getting into, and it's not a perishable skill. I still do it, and I'll be doing it for the rest of my life. Now, how did you know that tractor was going to be there?"

"I don't see what the big deal is," Erica said flippantly. "We're in farm country, and there are tractors everywhere." As though the universe was trying to help her make a point, they passed a field where a massive combine churned up dust as it moved through the rows.

"Hmph."

He didn't seem inclined to continue the argument, and Erica couldn't decide how she felt about that. She wanted to argue; it was easier than acknowledging the heaviness in the air between them. There was something about this man that got to her, something that poked beneath the protective wall she'd put around herself so long ago, some-thing that wouldn't leave her alone. At least when he spoke, she could focus on his actual words instead of his seem-ingly random thoughts, and now she distinctly heard one of them. "I am not."

"What?"

"You just said I'm stubborn."

Jack shifted in his seat, stretching his spine upwards until his head nearly touched the ceiling and then settled back down again. He let out a breath as he did so. "I didn't say that."

"You did. I heard you." And she'd heard it many other times from other people, especially men. It didn't bother

her in the same way that it used to. In fact, Erica had almost come to like the fact that people thought she was stubborn. Any remark on her character that came from Jack, however, was a potential point of argument.

"All right. I did say that, but only in my head. I never opened my mouth."

Damn! Had she really done that? Had this man gotten her so vexed that she'd mixed up her signals? Erica had done this before. It was, in fact, how her mother had come to find out about her talent. It hadn't always been easy to distinguish when someone was saying something instead of just thinking about it, particularly if the thought was a strong one. For a while, Erica made a point of pretending she didn't hear well and used it as an excuse to watch people's lips moving. It made her feel better in knowing that the words had actually been spoken before she acted on them or replied to someone. "People do that all the time, you know. They mean to keep their thoughts to themselves, but their mouths betray them."

His smile wasn't a pleasant one. "Erica, I don't know exactly what's going on here, but *something's* up. I suggest you tell me." He fully turned his eyes from the road to look at her.

Jack's presence completely filled the interior of the car and Erica thought she might choke on it. There was the man she could see before her, the soldier, the one who'd been called in as a consultant for the DHS, even though she didn't want him there. But there was someone else as well, someone with the cleverness of a wolf and the cunning of a cat, someone who spent a lot of time alone and had used his skills to slip around fences and penetrate fortresses. Winston had claimed they could trust him, that he was the best man for the job, but she now knew for sure. "I don't know why you're bothering to ask me. You're the one who's a spy." It was the only answer that made sense.

"Excuse me?" he practically laughed. "Who the hell am I spying for? I haven't done a damn thing since you met me besides sit through a bunch of meetings and drive a car."

Erica rubbed a hand over her forehead. No matter what she did or said, this wasn't getting any better. His spirit was incredibly strong, and it'd practically invaded her mind. Her skull was starting to throb. "I know."

"You keep saying that," Jack reminded her. "I'm starting to think that's just your sorry excuse for not having done all your work. I don't blame you. If it's worked for you so far, then that's great. You can go right ahead and keep fooling Winston and Mr. Worth with it, but that bullshit doesn't work on me."

Something exploded inside her. Erica felt a rage bubble up and detonate like a massive volcano of psychic energy, something she could no longer hold back. "I'm a fucking psychic, okay? Does that make you happy? Is that what you wanted to hear? I can feel both sides of you inside my brain. You're like two people wrapped into one, and it's completely overwhelming. If I have to spend another second in this car with you, I think I might explode."

Jack said nothing.

Erica stared through the windshield, but she wasn't looking at the road. She closed her eyes. What the hell had she just done?

"A psychic." It wasn't a question, simply a statement.

Erica swallowed. This was it. Jack was a trained military man, the kind of guy who didn't put up with crazy things like psychic powers. But she'd already said it, and there was no turning back now. She could blame him for ruining her career, but she was the one who'd opened her big mouth. Maybe she could go get a job working for Dionne Warwick. "Yes."

"That explains a lot."

She slowly turned her head and opened her eyes. Everything felt heavy and difficult, like she was moving underwater. "It does?"

"Yes. And you've got me on the dual personalities. I'm hiding something, but I'm not a spy. I'm a shifter."

"A *what?*"

"A shapeshifter." Jack's grip on the steering wheel tightened again. "I can morph from man to fox and back again at will."

Erica swiveled her head back to face the front. Her body sank down into the seat, too exhausted to do anything else. She felt too tired to even talk. Whatever had just happened between them, it'd sucked every ounce of energy out of her. She knew she should still be fighting for him to pull the car over and let her out, and there was no way they could actually make this mission work. She'd just have to try again later. At least, for the moment, the waves of energy Jack was emitting had settled down somewhat. The two of them continued on that ribbon of Kentucky highway in silence.

5

JACK TRIED TO IGNORE THE DIRT AROUND THE EDGE OF THE
sink as he leaned over and splashed his face. He'd been
driving for three hours, and he needed to get out of the car
for a bit. It wasn't just the ache of staying in the same position for so long, either. It was being stuck in there with
Erica.

He snagged a paper towel to wipe his face off and
glanced at himself in the mirror. *What kind of an idiot are
you?* he asked himself. *Actually telling her what you are, like
you're some kind of amateur? You've just sent generations of
hard work right down the shitter.*

He and the others like him had done a lot to maintain
their secret. Granted, there were a few humans here and there
who knew about them, but they were shifters' mates. They'd
forged distinct bonds that would never allow for betrayal.

Those with animals inside them didn't even go to normal physicians. Their anatomy was slightly different to accommodate for the movement of bones and organs as they went from one form to another, and anyone who noticed that would surely expose them. Max's mate, in fact, was even working on starting up a specialized (and very secret) hospital to ensure the shifters got all the medical care they needed. They had their own government in the form of conclaves, and now the SOS Force even served as a small Army. All of that was wonderful, but Jack had decided to just blurt it out.

Not that he could've helped it. Jack tried to comfort himself with that thought as he stepped out of the gas station bathroom and into the convenience store area. He perused the cooler, looking for something cold to slake his thirst and make him feel as though he'd been doing anything other than purposely not looking at Erica for the last couple of hours.

He was a fool like any other man around a beautiful woman, shifter or not. She gave him an unsettled feeling inside, one that he'd first interpreted as meaning she couldn't be trusted. But after their startling revelation in the car—and the way he'd just blatantly laid the biggest secret he'd ever been trusted with on the line—Jack had to wonder if he was wrong. There was more to it than that, though. No doubt, Erica was a knockout. From the way her dark lashes contrasted with the brilliance of her eyes to the tempting sway of her hips as she walked, his fox wouldn't let him deny that for a second. Regardless of how his inner beast craved her, he had a mission at hand.

Snagging a Coke and a can of Pringles, he headed up to the checkout just as Erica did the same. "Here. I'll get it." He gestured for her to put her items on the counter as he reached for his wallet.

Holding her shoulders back defiantly, her eyes met his. "It's all right. I can get it." She hugged her bottle of water and a couple of snack bags closer to her body.

He tipped his head toward the counter once more. "Come on. Just let me do this."

"I don't care who the hell pays for it, as long as someone does," said the cashier in a bored tone.

Erica pursed her lips for a moment, then took a step backward. "Fine."

Jack paid quickly and stepped outside, but he didn't get in the car just yet. He leaned against the driver's door, taking in their surroundings. They'd crossed the border into Illinois, but they hadn't exactly reached civilization. The worn wood paneling of the gas station made it look like something out of an old Western, and the counters on the pumps were still analog. Citizens who slowly drove by in their battered trucks eyed him suspiciously. He'd spotted a bank and a dollar store, but the place seemed to mostly be made up of bungalows and single-wide trailers. These extended even down the river, where old flood damage could clearly be seen.

It was, he realized, not much different than the way people lived in the desert. They eked out their living in any way they could, as evidenced by the logging truck that rumbled by at full capacity. It wasn't any place special, and there were far grander cities that people could move to in order to expand their horizons, but they chose to stay in a place they understood. It might not be a good plan from the perspective of an outsider, but it was what worked for them.

The car rocked slightly behind him as Erica got in the passenger seat and slammed the door. With a sigh, Jack followed suit. He put the key in the ignition, but he didn't start the engine. "Erica, I propose a truce."

Her thin brows drew together as she turned to scowl at him. "Oh?"

Jack waved his receipt in the air. "It's the closest thing I have to a white flag right now. I know this has been an odd trip so far, to say the least. But the fact is, the two of us are professionals. We have a job to do, and we've been selected for it because we're more than capable."

"Despite our little secrets?" she asked, arching a brow.

"Maybe even because of them." It was something he'd had a lot of time to think about as the road swiftly moved beneath them on the way there. Jack knew that being a shifter had made a massive difference in the success of his career. He wouldn't have made it this far if he hadn't been able to tap into the primal instincts of his fox side. Surely, Erica's psychic abilities had served her in much the same way. She knew when things were happening, and even if she couldn't always explain them, it had boosted her success rate on her missions.

"I suppose that's true."

He was making headway with her now, so Jack went ahead and started the car. "I think so. You also have to consider that the two of us are going to be working closely together while we figure out what's going on with this guy. Mr. Worth did say he wanted us to get to know each other."

That elicited a small but tired laugh from Erica. "I have a feeling that's not what he meant."

He looked away from her as he pulled out of the gas station. God, she was gorgeous when she smiled. She'd been a magnificent and spiritual creature earlier that day as she'd argued with him and tried so hard to sway him, and it'd been a completely different kind of beauty, one of power and passion. It was one that was better admired from afar, yet it drew him like a moth to a flame. But the light in her eyes was warmer when she wasn't engaged in a full-on battle, and he found it incredibly attractive.

Jack glared at a passing truck as he waited for his turn to pull out onto the highway. Erica was special, yes. She knew his true identity. But that didn't mean he should put his guard down for one second or let himself get sucked in by the allure of those brilliant eyes and the soft curves of her body, no matter how much he wanted to. His fox panted with urgency at being so close to her, and he chewed the inside of his lip in an effort to calm it down. Jack was level-headed and cautious. He didn't do anything impulsively, acting only on plans he'd carefully thought out. Erica was changing that about him, and it didn't seem like a good thing.

"No, probably not, but we'll have to work with what we've got," he finally said as he accelerated onto the main road and headed for the larger town where their destination lay. "After all, if we really had been best friends since childhood, we would've already known these things about each other. Tell me something else."

"What do you want to know?"

Jack was no psychic, but he could tell Erica was putting a wall up around herself. If she felt vulnerable after sharing such vital information, then he couldn't blame her. She was the first human he'd ever told, and it wasn't an experience he was eager to have again. "Something basic and simple. Where were you born?"

"Lake Placid, New York."

"I've heard that's a nice area, but I've never been there."

"I haven't either," she said with a shrug. "My mother was a travel writer, and being pregnant with me didn't stop her from doing what she wanted. She was constantly on the go, and once I was born, I was on the go with her. She slowed down a little once I was in school, but we still moved about once a year; that was the longest she could stay in any one place. She always made sure it was an area that had a lot of hotels and resorts so she'd have plenty to keep her in business for a while. I essentially grew up as a tourist."

"That had to be rough." It wasn't anything particularly deep, but it was a start. It was easy for him to imagine a younger version of Erica, exploring the world city by city. Those experiences had stayed with her, he could tell. They showed every time he looked in her eyes.

Erica flapped her hand in the air. "I managed, and I certainly learned how to pack a suitcase. I was more than prepared for my current career when it came to the traveling aspect, and I can't be upset about that. Mom still travels all the time, actually. She just takes cruises around the world and makes sure she sends postcards. What about you? Where are you from?"

"We moved around a lot, too," he admitted. "My father was a military man, and he was stationed at Fort Benning when I was born. We stayed there for a little while, but I've been all over the place."

"Did you ever settle down anywhere, or do you stay on the move?"

"I'm living in Dallas at the moment." That was where he'd been staying ever since he was recruited by the Force, but whatever happened after that remained to be seen. "You?"

"D.C. It's a bit too crowded, and there's a lot of tension there that's difficult to get away from, but that's where my job has led me."

The two of them continued their idle chatter for the next half hour, and Jack was sure that Erica was being just as careful to steer clear of anything related to their major revelation earlier that day. It was just as well. They needed things to be on a smooth, even keel when they arrived.

Hortonburg was supposed to be one of the largest towns in this area, but when they pulled inside the city limits, Jack couldn't help but notice it was only a bigger version of the village they'd stopped in just after crossing the Ohio River. It was spread out, with large strips of ragged grass between the buildings. The zoning laws there were loose or perhaps nonexistent, with homes and businesses mingled all along the main route. A group of teens ambled down the side of the road, where Jack noted there was no actual sidewalk, clearly looking for trouble.

Best Value Car Sales was just on the outskirts of town. Jack noted this was where the newest stores were opening, including a strip mall and a massive superstore. The lot itself wasn't much different than any other used dealership. Rows of vehicles were grouped together by body style, creating a section each of cars, trucks, SUVs, and even a few ATVs off to the side. A tall, electronic sign proudly proclaimed the best deals they currently had on the lot, with blinking prices and bids for urgency such as "Come in Now!" and "Get Them Before They're Gone!" It was all so very mundane, and it made Jack's suspicion increase exponentially. If this guy did have some sort of secret terrorist cell, then he was doing a great job of covering it up.

Jack parked between the rows of vehicles and looked at Erica. "Ready to go shop for a car, best buddy?"

"Only if we can get recruited into a strange cult while we're at it, my dude," she replied with a spark in her eye.

The air was hot and humid, but it wasn't nearly as bad there as it'd been further south near those old cabins. Still, it made his shirt stick to his skin. Jack plucked at the fabric as he felt his fox vibrate with vigilance. He kept a careful eye on Erica, feeling a surprising need to protect her from whatever they might encounter.

They'd only been on the lot for a couple of minutes when an enthusiastic voice hailed them from the small white building at the back of the property. "Hi there, folks! Is there anything I can help you find?"

Jack turned to face Ben Jones himself, who was walking toward them with large steps and a friendly smile. He was exactly the same as he'd been in the picture Mr. Worth had shown him, a salesman bent on pretending to be your friend so he could line his own pockets. Long gone was the idea of a used car dealer wearing a plaid polyester suit and cheap shoes. Ben was dressed in a short-sleeve button-down and khakis. Even his accent had been polished away into almost nothing, which Jack was sure was a good tactic for a rural area like this. "My friend here is looking to get a different car."

Erica waggled her fingers at the man in a girly way Jack knew she'd never do in real life. "I want something a little newer and a little cuter."

"Cute doesn't matter, Erica. It's about how well it runs and if you can afford it." They'd agreed to keep their actual names just so there would be less to slip up on. Ben wasn't going to bring them to his compound if he had any reason to distrust them.

She shrugged and rolled her eyes.

"What kind of budget are we working with, folks?" Ben asked politely.

"Ten to fifteen," Erica replied.

"More like ten," Jack corrected.

Ben slapped his hands together in a clap and kept them there. "Great. I've got plenty right here that will accommodate you. Please note that all the price breakdowns are posted in the windows of every vehicle. Here at Best Value, we always want you to know exactly what you're buying. This Toyota, for example, is only six thousand, but it's got low mileage and the history report shows no accidents. You can also see here that we've put it through our multi-point inspection to make sure it's safe and running properly."

Jack leaned over, pretending to study the price sheet

while Erica peered through the front window to check out the interior. This guy was trying to sell them a car that was only a fraction of the price they'd said they were willing to spend. The vehicle looked immaculate, too. "It's something to keep in mind."

"How about that one over there?" Erica trotted off to check out a little coupe.

The trio continued the usual banter for about half an hour. Mr. Jones was nothing less than polite, and he didn't give off the type of vibes that most people in his position did. If Jack hadn't already known about Ben's somewhat suspicious behavior—and if he lived in the area—he'd be sending all his friends to go buy vehicles from the guy. They gave him their names and told him all about how they were new in town, but they'd heard this was the place to go for a used vehicle. They talked about the weather and how the summer promised to be a nice one.

"I think your wife will be very happy with this car," Ben said as they headed inside to get started on the paperwork.

"Oh, she's not my wife. We're best friends, actually. We grew up together, and we've known each other forever." Jack was secretly glad that Winston hadn't insisted on some other farce, like honeymooners or even an engaged couple. Things were better between him and Erica now that they'd decided on their truce, but he didn't think they could quite pull that off. Whether Ben could see it or not, Jack could still sense a certain amount of tension in the air between them. He didn't know how to make it just go away, either.

"That's right!" Ben tapped his forehead. "You mentioned you were friends. I'm sorry."

"Nothing to be sorry for, especially with the price you're giving her." He glanced at Erica, who hadn't stopped smiling since they'd arrived. Clearly, she'd decided that the slightly ditzy female tactic was the best route for her. It worked well enough for their purposes, but he had to wonder how she felt about it.

Ben brought them into the building and sat them down in his office. "What can we do for you folks in terms of financing? We have a great local bank that we work with a lot."

"You don't do any in-house financing?" Jack asked. Many small lots did, and even when they had no ties to terrorism, they were usually a rip-off. He'd been cautiously watching for any signs of money laundering or other odd banking schemes that might have pointed to something shady.

Ben shook his head vehemently and waved his hand in the air, brushing away any notion of such things. "Absolutely not. I understand a lot of folks are looking for a second chance, and they're worried the banks won't touch them. I actually worked at a dealership that did just that sort of financing before I started this place. I saw how much it affected people's budgets when they were so severely overcharged, and they thought it was their only option. I don't like that idea."

"That's really great. In fact, everything about this place is great." Jack glanced at Erica. They needed to get in. Buying a car and going back to Kentucky wasn't going to get them anywhere. But Erica was just sitting there with her legs crossed, swinging one foot carelessly in the air.

Fortunately, Ben pulled out a form and poised his pen to fill it out for them, asking the one question Jack had been hoping for. "So, how did you say you heard about us?"

Jack rubbed his thumb across his upper lip. "Actually, it was your website that brought us here."

"Oh, you'd been shopping for cars online. That's great. I've really tried to improve our web presence." Ben made a note on the form.

"Actually, we've been looking for something much more than a car. We found your other website, the blog about peace, happiness, and a better way of life. We watched a few of your videos, too, and we really liked what we saw."

Jack's fox had relaxed somewhat while they'd been working on buying the car. Ben was surprisingly easy to be around. Now, though, it coiled its muscles, ready to run or strike, whatever might be necessary. Like most situations in his life, Jack had rehearsed this in his head several times over. The only thing he had to do right now was to wait and see what Ben had to say.

The salesman's face split into a grin and he leaned back slightly in his chair. "Really? That's fantastic."

"No, *you're* pretty fantastic." Was Erica batting her eyelashes at him? "Everyone these days is just out to make a buck, and they don't care how they do it. For me, I just want to be happy. I think modern life is all backward."

Jack was on board in an instant. "Things are supposed to be better in this day and age with all our technology, but I think it just inhibits us. We don't look up from our screens long enough to see what's actually going on around us." He knew he was just echoing some of the sentiments Ben had shared in his online videos, none of which were particularly extreme. They were a rebellion against first-world lifestyles in a very peaceful way.

"I completely agree," Ben enthused. "If I had it my way, I wouldn't even have any computers here in the office. It's a little hard to run a business that way, but in my personal life, I try to stay off the grid as much as possible."

Erica clapped her hands. "I've been reading a lot about off-grid living! I still have so much to learn, but it's a really exciting idea. How great would it be to actually not depend on grocery stores and utility companies?"

She was really selling it. Jack had to hand it to her. He only hoped that was what Ben wanted. The salesman smiled benevolently, steepling his fingers in front of his chest. "I do live that way, actually, when I'm not here at work."

"That's so awesome," Erica gasped. "Can you give us some tips?"

Ben pressed his lips together, but he was only suppressing a smile. "I can do better than that. I can show you. If you're truly interested, that is."

"We are." Jack didn't want there to be any chance of Ben recruiting Erica without him going along. "In fact, we were thinking about buying ourselves a plot of land and giving it a shot. It turns out we can't quite afford to get the acreage we'd need."

Ben pursed his lips thoughtfully as he looked from Jack to Erica and back again. "I can tell you're... *special* people, the kind who know how to get in touch with their more instinctive, natural sides. The kind who could go out into the wild, away from all society, and still survive. Yes?"

Jack's stomach stuck to his spine. So Ben could tell he was a shifter. He must have sensed something about Erica, the same way Jack had, and decided she was one of them as well. It'd been disturbing enough to tell Erica who he was, but now this stranger also knew. This was all part of the game, though. Jack nodded.

"You don't need any acreage at all, my friends." Ben held up his hand to stave off their worries, and Jack noticed a bit of his accent had come back. "I have a lot of land. I started out with just a few acres, but over the years, I've been able to buy up the surrounding plots as people have sold them off and relocated to the city. My friends have moved there with me, and we live in peace and harmony away from the prying eyes of the government and society who might judge us for our simple ways. They're the same kind of people you are: in touch with their true nature."

Erica reached over to pat Jack's arm. "Isn't that great?"

"Let's finish this paperwork, and then I'll take you out there. If you like it, maybe you can find a new home with us." There was that kind smile again.

This man was a charmer. Jack could sense the shifter inside him, but it was incredibly subtle. If he hadn't been looking for it, he might not even have noticed. Ben put out the side of him that he wanted everyone to see, and if there was anything beyond that, then he hid it carefully.

"There's nothing we'd like better," Jack affirmed. "We could learn a lot from you."

Ben's head bobbed. "I'm sure you could."

6

"THAT WAS ALMOST TOO EASY," ERICA SAID WHEN THEY WERE in her new car heading down the road behind Ben's vehicle. "It really makes me wonder."

"You figured it'd be harder?" Jack questioned.

"Well, yeah! I mean, this isn't my first rodeo. It usually takes a lot more time to get involved in someone's personal life. I don't like the fact that he's bringing us right back to his place. It makes me incredibly suspicious. What if he's decided we know too much and he's just going to get rid of us? I mean, when we went over all the other information the DHS has gathered, some of it pointed to the possibility of the recruits being killed off."

Jack adjusted his hands on the wheel and bit his lower lip, his jaw flexing. "Well, I have my own theory about that."

"Which is?" Erica glanced out the window. The land that held Ben's compound butted up to the national forest, but in a rural area like this, it didn't take long to get away from civilization. They didn't have long.

He hesitated for a moment, as if deciding exactly what he wanted to say. "I believe our new friend is a shifter. It could be that he's recruiting other shifters, and in that case, people might be coming and going from the property in other forms."

Erica closed her eyes and ran her hand across her forehead. "That's not good. I could hardly stand being around *you* at first. How the hell am I going to manage being with an entire compound of people with so much spirit energy? Christ." When she'd been informed about this mission, Erica had been convinced that it was simple; cut and dried, same old stuff she'd always been doing. Instead, her entire world was changing. The things she'd already learned before she'd even gotten to the meat of the operation were staggering, and she could only hope she could deal with them.

It would be a lot easier if she didn't have to fight with herself about Jack. She was a professional, and she'd long ago made a pact with herself not to get involved with anyone she worked with. It was just too messy, and simply being a woman made it difficult enough to climb the corporate ladder without a relationship cluttering it up. Erica could control herself, and just because a guy was good looking didn't mean she had to do anything about it.

But Jack was different in every sense of the word. Not only could she justify her feelings toward him by reminding herself that he was only a consultant for the Department, he was attractive on a different level. Sure, she'd met some handsome guys, ones with broad shoulders, muscular bodies, and relaxed grins that were both boyish and sexy. Jack had all that, but the rest of it went deeper. If she didn't know he was a shifter, she would've just said there was something about him. And maybe it was the fact that there was a whole other person inside him. Erica couldn't be sure, but she felt the ripples of energy between them. She could practically see them, like shimmering northern lights that pulled them together.

Unfortunately, there was no more time to talk about it. Ben's car had turned up a long driveway, and it now stopped just before a large gate. A man leaned near one of the gate posts. His stance was casual, but his eyes were watchful. Ben got out of the driver's seat and came back to Jack's window. "My friends, as you know, we strive to get away from the rigors of the world. I ask that you each give me your cell phones. This is my way of protecting you from such unhealthy things."

"Of course." Without question, they each handed their devices over. They'd known this would be part of the process.

Ben grinned, seemingly pleased with their cooperation. "Perfect. Follow me inside, and you can park over to the left."

The parking lot was the same as what they'd spotted on the satellite imagery, and the other vehicles already neatly lined up left no question as to where they were supposed to go. "You ready?" Jack murmured as he turned off the car.

Erica heard the gate slam shut behind them, echoing in her blood. "I don't think there's any turning back, even if I'm not." The one comfort she could take was in knowing that Jack was there with her. She wasn't alone. She might not have trusted him at first, but she definitely trusted him now.

Ben spread his arms as he welcomed them from the edge of the parking area. "I welcome you to our little corner of the world, where we can live happily and freely. Let me show you around."

Erica had prided herself on being a strong, independent woman who didn't need a man to lean on. She'd charged into plenty of dangerous situations, and she relied on her skills, experience, and innate talents to keep her safe. For some reason, though, she found herself wanting to wrap her hands around Jack's tight waist and lean her head against the hard planes of his chest. She could even imagine his fingers coming down to graze the small of her back in return.

She blushed and shook her head, grateful that Jack

wasn't the one with psychic powers so he couldn't read her thoughts.

―――――

ERICA SAT on the edge of the twin bed and looked around the small room. It had anything a person could need, if not necessarily what they wanted. As Ben and his website had promised, the electronics had been kept to the barest minimum. Even the clock was analog, and she hadn't spotted a single television or laptop since they'd arrived. Any electricity they did have was provided by the massive solar panels on top of the building.

It was getting late, and everything was quiet. Not just the noise in the building, but inside her head. The silence made her realize just how far she'd come in getting used to Jack and his extra presence. Being there in that room was like stepping out of a crowded elevator and finding herself in the middle of a remote forest. It was a nice break, but she wasn't comfortable enough to enjoy it.

She knew it was against Ben's rules. She knew she was taking a major risk by attempting to go against the grain on the first night. Still, she launched herself from the side of the bed and went to the door. Her hand rested on the knob for a long moment, almost afraid to turn it. Ben had said nothing about locking their new friends in, but he did say they were supposed to remain in their rooms until everyone arose at six in the morning. She cringed as she slowly twisted the brass handle, her eyebrows lifting when the door released with a small click.

The hallway was wide but plain, giving plenty of room to move around furniture or large crowds. The sealed concrete floor shone faintly in the interspersed wall lamps. Erica watched the pools of light and willed her heart to be quiet for a moment so that she might listen. No one was coming.

Erica was careful to twist the knob as she shut the door behind her, not wanting even the faintest click of the latch to give away her position. She flicked her tongue across the roof of her mouth, thinking. Each of the rooms was labeled with a number, and Ben had explained that men and women were all separated unless they were a married couple, but he hadn't told them if there was any kind of system that indicated who might be in what room. She turned to look at her own door, looking for her name or even some sort of mark that might indicate she was a newcomer or a female or something. It was all plain and clean.

In working with Winston and Mr. Worth, they'd decided against any forms of communication with each other or to the outside world. It wasn't worth the risk of Ben or his minions finding a wire on them. The only thing they'd smuggled in was a small, specialized transmitter from Hudson's communications company that couldn't be detected until one of them pulled a tab out of the back to activate it. This was to be used only in the most extreme emergency when requesting an extraction. While Erica had completely agreed with this idea in the first place, she cursed it now. She needed to find Jack, but she couldn't possibly break into every room until she found him. The longer she stood in the hall, the more she risked being discovered.

There's always a backup plan, she reminded herself as she closed her eyes. She reached out and placed her fingertips on the wall to steady her body as she opened her mind. There was only so much she could do to cut off other presences that invaded her head, but she now opened up every facet of her psychic powers in order to listen.

The thoughts of those peacefully slumbering the night away came to her like gentle curls of smoke on a breeze, carrying with them only the wisps of their dreams. Erica brushed these aside. She highly doubted Jack was any less awake than she was, and none of these hazy presences felt the same way Jack did. Erica reached out further, searching, testing her powers in ways she hadn't for a long time. She was always trying to get everyone out of her mind, and now she was trying to pull them in.

There he is. She'd only known Jack for a few days, but there was no mistaking his signature. He was strong and restless, his spirit so much bigger than his body. Erica moved more quickly down the hallway, turning a corner and trotting silently down the next hall. Her heartbeat picked up once again as she drew nearer. She needed her eyes only to make sure she didn't bump into a wall because her mind was leading her straight to Jack.

She paused for a moment outside his door. Was this a mistake? What would Jack think of her for coming to him in the middle of the night like this? She instantly chastised herself once again. The two of them were coworkers, partners. If she couldn't come to him, then what was the point of any of this? Just because it was late and she hadn't been able to completely set aside her desire for him in favor of doing the job they'd set out to accomplish didn't mean this was wrong. A knock would be too loud. She tentatively reached out a finger and scratched at the door.

It whipped open, the air from the movement pulling her loose hair along with it. Jack stood in the doorway, bare to the waist. He'd already been impressive to look at, but seeing the way his tight abs tapered into a V under the edge of his pants made her core ache with need. His chestnut eyes flashed in the dim light as they flitted from her face to take in the rest of the hallway. Seeing she was alone, his strong hand gripped her arm and yanked her into the room, closing the door silently behind her. "What the hell are you doing? You could get us both killed."

"I know that," she said impatiently. "I'm perfectly aware of the rules Ben set forth. Like I said, this isn't my first time doing this. But I can't sleep, and we need to talk. I'm worried he'll keep us separated and we won't get a chance to put our heads together and fully analyze this place. Besides, I can't stop thinking about what you said on the way over here." There were plenty of other things she couldn't stop thinking about, too, like how the warm skin covering his brawny arms would feel under her fingertips as she glanced at the intricate tattoo on his bicep.

"About Ben being a shifter?" Jack pulled a shirt over his head, something Erica was grateful for. She didn't need the distraction of his impeccably chiseled muscles.

"Yes. Well, but it goes back further than that. You mind if I sit?" The room was small, just as small as her own, and yet Jack's presence filled it completely. It was a different sensation than what she'd felt with him in the car on their way up from Kentucky. It was her awareness of him more than anything.

"Sure." He gestured her toward the bed while he occupied the firm chair near the wall, his feet spread wide on the hard floor and his elbows braced against his thighs.

Erica pulled in a deep breath. She hadn't wanted to go into all these details. Life, she'd learned a long time ago, was simpler when the hard stuff stayed buried. No one needed to know her secret or how difficult it was to deal with it. Even though Jack knew of her power now, there was so much more to it than that. "First, I need to apologize to you. I didn't trust you from the instant I met you."

He flicked an eyebrow. "So I noticed."

"You can't really blame me," she said with a glare. "I can feel people inside my head. It's like I can tap into their mental energies. In fact, I could sense both sides of you. I just thought it meant you were some sort of double agent. Up until earlier today, I had no idea shifters existed in anything outside of teen movies. Sorry." She realized after she said it just how much she'd cheapened his very existence.

Jack didn't seem affected. "There are a lot of us, actually. You've met others, I'm sure, but it's not my place to tell. We keep it to ourselves, for obvious reasons."

Erica nodded and licked her lips. "Can you tell me a little more about how it works? I mean, is it the kind of thing where you can turn into whatever you want?" It'd been a little difficult to imagine that anyone like him existed at all, and she felt so rude in asking, but she was desperate to understand.

"No, nothing like that. Each of us has an animal side, and it's only one animal. Some people are wolves, others are bears, and a few are dragons if you can believe that. I'm a fox."

"Oh." She stifled a smile. He was a fox for damn sure, but she wasn't about to say it out loud. On the more serious side, she could even see it in him now. Not just in the auburn tones of his hair, but in the intensity of those light brown eyes. "Do you have control over it? Shifting, I mean."

"Most of the time, I'm absolutely in control. There are

certain circumstances, like in the presence of the full moon or... strong emotions, that make it a little harder to remain human." He cleared his throat and glanced away. "But I've met plenty of shifters who hadn't let their other forms out in months if they didn't want to." He folded his fingers together and looked her in the eye. "No offense, Erica, but I thought you wanted to talk about the mission."

"I do. I mean, this is about the mission." She made a sound, disgusted with herself. Erica could be perfectly articulate during a business meeting, but there was something about Jack that made him impossible to talk to without sounding like an idiot. "It was difficult to be around you before I understood why you had so much extra energy surrounding you. Once I did, it helped me sort things out in my mind and block some of it out. My concern now is you said Ben is a shifter, and that maybe his recruits are, too."

"Yes."

"But I don't sense that same energy within them. Not in Ben, and not in the people he'd introduced us to here while he was giving us the tour. They were all so bland, if you will, that it's like they hardly have any mental energy at all. It's disturbing." Jack had really gotten her mind working when he'd mentioned that Ben and the others might be shifters, and Erica had been searching for similar cerebral patterns in everyone as Ben had shown them the gardens, the solar array, and the massive pole barn that had been converted to living quarters. There had been a man hoeing a row of corn who smiled pleasantly and touched the brim of his hat, a woman in the kitchens who beamed at them over a pot of stew, and several others gathered in a common area who enthusiastically hugged them and shook their hands while welcoming them to the fold. None of them, however, had given her anything to latch onto other than mild pleasant sensations.

"I see. That's interesting. You see, shifters can sense the animal inside others. We can't always tell what kind, and I don't think it blows us away like it did to you at first. But if I hadn't already known to look for it with Ben, I might not have noticed. It was very faint, barely even there at all." His gaze wandered up to the corner of the room as he thought.

"Wait, how did you know to look for it?" Erica was exhausted, physically and mentally, but that tiny phrase was an important one.

Jack cursed under his breath as his eyes flicked to her and then away again. "Like I said, there are other shifters you've met, but it's not my place to say. I shouldn't be telling you this either, but I actually work with a group of shifters who are all Special Ops vets. Coming in as a consultant for the DHS was just my way of paying back a favor for Winston."

"I see." She'd hoped for answers, but it only spurred on more questions. Just how many people like Jack was she surrounded by? Had it been Winston? Mr. Worth? Why hadn't she noticed it in them? This team he spoke of was certainly something she wanted to know more about, but first, she needed to understand just who and what he was. "Are some people just better at hiding it? I mean, in your experience, when it comes to sensing them?"

"It's not always that they're trying to hide it," Jack explained. "It might just be that the more feral side of themselves isn't as active at the moment. Honestly, I thought maybe you were one of us at first."

"Me?" she squeaked. Erica had always been getting into other people's minds, whether she wanted to or not. She'd never imagined it being the other way around. Somehow, the idea of Jack looking inside her like that wasn't as disturbing as she would've thought.

"There was definitely something... *different* about you." His eyes were intense on her now.

She turned away. Jack was just too much. Not in any way that she truly knew how to explain. It was just so easy to get lost in the deluge of his energy. "That's something I've heard plenty of times before. I was always the weird kid growing up, and it really hasn't changed at all in my adult life. I'm sure there are plenty of other agents who don't trust me or like me."

"I never said I didn't like you," he corrected.

Heat flushed her cheeks, and she chided herself for reacting to him that way. There was something so distinctly male about him that was difficult to ignore, and anything that could possibly be misconstrued as a sexual remark instantly got translated that way in her mind. "Maybe not, but you did say you didn't trust me. Everyone else I've worked with has had some notion of that. My boss doesn't like the reports I write up because he thinks everything should be hard and fast facts. No one wants to talk about intuition or instinct."

"Is that how you refer to it?" he asked quietly. "Instinct?"

Had the room suddenly gotten smaller? Why did she still have to be so damn aware of him? When they'd first started talking, Erica could've sworn he was across the room. But with her on the edge of the bed and him in the chair, their knees were practically touching. She could feel the heat radiating off his skin and smell the sandalwood soap he'd used. "It's one way," she gulped, trying to keep her mind on the conversation and not his body. "I can't exactly explain it to anyone else."

"Now that, I definitely understand," he remarked with a wry smile. "It's not easy to hide a secret from everyone you work with, everyone you run into on the street, and even people you want to be friends with. Not when your chances of them understanding are slim to none."

"But you said there are a lot of shifters," she countered.

"I only meant that there are probably a lot more than you would imagine. I've got my Special Ops buddies and other shifter friends, but humans still outnumber us by a long shot. I can't imagine there are very many psychics running around, either." His eyes danced over her features, lingering on her lips for a split second too long before returning to her eyes.

"No. I've never met another one, anyway." Erica frowned, thinking about how lonely her life had been. Even her friends and family had never truly known her, and she'd longed for a deep connection with someone. "It would be nice, though. I'd like to have a bond with someone who understood me like that."

He tipped his head. "Do you think if you did, it might be the kind of thing you just couldn't deny? Something that you felt in the very core of your soul and couldn't stop, no matter how hard you fought against it?"

Something about his words made a shiver of electricity course through her nerves. She bit her lower lip. Why did Jack do this to her? She should have been focusing on their mission and finding out who Ben and his recruits really were, but instead, she was getting completely lost in Jack's entrancing eyes and voice. Erica felt hypnotized by him as she slowly nodded. "Yeah, something like that."

"It's like that for shifters," he said quietly.

"Like an alliance? You have to be on their side?" She was getting into dangerous territory, and she knew it. Erica was about to botch this entire operation with whatever was going on inside her mind. "Is that going to be a problem if you have to fight shifters?"

The corner of Jack's mouth curved seductively. "That's not what I mean." He'd moved forward on the chair and reached out to pull her hands into his. Her fingertips crackled with energy as he ran his thumbs over her palms. "It happens with all of us, but not with every person we meet. Sometimes that person is another shifter, and sometimes they're not. But that one person, when we do meet them, makes it difficult for us to control our form. It's like we completely lose our heads when we finally meet the person we're destined to be with."

"Destined?" There was hardly any room in her throat for the word to come out. This wasn't happening. She'd fallen asleep and was having some wild dream.

But Jack had leaned forward, and their faces were only a few inches apart. "Destined. I can tell we're fated to be together. As mates."

Perhaps he'd been controlling his spiritual energy once she'd told him she was psychic, or perhaps she'd just been doing that good of a job of blocking it out, but neither was stopping the flow now. She could feel him, not just physically, but psychically. He'd wrapped around her as he delved into her mind. He was like cool water on a hot beach: refreshing, invigorating, and absolutely irresistible. "How do you know?"

"I just do. And I think you do, too." He pressed his lips to hers, a slow but deliberate gesture. "Mission or not, I don't know how long we can really ignore this, Erica."

She closed her eyes, savoring the sound of her name on his voice. "I know."

"Does that mean you feel something, too?"

Feel something? Hell, she couldn't get away from it. Jack was a blur of colors, images, and emotions in her mind, massive and engulfing and utterly delightful. Erica wanted to get completely lost in him and pretend the rest of the world didn't exist. "Like nothing I've ever felt before." Her lips found his again then, and Erica didn't know which one of them had initiated the kiss. It didn't even matter. His fingers twined in between hers and gripped them tightly as though he might lose himself if he let go as his mouth explored hers. His lips were warm and inviting, and their tongues were soon a tangle. At that moment, Erica allowed the rest of her concerns to float away. It didn't matter that they were in the middle of potential enemy territory or that they should be behaving like professionals. She just knew that she needed him.

He got out of the chair and pulled her to her feet along with him. Just as she'd envisioned before, she felt his hands on her lower back and pressed herself against him. The evidence of his need for her was hard against her stomach, which sent a spark of excitement through her core as their kiss deepened. Erica touched him tentatively, exploring his hard abs beneath her fingertips before bringing her hands up his back and into his thick hair.

He pulled back slowly, breaking their liplock with the

utmost delicacy. "Erica," he breathed.

"Yes?"

"I can see where this is going, or at least where I'd like it to go, but I don't want to do anything if it's not what you want." He pressed his forehead against hers, his shoulders tense with the effort of holding himself back.

She smiled. For all the distrust she'd initially held for him, Jack was a good guy. "I thought at first I was just attracted to you because we'd been put in a dangerous situation together. That makes people think and feel things that aren't quite true. I don't think it's like that with us." She dared to find his mouth with hers again.

He growled as his hands gripped her backside. "I mean it, Erica. Please don't do that unless you mean it, too."

She put her hands under his shirt, splaying her fingers against the muscles of his back and longing to feel more of his skin against hers. "I absolutely do."

His response was a strong one, gripping her body against his with such strength that he lifted her feet off the floor. The two of them tumbled into bed together, and the rest of the world melted away. Jack worshipped her mouth with his own as his hands worked at her blouse, pulling the buttons apart to reveal what lay hidden beneath.

She was already heated through, but the feeling of his hands on her stomach, then drifting up to the roundness of her breasts, set Erica on fire. Arching against him, needing more, she gripped the hem of his shirt and pulled it off.

She'd already seen him without his shirt, but it was different as they lay in bed together. He was stronger, bigger, and even more statuesque. She pulled him down to her as he stripped off her jeans, running his hands down the smoothness of each of her legs and sending a quiver through her body that made her gasp.

Erica ignored the soft thumps of their clothes hitting the floor as her skin met his. Fire blazed behind her eyes as she explored his body, from the hardness of his chest to the rippling muscles of his abs to the strength of his legs and the urgency of his throbbing manhood that lay between them. She wrapped her own legs around him, desperate and eager.

"Erica," he groaned into the crook of her neck as she writhed against him.

"Please." She couldn't remember the last time she'd yearned for anything so badly. There wasn't time for foreplay. Erica had finally found someone that she could connect with on the deepest level possible, and she didn't want anything to stand in the way of making that final bond. She pushed her hips against him once again.

Jack sank inside her, filling her completely. She opened her body and mind to him, willing him to be inside of her in every aspect. His presence was no longer random flashes of imagery that she usually got from other people. He was light and color, melding and swirling and then separating into a million suns that exploded into galaxies. She felt the animal inside him now, a raw and feral beast that needed her in the same way she needed him. They fastened to each other on an intrinsic level that Erica had never before accessed as their hips pulsed together.

Her body accepted him just as easily as her mind did, wrapping around his hardness and making it a part of her. She could smell him, taste him even, as her walls contracted around him more and more with each thrust. The low growl emitting from his throat as he gripped her hips let her know he was almost there. Erica clenched her body and bucked harder against him, sending them each over the edge.

Separating from Jack was like coming to after passing out in a strange place. Her consciousness returned to her own body as she looked around the room, hardly even knowing where she was for a moment. He'd rolled over and put his back to the wall with his arms around her, holding her from behind. She sank into the warmth and comfort of his body, and the reality of where they were and what they were actually supposed to be doing there was like a distant memory.

"You okay?" he whispered as he pulled her closer, wrapping his leg over the top of hers protectively.

She smiled. "Mhmm." For the first time in her life, she'd deliberately let someone in instead of pushing them away. Her mind was calm and relaxed, and she couldn't remember ever feeling more at peace.

7

JACK SCANNED THE LARGE COMMON ROOM THAT SERVED AS A cafeteria and general gathering place. There were so many people there, so many more than he'd ever estimated. When Ben had shown them around the day before, they'd only met a handful. Jack now felt like he was in the break room of some big corporation. Of course, it would've had to have been one of those newer places with good benefits and flexible work schedules, because everyone looked way too happy to be there.

Finally, his eyes landed on a woman in a blue shirt just getting in the back of the line for food. Her waves of hair were slightly rumpled, but her eyes carried a familiar glow to them as she, too, scanned the room.

He stepped up behind her. "I was worried about you

getting back to your room last night," he whispered in Erica's ear. "You should've let me walk with you."

"I can handle myself, thank you." Her words were tough, but the coy smile she gave him sent an entirely different message. "Besides, it wouldn't be worth both of us getting into trouble."

The line moved forward, and the two of them stepped up with it as someone headed toward the tables with a tray full of food. "We're in this together, Erica. We already were, but I would think last night more than proved that." He hadn't been able to stop thinking about her, and it wasn't just the sex. Jack had been honest when he'd confessed that he believed Erica to be his mate. Those were words he'd never thought to hear from his own mouth, but as soon as they were out, they made complete sense. No one else had ever sensed him in the way that she did, psychic or not. Never had he been tempted to reveal his own truth to a non-shifter, yet he'd just blurted it out to her in the car. There was no denying it for him. She was his.

"Yes, but at least some of that has to wait. We're supposed to be best friends, remember?" She glanced up at him again through her lashes.

He thought he might completely come apart inside seeing her like that. Jack had always relied heavily on his logic, and it was only the shifter portion of him that didn't like to obey practicality and reasoning. Whatever had happened between he and Erica had brought even more of that out in him, and he was struggling to have any control over himself whatsoever. "That's going to be a hard sell if you keep looking at me like that."

She turned away, and the conversation was suspended while they filled their trays from the generous buffet. Jack noted a wide array of quality, fresh food that even most restaurants didn't offer. "This is quite a spread," he remarked as the two of them sat down at a table near the corner. "It certainly helps rule out a few theories, too."

Erica looked up from her tray. Her eyes were soft and sweet, but she quickly hardened them. Jack wondered if she, too, was working hard not to let anyone see what had transpired between the two of them. "How so?"

He pointed with his fork. "Pork sausage. Most of these terrorist cells join their recruits based on religion, but he's clearly not some Islamic extremist. Or, if he is, he's decided to take a different tactic."

"He never once asked for our spiritual beliefs," Erica noted as she scooped up a spoonful of fruit salad. "I was thinking about that quite a bit myself. It's not like a typical religious cult. It's more like he's just promising peace and happiness, a utopia of sorts. Of course, we haven't been here long enough to really know what his motives are."

"The one thing I can say is that the peace and happiness he's promised seems to be a genuine offer. Look at everyone. It's bright and early in the day, but they're smiling from ear to ear. They all look so happy and healthy."

"Maybe that's all it takes these days," Erica reasoned. "He's not going to get anyone here by promising more of the stress and headache of our current lives. And he did tell us that he's protecting us by taking away our cell phones. I have to agree that social media and the constant screen time are bad for people in the long run. If we're lucky, this is more like a wellness retreat than anything."

He noticed the subtle shift in her eyes. It was like the color had changed slightly. "Can I ask you something?"

"Of course."

"You told me how hard it was to be around me, that you could even tell there was more to me than a regular human. Just how much can you see? I mean, can you actually see my thoughts?" Jack had been wondering this ever since she'd told him, and he hadn't been sure how to ask. It was funny to think that they were each practically fictional to each other up until yesterday.

"Not really. I mean, I can, but it's something that takes a lot of energy. If I'm actually trying to reach into someone's mind and get specific thoughts, I usually end up passing out afterward. I have to be careful about that, obviously. Most of the time, it's just a general notion of their feelings with a few flashes of imagery here and there."

She spoke of it to him like she was talking about going to the grocery store, and even though Jack knew that was how things should be, it was making him nervous. He wanted to know more, but it would have to wait. "Look, there's Ben right now."

The man had just walked in through the double doors. As soon as the others saw him, the crowd broke out in applause. He spread his arms and put his hands up in the air to acknowledge them, the smile on his face very similar to the one he wore on his sales posters. "Thank you! Good morning! It's good to see you." He made his way through the room, stopping here and there to put his hand on a shoulder or laugh at someone's joke. The center of the room had been left free of tables, something Jack had noted but hadn't known what to make of it. When Ben stopped and the crowd silenced, he understood. This was how Ben spoke to his followers, and they readily put down their forks to listen.

"My dearest friends, I hope you're having a fantastic morning. I know I am. I woke up today feeling so grateful for everything we have here. We're happy, we're healthy. We have plenty to eat and drink. Most of all, we have the fellowship of likeminded people who simply want to live their lives. I think those two things are incredibly important: gratitude and fellowship." Ben paused as several in the crowd cheered. "We are nothing without each other. I do my best to provide all of you with everything you could possibly need, and I do my best to protect you from the dangers of the outside world, but in return, I get so much from you that I'm grateful for. My mission and I would be nothing without all of you." Once again, there was a smattering of applause.

Jack knew he needed to pay attention to every word Ben was saying, but he was also very interested in seeing how the crowd reacted. In every situation like this that he'd been a part of, there was always someone who hadn't completely bought into what the leader was selling. There was someone who didn't feel they were getting what they'd been promised out of the deal. Or maybe they did and realized that wasn't what they actually wanted, and now they were just looking for a way out. They would do their best to hide this fact from the leader for as long as they could because, of course, it wasn't worth risking their lives, but it would be evident on their faces or in their actions whether they realized it or not. Jack looked around, watching all the nods, smiles, and occasional claps of encouragement. He watched for hard eyes, tightened jaws, or stiff shoulders and saw none.

None, that is, until he turned back to Erica. Her eyes had changed again, the verdant green having turned to hard stone as she looked not at Ben, but at the double doors where everyone had entered the room. Trying to be subtle, Jack let his eyes drift in that direction.

A man leaned in the doorway there. Most of the people in the room were the of the same demographic that was common in that rural part of the state. Whether because they wanted to be or because Ben had made them to be, they were clean cut and dressed conservatively. The man in the doorway could've just as easily been one of them, but the grease stains on his clothes and the dirt under his fingernails made him stand out. Even more than that, the hard look in his eyes as he watched the leader wasn't anything like the happiness that glowed from the other followers.

Jack was no psychic, and he was still getting used to the idea of such a thing existing, but he wished he could reach out and touch Erica's mind with his own. His fox was on alert, knowing there was something wrong with her. He could feel it thrashing around inside him, desperate to get out. At the very least, he wanted to ask her what was going on. He didn't dare to interrupt Ben, though. For the moment, he turned his attention back to the car salesman.

"Friends, we have two new people who have joined us. They, like the rest of us, are looking for a better way of life. They want the peace and harmony that everyone craves, but they've been brave enough to go out into the world and find it. Please give a warm welcome to Jack and Erica." He gestured at them to stand.

Jack pushed his chair back, glancing nervously at Erica. She'd pasted that vapid look on her face that she'd worn back at the dealership, the one that indicated she wasn't very deep or smart and certainly not capable of infiltrating a terrorist cell and tearing it apart from the inside. Erica smiled and blushed.

"Please, make sure they feel at home here, as all of you do. They've come at a good time," Ben continued, "since we are ahead on our work. It's time for a day of relaxation and fun, my friends. Enjoy yourselves, take a day off, and revel in the tranquility that you've come here for." A rather thunderous round of applause broke out this time. Ben thanked everyone with a bob of his head as he made his way over to Jack and Erica's table. "I take it you each slept well?" he asked.

Was it a test? Did he somehow know what they'd actually spent the night doing? Even if it was, Jack wasn't about to give the man what he wanted. "Oh, yes. It's so nice and quiet here."

Ben seemed pleased with this answer. "Good, good. I'll be going in to work today. You'll find activities throughout all the common areas here, including movies and games. But first, I'd like to talk to you about your role here."

"That's exciting!" Erica squealed. "It's so generous of you to support all these kind people, and I've been wondering what I can do to help."

"Everyone has their place," Ben assured her. "We strive to put people in the place where they will be the happiest, so that we may all find fulfillment in our jobs while we support each other. There are some who work in the kitchens or the gardens, and we even have some who prefer the laundry area. Tell me, what are your talents?"

Erica lifted a shoulder. "I think I'm a decent cook, and I'd really like the chance to find out more about gardening. It's so much healthier than buying all of our produce from the store, and the breakfast you've just served proves that."

She was laying it on thick, so thick that Jack wasn't sure Ben would buy it.

But the man once again looked pleased. "Great! As I've said, we'll have a relaxing day today, but I'll have Rayna guide you through some of our processes starting tomorrow. She's the head of our kitchens, and she oversees much of the gardening as part of that. She'll be more than happy to show you around. What about you, Jack? Where does your passion lie?"

This was their chance to get to know Ben a bit more and get a better insight into what he was actually doing there. Jack had to follow his instincts. They could put their heads down and simply do as they were told, but that wasn't going to get them very far. "I'm actually interested in your dealership. I'm pretty good at working with my hands if you need a mechanic to work on the cars you bring in."

Ben wasn't as agreeable with this as he had been with Erica's proposal. "No, I already have someone in that position. In fact, I've got to go see him in a moment. I'm giving my people the day off, but that doesn't mean I get one." He laughed as if this were a great joke, and Jack followed suit. "We could use your skills when it comes to building and repairing our structures, and there's always a lot of electrical work to be done. Do you think you could do that?"

It wouldn't get him right under Ben's wing where he needed to be, but it would at least keep their cover for now. "Sure. That would be great. Is there someone I should report to?"

"Kenneth will come find you after breakfast tomorrow."

"This is just so amazing," Erica gushed. "I know we haven't been here long, but we're really happy to be a part of such a great community. Is there anything else we can do to help?"

"Well..." Ben trailed off as he pursed his lips. "I hate to ask, but if there is any money you can contribute to our cause, we're in great need. As you can imagine, it's difficult to support so many people just by selling used cars here and there. We have to have some sort of sacrifice in order to gain the tranquility that we strive for here."

"I've got a little in savings. I was going to use it as a down payment if the two of us went in on a piece of property together, but you'll be able to use it much more effectively." Jack hoped his acting was up to par with Erica's. He wasn't used to being so ingratiating.

"How generous of you! Thank you, we'll get that all arranged, but for now, I want the two of you to enjoy your day. Get to know everyone. I'll be checking back in with you soon." He shook each of their hands before turning to leave.

"Um, sir?"

Ben turned to Jack, raising an eyebrow. "Please, call me Ben."

"Right. Ben. I wanted to ask you a question." This was going in more of a direct route than he normally preferred, but Jack was eager to get to the bottom of this. They hadn't discovered anything that seemed particularly odd just yet, and usually guys like Ben left their evil intentions simmering just under the surface.

"Of course."

"Why shifters? I mean, why don't you bring any regular humans in here with us? I'm sure they're looking for peace and tranquility just like the rest of us are." He widened his eyes a little to make himself look more innocent.

Fortunately, Ben didn't take this as an insult. He laid his hand on Jack's shoulder as he leaned forward. "You're right, I'm sure. But we're not like regular humans. We're separate from the rest of the world. We, carrying these animals inside us, know what it's like to live in a peaceful group. We understand what it means to be one with nature, to understand all the things the rest of man has forgotten. Humans no longer have a sense of passion and understanding. We're different."

"I get that. Makes perfect sense."

Jack watched him go, noting that the greasy man in the

doorway had been watching them. He turned away just as Ben approached him, and the two men walked down the hall together, their heads close as they talked.

"Seems to me like Ben is trying to make a point about shifters being different from the rest of the population. It's a pretty standard tactic for extremist leaders. They have to find some way to encourage you to cordon yourself off from the world. I still feel like we're missing something here, though."

"I wish I knew what that was." Erica pushed the remainder of her breakfast around on her tray. "I'm not liking anything I see here."

"What do you think is going on?" Jack knew something was amiss. Dozens of people didn't just get to do a few household chores and a little maintenance in exchange for three square meals and a solid roof overhead. "It's more like a hippie shifter commune than a terrorist cell."

"To the naked eye, yes," she agreed. "I was really looking for anything fishy from Ben himself, and of course I got nothing. It was the same way with all the other people here, except for that guy Ben just took off with."

"I was going to ask you about that," Jack admitted. "I could tell something was going on with that guy. What do you think his deal is?"

She gave a short laugh of frustration. "I wish I knew. I like to think I'm pretty good at what I do, but so are people who try to overthrow the government or make some pointed political statement. They've spent their entire lives covering up their true motives, and that's often reflected in their psychic energy. The only thing I can say for sure is that he's up to no good."

Jack rubbed his jaw. "Ben said he was a mechanic. I wonder if that translates to a bomb engineer."

"I don't know. But I *do* think we should enjoy our day, just like Ben wants. I say we split up and get as much information as possible. Your brain is geared more toward engineering, so I'll leave it up to you to map out the buildings and figure out anything you can about how they work or what might be hiding here. I'll work on the people. Someone's got to know something."

Jack's mouth twisted. "I don't like it."

"If you'd rather rub elbows, then have at it. I just think we'd be using our best assets the other way around."

He cut his hand through the air. "That's not what I mean. I don't like the idea of splitting up. This place is pretty big, neither one of us is completely familiar with it yet, and the only communication we have with the outside world isn't one we can use right now."

Now the resistant look in her eye had nothing to do with acting. "We haven't seen any actual threats, and I shouldn't have to remind you that I've been through plenty of training. I'm more than capable of taking care of myself."

That may be true, but it was hard for Jack to see her that way. She'd been soft and welcoming the previous night. Erica was a woman to be treasured and protected, not thrown out amongst a group of potential terrorists. "You don't understand. I know you're capable, but with what I am... what we did... what I feel..." He searched for the right words and cursed himself for being so emotionally wrapped up in this. Jack was a logical man, and matters of the heart always came second after matters of the mind. With Erica, though, the line blurred to the point of disappearing. How could he explain his incessant need to protect her?

She touched the back of his hand with her fingertip, a small gesture that wouldn't reveal just how intimate they'd been. "That's very sweet of you, Jack, but it's not going to get this taken care of. I'll be fine. I promise. Now if you'll excuse me, I'm going to introduce myself to that group of ladies over there." Erica rose from the table, bussed her tray, and approached the women she'd indicated.

Jack shook his head and cursed under his breath, but he had to be proud of her. His animal side told him to protect her and make sure nothing happened to her, but the other side of his brain told him she really was more than capable of handling herself. The only thing she needed from him was to do his job.

Reluctantly, he stood up and attempted to do just that. Jack strolled over to a man sitting by himself, smiling as he polished off a blueberry muffin. "Hi, I'm Jack. I'm new here."

The man eagerly extended his hand. "Ted! Ted Costello. It's nice to meet you. You're really going to love it here."

"I think you're right, based on what I've seen so far. I'm still new, though. I don't really know anyone except my friend that I came here with."

"Have a seat, Jack, and feel free to call me your friend as well. Anyone who's here seeking a better way of life certainly has something in common with me. Can I get you anything? Coffee, or a muffin?"

Jack took the chair but waved off the offer. "I just ate, thanks. So what brought you here, anyway?" The guy seemed more than eager to talk, which could only be counted as a good thing. Getting in good with the other recruits was always his first step. It helped him to blend in while he learned more about the actual operations. If he was lucky, Ted was some vital part of this compound and might let a few secrets slip.

"Oh, Jack. I'm happy to tell you. In fact, I've been thinking about writing a book and telling everyone. I thought about putting it online in a series of blog posts so I could make it free, but then I realized that is exactly the type of thinking we're supposed to be getting away from." He slapped his fingers on the side of his head. "It's crazy when you realize just how much all our societal norms are ingrained in us. You think you've gotten past them, and then they come creeping back up again. Now, where was I?"

"Um, you were going to tell me what brought you to this lovely place." Jack risked a peek at the other side of the room, where Erica and a few of the ladies were heading out the door. He could practically feel her presence diminishing, and he no longer had to feign his discomfort. Anything could happen to her there. They still had no idea exactly what Ben's movement was all about.

"I was working up in St. Louis, and I thought I had it all. Great job, nice house, fancy car, beautiful women on my arm. But I was always so stressed out, Jack. All that money I was making was getting taxed to death. The value of my home decreased every year. The women were taking just as much money as the government, and they valued me even less." He chuckled to himself. "It was a crying shame, Jack. I put in all that work and for what? Some material things? Not worth it. My inner groundhog gave me warning signs, but I truly found myself when I had a massive heart attack."

"I'm so sorry. Are you all right?" Inwardly, Jack was wondering just what the hell this guy was doing out there in the middle of nowhere if he had so much going on in the city. He and Erica hadn't seen any signs of brainwashing yet, but it had to be happening if it could make someone change his life so drastically. In other parts of the world, most people joined these movements to keep themselves or their families from starving to death. They had no money, and they needed a better life. They would've killed to live the way Ted had been.

The man thumped his chest. "Better than ever! The one thing my money did buy me was medical care, but did it buy me someone waiting at my bedside while I was in the hospital? Or waiting for me when I finally made it back home? No sirree. I started doing some real soul searching. I'm ashamed to say that at the time, that also meant searching the web, but it all worked out in the end. I stumbled across some of Ben's blogs and videos, explaining how I could live a life of purpose and peace out here. I sold everything I had and came up. Now, I've been able to shift more than I have in years, too."

"I see." And he was beginning to. Ben wasn't pulling people in based on religion. He was fighting against the difficulties of modern life, something almost anyone could relate to. The rich were working themselves to death and finding no comfort in the amenities they could afford. The poor were also working themselves to death, but with even fewer results. Either way, Ben was benefitting from the money they turned around and donated to him. At least, it was one theory. Hopefully, Erica would be able to confirm it with her own recon when they met back up later. "And how long have you been here?"

"Two months. I tell you, Jack, it's like going to a health spa. No massage tables or saunas, but there's nothing better for the soul than a little hard work. I feel like there's a real need for me here. If I don't do my share, then someone else might suffer. Someone I know and care about. That's what you'll come to find, Jack. We're all family here, like a new clan. We'd do anything for each other. Anything."

Including drinking poison? Jack had to wonder. He wouldn't have asked, but he didn't get the chance. A scream emanated from down the hall. It shivered in his bones and echoed in his soul.

Jack was out of his seat and across the room in a flash. He fought his fox, who snarled when Jack forbade it from coming out. Something was happening, and his animal instinct dictated he'd get there faster on four legs than on two. Jack barely kept himself in check as he raced down the hall toward the sound.

He rounded a corner, and it was then Jack realized just how far away the scream had been when he'd heard it. The group of women he'd seen in the common area stood at the other end of the hall, backing slowly away from a body on the floor. Jack's heart beat like a bass drum as he saw the dark hair and the blue shirt. He shot forward, shoving these women aside to get to her. "Erica!"

"I'm fine," said a voice just behind his shoulder as a cool hand touched his arm. Erica tugged him backwards.

Confused, Jack glanced from the woman on the floor back to Erica. They had similar coloring, and the woman's shirt was a close shade to Erica's, but it wasn't her. "I thought... I heard... I saw..."

"Your friend must have excellent hearing." This came from Ben, whom Jack hadn't realized was standing among the group. He held his right hand in his left as though in pain. "I'm sorry if I startled you. I hope you understand that I must do whatever needs to be done in order to keep my clan in check."

Jack swallowed as one of the other women bent to help the woman in blue off the floor. A bruise that matched her blouse was beginning to form on her cheek below her eye. Rage swelled up inside him. Jack didn't know this woman, but that didn't matter. There were no excuses for what had seemingly just happened there.

Ben smiled at him, but it wasn't the same smile he offered when he was selling a car. It was a placating one offered alongside a friendly nudge on the arm as he gestured with his head for Jack to step aside with him. "I pride myself on running a very tight ship, Jack. The only way I can do that is if everyone pulls their weight and does as they're supposed to. Anyone who doesn't cooperate risks ruining it for all of us. You can understand that, I'm sure."

Shit. This was a true test of his spying skills. There was nothing he'd like more than to lay this guy out like he deserved. The piece of shit had just hit that woman, and Jack highly doubted she'd done anything that would actually threaten him. But the way he'd acted when he'd thought Erica was down had already put him dangerously close to blowing his cover. He was painfully aware of her eyes on his back now, and he hoped she'd be willing to forgive him for going along with this. "Of course. I thought maybe someone had fallen or was in some other medical trouble. I'm terribly sorry for interrupting."

"Not at all, my good friend." Ben released his sore hand to pat Jack on the shoulder. "I knew you'd recognize what I'm doing here. You're a smart man with a good head. I need more men like you." He patted Jack again before moving off down the hallway.

The other women had picked up the injured one and were escorting her down the hall. Jack could overhear them shaming her as they went.

"Really, Mary. You knew better than that."

"It doesn't matter that you want to leave. You committed yourself to a life here, and you can't go back on your promises."

"I know. I deserved it. I was wrong." The now weeping woman clutched her cheek as the others guided her off to one of the rooms, presumably to get cleaned up.

Erica hung back just long enough to turn to Jack. "Her mother is sick," she whispered. "She wanted to leave to go see her, but Ben told her no. She tried to argue with him, and it escalated quickly."

"That's not right, Erica. I thought it was you. I thought..." And the very thought of it made him sick to his stomach. Something horrible could've happened to her, and all for the sake of the mission. Jack wasn't sure it was worth it.

She gave him a smile. "I think your mouth stops working when you get too caught up in things. Be careful with that, Jack. It could get us both in trouble."

"I know." He glanced at the women again, liking this situation less and less. At least knowing Erica was all right had calmed him down somewhat. "That could've been you, Erica. Maybe we should pull out. We haven't even been here for a full day yet. Ben might let us leave."

The glare she gave him was a serious one. "We've already been through too much to leave now. I'll be fine. And I know not to get into an argument with Ben." She patted his arm and turned to follow the others.

Jack headed back toward the common area, lacking any other direction. Never before had he been eager to abort a mission. He was always concerned for the safety of those involved, but he was a trained and hardened man who understood that sometimes sacrifices had to be made. Everything was different now. It would be a good kind of different if he was any regular guy, but he wasn't. And Erica definitely wasn't just a regular woman.

8

JACK JUST HAPPENED TO BE WAITING FOR ERICA OUTSIDE HER door when she went out for breakfast the next morning. He made it look casual enough, walking past at a leisurely pace, but she knew he'd been out there for at least the past five minutes. She'd sensed him.

Erica knew she had a lot to figure out once this mission was over. Jack affected her in a way no one else did, and staying away from him the previous day had been difficult. When he was too far away for her to pick up his signature, she fought herself on going to track him down. He'd been too much to handle at first, but now that she'd let him inside, she didn't know how to exist without him. It was troubling, in a way, because she knew eventually she'd have to go back to D.C. and return to a normal life, whatever that was.

"How did the rest of the day go yesterday?" he asked as she fell into step beside him. "I hardly saw you at all. I thought about coming to your room last night, but someone was up and roaming the halls."

"Not just someone," Erica replied with a shiver. "I think it was that mechanic. I don't like the feeling I get from him, Jack. I locked my door, but it's not a very secure one. I'm sure Ben and whomever else he fully trusts have keys anyway." Her back twinged as she remembered that horrifically negative energy that emanated from the man.

"Do you get that feeling from anyone else?" Jack asked.

She stopped and looked at him. "You know, no one has ever asked me that before. I've always had to lie and make some other sort of conjecture about why a person might be on our side or working for the enemy. It's kind of nice."

He frowned a little. "I have to admit, it's still something I'm getting used to."

"But you believe me? Or more to the point, you trust my feelings about these things?" She held her breath as she waited for the answer. There was no doubt that she had some sort of special bond with Jack. He might be able to explain it away as simply being fated to be together. It was a nice idea, but Erica wondered if true happiness might require more than that.

"I do. Which is why I'd really like to know if you get that feeling from anyone else," he reminded her.

Erica shook her head. She'd exhausted herself monitoring the mental waves from the others in the compound. "Not at all. They're the same on the outside as they are on the inside, just pleasant and happy."

"Any news on the woman Ben hit yesterday?" he whispered.

"No. They gave her a cold compress, and she spent the rest of the day in her room. I tried to broach the subject to the other women, but they changed the conversation quickly. I think they were worried for her, but they were more concerned about what might happen to them if they were caught talking about it. That was the only hint of negativity I got from anyone, just a bit of fear."

"Getting slapped around sounds to me like more of a reason to leave than to stay," Jack pointed out.

Erica pressed her lips together. She'd pondered this all the previous day as she'd worried about that poor woman and what she might be going through mentally. "It's not as simple as that. It's easy for us to think there's no reason for anyone to stay here. We've been trained, and we've got strong connections with the outside world. But Jenny, the girl he hit? She doesn't have anyone. Her pack is all the way down in Mississippi, and it sounded as though she doesn't have the best relationship with them or her sick mother. I asked Jenny if there were others that could be with her mom, and she just shook her head and fell silent. People get isolated in some form or fashion, and they end up in places like this."

"Or in other abusive relationships," Jack agreed. "You're right; I've seen it before. It's easy to pick out who the victims are and why they won't leave."

"In this situation, I'd say they're driven by money and loneliness more than anything. No one here has to worry about shelter, a steady paycheck, or buying groceries. They don't even have to worry about health insurance. One of the ladies told me there's an onsite shifter doctor. It's quite the promise of an easy lifestyle."

"I just have to wonder what sort of price they're actually paying for it," Jack murmured. They were nearing the common room now, where the line already trailed out the door. "A guy I was talking to yesterday sold everything he owned and gave all the money to Ben in exchange for this stress-free lifestyle."

Erica snorted, thinking about Jenny and how much stress the woman was still enduring. She had to wonder if the men were treated the same way, but they hadn't been there long enough to find out. "Anything else noteworthy on your end?"

He shook his head. "Everything is about as normal and boring as it gets. I explored as much as I dared. I didn't see any evidence of hidden rooms or a shed where someone is building a bomb or anything suspicious at all. It looks like there's a strong perimeter fence that's probably electrified, but that could just as much be to keep people out as in. I don't get it, and I don't like it."

"Either it's a very good coverup or we're wasting our time," Erica agreed.

Jack's hand was wrapped around her elbow then, pulling her slightly back from the end of the breakfast line and holding her close. "I want to do things differently today."

Her body reacted as she looked up at him and saw the urgency in his eyes. Instantly, her skin recalled the way it felt to be pressed up against him. Her heart thundered in anticipation, even though he touched her with only his fingers. She'd missed him as she'd spent the night alone. Jack had an uncanny knack for making all the danger that surrounded them melt into the background. "Yes?" she choked out.

"Let's stay together today. We should be a team."

The words were simple, yet they said so much. Erica wanted nothing more than to agree with him, but she knew it wasn't practical. "It won't work. We're supposed to learn our duties today. Ben will be suspicious if we suddenly change our minds."

"I don't know. I'm not sure anyone will notice. Look."

The common room seemed to be bustling with even more energy than usual. Clumps of people stood close together, chattering excitedly and gesturing with their hands. Erica sensed something big in the atmosphere, something that was about to happen, but she couldn't tell what it was. "I think we're about to get a little insight into our mission," she whispered.

Retrieving their meals, a man with a brilliant smile and slicked back hair waved them over to his table. "Jack, there you are! I was looking all over for you yesterday after you ran off."

"I'm sorry about that. I got a little caught up in other things. Ted, this is my friend Erica. Erica, meet Ted."

The shifter extended his hand to shake hers. Erica picked up waves of confidence, maybe a little ignorance, but nothing sinister. "It's nice to meet you. Tell me, is there something going on today?" She gestured with her head at the anxious crowd.

"Oh, yeah! Ben's going to talk to us!" Ted looked as if he were ready to clap his hands like a little girl on her way to get an ice cream cone.

"I thought he talked to us every day. I mean, he did yesterday." She knew she must've missed something when she was watching the mechanic.

"Sure, but this is different. Didn't you hear him yesterday? He said we were going to get our final missions very soon. I thought it might be another week or so, but rumor has it today is the day!" Ted's teeth flashed white as his smile broadened.

"Excuse me? Our *final missions*? What does that mean?" Jack asked. Erica could tell he was trying to keep the concern out of his voice, but some of it was leaking through. Not that she could blame him.

"Oh, I forgot what it's like to be so new here. We all have our normal chores and duties, but Ben has promised us that we'll be assigned a final mission that will help perpetuate our way of life here in more ways than we can imagine. It's some big project he's been working on, and almost no one knows the details. The one thing we do know is that it'll change our lives permanently."

Erica didn't like the sound of that, and she exchanged a worried look with Jack. For the moment, all they could do was wait.

Apparently, Ted wasn't the only one who'd heard those rumors, because Ben's arrival that morning was met with thunderous applause. It didn't cease even when he waved his hands humbly through the air, and Erica could feel the tension building in the room.

Finally, all was silent. Ben pressed his hands together in front of his chest and bowed his head so that his lips touched his fingertips. He closed his eyes thoughtfully and held the pose as he began speaking. "My friends, I can't tell you how much I appreciate each and every one of you. As I said yesterday, this place would be nothing without you."

Again, there was more clapping and cheering.

Ben opened his eyes, matching his gaze with his followers' as he looked around the room. "I have heard so many of your stories. I have heard from those of you who have left abusive relationships and needed a new clan. I have heard from those of you who were so desperate to find a different way of life that you turned to drugs and crime before you came here. Broke, broken, addicted, or just fed up, there are so many reasons that you have sought me out. Once again, I must say, for this I am grateful."

Erica looked to the doorway, expecting to see the man in the greasy coveralls again, but he wasn't there. She wished she knew how to interpret that.

"Some of you already know my story, but today, I'd like to make sure I share it with everyone. You see, when I was a little boy, I lived in the mountains near the Persian Gulf. You might wonder why anyone would try to live there for so long when it has so little to offer. But I say to you, how is that any different than the wastelands you've been living in? Country or city, hot or cold climate, we are all seeking a shelter that will keep us safe from the world."

His followers nodded and smiled, encouraging him.

"It was the same way for me and my family, and it had been that way for generations. Our little settlement was the only place we'd ever known, and we thought we were happy. Or at least happy enough. We worked hard to put food on the table and clothes on our backs, but that hard work meant we always slept well at night. Everything changed when the American government came sweeping in. I was only a little boy when they invaded our country and my hometown. I was just an innocent child when they came and took my father away from me. I can still see him turning to me as they dragged him out the door, telling me to take care of myself. It is still so vivid of a picture, and I've kept it with me all this time.

"That single day changed my life and the lives of everyone else in my family completely. I knew I had to do something to fix it, but as I said, I was just a little boy. I grew into a man, and still, I didn't quite know what I should do. But I came here with the assistance of some other family members who'd already left to seek a better life. Everything is better in America. Or at least that's what everyone believes.

"In my time here, I've learned that it wasn't quite true. Yes, there's more food. There's more freedom, or at least perceived freedom. But it's not as perfect as they would have you believe. I want you to think carefully, my friends, about my experience as a child. The American government came into my country and took my father away. They accused him of horrible crimes, and I nor anyone else ever saw him again."

The audience was shaking their heads and exchanging sad looks, but they were captivated. No one dared question Ben on exactly why his father was taken or what he might've done. This was all about sympathy for Ben at the moment. Erica knew he would soon turn the story around and make it about them. He would unite them with a common enemy, and it wouldn't be difficult to do since they already respected him so much. These people were beholden to him for their current lifestyle, and their choice would be to go along with whatever he said or face the harshness of reality once again.

"What I see here in America is that even its own citizens are falling victim to the same thing. Homes are being invaded; guns are being taken. Police are shooting innocent citizens simply because they can. Peaceful protests are shut down with violence and force. And it all makes sense, doesn't it?" Ben asked. "If they would invade a country on the other side of the world in an effort to control it, then why wouldn't they do the same thing right here on their very own soil? They do, my friends. They can, and they do. Every day. It's only a matter of time before we're next."

This caused a ripple of fear through the crowd. It was chokingly thick, and Erica fought to breathe through it. She felt Jack's hand on her thigh under the table, a comforting presence, but even he couldn't make this go away.

"All of you," Ben continued, "every single one of you, are different. We don't talk about it much here, because we shouldn't have to, but you are not the same as other people. You possess powers the rest of the country—and even the rest of the world—wouldn't understand. What makes you think the government would leave us alone to live in peace? What makes you think for one second that we would be allowed to have our own community?

"They know. They know that we are not like them. They know that we have animals inside us, animals with teeth and claws and fighting instincts, animals who don't hesitate to lash out when they're being wronged. And believe me, they're ready to do something about it. The American government strives to eliminate any threat or even potential threat. Anything that might take money from their pockets or control from their fists is absolutely a menace, and that menace is us, my friends. They've made us their enemy.

"The threat is already upon us. I wish I didn't have to tell you about it, but just as I expect you to be honest with me, I will be honest with you. There are already government officials keeping an eye on our peaceful village. They're jealous of the food we grow without interference from pesticides. They're determined to wipe out our happy lives free of taxes and fees. They want to have their hands in everyone's way of life, and that includes ours.

"Please," he said, holding his hands out in an effort to calm the restlessness of the gathering. "Please understand that I've known this day would come for a long time, and so I've been preparing for it. Who better than us to fulfill this mission? We have the skills to fight if we need to. We have the ability to become something other than the enemy they're looking for when it's time to get away. A man may attack the governor, but they won't see a wolf trotting off through the woods. We are a small group, too small to even be considered a village, but we will make a statement the United States government will never forget! They will think twice before crashing down on us!"

The room erupted in applause once again. This wasn't good. Whatever Ben had prepared, he had all his followers on board for it. They were U.S. citizens. They didn't have to agree with every single thing their government did, but they should be trusting it more than they did some charismatic stranger. Ben had won them over, though. He had them wrapped around his finger.

"For two years, I've been selling used cars. Each one of these vehicles has been outfitted with a special circuitry board, one that will make that statement for us. These vehicles are already parked at homes and businesses, and they will do the job they've been set to do. But I have many more vehicles, ones that I ask you all to take out into the world. Tomorrow is my father's birthday, and when you reach the destinations I assign for you, the world will know that we mean business!"

People were out of their seats now, clamoring to find out exactly what their leader wanted of them.

"Friends, please!" Ben shouted. "I will be speaking with each of you. There is plenty of time, and there are jobs for all of you. You can all help our cause."

Things settled down somewhat, but a massive ring had formed around Ben.

Erica and Jack hung back. "I don't like the sound of this,

and I can't believe they're actually going for it," she whispered. "Please tell me I misunderstood."

"I don't think you did." He gripped her hand under the table. "Those cars have bombs in them. I'm guessing Ben has them set to go off at a particular time. The ones that haven't been sold will be driven across the country by his followers. He'll probably have them headed toward national landmarks, churches, schools, places where they'll really make an impact."

"We've got to find some way to stop them." Erica thought back to their briefing when they'd first met in those rural cabins. It had only been a few days ago, but it felt like another lifetime. "Ben's dealership is a small one, but he's had to have sold hundreds of cars in the couple of years he's been operating. If all of them are active, we've got one hell of a problem on our hands."

"Ben likes you, and you're better at pretending you're on his side. You go up there and see what mission he wants to give you, and I'll head outside." Jack turned for the door.

Erica grabbed his arm. "Don't you think that'll be a little obvious?" she hissed.

"Everyone's pretty well occupied." He tipped his head toward the crowd. Some of them had already stepped away from Ben, apparently because they'd gotten the information they needed. Two people nearby were celebrating their upcoming trip to Mount Rushmore.

"Still, if he actually has everyone assigned, then he's

going to wonder where you are. We can't blow this now." Jack had reacted strongly when he thought Erica was the one Ben had hit. If he was feeling protective, he might do something stupid because he thought it would keep her safe. They couldn't risk that.

"I'll be back as soon as I can. Tell him I'm sick to my stomach or something. I'm heading out to the cars that are parked here to see if I can find out if we're right about the bombs. You go to Ben. See if he's got some sort of master list of where the sold cars are and where the unsold cars are headed. There's got to be one somewhere." Again, he stepped toward the door.

"Jack, we both signed on knowing we would be taking risks. Don't throw yourself into the fire because you think you're leaving me safe in the frying pan." She reached out to him with her mind, determined to make him understand —whether through words or through mental energy—that she didn't want to lose him. It wasn't worth it.

His lips twisted as his eyes skimmed her mouth. "I'll be fine. We both will. If anything goes sideways, you get Winston on the line."

Erica nodded and headed for the crowd. Her stomach churned at all the elation in the air. She wanted to put out a wavelength of peace and harmony, the kind of stuff these people had thought they were going there for, but she knew the energy it would take would only be wasted. They weren't going to listen to her. For now, she had to do what her job dictated and pretend she was going along with this plan. In the back of her mind, though, she could only hope that Jack was safe enough.

Ben was handing out small slips of paper. Erica watched as the people around her took them, noticing that each one had a location and a departure date. Some of them had addresses, others were names she recognized. A woman next to her had one that listed the Lincoln Memorial and a time of eleven p.m. Another listed Millennium Park in Chicago, leaving at six the next morning. Erica wiped her face of all the horror she felt knotting up inside her body as she drew closer and closer to the leader.

"Ah, Erica!" he beamed when it was her turn. "I know you're still new to the fold, and you probably weren't expecting this trip."

"Yes, you're right. I was worried when you made your announcement because yesterday, you said you wanted me to learn my way around the kitchens. I wasn't sure what the right thing was to do." She gave him a vacant smile as she tried to reach out to him. There had to be some way to find out more about his plan.

Ben's mind was well-guarded, though. "Don't you worry about any of that; I'll find someone else to do it. I've paired you up with Lucy. The two of you won't have a very far drive, just into town at a rather prominent church. She's already got the assignment." Ben pointed to a woman on the other side of the crowd.

Lucy, a tall woman with her blonde curls yanked back in a tight ponytail, waved the piece of paper excitedly in the air.

"That's so nice of you. Thank you." Ben had turned away, and Erica had no choice but to join Lucy. She bit her lip as she ran through what she knew. Ben didn't have a master list, or at least not on him. He'd only handed out those little slips of paper, most of which had already been dispersed through the crowd. Ben had eschewed electronics on the grounds, at least for his followers. All the departure times indicated arrival times of around noon the next day. If she and Lucy were only going into town, less than half an hour away, that would give her some time to come up with an alternate plan before anything drastic happened.

"Are you Erica? Oh, I'm so excited to meet you!" Lucy wrapped Erica in a bear hug that lifted her off the ground and set her down with a thump. "How great is it that so many women will be involved in a movement like this? You always hear about men making a statement. Don't get me wrong; Ben is a wonderful guy. We couldn't have done any of this without him. I just think it's so great that we get to make a difference, you know?"

"Yeah. Absolutely." Erica wasn't paying much attention to Lucy babble on. The woman was either someone Ben trusted implicitly, which was why he'd paired the two of them up, or she was someone he didn't think was capable

of much, which was why they were only going into Hortonburg. She peeked over her shoulder, hoping beyond all
hope that Jack had returned, but there was no sign of him.

"And to make things even better, we're one of the first to
go out!" Lucy squealed.

"Wait. What?" Erica snatched the slip of paper from the
other woman's grip. To match up with everyone else's
assignments, they should've been leaving late the next
morning. The scrap listed a time only an hour from then.
"This can't be right. Most people aren't leaving until tonight
or tomorrow."

"I know! We're going to be some of the first ones out the
door! Can you believe it? Oh, and I already asked Ben
which vehicle he wanted us to take. He said we can have
our pick!" She squealed again and clapped her hands.
"Let's head outside and see which one we want."

Erica hoped her horror didn't show in her eyes. "That's
even better. Look, I've got to run to my room for a second."

Lucy frowned. "What for? You look fine."

"I, um, I forgot my bracelet this morning. I wear it every
day, and it's got sentimental value. You know how it is. I'll
meet you outside." Without another word, she pushed her
way through the throng and out the door. As soon as she
reached the relatively open space of the hall, she burst into
a full run toward her room.

The muscles in her back contracted as she worried
whether she was being followed. Lucy didn't seem the type

to come after her, but Erica had realized it was hard to understand or estimate these people. They'd fallen under Ben's spell, and they believed he was giving them exactly what they wanted. Even worse, they were willing to commit horrific crimes.

Erica reached out with her mind, searching for Jack, and found only the other recruits.

She dove into her room and shut the door behind her, leaning against it for a moment and breathing heavily. It'd been easier to remain distant in her other missions, getting in and getting things done and getting out. But having Jack there had complicated things. She had so much more riding on the line than her job.

She'd brought only a small suitcase and her purse, both of which sat on the floor near a set of built-in drawers. Erica quickly dug her keys out of her purse, unfolding a tiny penknife. Unzipping her suitcase, she carefully ran her fingers over the lining until she found the small bulge. The slick fabric parted easily at the behest of the tiny knife. Erica hesitated as she held the tiny transmitter in her hands. It was only for emergencies, only for things going completely awry. Rarely had she needed to use the emergency backup plan that was put in place for every mission. This was one she hadn't even been familiar with, considering Jack had provided it.

Then she remembered just how many cars were out there. Even if she or Jack managed to find some list that told them how to locate every vehicle, there was no possible way she and Jack could stop them by themselves. Erica pulled the tab that engaged the battery and waited.

"I'm here." It was Winston's voice.

"It's me." Relief washed over Erica. No one should have been able to tap into their frequency, but she still didn't reveal her name just to be safe. "Listen, we've got a situation." She rattled off the details as quickly as she could.

"10-4. We'll work on things from our end, but keep me posted. I'll maintain radio silence unless you contact me first."

"Right. Over and out." Erica tucked the transmitter in her pocket, hoping no one would happen to notice, and headed outside.

Lucy was waiting for her in the parking lot as promised. "There you are! Did you get your bracelet?"

"Oh, um, I couldn't find it. I must've dropped it somewhere else. I'll get it later. What car should we take?"

"This little sports car is cute," Lucy enthused, "or we could take the convertible. Like Thelma and Louise!"

Bile rose in Erica's throat as she remembered just how that movie had ended. "Right. Well, you've been here longer. I'll let you choose." She swiftly turned her head as movement caught her eyes. Erica could swear she saw the tip of a furry tail disappearing behind one of the vehicles.

She dared to lean against the side of the car, even knowing it was probably hiding explosives somewhere under the hood. Erica closed her eyes as Lucy prattled on about her driving experience and reached out once again. The wave of emotion that hit her nearly knocked her down. It was Jack, but it was the side of him she hadn't had unimpeded access to when she'd known him in his human form.

Erica received his messages clearly, even though they were only in pictures. She could see through his eyes, suddenly much closer to the ground, as he made his way around the grid of vehicles in the parking area. They were massive hunks of metal, all of which smelled like different places and different people. Those scents varied depending on how long the cars had been there, and Erica could sense through the vision Jack was giving her just how much time had passed and where they'd been. More importantly, there was an acrid, sulfuric scent that made adrenaline shoot through her veins. *Explosives.* They were in every single one of those cars, just as she and Jack had guessed.

"Hey, are you all right?"

Erica snapped her eyes open, breaking off most of her connection with Jack. She knew he was still around, but those vivid images had disappeared. "Yeah. I'm fine. I think my breakfast just isn't sitting well. What about that car over there?" She pointed to a little blue coupe in the next row.

Lucy turned to look at it. "I guess that would be fine, if that's what you really want."

Erica braced her shoes against the ground, wishing for pavement instead of loose gravel as she took off and jumped against Lucy's back. Her would-be partner was tall and much stronger than she looked. Lucy's fingers dug into Erica's arm, trying to unfold her grip from her neck. This was the part of the job she hated, when she knew she was holding someone's life in her hands. Erica squeezed harder, her disgust powering her muscles as she pressed against Lucy's windpipe. The blonde woman began to sprout fur along her arms as she began to shift and managed to land a few blows, but she soon sank to her knees. Erica laid her gently on the ground.

The fox that emerged from around the other side of the convertible watched her carefully. Its brilliant eyes looked toward the gate for a moment, and then it began to change. Right before Erica's eyes, the fox stretched, twisted, and grew. It went from standing on four legs to only two, the brawny form of Jack arising out of the agile fox with ease until he was standing before her as though he'd always been there.

He stepped forward with his now very human legs and gripped her arms. "I think I found something. Come on."

9

THE LOOK ON ERICA'S FACE AS SHE WATCHED HIM TRANSFORM was a priceless one, but Jack didn't have the time to tease her about it now. "Lucy won't be out for long. What did you find out?" He'd grabbed her hand as they ran back toward the building.

Erica's feet were just as confident as his as they barreled across the yard. "I saw several of the assignments. If my skills at guessing travel times are still sharp, then everything should be going down at noon tomorrow. Or at least that's one phase."

He didn't like the hesitation in her voice. "What do you mean?" There was no doubt in his mind that the cars carried explosives. Whoever had done the work had done it well, and no human mechanic had happened to locate the material so far. Ben knew what he was doing, but that wasn't good news for them.

"Ben gave Lucy and me a special assignment. We were supposed to leave almost right away, and we were only going to a church in Hortonburg. I'd guess he wanted to get rid of me quickly, since I'm new, and you were probably going to get a similar assignment as soon as he saw you. For all I know, he's doing it in waves. Shouldn't we be heading away from this place?" she asked as they ducked back inside the building.

Jack yanked her to the left and down a hall before a group leaving the common area could spot them. "Sure, that would be great. But then we wouldn't be able to get to this." He reached for a door around the next corner, but the knob twisted before he could touch it.

The mechanic was standing there, his eyes wild. He immediately readied himself for a fight, his fists curling and his feet braced. Jack didn't hesitate, either. He launched himself at the man, knocking him backward into a metal desk. The mechanic's fists whipped through the air, missing Jack's head by only a hair's breadth. Jack's fox fought to get out, eager to sink its razor-sharp teeth into this evil man's flesh, but Jack resisted. His human form was bigger, and the mechanic didn't show any signs of shifting. The scent of grease and sweat filled his lungs as they grappled. Finally, Jack swung his head back and smashed it into the other man's face. The mechanic collapsed, and Jack let him fall to the floor.

Erica's had the foresight to shut the door behind them, and she flicked a small lock that should keep them safe for at least a short while. "I wish he could at least tell us what's going on," she remarked as she took in her surroundings.

Jack rubbed his arm as he straightened. The small room was filled with computer equipment. The heat from the devices and the closeness of the room gave off the distinctive smell of plastics and electronics. It was unmistakable now that he knew it was there, but before it hadn't looked like anything more than a janitor's closet. "I don't think we need him. We've got most of it figured out."

"I thought you said there wasn't a place like this here," she pointed out as she sat in front of one of the computers and began hacking the password.

"Yeah, because I was looking in my human form. I shifted almost as soon as I left the common room, and my nose led me here before I even made it out to inspect the cars. I should've done that as soon as we arrived, and then maybe I would have figured out Ben's plan before it was too late."

"We don't know that it's too late yet," Erica said through gritted teeth as she rattled away on the keyboard. "I guess Ben is only anti-electronics when it comes to his recruits. God, they followed him so blindly. I can't tell you how much it worries me that terrorists like him can brainwash people by offering so little."

"I wouldn't say that." Jack leaned down to look over her shoulder. "They couldn't deal with everyday life anymore, and he offered them something better. Religious extremists are basically motivated the same way, just in different dressing. There you go," he said as Erica finally made it into the system. "Those look like coordinates."

Erica pulled the transmitter from her pocket. "I'll start feeding these to HQ. They're going to have to activate every specialist in the DHS to stop this from happening."

"And probably all the local police, too, but it'll be worth it. It's hard to tell without getting inside the vehicles and inspecting them individually, but there's no telling just how much damage Ben is planning to do." While she began reading off what information they had to Winston, Jack used the password information she'd decoded to log in to one of the other computers and search for more data. Coordinates were great, but that would only help so much if they didn't know who and what they were looking for. "I'll see if I can find a roster of everyone here and maybe a list of cars."

Winston's voice came through the radio. "The local police are working on shutting down the roads nearby. That's going to help us filter through any vehicles that might have already been sold. We've got satellite imagery on the compound as well. I'm working on getting a force activated to get in there. What kind of explosives are we looking for? I need more details on that."

Jack and Erica exchanged a look. She knew; she'd seen those images. Jack had been startled to realize how easy it was to get inside her head when he stood on four legs, but he shouldn't have been. Shifters who shared the bond of a mate or clan could telepathically communicate with each other in an even more articulate way, and Erica certainly wasn't an ordinary human. Winston wouldn't be surprised at all if Jack told him he'd smelled out the bombs, but Jack had no way of knowing if Mr. Worth was sitting right there with him. Someone probably was.

Erica's mouth worked as she tried to formulate some way of explaining it, no doubt ready to use an excuse similar to the ones she used for herself when she got through a mission with more than just training and smarts.

He snagged the transmitter from her before she had to do it again. "You know how I am," he said drily into the radio. "I've got a nose for these things."

Winston didn't ask any further questions, even though Jack knew there would probably be a list of them waiting for him when they made it out of there.

"Right. Is anyone onto you yet? You're rural enough that I can't arrange an extraction for a while yet."

"I don't think so," Jack replied. "We've got a couple of minor casualties, but only control over one of them." Given that Ben had already hidden this massive computer system from them, Jack wouldn't doubt it if someone was monitoring the airwaves. Granted, the frequency should be encrypted, but he didn't like to take any chances and kept things as vague as possible. The blonde woman Erica had choked would either come to or be found soon, and that could mean the end of the mission for them if they were discovered. The mechanic was silent and still on the floor, a trickle of blood leaking from his nose and down his lips. The one saving grace Jack could latch onto was that there didn't seem to be many weapons on the compound.

"I'll see what I can do. I need the rest of those coordinates."

Erica had stilled in front of her computer console. "It looks like that's not going to be possible," she whispered.

Jack let go of the radio button, speaking to her directly. "What's wrong?"

"The file has been corrupted." She tapped angrily at the keyboard. "If I had my guess, I'd say Ben or one of his cohorts put a self-destructive virus in the system. As soon as it detected the hack, it started destroying the files. I got most of them, but it's begun erasing all the information." Erica worked away, but she shook her head in frustration.

He took over on the computer, using every skill he'd ever had hammered into him in the intelligence field. The graphic user interface was set up like most computers, only allowing the user into the part of the system that was easy to understand. Jack moved into the back side of the operating system, pummeling the keyboard as he typed in commands. "Here. Read these off to Winston. I've got some of them."

Erica stood at his shoulder and fired off the coordinates over the radio as quickly as they appeared on the screen. Winston reported that a few of them were repeats, but they were making progress.

"There's still one here," Jack growled. His focus was entirely on the screen. Vaguely, he thought he heard shouts outside the building. As long as no one realized where the two of them had gone, they'd be safe for the moment. "I can't get it. The virus has it."

A gasp sounded over his shoulder as Erica pointed to the column of numbers next to the coordinates. "Look. They're put in order according to when they were supposed to leave. The one right above it is the car Lucy and I were supposed to take. That should mean this last one has already left."

"Fuck." Jack slammed his fist into the keyboard. "We've got to get out there and find them."

"But all the cars are loaded with explosives," Erica argued. "We don't even know what will trigger them."

"Then what do you propose we do?" Jack rumbled. The only positive aspect he could concentrate on was the fact that they weren't in a metropolitan area. Even if everything went wrong, the casualties would stay low. He'd prefer none.

She put her hand on his shoulder, and when Jack turned to look up at her, Erica's eyes were blazing. "I'll find it."

He pointed helplessly at the computer screen. "How? There are traces of a file here that indicate Ben was going to track all the vehicles via GPS, but that's corrupted now, too." Everything he tried just turned to dust in his hands, and it unsettled him on a very deep level.

Erica set the transmitter on the desk, where neither of them was touching the button. "Astral projection."

She looked so calm and tranquil as she spoke, but Jack felt ripples of unease on the underside of his skin. His fox was anxious now, ready for action. "I think I've heard of that before, but I don't know anything about it."

"If I leave my physical body and go out into the world, I can find the car faster than even the DHS." Erica looked like a goddess as she stood before him, her tousled hair flowing around her shoulders and her voice quiet and steady.

"Have you done this before?" Jack could feel control quickly escaping his grasp.

"Of course."

"But on a mission?" he pressed. "When someone could burst in here at any minute?"

The corner of her mouth jerked. "Not so much, but it's the best solution I can come up with. It's either that or try to get all the information out of Ben, if we can even find him."

He swiped a hand over his face. Jack definitely wanted to get his hands on Ben, whether he gave them any further details or not. But Erica was right. They didn't have any time left to lose. "Tell me what I can do to help."

Erica launched into an explanation of how it worked as she cleared off one of the desks. "Astral projecting is basically what people refer to as an out-of-body experience. These happen when people undergo medical trauma or accidentally find themselves in an altered state that allows them to separate their minds from their bodies. The big difference is that I'll be doing it on purpose." She hoisted herself onto the surface of the desk and took off her shoes.

"That sounds dangerous." The room was getting hotter, smaller. Jack tugged at the collar of his shirt.

"To a degree, but I've done it before. It'll be fine." She shook out her hair and laid down, closing her eyes.

Jack swallowed. He wasn't the one who had brought Erica into this mess, yet he still felt incredibly responsible for her. That bond they'd forged the other night in his room hadn't been an accident. He knew she was his mate, and he wasn't about to lose her now; they shared a destiny. Seeing her laid out on the desk, she looked so vulnerable. What if she somehow got lost out there without a physical body to be attached to? He'd never forgive himself. "What can I do to help?" he whispered.

Shouts were emanating from somewhere just outside the building now, and her brow furrowed over her closed eyes. "I've got to relax every part of my body before I use something called the rope technique. It's basically like climbing right out of myself. But I've got to get into the right state of mind to do it." She chewed her lip. "Lay your hand on my shoulder."

He did as he was told and felt her body relax under his touch.

She sighed, a sensual sound that made his own flesh react, even though this definitely wasn't the time for it. "That's better. There's something about you that calms me down, Jack." Erica said nothing else as the rest of her body went slack.

Jack watched impatiently, looking for a sign that something was happening. Minutes dragged by in silence. Someone went thundering down the hall, but Jack kept his hand on her shoulder and waited. He pressed his forehead into his free hand and thought about the way the two of them had linked just a short time ago in the parking area. Jack's mind had automatically sought her out when he had something to tell her, and Erica was so receptive that she'd picked it up immediately. Could it possibly work the other way around?

Still keeping his fingers against her skin, Jack let his human body go. Shivers of concern rippled over his skin as the human side of him wondered if this was a good idea.

There were other shifters there, but they could be bears or lions. Ben had suppressed those urges to keep everyone placid, but all hell was about to break loose. Jack didn't know which of his forms he would need to fight them off. He did, though, know which form would work the best to help Erica.

What had only a moment ago been the faint sounds of the recruits outside sharpened into intense vibrations as his ears molded and moved. He only had to close his eyes to track each of them as they moved past the outside corner of the building, some of them running toward the cars. The concrete floor was cool to the touch under his paw pads, but still, he kept one black paw on Erica's shoulder. The room grew bigger as he grew smaller.

The power of his mind, however, had shifted completely. He was not just a former intelligence officer with the Army who had the training and skills to take down terrorists. He carried with him the knowledge of all the generations that had come before him, all the shifters who had honed their animalistic sides and understood their instincts. His mind reached out, a nebulous energy that sizzled through the air.

The link took his breath away as Jack was no longer in the computer room, but flying over the treetops. The creature alongside him was Erica, but not in the state he recognized. Her entire form sparked with blue light, a being of energy and not of body, and she was all the more beautiful.

Jack could feel the air through his fur as they scoured the road beneath them. His paw still rested on the area of her shoulder, even in this form. Erica's hand touched his and sent flickers of energy through him.

There! He heard the word as though she'd said it, but the current configuration of Erica hadn't moved her lips.

Jack looked down. He'd hardly even noticed that they'd reached the edge of town. A car, the same convertible Erica had been standing near not so long ago, was racing across city limits. It shot through an intersection, narrowly missing a grain truck before whipping around a corner.

Erica tilted, flying after it, and Jack automatically went with her. He studied the form in the driver's seat, wishing he hadn't just recognized Ted Costello. The shifter was flooring the vehicle, driving hell-bent for leather with that same brilliant grin on his face. Jack gritted his pointed teeth, impatient to see where this man was going. Erica had been destined for a church, the kind of place that was very prevalent in a small town like Hortonburg. Was Ted heading for another one?

But when Jack looked ahead, he could see that wasn't the case. The red convertible was zooming straight toward the town square, right where city hall and a big clock tower stood.

That's it! He could feel Erica's words inside his mind more than he could hear them. *Tell them, Jack! Tell them! I can't get back there fast enough!*

Jack had fought between his human and animal side on many occasions, but he'd never had to fight between his spirit and his physical form. Pain bristled through his body as he tore himself away from the scene before his eyes. He staggered against the side of the desk as he fell back into himself. The transformation back into his human form felt like a cross-country trip, a wondrous journey that left him exhausted. He grabbed the transmitter with hands that didn't even feel like his own. "City hall," he gasped into the device. "The square!"

The two seconds of silence that followed was an eternity. "We've got it. And I've got a unit coming straight up the road to your location."

———

CHOPPER BLADES THUMPED OVERHEAD, but this time, they weren't being operated by Max. Jack didn't know the pilot who brought them back down to Kentucky, and he wasn't sure that he cared. He leaned his head against the back of the seat and closed his eyes, feeling only Erica's serene presence next to him.

"That was an interesting run, you two," Mr. Worth said by way of greeting when they stood in front of his desk in the main cabin a few minutes later. "I'm still trying to figure out exactly what happened. I brought you here in the hopes of getting a more detailed explanation, but you look like you barely even have the energy to walk."

Erica slowly blinked up at Jack before turning to the director. "It's been a bit of a rough go, even if it was short."

"Well, the important thing is that you got in there just in time. I wasn't completely convinced you'd find any evidence against Ben Jones. He kept everything under wraps, and most of the recruits weren't even aware of the plan until this morning, from what I've been told." He slapped the desk and reached into a drawer. "The man is in our custody, though. Can I interest either of you in a celebratory cigar?"

"No, thanks." Jack figured he'd regret that later, but Mr. Worth hadn't underestimated his exhaustion. "I just want to get some rest."

Mr. Worth waved them off. "Your cabins are still waiting for you. Might as well get a little shuteye before Winston gets back. The man has been talking my head off the entire time."

The two of them shuffled back out the door, and Erica's footsteps fell in next to his. "Can I talk to you for a minute?"

"I'm not sure how good of a conversationalist I am right now, but sure." He managed a small smile.

The sun was sinking behind the giant trees, the pink light illuminating her face as she studied his. "As I told you, all my life, I've felt like I've been alone. We moved all the time, and I was never in one spot long enough to make any real friends. I've never even felt like I'm from any one place. As I've gotten older, those feelings stayed with me."

Jack listened quietly. He had plenty to say, and he'd thought about sharing it with her a thousand times since leaving Ben's compound, but he hadn't been sure when the right time was or if there would ever be one. "I know."

"Working with you has been completely different. I resented you. I didn't trust you. I didn't even know how to be in the same room as you. But now I feel like I've lived an entire lifetime just in the last few days. I'm not the same person I was a week ago."

Jack opened the door to his cabin. His body was completely drained from the lengths they'd had to go to in order to successfully complete this mission, yet he felt energy slowly flowing back into him just from being near her. He turned to Erica and ran his palms down her arms. "I understand that, too. I've almost always worked alone, and even when I didn't, I still kept to myself. You and I couldn't exactly do that, could we?"

Hope shimmered in her eyes. "I've never had anyone get inside my head like that before, Jack. And not even just in my head, but in my heart. In my *soul*. I don't know if it's fate like you mentioned or something else, but I love you. I know I shouldn't say it, but I've spent an entire lifetime covering up what I saw or felt because I didn't think anyone would understand. But you've been inside my mind. I like to think you've already seen it."

"I have." Jack ran the back of his fingers down her cheek. She could be so strong and stubborn, yet inside her lived a surreally beautiful creature who just wanted to love and be loved. "I have seen it, and it's the most incredible thing I've ever witnessed. I love you, too."

He couldn't say then if his head bent down to meet hers or if Erica rose to press her lips against his, but the two of them crashed together like two stars that'd been circling the same orbit for eons until their gravity finally pulled them together. His tongue danced with hers as they explored each other, the physical aspect of their relationship merely a reflection of everything they already knew about each other spiritually and mentally. Jack pulled her onto the bed with him, refusing to ever let go of this astonishing woman he'd finally found amongst all the other beings in the world.

His hunger for her couldn't be satisfied by touch alone and he sank into her with relief, knowing he was finally home. He didn't need to open his eyes to know every curve of her body, every strand of her hair. As he plunged his thickness deeper and deeper into her, Jack could feel his mate in his mind, a fire that sent cascading heat all throughout his body, making him so hard, he was on the verge of exploding at any moment.

Erica, he knew, was flying with him to some spiritual plane other than the one on this Earth. She gripped him with her thighs as she pressed her forehead to his. A heady mix of trust, desire, and passion swirled between them as her fingers rippled up his back and through his hair. Trailing his hand down her body as his thrusts intensified, Jack teased her slickness with the pad of his thumb, circling faster and faster, her breath hitching in her throat as the tension spiraled within her. She cried out in sheer ecstasy as his thick length continued to dive deeper inside her, her muscles shuddering around him as they both reached their pinnacles of pleasure. Their breath, their heartbeats, their very spirits were absolutely one.

10

ERICA SLOWLY OPENED HER EYES. SHE HADN'T BEEN ASLEEP, but she felt as though she'd gotten far more rest than she had in ages. The candles she'd lit had nearly guttered out, the incense a meager trace of smoke in the air. Meditation had become a part of her daily practice there in Dallas, one that was much easier to fit into her schedule now. It filled her body and her mind with such a pleasant energy, and she could feel her talents growing by the day.

She smiled as she felt him draw near. The thick door and the soundproof walls were great for keeping noise out of the room, but she couldn't keep Jack out, even if she tried. Not that she wanted to. Erica stood and stretched, waking her body from the long afternoon of being inert, and opened the door.

Jack yanked his fist out of the air and put his hand at his

side. "I was just about to knock, but I wasn't sure if I should or not."

She slid easily into his arms, inhaling that distinctly male scent of his that she'd come to find just as comforting as his touch. "I've told you, Jack. Nothing can hurt me in there. No matter how far I've gone, I'm in a peaceful place. If you need me, then you need me."

He pressed her body against his, the hard reminder of his need for her evident beneath his clothes. "You shouldn't say that. I'm supposed to be professional right now."

She bit her lip as she recalled just how unprofessional they'd been in Jack's apartment there at the Dallas Force headquarters the night before. He'd wrapped his arms around her as he'd taken her from behind, savoring her body with his hands and dropping climax-inducing kisses on the back of her neck. She was supposed to be the psychic, but he seemed to read her mind as his fingers roved to just the right places to bring her to her peak. "Don't worry, we can circle back to this later."

"I can try, anyway. I'm not sure if I'll be any good working alongside you." He kept his arm around her waist as they walked down the hall of the headquarters together. "You're very distracting."

"I'll do my best to keep it that way," she assured him with a smile.

Just outside the doors to the conference room, Jack paused and turned Erica to face him. Those caramel eyes searched hers, remnants of his wild side seeping through as he searched for truth. "Erica, are you sure you don't mind leaving the DHS? Don't get me wrong, I think you're going to be great here. I just want to make sure you're happy more than anything."

She sighed her content. Even in this form, and even when she wasn't actively reaching out to find the vibration that was so distinctly him, she could feel the smallest touch of his mind to hers. It was a comfort and a pleasant reminder that she wasn't alone, like holding someone's hand without really thinking about it. "I am happy," she assured him. "I'm excited to see what I can do as a consultant for the SOS Force. There's so much that I still have to learn about the world and about myself, things I never would've figured out if I'd just stayed in the same old rut. And I'm thinking about expanding this little gig into my very own business."

"Really? Does that mean...?" He let the question hang in the air.

"Yes. I'll fully advertise myself for what I truly am. There are plenty of people who pretend to be psychics just so they can give out common sense relationship advice and make a few bucks on it. Why not charge into the world as the real deal?" She'd considered it a lot after she'd turned in her resignation, knowing she could never go back to the way things were. Erica had changed on a deep level, and even though her work with the DHS was important, she had a feeling there were even bigger and better things in store for her.

With all thoughts of professionalism out the window for the moment, Jack tucked her in close and pressed his lips to her forehead. "I'm proud of you, Erica. I was fortunate enough to find my place in the world with these guys, and you deserve something like that, too. I love you."

"I know," she said with a grin. They'd said it constantly to each other, and it had yet to get old. "I love you, too. Now let's get in there and see what I can do for you."

Jack opened the conference room door. Erica straightened her shoulders and walked in, ready for the next chapter of her life. She knew it wasn't going to be easy. Her powers would be exposed, and she'd no doubt draw ridicule from those who didn't believe. She had Jack at her side, though, and that was all she needed.

THE END

BABY FOR THE SOLDIER COUGAR

SPECIAL OPS SHIFTERS: DALLAS FORCE

1

VANCE MORRIS STEPPED OUT OF HIS HOUSE AND TOOK A DEEP breath of fresh, Texas air. The sun was starting to sink toward the horizon, and the animals knew what time it was just as much as Vance did. The horses trotted to the edge of their paddock, bobbing their heads over the fence and whickering hungrily at him. The cattle that weren't currently out to pasture echoed the horses with long, low moans and constant shuffling. "Easy there, girls," Vance soothed as he stepped up to the fence. "I'll get you taken care of."

He turned from his work as a truck pulled up the driveway. Vance leaned against the fence, his body relaxed and casual, but his eyes and instincts ever vigilant. He hadn't spent ten years as a Green Beret only to let someone sneak up on him. It wasn't a vehicle he recognized, and he immediately noticed the out-of-state plates. Even though he was a rancher now, the soldier inside him would always be on alert—just like his inner cougar.

The truck rolled to a stop, but a glare of light stopped Vance from seeing through the windshield to find the driver's face. Vance had one arm looped casually around the fence post, but his right hand was still free to snag the pistol from the back of his waistband, should the need arise. He wasn't expecting company. His ranch hand, Daniel, had the day off, and he drove an old beater he'd dug out of a barn somewhere.

The driver's door opened. The man who stepped out was almost unrecognizable with a short beard clinging to his chin and the hair that he swooped back with his hand, but there was no mistaking those piercing eyes.

"Well I'll be..." Vance launched himself off the fence and strode forward. "Gabe Vinson, you damn fool. Is that you?"

"In the flesh." The man grinned as they shook hands. "I heard you'd retired to the country after your time in the service. I was picturing you'd be living somewhere a little more posh, man."

"Not exactly," Vance chuckled. "I'm covered with mud more often than I'm clean, and I'm always on duty. There's more work here than you can shake a stick at."

"Sounds like nothing's changed, then," Gabe chuckled.

"And I wouldn't want it any other way. What are you

doin' here, anyway? I thought you re-upped." Nothing could forge a bond between people faster than serving together, and Gabe was one of the soldiers Vance had come to think of as a brother. No matter how bad the situation got, Gabe never complained and always had Vance's back. He was always ready to charge forward and do what needed to be done, regardless of the consequences.

"I did. I was going to stay in as long as they'd have me, maybe teach at the JFK Special Warfare Center when they didn't want to send me overseas anymore. But then this happened." He lifted the side of his t-shirt to reveal a set of angry red lines that tore across his ribs and abdomen.

"Shit." Vance sucked in a breath through his teeth as he studied the scars. "Shrapnel?"

"You know it. Came out of nowhere, too. We were heading back onto the base; everything was quiet, technically in a safe zone. But no one expected that mortar—God knows I sure didn't. Ripped right through the hummer and straight into me."

"Damn. Is it still in there?"

"Fuck yeah. You know how those field docs are. They dug around a bit just to make sure I felt it and then decided it wasn't worth any more effort. I'll be setting off metal detectors for the rest of my life." He pulled his shirt back down and leaned against the side of his truck, his eyebrows twitching together for a moment as he glanced off toward the horses.

"That sucks, man. Really." Gabe wasn't just a Special Forces soldier; he, like Vance, secretly identified as a shifter. Their inner animals could sometimes rule their heads and hearts, and it was usually a situation of strong emotions or great need that gave them the urge to shift, but they still had some control. There were thousands of others like them all over the world, yet most people didn't know a thing about them. Shifters were careful to keep their secrets, and a situation like Gabe's made it difficult. The soldier would heal quickly and be perfectly fine to return to duty, while an ordinary human would've been discharged under the same circumstances.

But Gabe couldn't exactly explain that to his commanding officers, so he'd been sent home.

"It's just the way things were meant to work out, I guess. And hey, since I've got all this free time on my hands, I thought I'd come down to see you."

Vance clapped him on the shoulder. "I'm glad you did, buddy. You're just in time to help me with the chores. Come on, let's catch up." Leading him over to the nearest pen, Vance began tossing the best hay in for the waiting cows. "These girls are pregnant, so they're getting the special treatment right now."

Gabe followed Vance's lead and pitched in. It didn't matter that he hadn't done any farm work before. Over the years, the two of them had learned to work together like a well-oiled machine, quickly picking up any random task, whether it was one they were familiar with or not. "So, you like it out here?"

"I do. It reminds me a lot of my time in the Army, but in a good way. I've got a lot of responsibility on my shoulders because I have all these lives depending on me. There are times when I've got to react to an emergency, like when a calf gets stuck. In a way, I don't know that I could do all this if I hadn't been in the service." Vance was silent for a moment as he topped off the water tank and they moved out to tend to the horses. "Got a feeling you didn't come here to talk to me about ranch life, though."

"You're right." Gabe scratched one of the horses affectionately. "I don't know what the hell to do with myself now."

That was something Vance understood. There were many soldiers—shifter and human alike—who felt lost when they returned stateside. It wasn't even always a matter of knowing what they wanted, either, but a question of what they could handle. Some of them couldn't take crowds or loud noises or had various other triggers, and that made the transition even more difficult. "I get that. I got lucky, though. I always knew I'd go into something like this. It's in my blood, and sure enough, as soon as I was out, I was shopping for land."

Gabe scuffed his feet against the grass. "Rumor has it you're not just a cattle farmer."

"No?" Vance knew exactly what he was talking about.

Not too long ago, he'd been recruited to the Dallas unit of the Special Ops Shifter Force, an elite group of Special Forces veterans who also happened to be shifters. They were the ones the various clans and packs turned to when they needed help beyond what the shifter-governing conclaves could provide. It was the perfect fit for a soldier who still had all those skills, but no good way to use them. For Vance, it made his life incredibly busy, but also incredibly satisfying.

"The Force?" Gabe asked. "Don't tell me it's classified and you can't talk about it. If that's the case, then some tongues have been doing a lot of wagging."

"It's only a secret depending on who you're talking to," Vance admitted. He had to gauge who he could tell and who he couldn't, but Gabe was certainly trustworthy enough to know the real deal. "You interested?"

His friend rolled a shoulder. "Maybe. I just know I need to do *something*. My disability check from the VA is enough to get an apartment and a bit of a living, but it's not a life. I can't imagine just sitting around and waiting for my check to arrive for the rest of my damn life."

"Nah." Vance scratched his chin as he thought about it. The Dallas unit had initially consisted of four members, just like the D.C. unit. One of those members, Ash, had decided to serve as a remote consultant from his place up in Alaska. Technically, that left an opening, but it wasn't up to Vance alone. "I'll have to do a little talking, but let me see what I can dig up for you."

"I appreciate it, man. I don't want you to think I'm taking advantage of you, though."

Vance dusted off his hands. "I ain't worried about it. As the saying goes, it's not about what you know, but *who* you know when looking for a job, and in this case, I reckon it's both. You could be a good fit for the Force. As I said, I just have to talk to the guys, but I don't think it'll be an issue." In fact, Vance thought it could be a great thing for both the Force and for Gabe. He needed something to do to feel useful, and Vance often felt that the SOS Force was under-staffed. It seemed the more problems they solved, the more trouble they found.

"Thanks again. Let me get you my new number so you can get a hold of me."

Thumbing over his shoulder, Vance gestured at the old farmhouse. "It's not a mansion, but you're welcome to stay here if you need a place." He wasn't about to let a brother-in-arms go without a bed for the night.

But Gabe waved away the offer. "I've got some family that wants me to visit around the country, so I'll be doing a bit of traveling until I settle down. Keep me posted, though."

"Sure 'nuff." Gabe watched him go, the headlights disappearing down the long driveway. It felt good to see him again, and Vance really hoped he could set this up for him.

For the moment, though, he had something else he needed to take care of. The evening chores were done, but that didn't mean his work was finished. Vance backed the four-wheeler out of the lean-to, flicked on the lights, and headed across the field. He'd built his fences with the specific intention of leaving pathways in between them, and this particular one led to a perfect corridor of corn-fields and the O'Rourke ranch.

All the lights were on in the barn, creating a brilliance against the growing darkness. It showed the old farmer in stark relief as he fished around on his workbench for a wrench and then turned at the sound of the ATV.

Pulling up just outside the door, Vance cut the engine and walked up. "You didn't get it working without me, did you?"

Jim O'Rourke gave a wheezy laugh. "I wish! This tractor acts like it's older than I am. I'm starting to wonder if it's time to spring for a new one."

Vance let out a low whistle. "If you can afford a new tractor, then you must be doing things right. Seems like anything I make off those cattle just goes right back into feeding more of them."

"That's the way of it," O'Rourke agreed. "I did see an awfully nice harvester for sale the other day, though. I'm living in the dark ages over here without an enclosed cab, air conditioning, and Bluetooth. I can't even imagine what my grandfather would say if he could see how some people are doing it this day and age."

"Don't listen to him," Maggie O'Rourke said as she stepped into the barn. "He's afraid those robot vacuums will take over the industry and put him right out of business. Here, I brought some fuel for the two of you." She cleared a spot on the workbench to set down a jug of freshly-squeezed lemonade and a tray of warm chocolate chip pecan cookies.

That was one of the things Vance loved about going over there. It was like traveling back in time, when people didn't carry cell phones and life was a little simpler. The O'Rourkes were probably only about twenty years older than he was, but the generations of their family that had lived on the farm showed through. He picked up a cookie, closing his eyes as he discovered the chocolate chips were still melty from the oven. "Thank you. And he might not be completely wrong. I've seen articles about tractors with GPS that can plant, fertilize, harvest, you name it. It's too expensive right now, but it's comin'."

"And that's when I'll retire," Mr. O'Rourke grumbled as he knelt next to the bucket of the tractor and began fiddling with the hydraulics. "I don't want to be involved if I have to know how to build a computer just to plant a few seeds."

Vance polished off his cookie and glanced at the tray,

but he'd agreed to come over to help with repairs, not just stand around and eat. He moved to help Jim. "Don't you think that's how people probably felt when tractors replaced horses?"

The older man gave him a sour look, but they both knew it was in fun. "I don't think you can even say that since you still use your horses."

"Only because I'm as stubborn as you. There's something pleasant about tending the herd from horseback instead of buzzing around on a four-wheeler. I'm convinced the cattle feel better about it, too." If his inner cougar had an easier time around a horse than a loud engine, then he couldn't argue with that. Indeed, there was something peaceful about saddling up and heading out onto the massive acreage of his ranch: the creak of the leather, the smell of the horse, the thud of hoofbeats underneath him. It was difficult to imagine doing it any other way, yet most people did.

Mr. O'Rourke grunted as the two men removed the bucket from the front of the tractor. "Speaking of, I was wondering just how stubborn you truly are."

Straightening, Vance lifted an eyebrow. "Is it the roof again? I know this barn has been standing for a hundred years, and the dry Texas weather has kept it in pretty good shape, but it might be time for you to just break down and have a contractor put some metal roofing up there instead of trying to fix it every time it rains."

"That's not a bad idea, but it's not the roof." Jim ran a hand through his thinning gray hair. "My niece has just moved back to town after trying to make it in New York. She's a great girl, about your age, and she's got a good head on her shoulders."

Vance instinctively took a step backward as his cougar grew wary. "Are you fixin' to set me up?" It wouldn't be the first time someone had attempted to. He'd met plenty of people, whether it was at the farmers' co-op meetings, the cattle auctions, or even the local rodeos. Inevitably, someone would set their sights on him as the perfect match for their sister or cousin or friend who just couldn't seem to find anyone.

"I wouldn't put it that way...exactly. But I don't think you should dismiss the idea before at least knowing a little bit more about her," Mr. O'Rourke hedged.

"She knows a bit about country life," Maggie added. "I mean, she grew up right here in Texas. Pretty as a pie supper, too. Her father is a veterinarian." She glanced back and forth between her husband and neighbor, feeling some of the tension in the room. "I'll just go inside and check on things in the kitchen."

Pretty or not, Vance wasn't interested. Just to be polite, he'd allowed himself to be fixed up here and there, but it always ended in disaster. He began checking over the hydraulic lines, looking for a problem area—and desperately hoping for one so they could change the subject. "I'm really not interested."

"Don't you reckon it's about time you settled down with a nice girl?" Jim asked softly as he sat back on an old milking stool that was probably made back when the barn had been built. "You're a good man, Vance, the kind of guy plenty of young ladies would be crazy about."

"And plenty of those young ladies are crazy, too. Couple sandwiches shy of a picnic, if you know what I mean." He shouldn't have said it out loud and regretted it as soon as he did, but it was true. This niece of the O'Rourkes might have been a great girl, but so far, he hadn't found a single one who was worth the drama. Most of them were too clingy, needy, and emotional, demanding all his time and atten-tion. They simply didn't understand that he wasn't equipped to deal with that kind of energy. Cougars are soli-tary creatures, united with mates solely for reproducing before going their separate ways. That trait didn't translate to humans very well, and the two sides of himself constantly battled over it.

The old farmer sighed, but he had a small smile on his face as he looked over the tractor at Vance. "I'm not going to argue with you on that. Maggie has driven me crazy more times than I'd like to admit, but she's also sweeter than baby's breath. She's been at my side through some rough times, and I don't think I could've gotten through them without her. I guess I'd just like to see you have something similar."

Turning away toward the workbench for a different wrench, Vance shook his head. "I do just fine on my own."

"For now. It'll be different as you get older," Jim warned. "One of these days, you'll come home to that empty house and wish someone was waiting there to greet you."

Vance imagined that was exactly how things went for the O'Rourkes. When Jim came in from the fields at the end of the day, Maggie was no doubt standing there waiting for him with a kiss and a hot meal. That wasn't a terrible thought, and Vance couldn't deny it would be much better than shaking off his boots at the side door before sticking a frozen meal in the microwave, but he also doubted he'd find something like that even if he bothered looking for it. "Women aren't like that these days, Jim. They don't want to be at home, cooking and cleaning and raising babies. They want to be out in the work-force, making their own money. I'm not saying there's anything wrong with that at all; it's a good thing. It's just that the picture you paint isn't one that exists anymore."

"I reckon it's possible to find a version of it, one way or another," Mr. O'Rourke replied as he stood up and took a cookie from the tray.

"Maybe." Damn it. He'd gone over there to repair a trac-tor, not to discuss his love life—or lack thereof. "I'm not sure it would even be fair to whatever girl I tried to be in a relationship with anyway. Between the ranch and work, I'm not home much." Of course, Vance hadn't told Jim about his involvement with the Force. He'd glossed over it, explaining he was the operations manager for a small company contracted by the military. That'd been enough to satisfy the old farmer, who knew better than to ask nosey questions about anything that had to do with the government.

"Sounds like an excuse to me," Mr. O'Rourke teased. "You just think on it, okay? And if you decide you'd like to meet my niece, then you just let me know. In the meantime, I reckon we're about ready to get this put back together."

With the lines fixed and the hydraulic fluid topped off, the two men worked amicably to put the bucket back on the machine and test it out. Vance was glad for the work. Having something to do with his hands was always better than standing around idly. Between the visit from Gabe and the lecture from Jim, he'd been given too much to think about and it was nice to just concentrate on the task at hand.

When he headed home, however, he could hear the farmer's words echoing in his mind as he showered and made a sandwich. It would be a pain to have a woman there with him. She'd be complaining about his muddy boots on the floor. She'd get upset when the food would get cold because he didn't head in for dinner on time. Or maybe she'd be so busy working that it wouldn't be like having anyone there at all, and then what would be the point? He was a cougar, after all. He needed a single, peaceful life.

On the other hand, his human mind knew there could be some benefits. Vance certainly wouldn't mind the soft warmth of a woman next to him in bed, someone he could wrap his arms around in the middle of the night just to hear her breathing. And on the weekends, it could be nice to spend time getting to know the same woman instead of having random hookups all the time.

He shook his head as he locked the house before going to bed. As he tossed and turned, he realized he was letting Jim's words get to him. Vance just wasn't the settling type. He dated. He flirted. He went out with a woman once and decided she wasn't worth it, and then he never called again. It was the way things had been for Vance his entire life, and there was no point in changing now.

2

DELILAH HENDERSON TIPPED HER OFFICE CHAIR BACK AS SHE flipped through the stack of mail that had just come in for the day. Most of it was just junk with a few random bills, but one piece caught her eye. The address on the outside of the envelope was handwritten, and there was no return address. Delilah tore it open and removed a small piece of paper that'd been folded over several times. The handwriting was shaky and inconsistent.

You don't belong in office. If the voters don't remove you during the next election, I'm going to remove you myself!

Delilah sighed and opened her bottom drawer. She scribbled the date on the outside of the envelope, stapled it to the note, and filed it away. The folder of threats was getting thicker by the day, but it just made her smile. Even bad attention was still attention, and she'd been voted in for her position, fair and square.

Delilah was the vice president of the Dallas shifter conclave. Made up of elected members of all different species, the conclaves had started as an intermediary for the various packs and clans. Their roles had shifted in recent decades to a more government-oriented one, in which they not only helped solve disputes but established infrastructure for shifters. One of the current developments was a hospital of their own, a place where they could go without having to risk being discovered by a human doctor who didn't understand shifter anatomy and physiology. There had been too many close calls. Now that most of the hospital had been built, there would soon be one less thing for their community to worry about.

Gathering up several folders, pens, and clipboards, Delilah left her office and headed down the hall to the meeting room. She could feel several glares on the back of her neck as she strode through the cubicles. They weren't staring at her because they thought she dressed oddly or because she was one of those rude bosses who could never be pleased. The various administrative assistants and research aids would probably never even have the guts to tell her exactly why they had a problem with her, but Delilah knew.

Even though she worked amongst bears, tigers, wolves, and lions, she was a cougar.

A shifter like any of them, yes, but the isolated lifestyle of a cougar made it challenging to have any sort of political position. She had no pride to rally behind her other than the loose support of other cougars. Most clans could speak with each other telepathically when they were in their animal forms, but for Delilah, it had always just been her. She knew that others resented her for being different, but she also knew she was qualified for the job. Anyone who felt otherwise could kiss her ass.

"Oh, good. I'm glad you're here," President Whiteside said as Delilah pushed through the door of the conference room. Harris Whiteside sat at the head of the table, his laptop open in front of him, and a stack of paperwork sitting next to it. Considering the number of drips down the side of his coffee cup, he'd had several refills already.

"Always," Delilah confirmed. "At it early this morning?"

"I have to be, with the Austin conclave up my ass every time I turn around. Sorry," he muttered apologetically. "I just never imagined I'd have so much trouble with people who are supposed to be our equals. They're adults. They're elected officials just like we are, yet they act like children."

"Stop talking about me when you think I can't hear," cracked Rob Swanson as he swept into the room.

"This is no time for jokes." President Whiteside swept a hand through his thinning hair that was far too reminiscent of his last name. "We could be in dire trouble here, and all you want to do is crack jokes."

"I'm just trying to lighten the mood," Rob replied.

Whiteside worked away grumpily while he waited for the rest of the conclave to come in and get the meeting started. Delilah observed him, concerned. He was an older man, one who was never too quick to react, one who sat back and listened to all sides of a story before taking action. His calm demeanor was what had gotten him elected in the first place. So many shifters looked up to him.

Several of the other members greeted each other and chatted as they refilled their coffee mugs from the side table and took their seats. A few acknowledged Delilah, but none of them were interested in talking to her. Even they knew she wasn't like them. Fortunately, it was something she'd gotten used to a long time ago. Besides, she wasn't there to make friends.

When President Whiteside cleared his throat, the chatter died down instantly. The conclave members were friendly with each other for the most part, but they had complete respect for their leader. "I appreciate all of you coming in for this extra meeting. I know y'all have a lot to do, but there's an issue at hand that we need to discuss." He wove his fingers together and tapped them at the bottom of his chin, staring into the depths of the table's wood grain as though it might tell him something. "You all know that we've been having some problems with the Austin conclave. It started off with only a few minor infractions here and there, with one of their members racking up traffic violations while visiting Dallas. Then there was the wolf that snuck up here to sell drugs. We're lucky we got a hold of him before the human authorities did, because I have no doubt he would've told them anything and every-thing they wanted to know."

Somehow, the silence grew even deeper as they listened to the president. The threat of their secret getting out was one that constantly hung over their heads as shifters. Their world would change completely if the word were to get out. The humans didn't even realize how much things would change for them, as well. The last people they should need to worry about letting the cat out of the bag were other shifters, but it'd been made clear that they couldn't trust the Austin conclave. That made all of them uneasy, and Delilah could feel a ripple of anxiety thread its way through the room.

"Now," Whiteside continued, "we've got an even bigger problem." He turned his laptop to show a photo of an angry-looking man. His long hair and beard were scruffy, and the long scar along his jawline was unmistakably a claw mark. "This is Paul Grimes. He's the main suspect in a series of convenience store robberies, with charges of assault sprinkled in for good measure. His crimes are severe enough that the local police are looking for him, too. They don't have all the same advantages that we do, and I can say with confidence that I know where this man is right now. The problem is that the Austin conclave is refusing to allow us to extradite him."

Delilah sat up a little straighter at this news. "You've got to be kidding me. Let me make a few calls and see what we can do. That's not how we handle business and they know that."

Whiteside gestured softly with his hand to stay her. "I've already made a hell of a lot of phone calls, Ms. Henderson, and they don't want to talk. I agree that this isn't the normal way of doing things, but that's exactly the problem. I'm starting to see a pattern here, and I don't like it. It's one thing if they think a few small infractions aren't worth pursuing, but I only see it getting worse. It makes me wonder what their plans are and why they're targeting us."

"They may not be targeting just us," Rob replied. "This morning, I heard about some similar problems that San Antonio is having with Austin as well. I don't think it's anything particularly severe yet, but one of Austin's conclave members called me today and asked if we were still on good terms with them."

Whiteside pointed at him. "Call him back, and get me all the details you can. Gather up any available proof, too. I don't want this all to be based on rumor, especially if it ends up going to trial." He shook his head and sighed, suddenly looking even older.

"Sir," Delilah asked. "I know this is something we've discussed before, but perhaps it's time for us to build up some sort of armed force. It's clear that Austin is going to cause trouble in one way or another, and we need to be able to protect our territory."

But the president shook his head. "As we discussed before, that could be taken the wrong way. One conclave suddenly arming themselves is going to make it look like we're trying to attack. We have to be incredibly PC these days."

"Politically correct or not, isn't there at least something we can do?" Virginia Cowan asked. "It doesn't seem right that we should have to cow down just because we don't want to offend someone." The wolf inside her was obvious in the gleam of her eyes, and backing down wasn't something that sat well with her true nature. Several others nodded their heads and murmured their agreement.

"No," Whiteside said firmly. "It's not only risky in a political sense, but a logistical one. Where, exactly, do you plan on drawing these recruits from? Most of the shifters in our area are professionals; they're not soldiers. Even the guards that serve within the packs are already serving important roles for their Alphas. We have to put a lot in place to get something like that going. It wouldn't be quick or easy. We need to figure something out that's going to help us in the near future."

Ideas were beginning to brew in Delilah's head. She twisted her mouth as she mulled them over, but they weren't ready to be brought out into the daylight yet.

When no one volunteered any more information, Whiteside tapped his pen on the table. "All right, fine. I know the best ideas can come when you're not looking for them, so I'll give y'all some time. But tomorrow, I want to hear some answers. In the meantime, I want you to also be thinking about ways we can connect with our shifters. We need to make sure they're aware of the fact that we're here to protect them and take care of them. I don't want them to think we're some distant, disconnected committee that doesn't matter. Get out there and talk to people, make sure they remember that we exist." He held up a warning finger. "Don't treat this as an opportunity to get votes during the next election, either. That's not what this is about. Since we're all here, is there anything else we need updates on?"

William Pitts cleared his throat. "Dr. Barnett tells me the hospital is almost complete. They've already got most of the departments operating, at least on a basic level. They still have a bit of construction and finish work, but they should be able to handle almost all medical issues."

"Good. That's at least something y'all can spread throughout your communities, and it's better than making everyone worry." Whiteside looked somewhat relieved, but Delilah could still see the tension in small lines around his eyes. "Anything else?"

"Yes," Virginia said. "Taylor Communications has been keeping me updated on the database they started up a few months ago. It's greatly improved, and if you get a chance, I suggest you take a look at it since some of the interface has changed. I think it's safe to say that almost every shifter in our area is on there, though. The network that carries it is, of course, incredibly secure."

"I'll do that immediately," Whiteside promised. "Have they made any progress when it comes to adding criminal records?"

"Some," she confirmed. "It's going to be a long process. I spoke with Mr. Taylor himself, and he says he has plenty of workforce on the task, so we don't need any volunteers for data entry. I hope he's right since we can't exactly afford to pay anyone."

Delilah let out a small breath of relief at hearing this news. Hudson Taylor owned Taylor Communications, one of the biggest telecommunication companies in the U.S. He also happened to be a shifter, and he was committed to helping out his brothers and sisters of all species as much as possible. "If he needs anything from us, please let us know. We'd like to cooperate as much as possible."

"I think that about does it. Don't forget what I said, though. We need ideas. We need solutions, and y'all know how to get a hold of me." Whiteside remained seated as the rest of the conclave gathered their stuff and left.

Delilah remained seated to his right, not liking the waves of uncertainty that rolled off of him. She waited until the door closed and the two of them were left alone. "What is it?"

The older man smiled. "You know, I didn't know you at all when you were elected into this position, yet you can always tell what I'm thinking, can't you?"

The two of them were completely different people—and even different animals. Harris Whiteside had a bear inside him, a creature that didn't automatically get along with Delilah's cougar. But they'd been working side by side for the last couple of years, and she'd come to know his little quirks and tells. Delilah thought of him as an uncle, someone to be revered and admired, but whom she could still kid around with when the time was right. "I try, but I don't think it's all that hard to figure out this time. Everyone here knows you're upset."

"And I have every right to be." The president stood up and strode to the long bank of windows along one end of the conference room. He scratched his chin as he stared out over the city. "I can't help but think this is a bad situation. I don't have anything beyond small offenses and a general pattern. It's not as though President Kelso has come right out and declared war on us. In a way, I'd prefer it if he did."

"It would stop this guessing game," Delilah agreed. "I do have a thought, but it's not one I was quite comfortable sharing in front of everyone."

He glanced over his shoulder, one thick white eyebrow raised. "I'm listening."

"We've brought in the Special Ops Shifter Force before

when we had security problems we couldn't quite solve on our own." Delilah knew it was a risk. The Force was as close to an army as they could get, even though only a handful of men were members. She'd never actually dealt with them herself, but she knew they had some exceptional talents that could come in handy.

Now President Whiteside turned to her fully. "We have, but what exactly are you suggesting?"

"To arrange a meeting with them, maybe see what they could do for us. There's no telling what kind of connections they might have when it comes to intelligence, surveillance, and even just sheer firepower. We're talking about Special Forces vets who don't exactly operate under the limits of the law." While Delilah had always been more of a rule-follower than a rule-breaker, she had to admit the idea sounded exciting. Her life had been one of education and civil service, one in which she'd had to work very hard for very little return. A bit of adventure peppered in wouldn't be a bad thing.

"Oh, I know just what kind of connections they have: plenty. They're the most talented and skilled group of soldiers you're going to find. It's too bad we don't have the time and the resources to make a security team of our own, because those would be the kind of men we'd want to run it."

This was a solution to one of their problems that Delilah hadn't quite seen yet, but now that she did, it made perfect sense. "That's even better, then. We ask them to do a little work for us and talk to them about recruiting and training some sort of regiment. That would take care of everything at once."

But Whiteside was shaking his head. "No, Delilah. I'm sticking with what I said about a military. We can't do it. It's practically an invitation for another conclave to attack us. That's not the sort of thing that's happened in probably a century, but I'm not willing to be the one to deal with it in the modern era."

"Can't we at least talk to the Force? We don't have to hire them in any official capacity in order to, say, retrieve Paul Grimes from Austin." That would be a nice stab in the eye to the other conclave. She shouldn't be thinking that way, she knew. Everything a conclave member did was supposed to be official and polite and carried out with dignity. But seeing such distress in the president's face made most of that easy to cast aside.

Harris returned to his seat. He leaned back in his chair, folded his hands in his lap, and took a deep breath. "Talk to them," he finally said, so quietly, she could hardly even hear him. "Talk to them and just make sure they're on our side. Ask them if they'll be ready to stand with us should the need arise. Yes, we've asked them for help before, but never with an inter-conclave issue. It's different, and I don't want anyone thinking we've got them in our pocket for the wrong reasons."

"Right." A thrill of excitement zipped through her ribcage at the thought. The issues with the Austin conclave might not amount to anything, but this task she had before her was a bit different than anything else she'd had to do in her time as VP. Most of the people she dealt with were bureaucrats just like she was, people who rarely even let their inner animals show if they could help it.

"I'm also very serious about getting in touch with the community," the president continued. "I know you're not part of a clan. I get that, and I know that means there's a bit less you can do about it than the others can. I still have every bit of confidence in you, though. You're here because people believe you can get the job done, and I want you to remind them of that. Find our shifters. Talk to them. Until the database turns into some sort of mass communication system—something I'm hopeful for in the future—we have to keep this as a grassroots effort."

"I can do that, sir. I'll get on it right away." Delilah headed back to her office and sat behind her desk. She twisted her honey-blonde hair into a chignon and secured it with a pencil before diving into her work.

———

BY THE TIME Delilah made it back to her apartment that evening, she was exhausted. It wasn't really that the work was all that hard; it was the emotional stress that came along with it. No matter what was happening within the conclave, Delilah always felt the pressure to perform. She wanted to do everything she could for her constituents, even if she was solving problems they hadn't realized they had. This issue with Austin only made things more complicated.

Flicking on the lights, she frowned at the cardboard boxes still stacked in the corner of the living room. Delilah had told herself time and time again that she'd get to them when she had a free evening or weekend, and that hadn't happened yet in the six months she'd been living there. Oh, well. It could wait a little longer.

Her phone rang from her blazer pocket just as she was setting her keys down. "Hey, Anita."

Loud music thudded in the background, and Anita had to shout to make sure she could be heard over it. "Where are you?"

"I just got home from work. Where are *you*?" It was hard not to shout back, even though the noise wasn't coming from her end. Delilah pulled the phone away from her ear and wondered how anyone could stand to hear it in person.

"At the Club Royale, remember? You were supposed to be here an hour ago! I've already had two drinks for you."

"Shit." Delilah pressed her fingers to her forehead and closed her eyes. She'd completely forgotten, although that was rather convenient on her part. She hadn't wanted to accept Anita's invitation in the first place, but she'd already turned her down so many times. Eventually, she'd stop asking. "I'm sorry. I had to work late and completely spaced."

"Come *on*," Anita urged. "Just turn your ass around and go right back out the door. I plan to be here all night!" Someone screamed their agreement in the background.

Delilah felt her shoulders slump. She liked Anita; she really did. But Anita just couldn't understand how much Delilah hated crowds. Her idea of an evening out was more along the lines of dinner and movie before hitting the bookstore to check the clearance rack. Being packed into a club full of sweaty strangers who had no respect for personal space simply didn't do it for her. "I'm sorry. I'll have to catch you another time. Have another drink for me, okay?"

"Okaaaay," Anita called back in a singsong voice, "but you don't know what you're missing!"

"Yeah," Delilah said when she hung up, "I most definitely do."

She put her phone away and changed out of her work clothes. It wasn't easy being a cougar. She liked her solitude. The human side of her still secretly craved being around other people, but the beast was stronger and usually won the contest. That night, she'd be perfectly happy to kick back with a glass of pinot noir and a good novel.

3

VANCE LEANED ON THE FENCE, WATCHING THE LAST OF THE rodeo wind down. A dusty wind kicked up, carrying with it the scents of horses, cattle, and corndogs. Brilliant lights shone down on the arena to showcase the barrel racers as they urged their horses in tight circles and then rode hellbent for leather back to the gate. The air was just starting to stay warm at night, bringing the excitement and activity of summer along with it. This was one of the first shows of the season, and he was looking forward to more.

"Hey, good lookin'."

He turned to see a girl standing next to him. Vance was pretty sure he'd seen her before, hanging around the bull riders. Her tight black tank top sported the Cruel Girl logo above a shiny belt buckle that she definitely hadn't earned. Considering how clean and stiff her boots were, Vance doubted she was the type of woman who knew her way around the ranch.

Vance touched the brim of his hat. "Howdy."

"You come here often?" she asked, batting a set of fake eyelashes.

More often than she did, that was for sure. Vance could see right through her. She was what those in the business called a buckle bunny. Most likely, she'd never pitched hay, cleaned a hoof, or had been bucked off a horse, but she wanted to pretend she had just to pick up guys in tight jeans. Vance knew her type, but he also knew he could be just as shallow. He'd done his share of posing when he wanted to attract the right attention.

"All the time. The name's Vance."

The girl let out a ridiculous giggle that was cut off by the horn as another racer finished her set. "My name's Brooke. Do you compete?"

"I just have a few friends in the business. I raise cattle, but you won't see any of them here." Vance's cattle were well known for their quality beef. He'd been tempted to switch over a small amount of his herd and see what he might be able to make on a good mean bull—the kind that all the showoffs were terrified of—but he was too busy to manage two breeds with entirely different needs. His work with the SOS Force took up enough of his time as it was without having a whole other market to worry about.

Those eyelashes fluttered again as she ran her gaze

across his arms. "I guess all that work makes you pretty strong, huh?"

Well, damn. He had plenty to do that night when he got back home, but some of his chores might just have to wait, depending on how far she wanted to take this. "Strong enough, I reckon."

Brooke giggled again, and this time she dared to run her fingers down his sleeve. "You know, I could really use a beer. How about you?"

"Sounds good to me." Vance turned and made his way through the crowd toward the beer tent, shaking his head at how easy it was sometimes. The other guys complained —or at least some of them did, before they decided to settle down—but Vance knew you just had to look for the right opportunities. There were plenty of women out there, and they weren't all looking for a deep commitment. Girls like Brooke were a dime a dozen. They'd have a good time, and when Vance never called her again, she'd complain to her girlfriends and move on to someone else.

He was just trying to decide if he was willing to take Brooke back to his place as they stepped up to the back of the line. Someone tapped his shoulder, and Vance turned to find himself staring into a set of very serious blue-gray eyes. He froze like an animal caught in a trap as he studied her, the sound of the rodeo and the carnival-like atmosphere behind them fading to a dull roar.

"Vance Morris?" she asked. Her sandy hair, the strands

varying shades of everything from palest platinum to deepest honey, was tied back in a thick but loose braid. Her plaid button-down was tucked into her Wranglers, which bore faint dust stains on the thighs. She was vaguely familiar.

"You're looking at 'im." Vance recovered somewhat from his initial shock as he tried to place her. He knew he'd seen her somewhere before. Clearly, his cougar recognized her. The animal inside him, if he were to let it out, would be walking slow circles around this woman. It sensed a familiar beast inside her, which wasn't always a good combination for solitary cougars. But this time, he didn't feel the need to back away.

Her manner was much more professional than Brooke's had been as she extended her hand. "Delilah Henderson. I believe we've met before."

Shit. They sure had. It'd only been brief, and Vance wasn't even completely sure they'd been officially introduced. It was at the end of one of their previous missions, and Vance had noticed her instantly. He'd tried not to worry about it, since he had plenty of other things to deal with at the moment.

"Excuse me, but we're kind of busy." Brooke looped her arm through Vance's elbow and tucked herself in close to his body. She shot Delilah a possessive look.

It was a bold move for someone who was practically a stranger, but Vance wasn't surprised. He didn't exactly mind it, either, but Brooke wasn't going to get her way, no matter how much she fluttered her eyelashes or how tight her clothes were. Vance extracted his arm from Brooke's grip. "I'm sorry. I'll have to owe you a beer some other time. I've got some business to take care of."

Brooke stuck out her lower lip, but her eyes didn't show even the gleam of tears. "Come on, Vance. You promised."

"Another time," he repeated as he stepped out of line and headed off toward the horse trailers. He sensed Delilah walking next to him more than he actually saw her. Now that he knew she was there, Vance figured there was no getting away. A woman like her wouldn't take no for an answer. He rubbed his hand along his jaw as they stepped into the shadows.

"I figured I'd find you here." Delilah folded her arms in front of her, continuing to give him that look. Her lids hooded her eyes, making it hard to tell if she was amused or grim. The vice president of the Dallas conclave looked far calmer than Vance felt, but the tremble of her pulse in her throat told him maybe she wasn't as unruffled as she wanted to make it seem.

Vance glanced over his shoulder to make sure Brooke hadn't tried to follow them. "Not a surprise to find me here at all, actually, but I have to say I'm not sure what brings you to a place like this."

Her lips curved into a smile. "I may not look the part most of the time, but I was born and raised here in Texas just like you were. President Whiteside sent me here to make sure we could count on the Force's help." Her tone started out light enough, but there was no mistaking the gravity of the last sentence.

A shiver threatened to twitch down Vance's spine as he studied her. She was gorgeous, yet not in the same sense that Brooke had been. That girl was only appealing because she was young and fit. Delilah had a knockout body of her own, but the experience and depth in her eyes created a completely different allure. Vance could sense the cougar inside her, and he wondered if she had to struggle as much as he did to keep this professional. He'd only seen her from a distance before, and whatever brief meeting they might've had had been busy and cluttered with conclave business. This was different, there in the dark shadows of the trailers with the horses dancing anxiously as their owners leaned on the arena fence or picked up souvenirs to bring back home.

He cleared his throat. "Look, I don't know exactly what the situation is, but I'm not sure we should be discussing it here. I should be getting home, anyway. I've got chores to do back at the ranch." He glanced at the sun, which had nearly sunk to the horizon. The truth was that the animals would be fine for a little while. He'd fed them late plenty of other times when he was on a mission or had something come up, but it was a good excuse so he wouldn't get cornered into anything.

"I completely understand that; we had a few animals around when I was growing up." One of her eyebrows quirked up slightly in challenge. "I've got time; why don't you let me help you."

His eyes flashed in surprise. "All right," he drawled out slowly, unsure of exactly what was happening. But as he headed toward the parking lot, there was no mistaking it: Delilah was coming back to the ranch with him. As he climbed into his truck, he watched her get behind the wheel of a sleek black sedan. He cursed as he drove out onto the road, knowing she'd likely be pissed by the time they pulled in front of the barn because that black paint would be caked in dust.

Her headlights followed his steadily for the short drive, and Vance took advantage of having a moment to himself to try to calm his cougar. He'd noticed the magnetic energy radiating from hers, and he had a feeling she'd picked up on his, too.

On the whole, he avoided most people like the plague. But Delilah was different. She created an urge deep within his core to reach out, to touch, to explore. One glance from those captivating eyes of hers made his stomach ricochet inside his abdomen

Hell, he knew what it felt like to be attracted to someone. He was a man, after all, and he most definitely enjoyed the company of women. But this was something else. Delilah wasn't just a new, shiny toy he wanted to take off the shelf and play with; every second they spent together, a surge of intensity wrapped around him like a lasso, yanking him closer toward her. If he hadn't been steady on his feet, Vance wondered if he just might have tipped forward and stumbled at her feet.

Stop it, you idiot, he chided himself as he made the last curve in the highway before turning off onto a gravel road. *She's the vice president of the conclave, and she's here on business. They need your help, and that's all there is to it. Control yourself.*

Unfortunately, that was even harder than he imagined once he'd pulled up his driveway and realized Delilah was now on his territory. The big cat inside him knew that a female—and not just any female—was right there, willingly within his boundaries. It put him in charge in a wild, feral way that humans wouldn't understand, but that Vance most definitely did.

He waited only long enough for her to get out of her vehicle before he headed to the barn. "You really didn't have to come out here with me," he said. "I'm sure we could've waited to talk to about this at headquarters or something."

To his surprise, Delilah moved in much the same way as Gabe had when he'd visited. She watched him for only a moment before stepping up and pitching in. When pasture grass was short, most of the cattle were fed with big round bails. The cows he was babying got the good square bails

Vance kept in the barn. Delilah easily jumped up through several levels of them to retrieve a few from the top, dropping them down to him. "I didn't want to wait, and I didn't want to do anything official. This is all supposed to be kept under wraps for the time being."

Vance tossed the flakes of hay to the cows, trying to focus on the sweet scent of the dried grass instead of the way Delilah looked as she pounced down the haystack. Human form or not, she was lithe and able. It was hard not to think about what else she might be able to do with that body. "Why's that?"

Delilah smiled at the cows as she helped feed them before her face took on that solemn look again. "We're having some issues with the Austin conclave. There have been several problems, but the one we're having right now is their refusal to allow us to extradite a known criminal."

He thought he was beginning to understand. "So, you want the Force to go retrieve this guy." That would be an easy enough mission, and it wouldn't even take them all that far from home base. "Just send the details to HQ and we'll git 'er done."

"I'm afraid it's more politically sensitive than that," she quickly corrected. "I'm not even asking you to do anything specific right now except to be there for us when we need you. It might be tomorrow or it might be months from now. President Whiteside is concerned about the Austin conclave's plans, and he'd feel better knowing we have shifters like you on our side." She strode confidently next to him as they headed over to take care of the horses.

Vance flexed his jaw as he tried to think with his brain and not his groin. "You know the Force has always tried to help any shifter in need, whether it's someone from a clan or the conclave. In that sense, I reckon you have your answer. But I can't give you any kind of commitment without clearin' it with the others." He wouldn't say it out loud, but someone in her position should know that. They'd worked with the Force before, and they knew how any group of shifters usually functioned. Vance, Max, and Jack might be a bit of a ragtag bunch, but they still relied on each other and kept the best interests of the group as a whole in mind.

Delilah didn't seem to be listening at this point. She was watching the horses as they shuffled along the fence, moving into place according to the order of the team. In the next moment, she'd ducked through the split rails and was running her hand down Cedar's front leg. The horse easily shifted his weight and picked up his hoof for her. "Do you have a knife or a pick?" Delilah asked as she squinted down at the horse's foot in the dim light and held out her hand expectantly. "He's got something stuck in his frog."

Who the hell was this woman? Vance reached in his pocket for the knife he carried every day and handed it over. He watched as she glanced at it, flicked it open, and used the tip to fling a sizable piece of gravel out of the vshaped area on the bottom of Cedar's hoof. Folding the knife and handing it back to him, she gave the horse a pat and climbed back out of the fence.

He didn't want to admit he was stunned, but Vance knew he was watching her like she was some sort of magician. "How did you know?" he asked quietly.

She was standing close to him, so close that he could feel the heat of her body radiating out into the night, swirling around him before it drifted off into the sky. As she tipped her head up towards his, his heartbeat picked up until he thought it might actually be some other noise from a neighboring farm instead of one that came from inside his chest. "Like I said, we had a few animals around. It's been a long time, but you and I both know that sometimes an animal just speaks to you."

Yeah, like the way his cougar was speaking to him, demanding that he claim her instead of just standing there in front of her like a damn fool. "Still, I'm mighty impressed."

"I pay attention to things, Mr. Morris. I kind of have to in my job. I'm sure it's not much different for you." Her eyes met his, the stormy blue of them darkened by the coming night. There was so much more hinted at behind those eyes; far more than two people simply talking about business or even horses.

Vance felt his body leaning toward her, his hands itching to close around her hips and pull her forward. He took a deliberate step away from her and toward the barn. "Yes, speaking of your job, is that all you wanted to ask me? For the promise of some loose allegiance between the Force and the conclave?" Work was a much safer subject than anything else, and he would stick to it as much as he could. Maybe if he could focus on the idea of missions or battles, he could keep his beast in check.

Maybe.

He stepped into the barn and flicked on the light. The animals had their own run-ins in the pastures, buildings where they could come and go as they pleased. Vance had long felt these were much safer and healthier for herd animals, who could stand close to each other for warmth or a feeling of security when they needed it. That kept this barn free for a tack room, spare hay, and other equipment. He plucked a broom from a rack on the wall and began sweeping. Vance was just killing time, and he knew it, but there was little else for him to do when it was already dark outside.

"That's essentially the idea, yes. It's just a precaution at this point, and nothing else." She'd followed him inside, her eyes scanning the room before they slowly lifted up to his. Their color had changed again to one of an almost crystalline blue as she drew her plump lower lip between her teeth. "No true commitment, you understand."

His throat went dry. Such a simple thing, the color of someone's eyes. It wasn't anything that should matter at all, yet he found himself studying every tiny detail of her. He noted the way she stood, with one knee bent to exaggerate the curve of her hip. Even the way the fabric of her shirt fit over her body was enticing. "Right," he murmured as he stopped his sweeping, "no true commitment."

"We're just doing what we have to do." Delilah's voice was a purr as she watched him, those heavy lids suggesting so much more than what her sweet, pink lips were saying.

Leaning the broom against the wall, Vance dared to step toward her once again. "I'm glad both of us understand that." They most definitely weren't talking about the conclave anymore. At this point, Vance wasn't even completely aware of what the hell a conclave was. He only knew what *she* was, and that was because his inner cougar was telling him. The hair on the back of his neck stood up as he took another cautious step, gauging her reaction as he did so. "It's just the way it is."

"I know." Her body fit perfectly against his as their arms moved around each other. Delilah's lips reached up to meet his, soft and inviting.

Vance sank into them. This was crazy. Somewhere, in the furthest reaches of his mind, he was aware that she was the vice president of the conclave. She was one of the most powerful women he knew, and he had no business standing with her in his barn, exploring the warm heat of her kiss. But all logic and reason were quickly drowned out by the exquisite feeling of her tongue against his own; the way her lips moved to keep him captured in place.

There wasn't any choice in the matter; she was his mate. Cougars always knew exactly what—and who—they wanted. While their solitary natures would soon be leading them in different directions, in that moment, she consumed him. Vance reached out blindly and flicked the lights back off before scooping Delilah off her feet, making his way through the barn with the ease of a big cat hunting at night.

Delilah's body leaned heavily, desperately into his as she wrapped her arms around his neck and trailed her fingers along his firm shoulder muscles. Her lips and tongue made trails from his jawbone down his neck, pausing in the crook of his collarbone as she inhaled his scent. "I don't know if you can handle me, Vance," she breathed against his skin.

Her words shot through him like lightning, making him rock hard in an instant. "We'll see about that, now won't we?"

He'd reached the spare stack of hay, the good stuff he made sure to keep out of the rain. It was stacked in bales as it'd been when they'd done their chores, but some of it came loose and spread like a pallet on the floor. Vance swung her down so that she landed on her feet, but by some silent agreement, the two of them went tumbling down to the sweet-smelling bedding. Vance kissed her again as he curled his fingers up the backs of her thighs, over the back pockets of her jeans, and up to clamp around her waist just under her shirt. Her skin was like velvet under his hands.

She yearned for him just as badly, wrapping her legs around him and pulling him down toward her, yanking hard enough that the stitching of his belt loops tore. Delilah stripped him of his shirt, smoothing her hands over his chest. "I sure do appreciate a powerful man," she growled as her fingers glided down his strong arms, tracing every muscle slowly as though they might tell her of the work they'd done.

The intensity of the heat between them was too much to bear. Vance groaned as he felt her release his cock from the confines of his jeans. He'd taken his share of women, but none of them compared to Delilah. She claimed him just as much as he claimed her, and it ignited him with a fever down to the very marrow of his bones.

Those muscles she'd proclaimed to be so strong and powerful were quivering with anticipation as he returned the favor, taking satisfaction in the pop of snaps as he pulled her blouse open. He explored her curves with his mouth, roving over the hills and valleys of her breasts, claiming the peaks as his own with his tongue.

Delilah's back arched, pressing her harder into him and encouraging him. She could demand anything of him and he'd do it, like a man bewitched. His cougar was demanding, too, demanding that he get things going already. Instead, Vance moved backward on their berth of soft hay and clamped his teeth around the leather of her belt before yanking his head back. The gasp of surprise from that sweet mouth of hers was enough to keep him going, and he ripped open her belt and zipper. His fingers joined in to pull the fabric away from her hips, and he claimed her soft folds with his mouth.

Vance was a man possessed as he teased and licked, exploring this most secret place as her hips bucked against him and her fingers swirled through his hair. He tucked his hands around the backs of her thighs and clenched them around her hips, keeping her in place as she writhed and trembled beneath him. God, she was sweet, and Vance thought he could worship her right there forever.

But his body had other wishes, too; ones that could only go unanswered for so long. Vance gave her one final caress before he climbed back up on top of her, his thick shaft sliding along her leg as he leaned down. "Is this what you want?"

Her eyes blazed with desire. "Don't tease me, Vance." Her legs gripped him around the waist and pulled hard, leaving no question as the two of them melded together.

Explosions rippled through Vance's body the moment he sank into her. The burning that had started as a mere matchstick of flame when he'd first encountered her at the rodeo—how long ago had that been now?—had billowed into a massive bonfire that raged inside him as Delilah's hips moved enticingly against his.

Her nails dug into his back, tiny stabs of pain like pinpricks of light that kept him from completely losing control of himself and shifting into his feline form. Vance knew she was suffering on the edge as well as she sank her teeth into his shoulder. Her thighs clenched as she tightened around him, and she arched her back even further as their pace increased. Delilah thrashed her head in the hay as she let out a wild cry of ecstasy that echoed through the barn.

Vance gripped fistfuls of hay, knowing he was right behind her, and picked up the pace. As beads of sweat traveled along the hard lines of his chest and back, he thrust into her one last time, his entire being cascading into her.

4

THE HARD PLASTIC CHAIR WAS UNCOMFORTABLE AS HELL, AND Delilah had only been sitting on it for a few minutes as she waited. She glanced around the room, wishing there weren't so many other people there. They were all shifters, just like she was. That was one saving grace since they were at the new Dallas Center for Shifter Medicine. That was the official name of the hospital, even though the sign out front only had the stylized acronym.

The fact that the new medical center had been made with people just like her in mind didn't make Delilah feel any better about why she was there. She leaned forward, bracing her elbows on her knees and putting her forehead in her hands, trying to understand how she'd managed to let this happen. She was a smart woman, a professional woman, one who was always careful.

Or maybe she wasn't after all.

The door on the other side of the room opened, revealing a young nurse in scrubs. Every face turned to her expectantly, waiting to see if it was their turn yet. The nurse checked her clipboard. "Delilah?"

The very pregnant woman to Delilah's right groaned impatiently, knowing she'd be stuck in that damn chair for a little while longer.

Delilah popped to her feet, immediately regretting the action as her stomach revolted and the floor tipped beneath her. She pushed through it, not wanting anyone to know how she was actually feeling as she made a beeline for the door.

"Hi, there," the nurse said sweetly. "My name is Jamie. Just come right around this corner and step on the scale for me, okay?"

She was just doing her job; Delilah knew that. Still, she was finding herself far more irritable than usual lately. "Can you please just tell me my test results?"

Jamie gave her a sugar smile as she adjusted the weights on the scale. "I'm sure Dr. Eisert will go over everything you need to know in a moment."

Delilah didn't like the way that sounded. "I'm sure Dr. Eisert wouldn't know the difference if you just took a little peek at the chart and told me yourself." The waiting was killing her. She'd already waited long enough, taking note of her symptoms and trying to ignore them as long as possible before she gave up and finally admitted she needed to see the doctor.

Still, the nurse with her rosy little cheeks wouldn't budge. "Have a seat right here, and I'll take your temperature and blood pressure."

Delilah glared at her as she went through the process, wondering what kind of shifter this girl was. Sometimes it was easy to tell, and others not so much. But Delilah would bet she was something just as bright and perky as her personality, like a rabbit. She bit the inside of her cheek to keep herself from saying anything rude. After all, she had a reputation to uphold. If this girl did happen to peek at her file, then she knew she was dealing with the VP of the local conclave. The last thing Delilah needed was for her to start spreading rumors about her.

When she'd gotten everything she needed, Jamie escorted Delilah down a long hallway of exam rooms and motioned for her to enter the one at the end. A saw buzzed in the distance. "Sorry for the noise. The wing right next to us is still under construction. There's a gown here on the table. Dr. Eisert will be with you as soon as possible." The nurse closed the door, leaving Delilah with only the sound of a loudly ticking wall clock.

The scent of fresh paint was still thick in the air, and the exam room had the cleanliness of new construction as well as the sterility of a hospital. Instead of the cold blues and grays she'd seen in other places like this, they'd painted the walls a dark mauve and installed blonde wood laminate flooring. A print of a watercolor landscape hung on the wall, surrounded on either side by closeups of wide-eyed babies. Why they always put those kinds of pictures in these kinds of offices was beyond her. Not everyone was there for the same thing.

She glowered at the gown folded neatly on the table. It was fabric, at least, instead of those miserable paper jobs, but it still didn't afford much privacy with the giant gap in the back. Delilah closed her eyes and took a deep breath, trying to center herself and regain the sense of logic and practicality that had taken her so far in life. There was no point in being angry about any of this. Being impatient wouldn't make this go faster, either. She just had to wait it out, and everything would be all right, no matter what happened.

The paper on the exam table crinkled underneath her as she waited, but fortunately, she didn't have to wait very long. A gentle rap sounded on the door just before it opened, revealing a tall woman with short hair. Her glasses had brilliant frames in multitudes of color that matched the smattering of funky necklaces she wore. She didn't look like a doctor at all, but she charged into the room with her laptop as though she owned the place. "Well, Ms. Henderson," she said as she shut the door behind her. "I think we should get right down to business. You're pregnant."

A tiny prickle started at the back of her neck and spread

out over her body, making its way down her back and legs, around her arms, and curved toward the front of her body until it coalesced in her chest. Delilah had already known what the answer would be. As much as she'd tried to make excuses for the symptoms, there was no other way to add them up. She'd allowed her cougar to get carried away that night. There was something about the excitement in the air at the rodeo and the way Vance's eyes had sparkled when he'd turned around and looked at her for the first time. At that moment, her feline side had come alive in a way she'd never experienced. He was handsome, sure, with his rugged good looks and those strong arms that had been built through his military service and ranching. But Delilah had instantly seen past that to the beast inside him, one that was just as urgent for her.

"Based on the information you wrote on your patient intake form, my best guess is that you're about a month to a month-and-a-half along. Your alternate species is *Puma concolor,* correct?"

Delilah blinked, barely even aware of what the doctor was saying now. "Um, yes. That's right."

Dr. Eisert nodded. "Then I'm sure you're aware this means you're likely close to halfway through your pregnancy already. Your cougar side will likely be very dominant during this time. Not only does it affect your gestational period, but you may find yourself feeling a little extra cranky and wanting more alone time. At this point, you should be fairly well past most of the nausea, dizziness, and things like that which are more prevalent in the first trimester." She smiled as though this was all good news.

But Delilah wasn't sure what to make of it at all. She had so little time to prepare, even though she knew she'd never be ready. The idea of a child had been a sweet dream, a distant fantasy that might come true one day when she had the time, but not something that would happen right in the middle of her term as vice president. She had so many things she was doing with her life. The threat to the conclave wouldn't just go away simply because it was inconvenient for her now, either. President Whiteside was still very much concerned about what the Austin council might do.

With a snort, she realized it was that very threat which had gotten her pregnant in the first place.

"Do you have any questions so far?"

Delilah wondered if she'd missed anything. Her mind didn't seem to be working properly lately. It most certainly hadn't been working that night in Vance's barn. "No. I think I'm good."

"Wonderful. We'll just do a quick exam, and then we'll get you over to ultrasound so we can confirm a solid due date. Jamie will get you set up with some nutritional supplements and she'll book a few more follow-up

appointments for you. As you know, we're still under
construction here, but we do have a mothers-to-be class
that meets in the cafeteria on Fridays. There's a lot of great
information, and I'll make sure you get a pamphlet on
that."

The next half hour swept by, and Delilah was soon
walking back out to her car with a complimentary tote bag
full of appointment cards, pamphlets, vitamins, and book-
lets. She slung it into the passenger seat as she got in,
bracing her forehead on the steering wheel just so she
could try to think for a moment.

She'd known. She'd known for at least a couple of
weeks, and yet it all seemed like it was happening so fast. It
was easy for the doctor to treat this like an everyday event,
because for an obstetrician, it was.

But it wasn't for Delilah.

She dared to touch her fingertips to her lower
abdomen, which was only just slightly rounder than it'd
been on that fateful night. Delilah had tried so hard to
make it purely about business as she spoke to Vance, but
neither one of them had been able to fight it. The instinct,
the urge had been there, no matter how much she wanted
to deny it. She couldn't exactly blame it on the romantic
atmosphere, either, unless she was suddenly turned on by
the scent of livestock.

With her eyes closed, she could easily drop back into
that night with Vance. It'd been carnal desire that had

brought the two of them together, but as their cougar natures dictated, it'd been just as easy to part ways at the end of the night. She'd gone home, her sedan gliding down the country highway through the night, feeling satisfied and unconcerned. They'd agreed beforehand that there would be no commitment, so what was there to worry about?

This. This was most definitely something to worry about.

Swallowing a wave of nausea that had nothing to do with her pregnancy, Delilah started her car. She pulled out of the parking lot, uncertain as to where she was even going. She'd already told President Whiteside she'd be taking the day off, although the distraction of the office sounded like what she needed at the moment. Going home meant she'd just have to rattle around inside her apartment and think. And God, she was already tired of thinking.

There was no getting away from it. Delilah punched the speed dial on her cell, and Anita picked up right away, sounding sleepy. "Hey."

"Hey. Are you available for an early lunch?" Delilah set the phone in the dashboard holder and gripped the steering wheel.

Rustling noises sounded from the other end of the line. "I'm just getting up, so I guess that depends on where you want to go. I probably don't have time to get dressed for anything fancy." Anita worked the late shift at a big box store and was usually in bed until almost noon.

"How about I just bring it to your place?" That would've been far easier than trying to explain all this in the middle of a crowded restaurant where there was a chance anyone in Dallas could hear.

Anita perked up instantly at the thought. "I'm not going to turn that down!"

Delilah showed up at Anita's apartment twenty minutes later with two bags from the Beijing Buffet.

"You're my favorite person," Anita enthused as she let her in and took the bags, unloading them on the small kitchen table. "I think you must be psychic, too, because right before you called, I was tossing and turning in bed, trying to decide what to eat. I woke up starving."

"Not psychic," Delilah replied. "Just eating for two."

The chopsticks Anita held in her hand hit the surface of the table and bounced onto the floor. "What?"

Delilah sat down and ran through the whole story as quickly as she could, desperate to get it out. The knowledge was like a thing inside her that was clogging her throat and fogging her brain until she shared it. "I just can't believe I let myself get into this situation. I'm not some seventeen-year-old girl who doesn't know any better."

Anita blinked her big blue eyes as she reached over the box of sweet and sour chicken to rest her hand on Delilah's. "Hey, don't beat yourself up. It's not like you're the first person who's had an unplanned pregnancy. And you have a lot of advantages over those teen moms, anyway. You're strong and independent, and you've got about the best job anybody possibly could. It's not like this is something you can't handle."

"I hope you're right." Delilah had already tried to tell herself this about a hundred times, but it was a relief to hear it from someone else.

"So..." Anita pursed her lips and poked a chopstick into a box of rice. "What did this Vance character say?"

"I haven't decided whether or not I'm going to tell him. Don't give me that look," Delilah warned, seeing Anita's jaw drop. "I've seen women that have these surprise babies, and they only suffer for having to make accommodations with whatever man they'd fallen into bed with. There are arguments over how to raise the child, who's going to pay for everything, and then jealousy and anger when one of them moves on and finds a new partner. I'm not sure it's worth it, either for myself or for the baby." Delilah shoved an egg roll into her mouth, hungry and angry.

"Partner? But you said Vance is a cougar like you, right?" her friend challenged. "That means the likelihood of either one of you moving on to someone else for just another quickie is likely." Anita was a tiger, but she understood how her stripe-less counterparts worked.

"That part is something I can handle, regardless." Delilah frowned at her meal. The way she and Vance had come together had really been something else. It wasn't just the physical interaction, either. He'd affected her, as though his very being had been twisted together with hers. Sure, she'd enjoyed the sex they had, but that inexplicable bond had been what had woken her up several nights during the week following their tryst. She had to forget about that. This was no time for ridiculous romantic feelings.

"But what about the rest?" Anita pressed. "Do you think the two of you would have such a terrible time doing this together?"

Delilah rolled a shoulder. "I don't know for sure, but I know it wouldn't have to be that way. I can raise this baby on my own, and I don't have to tell anyone who the birth father is. There could be some distinct advantages to single motherhood. I make all the decisions without anyone trying to tell me otherwise. I never have to check in with anyone or get any approval. If I've had a rough day and I decide we're having cereal for dinner one night, then that's what happens, no questions asked."

Anita squinted across the table. "I don't think this is really about having cereal for dinner. What are you afraid of?"

"Oh, I don't know. *Everything.*" Delilah slumped forward onto the table. "I just don't know what to do next. It all seems wrong and surreal, like some sort of strange, waking nightmare."

A cool hand reached out and stroked her hair. "I don't know this Vance guy, but you might not be giving him enough credit. Rumors about the SOS Force have been spreading in the shifter community, and I doubt any guy who qualifies to be on their team could be such a bad person. He'd have to be responsible, experienced, and capable of making good decisions if he's a Special Ops vet. You could even give him the choice of how involved he wants to be, if that makes you feel any better."

Delilah slowly lifted her head from the table. "You know, that's not a terrible idea."

"I like to think I have a few good ones every now and then," Anita replied with a sly smile.

"If Vance doesn't feel like I'm backing him into a corner, then he'll have time to figure out exactly what he wants from this. No pressure, no commitment, just like it's supposed to be." Her stomach rumbled, reminding her that she'd need a little extra protein for the next couple of months. Delilah obliged with another bite of chicken.

"From what you've told me, he seems like a good guy. Even if he doesn't want to be an active father, your little one will always have her Auntie Anita to count on." She grinned as she dug the fortune cookies out of the bag.

"You're absolutely right. I've been so stupid about all of this. I'll just send him a quick text to make sure he's in town, and I'll get it off my chest right away." Her fingers flew over the touchscreen of her phone. Now that she'd made the decision, she wanted to get it over with as soon as possible.

Still, her hands shook when she pulled up to the garage door on Dragon Street. The SOS Headquarters was in an old building, squished in right alongside all the other shops on that road. The plain white front with a cracked concrete driveway was entirely unassuming. Vance was expecting her, and the overhead door rolled up slowly. Delilah pulled inside, peering into the dim interior. As much as she'd heard about the Force, and even though she knew exactly where their headquarters was located, she'd still never been inside.

The door rolled back down behind her as she swung into a parking spot. "This is the right thing to do," she reminded herself. "Anita agrees, too. You've just got to tell him and get it over with." Delilah turned off the ignition and opened her car door.

Vance had just emerged from a door off to her left, and he was striding casually toward her with that easy grin of his. Just being in the same building with him had a distinct effect on her. Delilah's human side had been hard at work most of the day, combatting the animal instincts that had her so riled up. The cougar instantly sprang to life again upon seeing Vance, though, reminding her in exquisite detail of their time together. He was a man like any other, yet her very blood seemed to surge toward him.

His smile faded slightly as he got closer. "Are you all right? You look a little under the weather."

Delilah wouldn't doubt it; she certainly felt that way. "I'm okay, thanks. Listen, I'm sorry to call you on such short notice—"

"No, no. That's fine. The gang's all here anyway since we've got a meeting. Come on in and I'll give you an official introduction, and then you can tell us just what President Whiteside wants." He guided her into the building through the door he'd come through a moment ago.

At one point, the interior had been an ample open space, but someone had divided it off into living and work areas. Delilah hardly noticed the modern décor as she moved through the place. Vance's hand was on her elbow, but she knew that was simply the Texan gentleman inside him. "Actually, I just needed to talk to you."

The rancher stopped, turning to her with a crease in his brow. "Me?"

Her cheeks heated and her stomach threatened to drop straight through the floor. Delilah was a diplomat, someone who'd been elected to her position for good reason. She'd dealt with all sorts of people; even death threats didn't bother her. Yet somehow, standing there in front of Vance felt like the worst torture in the world. "Yeah, just you—alone, if we could."

He glanced over his shoulder down a hallway and rubbed the side of his cheek uncertainly, but he nodded.

"Sure. I reckon I misunderstood. I assumed you wanted to talk about conclave business, so the guys are expecting you."

"This won't take long, and I don't mind talking to them for a minute if it will make things easier on you." That would be a small price to pay to save them both from a bit of embarrassment, especially if Vance didn't like the news she'd brought.

Vance led them to a common area with comfortable couches, a coffee pot, and a window with privacy tinting that looked out over a backlot. "Can I get you a drink or anything?"

There were those Southern manners again. "No, thank you." She could have used a cold glass of water, but Delilah wasn't sure she would've been able to keep a good hold on it. Delilah stepped to the window and concentrated on the industrial area pictures below. It was hard and hot and utterly real, even though this moment felt like something out of a movie. "I wanted to tell you something."

Vance perched on the arm of a couch. "I'm listening."

"That night..." Delilah trailed off. Making the choice to tell him had been much easier than figuring out exactly how to do so. "You and I..."

He was at her elbow now and she hadn't heard him walk up behind her. "Is someone giving you a hard time because of our little get-together? I know how tongues like to wag in these parts, but I wouldn't pay it any mind if

I were you. I'm sure there are plenty of other rumors that'll start flying and everyone will forget it soon enough."

"Oh, you might be right about that." Yes, there would be plenty of rumors when the local shifters found out their vice president had not only slept with a member of the Force, but had gotten knocked up in the process. She knew that wasn't what Vance meant, and he was trying to be nice, but it was hard to see the positive side of this just yet. She looked up into those green eyes of his and it was easy to remember how this had all happened in the first place. "Vance, I'm pregnant."

The words had squeezed out of her throat with great effort, and then they hung in the air. Vance didn't move, staring at her without so much as a blink, and Delilah thought she might have to push those words toward him to make sure he understood. "Are you sure?" he finally asked breathlessly.

Delilah nodded. "Completely. I was at the medical center today. Blood tests and an ultrasound and everything." The odd blobs the ultrasound technician had pointed out hadn't looked like much to her, but she had no doubt.

Vance was wearing the same black Stetson she'd seen on him when they'd met at the rodeo. By the end of that night, it'd been thoroughly covered in hay, but now it was clean again. He swept it off his head and ran a hand through his short hair. "I take it you're telling me this because it's mine."

It was a silly statement, in a way, but Delilah understood why he was confirming it. She nodded, her mouth dry as she waited for him to yell or curse or even turn around and stomp off.

Instead, one corner of his mouth tweaked up as his eyes drifted down to her stomach. "Really?"

"Yes. One hundred percent."

His eyes flickered in a double blink. "Wow."

Delilah could tell he was stunned, and she couldn't blame him. This was the very last thing he'd been expecting from her visit. "I don't want you to think I came here looking for money or support or anything. You don't have to be involved any more than you want to be. I know neither one of us was looking for this, Vance, and I'm sorry, but I can manage on my own."

Now the other side of his mouth crept up, and he closed the distance between them. "Delilah, don't be ridiculous. This isn't your fault. Neither one of us was careful, and I'm certainly not going to just let you deal with this alone. This is our child, and I'm going to be there every step of the way." He reached out and gently touched her belly with his fingertips.

Delilah felt a rolling sensation as the unborn child lurched toward its father. Her cougar was fighting this, demanding that she be alone and not have to deal with anyone else. She was the mother, and she knew best. She'd always thought her animal side was the most primal, but she realized as she stood so close to Vance that maybe her human half could be just as demanding. There was something appealing in that moment about knowing she truly wasn't alone, and she let her head fall forward onto his shoulder. Vance took her weight easily as he wrapped his arms around her.

5

"ARE YOU GOING TO STARE AT YOUR PHONE ALL DAY?"

Vance looked up from the screen and over to Max in the pilot's seat. They were just returning from a mission. The action and adventure of saving a shifter from the human mob he'd accidentally gotten involved with should've been on the forefront of his mind, but lately, there was only one thought in his head. "Until Delilah goes into labor, yes. Every morning I wake up and wonder if today is the day."

"Blows my mind that it's only been a couple of months and you're already talking about delivery plans," the tiger said with a shake of his head. "You cougars sure work fast."

"What do you know? You don't have any kids. You and Sabrina ever talk about it?" He glanced down out of the helicopter at the map of rural homes that spread out before them. It was a beautiful scene, but it was one he hardly paid attention to these days.

Max shrugged. "A little, but she's busy with the medical center. You know, the board was really trying hard to name it after her, since she put so much time and even some of her own money into it. She wouldn't hear of it, although personally, I think she deserves it. She already opened a new surgery wing at the human hospital, but now she's completely changing medical care for shifters. That's a particularly important issue for you and Delilah right now."

"Yeah, I reckon so."

"What's that mean?"

Vance sighed. He'd tried hard not to talk about it, but it was difficult not to mix their personal lives with business when they worked in such a small group. The other members of the Force were like brothers to him. "Well, that there is no 'Delilah and I.' I know we didn't plan any of this, but it happened, and I'd like for the two of us to really be a team."

"Oh, so she dissed your sorry ass?" Max asked with a grin.

"Asshole. I'd punch you if you weren't responsible for my life right now." Vance folded his arms in front of his chest. "Look, I don't expect some whirlwind romance. It's just that she's stubborn as a mule, not wanting to rely on me for anything. I asked her to move in with me right after we found out she had one in the chute. I thought it would be good for both of us. I could be there for her during the pregnancy, and then once the baby arrived, it would just make things simpler. She wouldn't hear of it." He felt sour about the whole thing, and it was clouding how he felt about having a child.

"Listen, I may not know a whole lot about this stuff, and I might not be the same species, but she's hormonal right now. Just give her time, and know that you're doing everything you can. It'll all work out." Max swooped the chopper toward the landing pad, set it on the roof of their headquarters, and began the long process of slowing down the rotors.

"I hope so. I don't want to be one of those dads that only sees his kid every other weekend. I want to be there all the time, for everything. Delilah sure wanted me that night at my place, but she doesn't want a damn thing to do with me now." He felt like a heel for even mentioning the encounter, but it was too late now.

"Then why's she calling you?" Max asked as he pointed to Vance's phone.

"Shit!" He hadn't heard the ring nor felt the vibration through all the noise and clatter of the chopper. Vance answered as he hopped out of the aircraft. "Sorry about the noise."

"That's okay." Her voice was strained, but not with the

usual amount of irritation she'd shown over the last couple of months. "I need you to come over."

"What do you need?" he asked as he swung the door open to access the staircase that led down from the roof. Vance and Delilah had been at odds, but he'd still been more than game to bring her hot fudge sundaes in the middle of the night. "Pickles? Chocolate? Bacon?"

"No," she panted. "I think I'm in labor."

His boots froze underneath him as his claws shot out from the ends of his fingers and dug into the wooden railing. "Are you sure?"

"Yes, I'm *sure!*" she snapped. "Or at least I'm as sure as I can get without being a doctor. I just need you to take me to the hospital."

Vance swiveled and shot back up the stairs. "Max is just winding down the chopper. I'll have him get it started back up and we'll have you in two minutes." His heart thundered in his chest, and he continued to fight the urge to shift. He could move so much more quickly if he were on all fours, his claws and paw pads gripping the pavement of Dallas as he pounced toward her.

"Please don't do that," she replied sharply. "You can't get that big thing in here, and even if you could, I really don't want that sort of attention."

Vance cursed under his breath, wanting to argue with her. But he'd been to her place several times now. The condos were modern ones not far from the center of the city, and they faced a park area that was full of trees and gazebos and had a massive swimming pool. Max was an excellent pilot, but Delilah was right. "Roger that. I'll be over there as soon as I can." Vance dashed through the building and down to the garage, jumped in his truck, and flew out of the garage.

He laid on the horn as he threaded through traffic, maneuvering the large truck as if it were a sports car. Vance was desperate to get to Delilah. What if the baby came too quickly and they didn't make it to the hospital? What if there were complications the doctors hadn't anticipated? Delilah kept telling him everything was fine, but that hadn't abated the worries that lingered in the back of his mind.

Pulling into the handicapped spot, Vance dove out of his truck without turning it off and charged up to her front door, covered in cold sweat. He reached for the knob just as the door opened. Delilah stood there, holding her overnight bag in one hand and her round belly in the other.

Vance darted forward and snatched the bag out of her hand. "You shouldn't be carrying that! I'm not even sure you should be carrying yourself. Let me get you to the truck, and then I'll come back for the bag."

The look she gave him was both pitying and amused as she stopped him from scooping her up off her feet. "I can walk, Vance. It's actually good for me if I want to make sure this labor doesn't last all day. There's no rush."

"Of course. Right." He fought to keep his feet at a reasonable pace as he ushered her to the parking lot when what he truly wanted to do was run. "Do you have everything you need?"

"I've been packed up and ready for almost a month now." Delilah paused, gritting her teeth as another pain shot through her body.

Vance felt his heart constricting. "What can I do?"

"Ah! Nothing," she panted. "It'll pass in a minute."

He knew it wasn't a long time, but it felt like an eternity. Vance was helpless, standing there watching her, holding out a hand for support that she didn't even need. He wondered for a brief moment if the child she was about to have would be just as stubborn as she was.

Finally, Delilah pursed her lips and let out a breath. "Okay. I think I'm good to go now."

If things didn't start moving faster, he was going to go crazy. Every horrid scenario he'd ever seen on TV flashed through his mind in an instant, including a traffic jam on the way to the medical center or even his truck breaking down. When they finally stepped off the curb, Vance dashed forward to open the passenger door and help her in. For the first time, he regretted having a big truck instead of a car. His nerves jangled as he helped her climb inside.

"Are you all right?" she asked when he hopped into the driver's seat. "You look a little pale."

"Me? I'm fine. You're the one that's in labor." Vance clenched his fingers tightly as he put the truck in gear and backed out of the space so he wouldn't see how much they were shaking.

Delilah let out a hint of a laugh. "Cool as a cucumber, eh?"

"Well, sure. I mean, I've delivered plenty of calves. I don't imagine this will be much different except that we're going to the hospital instead of a barn. I could probably deliver the baby myself, if need be." He'd thought about that quite a bit, actually; wondering how much his ranching experience might help him in the delivery room.

"I don't think that'll be necessary," she said with a shake of her head.

"No, but it's a possibility. And you sounded pretty worried yourself when you called me." Why did he feel the need to justify every tiny thing when he was around her? She'd driven him crazy over the last couple of months. Both of their cougars had been reacting in similar ways when they spent time together to make plans for the child, desperately seeking solitude once again. Everything past that first night had been so difficult, and he didn't want it to be that way. Panic was flourishing in his bloodstream.

"I was in the middle of a contraction," she snapped,

rubbing her belly as she rolled her head back against the seat.

"I'm sorry. I'm sure that's rough."

"You're goddamn right it is," she growled.

"I'm just tryin' to help."

Delilah's response was only a sigh as she looked out the window, unwilling to further the conversation. That was probably for the best, considering he wasn't doing anything but making it worse. He clamped his jaw shut and promised himself a good long run in the back fields of his property as soon as he got the chance. He needed a moment to let out all the pent-up energy and anger that had been building inside him. He swept into the emergency driveway of the medical center.

To Vance's surprise, an orderly instantly stepped through the sliding doors with a wheelchair. "What's the situation?" he asked.

"We're having a baby." Vance dashed to open the passenger door and help Delilah into the waiting wheelchair. She didn't need his help, but this time, she at least did allow him to do so. "I'll just pull the truck into a spot and I'll be right in," he promised her.

As he parked his vehicle, the full force of what Vance had told the orderly hit him.

They were having a *baby*.

There would be no more wondering or planning; it was happening. *We're having a baby*. He felt almost numb as the thought rang loudly through his mind. There were so many things to think about as he walked through the emergency room doors. Vance thought he'd already pondered most of them, like where he was going to get the tiniest set of cowboy boots and the curtains for the nursery he'd set up in his house. But now a sudden flood of terror washed over him as he asked a nurse where to go to find Delilah. There would be illness, homework, bullies, friendships, good days, and bad ones. It was both incredible and overwhelming at the same time. Vance had seen warfare at its very worst, close up and personal, and yet none of that would change his life as much as what was about to happen. He barely even heard the construction noises coming from a nearby wing as he wound his way around to the maternity ward.

The hospital staff had worked quickly. Delilah was already dressed in a cotton hospital gown. The nurse standing next to her bed was strapping monitors around her belly, but she looked up when Vance walked into the room. "Are you Dad?"

He blinked and swallowed. How could it be that in all the discussions he and Delilah had already had about this baby that such a question from a stranger could nearly knock him over? "Yes," he finally said.

"Good. You can have a seat right there. I was just telling Mom here that the contractions do seem to be very regular and growing closer together. Things are looking good for having a baby within the next few hours if all goes well." The nurse secured the monitors with strips of Velcro and headed for the door. "The doctor will be in to check on you in a moment."

"Are you all right?" Delilah asked as soon as the nurse gently shut the door behind her. "You look like you're going to be sick."

And he felt that way, too. His stomach churned, and his skin had grown clammy. Vance would've laughed at himself if he could've managed to. Birthing was nothing new to him, not when he was breeding cows and occasionally bringing one of Mr. O'Rourke's studs over to cover one of his mares. It was just part of life—and far more beautiful than all the death and destruction he'd seen. Even so, this was getting all too real. "Of course. I'm fine. The real question is, how are you?"

Delilah shifted slightly on the bed, turning to face him completely now. Her brow was wrinkled and her lips were dry, and those hooded eyes were full of more fear and anxiety than he'd ever seen on her face before. She'd always come across as being so calm and in-charge, and it was disturbing to see that she was just as frightened as he was. "I'm in pain," she moaned. "And I'm a little scared."

Instinctively, Vance reached out and covered her hand with his own. "It's going to be okay. You couldn't be in a better place to have this baby. Everyone here knows what they're doing, so just trust them. And I'm going to be right here by your side through the whole thing."

Her mouth twitched as though she wanted to argue with him, but then she nodded. "Thank you."

He hadn't lied. Vance might not have gotten along with Delilah very well, but he'd be damned if he was going to be one of those men who'd just stand back and let the woman take care of everything alone. It wasn't just because it was the right thing to do, either. He wanted to give Delilah every bit of strength he had, and as he saw her face twist and her body writhe in pain, he felt his heart reaching out for her. Once, as the doctor was urging Delilah to push harder, Vance had to fight down his inner cougar from lashing out.

Finally, after a lot of sweat and tears, the nurse placed a squirming bundle in his arms. "Here's your little girl, Mr. Morris."

Gently, Vance pulled back a bit of blanket to get a better look. She had perfect little rosebud lips, flushed cheeks, and a mop of brown hair. The baby blinked bleary blue eyes up at him as she curled her fists angrily at the world she'd just been brought into. "Hi, sweetie," he whispered. "I'm your daddy." He felt a crack in his heart, but not the kind of heartbreak people lament over. His life had changed forever, and all because of this tiny little she-cub.

———

"Sorry, I'm running late." Delilah dumped the diaper bag by the door, but she gently set down the car seat holding sleeping little Rose in the middle of the living room floor. "She kept me up half the night, but of course she was out like a light when my alarm went off. It's just one of those mornings." She turned for the door. "I'll see you after work."

Vance knelt by the car seat, admiring his daughter. She'd changed a lot in the first few weeks of her life. Her hair had lightened and her eyes had become more clear. All the baby books claimed she couldn't see yet, but he would swear she was assessing her surroundings carefully. "I wish you'd just moved in with me."

"We talked about this, Vance," she replied with a sigh.

He glanced up at her, ready to argue. Delilah wore a summer-weight pantsuit for work, a far cry from the Western attire she'd worn on that night in the barn. She was one of those women who looked natural in almost any style, and he thought she looked hot, even in sweatpants. But there was no missing the circles under her eyes and the way her mouth turned down at the corners.

"Only a little," he reminded her. When Delilah had first come to him and told him she was pregnant, moving in together had been one of his first thoughts. But she'd been quick to dismiss it. "I really think it would be a lot easier on all three of us. You wouldn't have to be the one getting up all night with her. We wouldn't have to track each other down to figure out our schedules for the week to see who would need to be with Rose when. The baby wouldn't have to travel back and forth so much, and we'd both save a lot of gas money. It's just practical."

Her frown deepened as she glanced around the living room for a response, and her hands twitched as she brought them together in front of her. "The last thing I want is to be a burden on you."

"It's not a burden." He dared to move a step closer. Vance had hoped that once the pregnancy was over, the two of them would get along a little better. Most cows became a lot more pleasant after they'd calved, and for all he knew, it would be the same for a woman. Delilah wasn't as snappy as she'd been a month ago, but she was still just as stubborn and hard-headed as always. "It would be a good thing. We'd be giving Rose a more stable lifestyle."

"Rose, yes," she conceded. "But I know you don't actually want me here, and moving in together will only make you and I more miserable. That's not going to be good for the baby if she has to listen to us arguing all the time."

Vance sighed. He stood exactly halfway between his sleeping daughter and his so-called mate, not knowing what to do. "Maybe we'll argue less if we get a little more sleep and do a little less traveling."

"I won't be an obligation to you, Vance. You don't want me here."

"Who says I don't?" he snarled. "I'm asking you, aren't

I?" Damn it, she could get him riled up. Vance couldn't figure himself out sometimes when he was around her. He found himself wanting to be gentle and loving, yet in the next second, he just wanted to be alone like any other cougar would. When she walked into a room with Rose in her arms, it was the most beautiful sight in the world. On the back end of that thought was always an immediate, instinctive pushback on anything that meant sacrificing his own needs.

"Only because you feel like you have to. Let's stop talking about it now before we wake her up." She gave a quick lift of her eyebrows to indicate her anger.

He glanced at the car seat. Rose's eyes were still closed, but she was beginning to squirm. That was fine. He'd offered at least twice for Delilah to move in. He'd even gone so far as to draw up plans for modifying the old house to make it work for them as best as possible. The spare room at the end of the hall could be Delilah's with her own bathroom and easy access to the nursery. But if she didn't want that, then he couldn't make her. "Fine. Then let's talk about finding a nanny of some sort. You've got a lot going on with the conclave. The Force has been kind enough to give me more time off to help take care of her, but we can't both keep doing this with our careers."

Delilah cocked a hip and rested one fist on it. "You can't be serious! We can't just leave her with someone!"

"Obviously, not just anybody, no. But it's hard for me

even to get my ranch work done. I've got to get up an hour earlier than usual to do the morning chores, and I can't do the night feeding until you've arrived. I've been able to take her out to the barn in her car seat a few times, but it's just too difficult with a newborn." He didn't like to admit there was anything he couldn't handle, but ranching was hard, dirty, and hot work. Vance worried too much about Rose. "I'm sure with your connections and mine we can find a shifter sitter who's qualified. We'll screen them carefully. I'd stay with her all day if I could, but it's just not practical." He turned back to the dozing baby, bending down to touch her soft cheek with the back of his finger. Rose was the most angelic creature in the world. He could easily just sit back and watch her grow instead of going to work, but his livestock and the shifter community needed him.

"I don't know." She turned slightly away, trying to hide the fact that she was wiping a tear from her eye.

Shit. It was happening again. Delilah could get him in a horn-tossing mood in less than eight seconds, and in the next instant, she had him wanting to wrap his arms around her and tell her it was all going to be all right. "Let's just think about it, okay?" he said gently. "I won't do any of that without your approval."

"All right. We'll think about it." Her shoulders were hunched, and never had Vance seen her look so defeated. "I've got to go. I'll be here as soon as I can get off work."

"Okay." Vance waited until her sedan was halfway down

the drive before he turned around, finding that Rose had awakened and was watching him peacefully with those big blue eyes. They were a brilliant shade of cerulean. He knew time would only tell if they would remain so or if they would turn the steely blue of her mother's or the green of his. Whatever color they were, Vance couldn't get enough of them.

"Good mornin', little cowgirl," he said as he unfastened her buckles and lifted her out of her car seat. She was a warm, soft weight against his chest, and he adored it. Rose made the whole world different. "Don't worry about your mommy. She's worried enough about you, and I have to admit, I'm a little worried about her. You know, I think there's a different reason she doesn't want to leave you with a sitter."

Rose watched his mouth move and her tiny fingers grasped for his lips.

Vance nibbled them obligingly. "She's worried you're going to do something amazing, like shift for the first time, and she won't be there to see it. Yeah, we've got to make sure we choose the right person. We need a Mary Poppins who turns into a cougar at the end of the day. But really, I think that's what it is. She feels bad that she doesn't get to spend all her time with you."

The baby squirmed in his arms, kicking her feet and grunting.

"I see. Time for a diaper change. We can do that." He

brought her upstairs into the nursery and laid her on the changing table. This room had obviously been used for a little one before he'd bought the place, the vintage wallpaper showing scenes from various nursery rhymes. Vance had repaired the few spots that were beginning to peel, tacked in new trim, ordered a set of lace curtains, and spread a large pink rug on the floor to make space for his baby girl.

"Anyway," he said as he got a clean diaper and wipes, "your mommy wishes she could be with you all the time, and so do I. It's tough for us because we have to work, but we also have to be parents now. I guess it's not any different than trying to be both a human and a cougar, which is something you'll have to learn to deal with someday."

Rose squirmed and wriggled, making Vance's efforts all the more difficult as she looked around the room.

He managed to get her snaps all lined up and back in place before he sat down with her in the rocker, his thoughts growing deeper. "And that's the problem your mommy and I have with each other, too. I *want* to be near her. I like the idea of having a family. She thinks I don't want her here and that I'm only offering for you both to move in for your sake, but that's not really true. On the other hand, there's this big beast inside me, an animal that's very demanding and wants nothing more than to be on its own in the middle of the wilderness."

She nestled against his chest, her awkward little hands batting at the fabric of his shirt.

It didn't matter to him that she couldn't hold a real conversation yet. Rose was very easy to talk to. "Yeah, you're right. We'll work it out because we both love you. That's all that really matters. But do me a favor. Give your mommy a break and get plenty of sleep tonight." Vance brushed his fingers through her fine hair, wishing he could get all these feelings sorted out once and for all.

6

DELILAH ROSE FROM HER SEAT IN THE CONFERENCE ROOM AND refilled her coffee mug. She's seen the dark liquid drain and refill in her mug so many times that day, she could no longer keep track of it. At some point, she knew she'd kept her caffeine intake under control. Now, she wasn't sure if there was any coffee strong enough to meet her demands. "Okay. So, if they want to meet up with us, then we need to make plans upon plans," she said as she sat back down.

"Meaning?" Virginia asked.

She pulled in a deep breath, fighting against her lack of sleep to get her thoughts together. President Whiteside had just called them in for a special meeting to let them know the Austin conclave was willing to meet face-to-face. The news was huge, but they couldn't be gullible enough to assume everything was aboveboard. "Meaning, President

Kelso said he'd like to meet with just the president and me. That's fine, and we should stick to that as a symbol of good faith. But I don't think it would be a bad idea to have someone with us, maybe a bodyguard of sorts."

"I don't like the idea," Whiteside responded instantly, as she knew he would. "It's a threat. It shows them we don't trust them."

"But they already know that," Delilah pointed out, "and we have *no reason* to trust them. They're idiots if they don't see that, and they'll think *we're* idiots if we just keep letting ourselves be intimidated by them. I say let them see that we have a bit of muscle under our shirts. Maybe part of the problem is that they see us as a bunch of weaklings they can just run over."

Whiteside tapped his lower lip with his fingers. "I suppose you're right. I've been very caught up in the political correctness of all this simply because we're dealing with another conclave, our theoretical equivalent. If we were dealing with local shifters who were getting out of hand, we wouldn't hesitate to make them understand who's in charge."

"Exactly." Delilah felt some of her old energy coming back, spurred by her work. Those long evenings and nights were such a drain on her spirit, even though she loved Rose more than anything. There was no question that Rose was a good baby, but that didn't mean she wasn't exhausting. Her mouth quirked up a little at the corners at the thought of Rose curling her fists in the air when she was hungry. "I say we bring a body-guard, and I also think we should have some sort of backup. Not immediately with us, but close by in case we need them."

Rob nodded. "We could arrange for someone to be in the same hotel. We could even put them in the rooms that adjoin yours and just have them check in at a different time so it's not too obvious."

The president nodded, but he looked worried. "I suppose you're right. Folks, I want to apologize for this whole thing. Perhaps if I had been more firm with the Austin conclave at the very start, we wouldn't be where we are now. I miss the peaceful times when we didn't have to worry about things like this."

"Don't you dare take this on your shoulders," Delilah warned him. "They knew what they were doing, and I have a feeling they still do. If they can take advantage of us, then they will. It's our job to figure that out."

"You're right." He nodded again, rubbing the back of his neck. "Where do you propose we get a bodyguard and the rest of our backup? A security agency?"

"Of sorts." She had a thought in that regard, but Delilah wasn't ready to say it out loud just yet. "I'll work on a few things."

"Very well. I think that's all for the time being." White-side dismissed them, and they all headed back to their offices.

Delilah automatically checked her cell as soon as she reached her desk. She'd been glued to the screen ever since having Rose. What if she took a tumble off the couch? What if she shifted? What if she came down with a fever? Her mind whirled constantly with the possibilities, and she knew it wasn't going to get any better even once Rose got older.

A jolt of energy ran through her body when she saw she had a text message from Vance: *Meet me at Saint Martin's tonight when you get off work. I'd like to talk with you about a few things. I've already got a sitter.*

Her heart fluttered at getting a dinner invitation from Vance, but her stomach sank on the back end of it. What did he want to talk about? Concerns swirled in her mind, and most of them were far too uncomfortable to think about for long. She tapped the screen to reply but hesitated, uncertain about Vance's true motives. But she couldn't avoid him forever, especially since he was Rose's father. She typed out a reply and sent it before she could change her mind.

That evening, it was impossible to get ready for dinner. "It's not a date," she said to Anita, who'd come over before her shift, "but it *is* at a very nice restaurant. I want to look nice, but not too…"

"Sexy?" Anita filled in for her with a laugh. She sat on the edge of the bed in her work uniform, a polo and khakis.

"Delilah, the guy has already seen you naked. I don't think it matters what you wear."

Delilah pulled a dress out of the closet and frowned at the plunging neckline. "I disagree. Clothing says a lot about a person."

"All right, I'll play. What do you want your dress to say about you?" She got up off the bed and pulled a skimpy black number from the rack. "This one says you're up for anything, including what got you involved with Vance in the first place." Anita snagged another black dress, but this one had a boxy look and a high neck. "This one says you're ready to join a convent."

Delilah huffed playfully at her before putting both of them back in the closet. "How about something in between? Something that says 'I mean business.' "

"Then just wear what you've got on."

Looking down, Delilah took in her pantsuit. It was fine for work. Technically, it was even fine for going out to dinner, but it wasn't quite right. "Okay, more like, 'I mean business, but I'm not just a callous bitch, either.' "

Anita grabbed her friend by the shoulders and turned her so that they were looking in each other's eyes. "Okay, I think what you're worried about here is not what your outfit says about you, but what Vance might say to you."

Delilah wanted to turn away, but mostly because she thought Anita was right. "You don't even want to know the possibilities."

"Sure I do. Hit me with it. Get it off your chest, and then you'll be all set to face him."

"Fine, but I'm going to say it fast before I change my mind. I'm worried he'll tell me he wants to take custody of Rose instead of doing this together. And I'm also worried he's going to say something really stupid like he loves me, but I'm also terrified that he hates me. Ever since he and I met, I've been waffling back and forth on how I feel about him and what I want to do about it. I don't know! The whole mate situation is so damn confusing when you're a cougar shifter. It's like a never-ending war between my human and cougar sides, and it's fucking exhausting." She collapsed onto the bed, her head in her hands.

"It'll be all right, kiddo." Anita rubbed a hand on her back. "I don't know Vance very well, but I do know he cares about Rose. In some sort of way, he cares about you, too."

"But it's just so hard." She was crying now, the tears audible in her voice. Delilah didn't like sounding so weak, but at least only Anita was there to hear it. "I don't know what to think when I'm around him. He's so damn hot, but I get mad at myself for thinking it."

Anita shrugged. "There's no denying he's a fine piece of ass."

"Sometimes, I wonder if it's more than that," Delilah admitted. "I don't see what it could possibly be, really. I mean, I'm supposed to be by myself. I shouldn't want to have anything to do with him beyond letting him see Rose when he wants to and asking him to help pay for her college tuition someday. It should all be nothing but business."

"But you don't really believe that, do you?" Anita asked gently.

Delilah wiped her face and marched back to the closet. "I don't know what to believe, but for now, I've just got to get myself to Saint Martin's and see what he has to say. I'm not the kind of person who likes taking things day by day, but I don't see what other option I have."

Finally deciding on a pale blue dress with a touch of lace along the neckline, Delilah showed up at Saint Martin's as Vance had asked. As she checked in with the hostess, she was more and more certain that she was there for bad news. Vance wanted Rose to himself. Vance was going to leave the country on a mission and leave her to care for Rose alone. Vance had hired a human nanny who promised to keep their secret but had actually exposed them to the tabloids...

He stood as she approached the table and moved to pull her chair out for her. "There you are," he said with a smile. Delilah was used to seeing him dressed in dirty jeans and boots for working on the ranch. He'd traded that for a tailored charcoal gray suit and a crisp white button-down. Leaving the tie off was a good look for him, and she scolded herself for the heat she felt in her cheeks.

A waiter appeared instantly, smiling and asking for their drink order.

"How about a bottle of wine?" Vance asked her.

She didn't know how to answer, especially considering she didn't know why he'd invited her there. For all Delilah knew, this was going to be a whiskey night. But she nodded her assent, and the waiter disappeared.

"I'd like to cut right to the chase," he said, leaning forward. The candlelight danced over the angles of his face and made his green eyes the color of the deep sea.

"That sounds good to me." It was much better than waiting for him to get to the point of this dinner, which she was still afraid she wouldn't like. The big cat inside her was pacing restlessly, ready to pounce or run, whatever the case might be.

Vance pulled in a deep breath. "When you and I... got together, we really didn't know each other. We were operating on instinct, and as incredible as that night was, we didn't expect it to turn into all this. We both love Rose, but we never got a chance to know each other as anything other than parents. I thought we should take the time to just talk without the baby here as a distraction."

A melting sensation of relief started at the top of her head and crept slowly down her neck to her back as many of her troubles evaporated into thin air. "Really? You just brought me here to get to know me?" Delilah could hardly believe it was true, and she wanted to laugh at herself for all the horrible things she'd concocted in her mind. A snicker rose in her throat. "Oh, Vance, you must hate me."

He cocked his head. "I don't hate you, Delilah. Wouldn't have asked you here if I did."

"I've been an absolute beast to you."

Vance's mouth turned up slightly, but confusion remained in his eyes. "We've been getting along like a house on fire, that's true."

"I just... I just... " Delilah gasped as the waiter brought their wine and poured them each a glass before giving her a look and retreating to the kitchen. "Oh, I'm so sorry. I was just so worried that you were bringing me here for bad news. I think that's part of our problem, Vance. Every time I see you, I expect the worst." She sobered as reality loomed large once again. "I don't know what to think at all, really."

"I don't either, but I'd like to fix it," he said gently. "No matter what happens with us, we've got Rose to take care of. I think it'd be best if we at least spend some time together, just us."

It was possibly the nicest thing he ever could've said, and Delilah knew she'd be crazy to say anything but yes. "That sounds good to me, as long as you think we actually have something to talk about besides Rose. I think she pretty much occupies my entire mind these days."

"You can start by telling me about yourself. The only thing I really know is that you're our VP—that, and you mentioned having a few animals while you were growing up." He looked so genuine as he asked her, so eager.

She felt the twitch of a smile as she realized she'd told him that on that fateful night they'd spent together. Delilah hadn't given him much credit, but the man did pay attention. "That's true. I grew up just west of here, near Palo Pinto. It was a small community with a tiny school, the sort of place where everyone has known everyone else since kindergarten. There are a lot of good things about a small town like that, but I was in about sixth grade when I noticed this one kid was getting picked on a lot. He was really shy and didn't want to have anything to do with the other kids, even when we were playing games or having a free day. I won't bore you with all the details, but it really bothered me that he didn't fit in, and one day I realized he was secretly a shifter. That's when I decided I wanted to do something to help people like us. Lots of kids get picked on. We all go through our awkward phases. But it was different for him."

"Does this guy know how much he influenced you?" Vance asked.

Delilah smiled and took a sip of her wine. "Probably not. He moved away in junior high; I like to think he found a better place for himself. I know we're not supposed to talk about Rose right now, but I worry about that with her. How hard will it be for her to fit in when she has an entirely different set of genes from the human kids?"

"We both managed to survive, didn't we?" he said softly, putting his hand over hers. It was warm and calming, and the glow of the candles encompassed everything in the room as the rest of the restaurant disappeared. "Look, I know you worry about her. I know that's why you get a little upset sometimes. I think it's normal, and I also like to think it's a good thing."

"You're mighty nice, Vance. Sometimes I think you're too nice."

"Is that why you won't move in with me? Because you think you'll be taking advantage of me?" His finger traced a circle on the back of her hand, and his eyes glittered with amusement.

"I just don't want this to turn into the sort of situation where we resent each other," she explained. "I mean, you wouldn't have asked me to move in if it hadn't been for Rose." She'd already told him this before, but she could say it without spitting fire at him now that it felt like they had all the time in the world.

Vance lifted a shoulder. "Maybe not. I don't really know. But we do have Rose, and I think it would make our lives a lot easier. I know our animals both need their space, so you'd have your own room and I'd have mine, and the nursery would be in the middle. It's not like I'm going to demand you come to my bed every night."

He'd said it jokingly, but Delilah felt a very real thunderbolt of energy ignite in her body at the thought. He was, as she'd told Anita, incredibly sexy. Delilah couldn't help but be intrigued by the mix of roughrider and teddy bear that he could be, depending on the situation. He was strong and commanding, an Alpha by all means if cougars ran in prides, yet she'd seen how tender and compassionate he could be when given the chance. She cleared her throat. "Right."

"I can't say I'd mind seeing those stunning eyes of yours across from me at the breakfast table every morning," he murmured.

Delilah yanked her hand out from under his. "No one has ever referred to my eyes as stunning before," she remarked coolly. "Intense, maybe, but not stunning."

"They are, though. We might have a few differences, but there's no denying how tempting you are. Sometimes I wonder if that's part of what gets us so messed up around each other."

"I think you might be right." Delilah felt a prickle of fur emerge on the back of her neck and quickly smoothed it down with her free hand, the other wrapped tightly around the stem of her wine glass. It was hard not to look at his handsome face or hear that slow drawl of his and not remember how things had been between the two of them that night in his barn. He'd been slow and passionate, attentive and generous. He was the type of lover any woman would want, and yet she'd been fighting so hard to keep her distance from him.

They passed the rest of the evening over grilled salmon and scallops. The wine went down easily, and Delilah felt herself being lulled into a heady mixture of romance and desire. She listened attentively as Vance told her about his time in the Army—or at least as much as he was allowed to tell her—and how he couldn't imagine living in the city because of his love for ranching. For the first time in months, she was seeing him as a real person instead of the man who happened to father her child.

Unbidden, her work returned to her mind. In the dark booth in the back corner of Saint Martin's, it was easy to forget the rest of the world. She blinked as she recalled the upcoming meeting between the two conclaves.

He picked up on her change of mood. "What is it?"

She clenched her teeth together, wondering if she should dare to ask what was truly on her mind. Delilah had been uncertain of it even when she'd first had the idea after her meeting with President Whiteside, but now, with this dinner and everything that was happening between them, it seemed much more complicated. "I'm sorry, but it's about work."

"So shoot. Maybe it's something I can help with."

"Actually, I'm hoping you can." She hated to ask him this, not because he wasn't the most qualified person for the job, but because it put him in the direct position of protecting her, should she need it. To someone who'd always been fighting for independence, admitting she needed help went against everything she'd believed in—not to mention the fact that it would very much feel like mixing business with pleasure. "You remember when I told you our conclave was having trouble with Austin?"

"How could I forget?" he said with a spark of knowing in his eye.

She studied the weave of the tablecloth in an effort to stay focused. "They've agreed to meet with us, but they only want the president and me to attend. We'd like to take security just in case and, well, I was wondering if you'd be willing to do it."

His face changed, no longer soft and open, but hard and solemn. "Of course I am. How dangerous do you reckon this will be?"

"We're not sure," she replied with a shake of her head. "I'm hoping it won't be any more complicated than a typical political summit, and that we'll have been overcautious in using your services. But we did talk about having someone else stay in our hotel as backup."

"A smart move. I'll arrange for the Force to be there."

Delilah shook her head. "I don't want this to be any sort of inconvenience or take you and your men away from what you're already doing."

Reaching across the table, Vance took her hand once again. He held it firmly, and Delilah could swear she felt the electricity of his pulse flowing into her body. "It's not an inconvenience from any standpoint. I'll get my cousin

Caroline to stay with Rose. That's who she's with tonight, and she's excellent with children. As for the rest of the Force, this is our job. We're here to protect the shifters of greater Dallas, and that includes the conclave."

"You're sure?" Somehow, she still worried she was doing something wrong.

"Absolutely. Now, let's forget about all that and have some dessert." Vance guided the conversation away from work and future troubles. Delilah allowed him to, preferring the easy conversation they'd been having before she'd brought the whole thing up.

Vance walked her out to her car at the end of the night, tucking her hand in the crook of his elbow as they made their way through the dark parking lot. "I appreciate you coming out with me tonight, Delilah. It means more to me than you can imagine. Now I just have to ask you for one more favor."

She trembled slightly as they stood next to her car, with Vance gazing so earnestly into her eyes and still holding onto her hand. "Yes?"

"Let Rose stay with me tonight. Go home, and get some rest. I know you've been exhausted, and you deserve a break."

Something snapped inside her, but in the best way possible. He'd been caught up in this situation just as much as she had, yet he refused to let it get the best of him. He was steady and strong—and undeniably sweet. He truly seemed to want the best both for her and for Rose. "Thank you. I have to admit the idea of a full night's sleep sounds amazing."

He pulled her close and dared to kiss her on the forehead. "Enjoy it, Delilah. I'll talk to you tomorrow." Vance opened her car door for her.

When she arrived home, it was strange to know that she was actually alone. Ever since Rose had been born, Delilah had been either at work or with the baby. The silence in her apartment was both shocking and exciting, and despite a small pang of guilt, she knew she had to take advantage of it. Rose was with Vance, and that was the best place she could possibly be other than there. After a long shower, Delilah fell into bed with a book she'd been meaning to read for months. The words blurred after the first chapter as she started to doze, and she laid it aside.

Drifting off to sleep, she thought about Vance. He really was something else, and she was lucky that if she had to accidentally get pregnant, it happened with him. Maybe, just maybe, there was something more between them than physical attraction. Maybe.

7

"I CAN'T THANK YOU ENOUGH FOR COMING ALONG ON THIS little business meeting," President Whiteside said from the back seat of the rental car. "The rest of the conclave agreed that we'd be much smarter if we brought some protection with us, even if the Austin leaders take it the wrong way."

Vance glanced at him in the rearview mirror, noting how old he'd gotten recently. He was a great man, one whom all the local shifters revered as their president. Whiteside had served several terms, something that was rare in most conclaves, but the votes spoke for themselves. "I'm happy to help, sir."

"And the rest of your men, did they get settled in all right?"

Vance smiled. The man was always polite and concerned about everyone he met, even though Vance

knew the members of the Force could take care of themselves. "Yes, sir. I'm told they're at the hotel right now. I can
contact them quickly, should we need them." The special
phones supplied by Taylor Communications were better
than any typical cell.

"Good, good. Glad to hear it." Whiteside turned to look
out the window, anticipation clear on his face.

"You didn't have to offer to drive," Delilah said quietly
from the seat next to him. She gave him a teasing smile.
Vance had a good feeling that if they'd had this conversation a week ago, she would've been much more critical of
him. Things had changed between the two of them ever
since that night at Saint Martin's, and only for the better.

"It's the least I can do," he countered. "Besides, nothing
crazy is going to happen at this meeting, and I want to be
able to say I did something useful."

"Do you really believe that?" She was dressed in a black
suit that made her eyes look a more brilliant blue than
usual. Delilah was the image of a strong, powerful female
politician, yet she nervously twisted the rings on her
fingers.

He'd started to make a habit of touching her hand, but
considering their company, he refrained from the gesture.
"I'd like to." He was a little on edge himself as he pulled
into the location the Austin conclave had given him. It was
a large mansion in the West Lake Hills area, complete with
a massive pool and more land than most city dwellers

could afford. Vance had already checked it out thoroughly via satellite and gone over all the details with Max and Jack. He hoped he wouldn't need them, but steeled his jaw as he drove through the gate.

Sliding into the driveway right in front of the house, a man with jet black hair and a thick mustache stepped out the double front doors of the house. He stood solemnly at the top of the steps, waiting for them.

"That's President Kelso," Whiteside murmured.

Vance thought he looked like a cartoon villain, but he kept his opinion to himself. He put the car in gear and turned off the engine, planning to get out first, but Delilah beat him to it.

"President Kelso, it's nice to finally meet you in person." She strode up the steps confidently, extending her hand.

His eyes raked down her body as he shook her hand, and Vance felt a stab of jealousy streak through his core. He kept his eyes on the man as he opened the car door for President Whiteside.

"I can't tell you how much I appreciate you coming today," Kelso replied, his voice far more stiff and formal than Vance would expect out of any native Texan. He turned to Vance, narrowing his dark eyes. "I don't recall there being a third name on the invitation, however."

"I'm sure you don't mind that we have our escort with us," Whiteside remarked with a genial smile. "You can't expect a young lady and an old man to make an out-of-town trip all by themselves, can you?"

"Of course not." The waves of discontent continued to roll off of President Whiteside, nearly palpable in the thick air. "Let's go inside and get started, shall we?" He opened the door and guided them through the home. "Welcome to our meeting space. We like to keep things as casual as possible around here."

Yeah, as evidenced by your lack of control over the local population, Vance thought. He followed at the back of the group. The place was top-of-the-line, with custom cabinetry, marble and hardwood flooring, and massive windows, but he only took small note of that. His true concern was in noting escape routes should anything go sideways.

They were soon in a large room at the back of the house. With a large fireplace on one end and vaulted ceilings, Vance guessed that at one point, this had been an extra living room that they'd converted into a conference room with an arrangement of comfortable chairs that faced the center of the space. To an outsider, it would look like nothing more than a conversation area, but Vance prickled as he realized they were far outnumbered. There were at least five other people besides President Kelso, and that only included those who were in the room at the moment.

The hosting president made the introductions and invited their guests to sit down. "Please, make yourselves comfortable. Tell Jenny if there's anything you'd like to eat or drink, and she'll make sure you get it. A blanket, a pillow, whatever will make you happy while you're here with us." He gestured without looking to a blonde girl standing in the corner near the door, at the ready for any possible orders.

Vance didn't like the look of her. Her eyes were alert for a command, but they were otherwise dead inside. She'd been trained like an animal, but she no longer had the strong independence of a shifter. That was likely thanks to their overly gracious host, and Kelso had another demerit against him in Vance's mind.

"If you don't mind, I've got a little something prepared." President Whiteside stood. He might have been a little gray around the muzzle, but he'd brought all the confidence of an experienced leader. "Vice President Henderson and I were delighted to hear that you were willing to meet with us. We are conclave leaders not only because we were elected, but because we care deeply about the shifter community and what happens to it as society continues to evolve and change around us. This includes not only folks in the Dallas area, but all over the world, and we believe that involves working with other conclaves and leaders to achieve common goals. Diplomacy and communication are the keys to our future."

"Very nice," President Kelso responded over the smattering of applause, though the smile on his face was a hard one that matched the look in his eyes. His cheeks were too round and his jaw too angular, and Vance had to wonder what sort of animal was hiding inside the man. A snake, perhaps? "I think we should get right down to business. Over the last several months, you've been claiming you have some issues with our community members. Let's talk about that, shall we?"

Whiteside resumed his seat next to Delilah. Vance saw how she looked at the man with utmost admiration and respect, like a father figure.

"Yes, I think that's a good idea. First, we need to discuss Paul Grimes. I understand he's a registered shifter here in your area, but he's been coming into Dallas on a bit of a crime spree. He's knocked over multiple convenience stores, and in some cases, the clerks have been severely battered in the process. Though he lives here, we do firmly believe that we should be able to bring him in for justice." Whiteside curled his fist slightly for emphasis on the last word.

Kelso shook his head and gave another one of those slick smiles. "Who's to say that we haven't already taken care of the matter here?"

"It should be addressed in the district where the crime is committed, as is commonly done," Delilah countered.

Vance felt the tendons stand out in his neck as he watched the way Kelso eyed her, like she was just a toy and he was trying to decide if he was going to play with her.

"Ms. Henderson, just because your conclave likes to do things the old-fashioned way doesn't mean we have to play along. I assure you, Mr. Grimes has been taken care of."

"What about the similar instances that are happening in San Antonio? We're in good standing with them, as we strive to be with all other councils, and they report that they haven't been able to extradite known criminals." Whiteside lifted one grizzled eyebrow in challenge. "This, as well as several other issues, have certainly made us wonder about your motives."

"I see." President Kelso stood up. He was a slim man, but his height made him imposing. That effect was only enhanced by the fact that everyone else was still sitting down. "First, you want to complain about a few petty criminals who've gone off to other cities to have a good time. Then, you assume that we're not doing anything about it. It seems to me, Whiteside, that you're putting all the focus on us to keep it off yourselves."

"What do you mean by that?" Delilah asked.

The man's laugh was as sharp as his shoulders in his suit jacket. "It's so easy for you to forget about all the land you're buying up in the Austin area, the educated shifters you're sending down here to start businesses or take over managing the current ones, and the string of violent offenses that happen when anyone stands in your way."

"Patently untrue," Whiteside responded.

"You have your accusations, and I have mine." Kelso

lifted one hand in the air, indicating nothing about this situation could be helped.

Vance was certainly starting to think it wouldn't be helped by any of this charade. The Austin members had invited them there for a meeting, but they weren't interested in getting anything done. Vance watched Delilah intensely, trying to get her to look at him. He wanted to know the truth before things went any further. As though she'd heard his thoughts, her eyes swept over to meet his gaze. Vance met her with a quizzical look, and her response was a subtle shake of her head. Good. Kelso was just spewing lies.

Whiteside moved to the edge of his seat, sitting up straight and bracing his hands on his knees. The over-stuffed furniture had kept him slouching and reclined otherwise. "If you care to see it, I do have proof of the crimes I'm speaking about, among several other offenses from your community members."

"Proof? What's proof these days? I can offer you proof, too, but you'll just tell me I had it manufactured. No, I might be younger than you, Whiteside, but that doesn't necessarily make you wiser. The fact of the matter remains that you're trying to hijack our territory. Dallas isn't enough for you, and you're making moves to expand. I wouldn't be surprised if you've got some grand plan of becoming the Alpha over all the shifters in the country. I'm not going to stand idly by and let you get away with it, not if we can stop it here."

"Such allegations are preposterous." Whiteside was getting angry, Vance knew, but he was doing his best not to show it. "We're simply trying to protect the safety of our people, and not just the shifters in Dallas, but the humans, too. It's our job to care about all the shifters in the world, but they have to be governed in some way."

"Right, you care so much about all your dear shifters," Kelso oozed. "I suppose that's why you had a medical center built right in the middle of your territory, yet you won't let anyone else obtain care there."

Delilah's eyes snapped. "What?"

"Oh, you heard me. One of our members happened to be in your area to visit family. She grew ill, but she knew she'd be all right, thanks to the Dallas Center for Shifter Medicine. What better place to go, after all? But the intake nurse said she wasn't in the Dallas registry and therefore couldn't be seen." President Kelso ran his long, pale fingers down the back of the couch. "Not very generous of you folks."

"That's not how it works." Delilah was calm on the outside, so calm that she looked stiff. But Vance could see and almost feel the fire blazing inside her. "We worked very closely with Dr. Barnett to create that hospital, and I can tell you with full certainty that medical care is available to any shifter who shows up. If there was any sort of problem, you should've simply asked us."

"And while an ill shifter is certainly something to be concerned about, so are the crimes that your shifters are committing. They run the risk of calling attention to our kind, should they be caught. You know how important it is to keep our secret from the general public, and there's a lot more than goes into that than simply keeping our mouths shut."

Kelso was bobbing his head far too enthusiastically now as he paced in front of the long couch. "You're right. You're absolutely right. There's a lot to think about, but I have to wonder what you're thinking of when you hire a group like the SOS Force."

Vance felt his lips tightening. He was several seats away from Delilah, yet he had the distinct feeling he was going to need to be much closer so he could protect her. This wasn't going at all like they'd planned, and why should it? This Kelso was a nut job. Still, he remained seated. Acting too quickly could cause more trouble.

"Interesting that you should even know such a thing," Whiteside countered. "It doesn't make a man feel much in the mood for negotiating when a man who's supposed to be his equal—and who ought to have the same goals—is apparently spying on him."

"Neither does it make a man want to negotiate when he finds out his equal—or rival, I have to wonder—has hired the most elite group of military-trained shifters to stand beside him. I don't know what kind of war you're preparing for, Whiteside, but don't think for a second that I won't stand up against you."

The old man's eyes narrowed. Vance could just imagine what he was thinking, wondering if he'd done the right thing by bringing Vance along and if it would be even more of a problem if Kelso knew Jack and Max were waiting for them back at the hotel. Delilah had told Vance that Whiteside didn't want to make a show of force, but it seemed the Austin president was determined to see what he wanted to see.

"I should hardly think that the presence of a few men with military experience should constitute a war," Whiteside riposted. "And if you think it does, then perhaps we have more of a problem on our hands than I ever expected."

President Kelso finally stopped moving, and he turned sharply to face Whiteside. The gleam in his dark eyes wasn't a pleasant one. "Here's the thing, old man. You think you know how the world works, but the world has changed without you. No longer are we living in a time when we can simply hide in the shadows and pretend everything is fine and dandy. My voters elected me because they want a man who's going to take action against our enemies. And if one of those enemies happens to be the Dallas conclave, then so be it."

Whiteside lifted his chin indignantly. "Is that a threat of war, President Kelso?"

"Of course not," the man said with that snide smile of his. "It's simply a reminder that we won't let you trample all over us."

"I hope you'll come to understand in time just how foolish you've been." President Whiteside stood and straightened his suit jacket. "I believe this meeting is over. Don't bother showing us the way out." He gestured Delilah out of the room ahead of him.

Vance followed on their heels, listening attentively for any sound of pursuit. He'd gladly take the chance to lash out at any asshole who tried to run after them and attack them when they weren't looking. God knew he needed an outlet after all that tension. But the Austin conclave let them go without a further word.

The three of them were silent as they made their way back to the hotel. Vance knew Whiteside and Delilah were in deep thought as they pondered their next move, but he'd already been forced to stay silent long enough during the meeting. He was in his room for only a brief time before he headed down the hall and knocked on Delilah's door.

She opened it quickly, as though she'd been expecting him, and held the door wide to admit him. "Good. You can join me for a drink." Delilah retreated to the minibar on the other side of the room and poured them each a whiskey.

"I think we need to get out of Austin as quickly as possible," Vance said as he took the glass from her. The liquor was cheap and burned all the way down, but that was just what he needed to stay focused. He'd gone there to talk business, but there was something about being alone in a hotel room with Delilah that made other parts of his mind—and body—want to take over. It wasn't exactly the barn on a warm spring night, but he could certainly make do.

"Why do you say that?" Delilah took a conservative sip of whiskey, considered the glass, and then knocked the whole thing back. She turned to the bar to pour another. "The ravings of a lunatic aren't enough to make me run away."

"I'm sure that's true." And he was. Vance still had a lot to learn about Delilah, but he knew she wasn't easily threatened. "I thought it interesting that he wanted only you and Whiteside, yet he had his entire council there with them. Even more to the point, he didn't offer any of them a chance to speak."

Delilah nodded. "You noticed, I'm sure, how Kelso spent most of our time turning accusations around on us instead of trying to resolve any of the real issues. He's one of those fanatic leaders that gets the voters excited by promising all sorts of action, even when it's toward things that the populace doesn't need. He could get them riled up about having fucking spaghetti every Wednesday night, and they'd vote him into office because he'd make them believe they deserved it."

"That's exactly why I'm concerned. I've seen men like him at work before. They get even crazier when times are desperate, whether that desperation is an illusion or not." He sat on the edge of the loveseat in the living room area of the suite, perched on the edge of the cushion and ready to jump back up again if need be.

Delilah turned to him, her fingers wrapped around her glass, curiosity narrowing her eyes. "What do you mean?"

Vance licked his lips as he replayed the meeting in his mind. "There were a lot of things Kelso said that were a bit off, but it was right at the end that he showed his hand a little. He said we can't just hide in the shadows and that times have changed. The man absolutely has a plan. I'd say he's getting ready to do exactly what he accused Whiteside of. He wants to take over other conclaves, gobbling them up one by one until he's made himself a shifter emperor of sorts. If he has enough people underneath him, then I wouldn't put it past him to tell the world our secret and perhaps try to hold some sort of power over the humans simply because we're stronger." Some of it was pure specu-lation, seeing as how he didn't know the man well enough to say otherwise. The one thing that was profoundly clear was just how much of a zealot Kelso was.

"I see. Yet another battle about shifter rights," Delilah said with a sigh as she sat down across from him, swirling the amber liquid. "It's funny, because within the Dallas region, we think we've made a lot of progress. We're a very active conclave compared to some of the ones in the past, working hard to improve social infrastructure for our kind. The hospital was a big step, but it was just one of many that we'd like to carry out. And yet you have only to go a few hours away to find someone like Kelso who still somehow thinks the right way is to stand up to the world, kicking ass and taking names. He doesn't realize that it would never work."

Vance ran a hand over his face, smoothing out the lines that were becoming permanently etched in his forehead. "I know Whiteside is a peaceful guy. He wants to focus on keeping everyone safe and happy, but he's going to have to take some real action to make it happen. We need to get back to Dallas. You need to talk to your constituents about being vigilant. Jack needs to work with our D.C. unit to put the final touches on the shifter registry. And Whiteside needs to seriously think about constructing a military."

Her mouth was a slanted line as she shook her head slightly. "It's already been discussed once, and he didn't like the idea."

"That was before meeting with the mayor of Crazytown. I'm sure Whiteside is starting to understand that negotiating with Kelso is going to be about as easy as putting socks on a rooster. I know he's a pacifist, but if he cares enough about his people, he'll see that this is the right thing to do." It bothered even Vance to think of raising a small, local army. It was too reminiscent of the militias he'd seen fight each other overseas. They were small groups who hardly even had the strength to carry out the battles they engaged in, and more often than not, their fighting ended in death and destruction instead of any real victory. Still, there was no telling what they'd face if they succumbed to the radical Kelso.

She let out a long breath before draining her glass and setting it on the coffee table with finality. "You might be right. Let's go talk to him." Delilah rose and headed for the door.

Whiteside's room was right next to hers. She knocked and then knocked again when there was no answer. Vance reached around her to knock himself, harder this time, and then he pressed his ear to the door. He hoped to hear the shower running or the TV blaring, but only silence issued from the room.

"Shit," he murmured, feeling defeated before they'd even started. "Did he give you a key to the room?"

"I'll get it." She jogged back to her room and returned with the card.

Vance slipped it in the lock, impatient for even the split-second it took for the light on the electronic pad to turn green, and shoved the door open. He charged into the room, still desperately hoping they'd find that the old man was just asleep on the couch after having a few drinks himself. "Stay right with me," he growled.

It didn't take long to search the hotel room, and he definitely wasn't there.

"Maybe he went downstairs. I can give him a call." Delilah pulled her cell out of her pocket.

Vance didn't think so, but the vibrating phone on the coffee table really only proved that wherever he went, he'd forgotten it. He scanned the room, using every sense he had available. Vance scrutinized every aspect of the space with both human instincts and animal, both of which had been honed and trained by his time in the Army as one of the quiet professionals and on the Force.

"The sliding door is unlocked," he said, noticing that even though the door was firmly shut, the latch wasn't in the correct position. He advanced across the room toward it, his eye catching on a dark scuff against the white wall. Vance brushed the curtains back to reveal a deep mark in the drywall. It was narrower at one end but not sharp, and it'd gone deep into the sheetrock before pulling out and gouging a scratch across the door trim. "Whiteside is a bear, isn't he?"

She was at his shoulder, her eyes focused on the same part of the wall. It told a story that was impossible to deny. "Yes," she whispered hoarsely as she reached out a shaking finger to touch the mark.

8

DELILAH FELT PANIC CONSTRICT HER CHEST AS SHE FOCUSED intently on the small amount of damage Whiteside had been able to cause before being dragged forcibly from his hotel room. In her mind's eye, she could almost see him, shifting partially out of fear and anger, yet still overpowered by his captors. Had they hurt him? Drugged him? Harris Whiteside wouldn't have gone willingly, that she knew, and she couldn't understand how this had happened without her and Vance at least hearing a scuffle.

"Come on." Vance's voice jerked her from her horrified thoughts and got time moving again. Unfortunately, it was ticking by too quickly. He took her by the hand and pulled her out of the room, shutting the door behind them as a precaution as he walked down the hall.

Her mouth refused to move, but inside, she was

screaming. Why weren't they running? Why was he just casually walking down the hall with his fingers wrapped her hand, looking no more in a hurry than if he needed to get home to do chores? She watched as his hand lifted slowly, so slowly, to rattle out a specific knock on the next door. Jack swung it open, and Vance pulled her inside along with him.

"The president has been taken," he informed the other men. "Jack, get online with Hudson to tap into any area security cameras that might help us locate him."

Max cursed under his breath and ran a hand through his dark hair. "At least we won't have to waste any time wondering who the hell it was."

"Right. We should check their meetinghouse, although I have a feeling they wouldn't be so obvious about it. Delilah, you contact the rest of the conclave and let them know what's happened."

Numbly, she tipped her head back to meet his gaze. She was having a hard time focusing on him. Whatever was happening around her had to part of some strange dream. "What?"

Vance gripped her by the shoulders, his fingers holding her firmly enough to make her pay attention. "Snap out of it, Delilah! Until we know what's happened to President Whiteside, you're in charge of the Dallas conclave. We don't know what the future may hold. Call your council and inform them right now. We'll take care of the rest of it."

She rolled her shoulders, trying to center herself within her own body again. It'd been enough of a shock to hear that the man she revered and respected was gone, but the implication that something truly terrible could've happened to him made her cold and stiff inside. But Vance was right. Until Whiteside was recovered, she had to step up. For all intents and purposes, she was the one running the show. Her phone was still in her hand from when she'd tried to call him a few minutes ago, and she used it now to dial the office.

By the time she'd given them the run-down on what was happening, the Force had already dove head-first into action. Someone had pulled a large case out from under the bed and opened it to reveal a portable arsenal. Jack had several laptops arranged on the desk in front of him, his long fingers flying over the keyboards. Vance hung up his cell and turned to her, peering into her eyes to gauge how she was doing before he continued giving orders. "It's going to take Jack some time to go through all the footage that's about to start coming through. You stay here with him. Max and I will head to Kelso's meetinghouse, since that's the most likely place they took him."

Delilah snagged his arm as he tried to move past her. "I'm not staying here."

He glanced at his men, who were trying hard not to pay attention. "Delilah, you're obviously shaken up by what's happened. I understand, and it's okay. I don't feel comfortable just leaving you alone, though. If Kelso took White-side, then he won't hesitate to come for you, too." He lifted his hand and laid it along her jawline, his worry evident in the softness of his emerald eyes.

She allowed herself to lean in ever so slightly against his touch. Vance had been her adversary at the same time that he'd been her lover, someone to overcome. She'd had a difficult time getting past the idea of becoming partners with him in any way because it went so steadily against her feline nature, but she was beginning to see him differently. He was steady as a stone in the middle of a stream, a rock for her to lean on when things got tough. Right now, he was also a boulder to leap off of. "Vance, let me go with you."

He straightened, his hand slipping to her shoulder. "It's dangerous, and you're not trained for this sort of thing."

"Trained or not, I've got the same beast inside me as you do. You know what that means." She willed him to understand because she was determined to go, regardless of what he thought. As a cougar, Delilah was also a huntress and a killer. She might not have the military back-ground Vance did, but that didn't mean she couldn't stand up to these assholes.

Vance still hesitated.

Max let out a gentle cough. "If she goes with you, I can grab the chopper and get eyes in the air in less than half an hour. They couldn't have taken him long ago, and there's a possibility they're still on the move."

Vance couldn't deny the logic in that. "All right. Delilah, you'll be with me. Jack, Max, you two keep us updated on anything you might find. We'll head straight for their compound, but I want to be able to change direction as quickly as possible if need be." He gestured toward the suitcase full of arms in the middle of the floor. "What's your poison?"

There was quite the assortment, and Delilah didn't even recognize some of the weapons. No doubt, the SOS Force had commissioned them as custom pieces with the help of Flint Myers. She reached for a 9mm, having used one at the range before, and tucked it under her blazer. "What about you?" she asked as Vance turned to the door.

"What about me?"

"Aren't you going to take anything with you?" She knew Vance could handle himself in many respects even in human form, but it seemed crazy to go into this situation unarmed.

He grinned that relaxed smile that was his signature look, even when everything was going to hell in a hand basket. "Trust me, Delilah. I've got weapons on me like fleas on a dog." He moved closer as he opened the room door. "Care to find them?"

Despite the situation, she blushed hotly at the thought of moving her arms around his waist and skimming her palms over his muscles to find what he might have tucked away for her. She flicked her head away from him and refocused on the task at hand. "I'll have to take a rain check."

Vance chuckled.

They took the stairs and a short bridge to the parking garage before jumping in the rental car. Vance swept down the ramp and outside, zooming through town as fast as the engine and traffic would allow and glanced in her direction. "We'll find him, Delilah."

"I know." She hoped he was right—more so, that they would find him safe and sound. "I just don't understand what they expect to achieve with this."

"Leverage," he answered instantly, dodging around a moving van and swerving back to the right to avoid a car waiting to turn. "We've already discussed what a psychopath President Kelso is. You and I both know this isn't the right way to achieve anything, but he's become desperate. He probably figured he could cow Whiteside enough with those false accusations and make him concentrate on that instead of Kelso's own flaws. And please tell me I'm correct about those being false accusations."

"Absolutely." Her anger mushroomed inside her at the reminder. Kelso just didn't know when to stop. "I have to wonder if his voters have any idea who he really is and what he's about."

"I have a feeling we'll find out soon enough." Vance growled as he shot through an intersection, barely making it through a red light. "If they're as loyal to him as his ego hopes, then I'm sure he can get them to fight with him. My guess is that they're normal people who don't have a clue."

His phone crackled from its holder on the dash and Jack's voice soon followed. "We've tracked all the cars that left the hotel within the last hour. Most of them are dead ends, but there's a black Mercedes heading west of town on 1431."

"What's out there that they might be heading toward?" Vance answered as he changed lanes and picked up a highway ramp.

"I'm not sure," the fox answered. "I've got a search going for any properties they might own besides the house in West Lake Hills. It could take some time, since I don't have all the same reference material we do for our own territory. In the meantime, I'll forward the vehicle location to your phone. Max is heading that way in the chopper as soon as possible."

Delilah racked her brain. She'd studied the area, wanting to gather as much information as she could have before the trip. Preparation had always been key, she felt, to any situation. She hoped it would pay off this time as well. "Maybe something like a national park? The Balcones Canyonlands are out that way. I don't know much about them, but it would make sense if Kelso wanted to get the president away from civilization."

"That's a good guess," Vance agreed. "Did you get that, Jack?"

"Sure did. The route matches up so far. I'll keep you updated."

Delilah pursed her lips as she let out a breath. Her nerves were overtaking her, and it wouldn't get better until she knew the president was safe. It took almost an hour to reach the park entrance, and by then, the sun was working its way toward the horizon. Jack had reported that the Mercedes had reached Balcones just ahead of them, but Max had yet to locate them.

"There's one thing I ask," Vance said as he put the car in park. "Stay with me. I know you're passionate about this, but that's exactly what worries me. People who let their emotions get wrapped up in a mission end up costing lives."

"Then I'd say you're talking to the right person," she sassed.

They left the car, and Delilah immediately had the sensation of being watched. "They're not far," she whispered.

His fist curled, a shimmer of golden fur showing on the back of his hand as he removed a pistol from his waistband. "I know. There's one thing I forgot to tell you."

"Yeah?"

"If you see anything, make sure you look before you shoot."

"Please!" She shot him a dirty look. "I'm not that stupid, Vance."

He huffed an impatient sigh. "I mean that if they show, they might have Whiteside in front of them. It's a trick I've seen played in situations like this. If they feel cornered, they get you to shoot your own man."

Delilah's throat tightened as she realized how terrible it would be to catch a flash of movement and fire, only to discover she'd slaughtered the very man they'd gone there to save. It was hard to believe anyone would feel cornered in a place like this, but it could be figurative instead of literal. "Right."

Things were quiet as they moved through the main trail that led into the park, far too quiet. Delilah almost wished someone would jump out and ambush them just to get it over with, but then, she spotted movement at the top of the next hill. "Over there," she whispered.

Vance didn't answer at first, assessing the situation. "We're still far enough away that they probably don't know we're here. I don't hear the chopper yet, so let's use the night and our other forms to our advantage. You can head east, I'll head west, and we'll come up on them from behind. But together." He emphasized the last word.

"Works for me." Delilah tucked the pistol away as she lifted her face to the sky and pushed her shoulders back. Stressful situations could make her want to shift, but it wasn't always easy to relax her body enough to let the metamorphosis happen. She'd never shifted in a situation quite like this, and the idea of being caught by the enemy mid-change when she was most vulnerable wasn't appealing to her.

Still, she felt the deep gravity of her tail as it extended from her lower back, swishing angrily at having been kept pent up for so long. Her back curled and hunched as her bones fought with each other over the proper form, and Delilah heard a crack from deep inside her flesh as her head moved to a different position on her spine. Long teeth extended from her jaws until they poked through her gums, and she ran her tongue along them to test them out. Her paws carried the full feeling of her retracted claws, and Delilah stretched forward to touch the grass with all fours. Yes, these were her weapons. Guns could be appropriate for combat at times, but this was a shifter situation, after all.

A figure stepped up next to her, and Delilah's breath froze in her lungs. She'd been so consumed with her own transformation that she'd hardly noticed what Vance was doing, but she could have recognized him anywhere, even with his current profile. His solid figure was breathtakingly strong, and her eyes roved over his massive paws and his thick tail. The human side of her that still resided within longed to reach out and touch the varied tones of his golden fur, tracing her fingers over the deepest hues on his face that served as such a striking contrast to the stark white of his muzzle. As a cougar, however, she would never dare.

She reminded herself of this as she moved off toward the right, leaving the path and Vance behind as she slipped silently in and out of wooded coves. She was on a mission, and she had a life to save, but it was impossible not to notice how good it felt to be in this form. How long had it been since she'd just let herself go? Delilah spent so much time tightly wound, trying to be the perfect vice president. She worried about her constituents themselves as well as what they thought of her. And yet her feline form was exactly why she'd been voted into office. She was one of them. She had a wild side, a side that didn't care so much about the laws of the human world.

Slipping down a hillside into a valley and up the next one, Delilah felt something inside that nearly knocked her over.

Delilah?

She panted in surprise and wanted to bite her own tail for not anticipating this. His presence inside her head was almost too great, and she narrowed her eyes in the dim light as she tried to keep her focus. She knew about fated mates amongst the shifter world: two creatures who were absolutely meant to be together, ordained by the universe to be the perfect match. While this pairing was far more common in bears and other animals, it rarely happened between cougars. They were too antisocial to spend much time together.

But was that truly what they were?

Delilah? he asked again.

She'd never felt the telepathic link that came along with this type of bond. It was not only reserved for certain relationships, but it was also only accessible while in animal form. There was a ritual that made it happen for those welcoming a new member of a clan, but that fateful night must have forged the connection between them forever. *What?* she finally snapped.

Good, you're there. Just checkin'.

I'm fine, thank you very much. I think I can handle a walk in the woods. His question made her realize, however, that their communication was more of a distraction than an advantage right now, and she twitched one sandy ear to listen for anyone or anything that might be approaching.

Yeah, but I don't trust these guys. I doubt they're all standing out there with Whiteside, and I wouldn't be surprised to find them stationed throughout the woods.

Well, there's nothing here. Delilah stalked on, wishing he'd never spoken up. She'd been rather enjoying her time as a big cat all on her own.

Let me know if anything changes.

He stopped talking, but Delilah had a feeling he was still in her head. She didn't need this moment to be clouded up with worries about how much of her mind he could access when they'd shifted. Delilah opened her mouth to pull in more scents and tried to concentrate on the forest around her. She circled up the back of the hillside, and when she saw another pale form emerge into the moonlight, she instantly knew it was Vance. She glanced only once into his eyes before turning toward their target.

Two men stood at the top of the hill, checking their watches and spatting impatiently.

"How long you reckon it'll be?" This came from a short, skinny man with a shaved head Delilah had seen at the summit. Kelso had introduced him as Mark. He paced in a circle, puffing out his chest and slamming one fist into another.

"Shut up. It's not like our job is all that hard. All we have to do is wait." The woman was the complete opposite of her partner. She was tall and dark, with her hair in tiny braids that reached to her waist. She exuded strength and patience as she stood with one foot slightly forward, ready for action as she glared at Mark. Delilah thought the woman's name was Edira.

"I don't like waiting," Mark replied with a pout. "I'm ready for some action."

Edira placed her hands on her hips, looking every bit like a gymnast preparing for an Olympic run. She glanced down at the ground between them. "I think you've had enough for tonight."

Delilah heard a low rumble as she spotted the limp form. It was President Whiteside. He still wore the same suit he'd had on during the summit, but it'd become rumpled, dirty, and torn during his abduction. A massive bruise showed darkly against his skin even in the dim light, and blood trickled down his temple. Delilah realized the low rumble was coming from her own throat.

The two enemy shifters swirled, caught unawares just as Vance had planned, and Delilah let her primal impulses take over. Her claws dug into the ground, giving her traction as she shot forward and leaped into the air. She barreled into Edira's chest, sending her flying backward. Mark jumped ahead to protect her, but Vance was too fast. The male cougar was too heavy and strong for a human. He slashed his claws across the man's throat, sending a dark spray out across the grass. Mark's hands swiped uselessly through the air before he dropped to his knees, his eyes rolling back in his head.

Edira was still fighting with Delilah on top of her. She swung and kicked, her long legs landing several blows to the cougar's back legs and flanks. Delilah liked to think she had the advantage, and she sank her teeth into the woman's neck. The warm, salty jet of blood made her gag, but she glanced at Whiteside and bit down harder. If this bitch had allowed him to be harmed, then she didn't deserve to live.

A set of thin fingers wrapped around Delilah's ear and twisted. Howling in pain with her mouth full of flesh, Delilah refused to let go. She didn't need to, as Vance appeared from his fight with Mark and sank his own teeth into the offending limb. Edira let go, and her body went limp.

Delilah backed away, angry and bloodthirsty, but there was no one else to fight. She flicked her tail in agitation as she turned in a slow circle waiting for the next adversary to show. Surely, they didn't leave him out there with only two to guard him.

I'll stand guard. You go to him.

Knowing Vance had her back allowed Delilah to focus her attention on Whiteside. Seeing him laying there like that drained the fight out of her and replaced it with pity and regret as she paced toward him. Her claws retracted as she reached out to touch him, the toes on her paws lengthening to fingers as she desperately hoped for some sign of life. Her tail reabsorbed into her body, and pain took over her joints as her human form adjusted to the trauma of the battle she'd just gone through. Sound popped and echoed in her ears as they returned to their rightful places, but she ignored it as she knelt next to the president.

Whiteside groaned and his body tensed. With his eyes still shut, he thought his attackers were still with him.

"It's all right, Harris. It's me. Delilah." She touched his face, frowning at the wound on his temple. "Vance and I are both here. And we're going to get you some help. I promise."

He reached out blindly for her hand, and when she took it, he opened his eyes. "Delilah. I'm sorry. I'm so sorry."

"Don't apologize," she reprimanded gently. "None of

this is your fault. We'll go home and we'll get an army together. We'll defend our territory against these lunatics, and we won't let them get away with this."

A tear slid from the president's eye and down his temple, lingering for a moment against his skin before it fell to the grass. "I'm sorry," he repeated.

"Stop that," she soothed. "Everything is going to be all right."

Vance was behind her now, and even though she didn't turn to look at him, she was aware he was in human form. She didn't feel his presence in her head in the same way. "I can hear the chopper. Max can track my location, so he'll be here any minute."

"There, see?" Delilah said to Whiteside. "We'll get you to the hospital and you'll be fine."

"No." He shook his head slightly and winced from the pain. "You've got to find Rose."

Her blood reversed in her veins. "What did you say?"

It took an eternity for Whiteside to speak again. He swallowed and panted, gripping her hand harder. "They didn't just get me," he muttered. "They wanted as much influence over you as possible, so you'd give in. I heard them. They went to get Rose."

Vance was crouched next to her, rage rolling off him in waves. His voice was hoarse. "*What* did he just say?"

Delilah felt as though her jaws were glued together. Her eyes were aimed at a random spot on Whiteside's chest, but she wasn't seeing anything in front of her. She was three hours away, holding Rose in her arms and savoring the feeling of cradling her sweet baby. "No."

Whiteside's grip tightened on her hand, and his eyes opened further with great effort. "Don't worry about me, Delilah. You've got to get her. For her sake and for the sake of the conclave."

A blast of wind brought her back to the present as the chopper landed close by. She ground her teeth together as she and Vance carefully lifted the president and moved him into the aircraft.

"Sorry guys," Max called over the whir of the blades. "Had some mechanical issues."

"That's okay." Vance slid the door shut and clapped the pilot on the shoulder. "We've got a bigger problem on our hands."

9

"I can't believe we didn't think about this." Delilah sat in one of the mismatched chairs in the waiting room, her head on her hands. "Why didn't we put her in the hands of someone more trained? Some sort of...bodyguard or something?"

She'd been sick and dizzy ever since Vance had called a sobbing Caroline and confirmed that someone had taken the baby. He felt the same way, but he couldn't show it. Delilah needed him right now, and Rose needed both of them. "We had no way of knowing. We thought the trip to Austin was a political situation, not a hostage negotiation. It's obvious Kelso is determined to get one over on the Dallas conclave one way or another, and he'll do anything he can think of to make it happen."

When she lifted her head, her red-rimmed eyes were full of hatred. "He's going to fucking pay for this."

He rested a hand on her shoulder, both proud of her and determined to protect her. "I know. He will."

"So what do we do?" Delilah sniffed and wiped her face on a tissue. "We can't just sit here."

They'd remained at the hospital after getting Whiteside admitted. Delilah was ready to run right back out the door, but Vance knew that wasn't going to do them much good at the moment. "We've got to wait for the intelligence reports to get back to us. It won't help to run around like chickens with our heads cut off, darlin'. Have a little to eat and drink, and Max can get us anywhere we need to go just as soon as we've got word." The pilot was on the roof of the hospital now, where he kept tools for working on the helicopter. Considering it was his mate who'd created the medical center, he had everything he needed.

"It just seems like we should be doing something."

"I know, Delilah. I know." His own heart twisted in his chest at the thought of his baby girl. Was she crying somewhere, scared at being with strangers? Did Kelso himself have her? What lengths might that crackpot have gone to in order to get Whiteside and Delilah to cooperate? He didn't want to know, not really.

His phone beeped, and he whipped it out of his pocket and to his ear in an instant. "Yeah?"

He expected Jack, or maybe even Hudson from the D.C.

unit, but the voice on the other end made his skin crawl. "Mr. Morris, how quickly you answer your phone. It's almost as though you expected my call."

If he could've transformed into some creature that could leap through the phone and come out on the other end to rip out President Kelso's throat, then he absolutely would have. "Where's my daughter, Kelso?"

The breathy laugh made the skin around Vance's ear crawl. "You think it's all so simple as that? I tell you where we are, and then you show up and kill us all? Is that it? Just like you did when you 'saved' President Whiteside? Oh, no, my dear boy. There's much more to it than that."

He gritted his jaw. Vance had been through some training on hostage negotiation, but they never told him what to do if his own offspring were in danger. "It doesn't have to be like this, Kelso. We can talk. Just tell me where to meet you." *And then I'll rip your black heart right out of your fucking chest.*

"Yes, talking is exactly what I'd like to do, but not with you. I need Delilah. She's the one in charge of the conclave and thus in charge of your territory right now. She's the one who can make me the deal I want."

"Just say where." He felt the resistance of his body against sending Delilah anywhere to talk to this man. Vance would just as soon keep her out of it if he could, but he knew it would never happen. She wanted to fight for

Rose just as badly as he did, and for the moment, Kelso had the upper hand.

"Oh, not far from you, really. I didn't want to wait around for you to get back to Austin, so we stayed in your area. I've got a nice little place by Lavon Lake. I'll send you the address, but I'm very serious about how we do this. I want Delilah and only her. No SOS Force. No crazy tactics. You hear me?"

Vance turned away and pounded his fist against the wall. He knew Delilah was watching him, but it was hard to keep himself together. There was so much at stake. "This is *my* daughter we're talking about."

Kelso sighed audibly. "Fine. I knew you'd show up anyway, so I suppose we can make it a formal invitation. I'll be here waiting for you." The phone went dead.

Delilah was already on her feet when Vance turned back around. "Let's go."

––––––––

THE SEDAN BUMPED over the pitted gravel road. Vance had been expecting a place similar to the house in Austin where they'd initially met Kelso. After all, there were plenty of nice houses out in that area. He could even set aside the fact that anyone from the Austin conclave owned a piece of property in this territory for the moment, but it disturbed him deeply as he pulled up in front of the abandoned farmhouse.

Dark shadows of former flames licked around the windows on the second story, indicating a fire had run through the place at some point. An old sun porch on the east side was crumbling in on itself, and even the porch boards didn't look safe enough to walk on. He shivered at the thought of his baby girl being in a place like this.

"Max and Jack are working their way here on foot," he said to Delilah, who'd been gripping the oh-shit bar over the door for the entire drive. "Max wanted to drop us off in the chopper, but this was the safest way to make sure Kelso didn't do anything drastic. They'll keep an eye on things, and we'll have them nearby just in case."

She pulled in a shuddering breath. "I just hope Kelso doesn't find out they're there ahead of time. There's no telling how many people he might've stationed around this place. With as many surprises as he's already thrown us, I expect more."

"I'd really like to disagree with you." Vance unbuckled his seat belt and got out, waiting for Delilah to shut her door before he advanced on the house. "Remember what we went over. Just tell him whatever he wants to hear to get Rose back. Nobody is going to hold you to what you say to him under duress. You can promise him the whole Lone Star State if he asks it, and we'll sort those details out later."

Her fists were curled as she marched forward alongside him, her face hard and serious. Vance had thought she was rather severe when he'd first encountered her at the rodeo, but she'd been lighthearted compared to the way she was now. "If Kelso gets out of this alive, I'm going to destroy him."

"I know." And he did. Vance thought of himself as the trained killer, the one who'd gone overseas into enemy territory to fight for everything he was worth with the Green Berets. If he'd made a tally mark for every man who fell at his hands, it'd take too long to count them. Now, though, he started to wonder if the U.S. Army should've been sending angry mothers to the Middle East instead of young boys.

They stepped carefully up onto the porch, but there was no need to knock. A man with a scarred face swung the door open and held it wide, bidding them silently to enter. Vance wished for all the world that he could send Delilah away. She'd hate him for it, but at least he'd know she was safe.

They stepped into what had once been the living room of the place. Wooden floorboards warped and curled under the soles of his boots. Faded floral wallpaper hung in sagging strips, and the remains of the tumbledown fire-place hadn't been used in decades. Someone had moved some old furniture into the place, but the scarred man remained standing near the door. Another man—this one with shaggy hair and his arms covered in tattoos—stood in the opposite corner.

Footsteps echoed and Kelso strode into the room. He'd taken off his suit jacket and wore his white button-down and trousers. What Vance noticed more than anything, however, was the bundle of pink blankets in his arms.

Delilah gasped, and Vance impulsively reached out to put his hand on her forearm. The last thing he needed was for her to dart forward, although he understood just how badly she wanted to do it. There was nothing more powerful than the pull of family, no matter how much he'd tried to deny that just a few months ago. Everything—his entire world—was there in that room, and he had to make sure he got them back out safely. He'd never forgive himself if he didn't.

"Well, well. So nice of you to come," Kelso said with a grin that tweaked the ends of his thick mustache upwards. "I'm afraid I'm a terrible host. I can't even offer you a cup of tea."

"Just tell us what you want," Delilah demanded. "Let's get this over with."

Kelso raised his eyebrows in mock surprise. "Is that how you conduct business in your conclave, Ms. Henderson? I have to say, it's not very polite. I thought perhaps we should chat a bit about what's best for each of our territories and how we'll get to that point. You know, the kind of conversation we should've been having at our little summit before your president began flinging accusations."

"There was something being flung all right, and accusations were the least of it," Delilah replied. Her feet had remained firmly rooted to her spot on the floor, but Vance could tell it was taking all her resolve to keep them there. He couldn't blame her, considering he wanted nothing more than to tackle the man and take their child. They had to hold off for the most opportune time, and he hoped Delilah would remember that.

President Kelso shook his head. "You've got a bit of a temper. Let's hope we can cool that down. Please, have a seat." He gestured grandly at a battered sofa as though it were an antique Chesterfield.

The cushions sank underneath their weight, raising their knees toward their chests, and Vance narrowed his eyes at their opponent. Kelso was doing every tiny thing he could do make sure they were at a disadvantage, including keeping them from jumping up too quickly. Even more so than before, they'd have to make sure they waited for the right moment to act.

"All right," Delilah said, crossing her legs at the knees and looking as proper as a vice president could in such conditions. "I'm listening."

"You and your president, as I said, have made several accusations against me and my conclave." As was apparently his habit, Kelso paced as he talked.

The motion pleased Rose as she slept in his arms, but it still made Vance's skin crawl to see his child in that man's grip.

"While I can't say that we've always been perfect, I must point out that you don't understand the deeper work we have going on. You see a man who's knocking over convenience stores. I see a man who's testing the waters, finding out where the faults are in our current systems. Just how governed are shifters these days? Do we truly have control over them? Are they getting everything they need out of our current—and very loose, I might add—system of government? Are we spending so much time hiding our identities from humans that we're forgetting who we really are?"

Several lines appeared around the corners of Delilah's mouth as she pursed her lips. "And what is it you'd like to do to change that?"

"I'm glad you asked!" His dark eyes saw a vision that existed only in his mind as he swept his free hand through the air and laid it all out for them. "You see, the humans of this country are kept apart by many things. City limits and state borders, political parties, even their favorite football teams. But they're all Americans, and there is one person who is their leader, no matter who they're cheering for or who they voted for."

"The President of the United States," Delilah said, playing along.

"Exactly!" Kelso held one finger in the air. "It might not always be the man or woman they chose, but that person is the leader of the free world. The president is revered in an extraordinary way, and despite the limits of checks and balances, he has an incredible amount of power. I think it's about time we put that power in the hands of the shifters."

"Wait a second." Vance glanced at Delilah and then back at President Kelso. "Are you saying you want to run for president? As in, of the country?" It was ridiculous. Never had a shifter held that position in the history of the U.S., and for a very good reason. There were too many eyes watching such an important person, and the chances of their secret getting out would increase exponentially.

"Yes! And I can see the looks on your faces, but it's not such a crazy idea after all. Just imagine what a glorious world we'd live in. Shifters could be out in the world without any fears. We'd no longer have to worry about being hunted down or shipped off to government labs. We'd be open and free, and we'd rule this country with a type of power the humans can only imagine." He strode forward, pointing a long finger at Vance. "You, especially, should see the advantage here. What's a military run by puny people who concentrate so much on making weapons out of metal and gunpowder instead of having their own weapons built into their bodies? Think about a shifter as the Secretary of State or a Secretary of Defense, most likely a member of the SOS Force. It would be incredible."

"It would certainly be a different world for us," Vance conceded. His mind began filling in the blanks in this fantasy Vance was creating. Yes, there would be some benefits, but the risks still didn't outweigh them.

"That might happen someday," Delilah said smoothly, "but I think we've still got some work to do before we get close to that." Her brow creased as the baby stirred.

"We do," Kelso agreed. "And the first step is to create a force powerful enough within the shifter community to make it happen. Think about the people who currently run for president. They're either billionaires or they've already held a significant political office. Nobody's going to vote for a nobody, and as much as I hate to admit it, that's what I am right now to the general population." He was gaining momentum and talking faster, taking advantage of his captive audience. "The work starts right here, in joining the conclaves together. We make a shifter community that spans the whole state and expand outward from there."

"So, you become the president of all the shifters in the country, and from there, you can become the leader of every single citizen in the country." Delilah tapped her chin and tipped her head slightly to the side. "It's an interesting idea."

"I'm glad you think so, because it's happening." Kelso wasn't placated yet. "We're going to start with an official writ. You sign the Dallas conclave and all its territory over to me. If you're cooperative, I'm sure I can find a place for you on my cabinet."

"And from there?" she urged.

"From there, it's San Antonio and Houston, then Amarillo. The state will be easy to sweep if we all join forces. You can see now how it will all come together, can't you? Within a few years, we'll be the reigning demographic in the House and the Senate. But it has to start here, and it has to start now. What do you say?"

Delilah's mouth opened and then closed again.

Vance had yet to take his eyes off Rose. She was squirming in earnest now, awake and uncertain of her surroundings. The child had her routines, and she was always ready for a good meal and a diaper change when she woke up. Her fists thrashed through the air, and the blanket moved as she kicked her legs. It was only a matter of time before the ticking time bomb went off.

"Well?" Kelso pressed.

"I think it has a lot of possibilities," she finally acknowledged.

"Keep in mind that I have ways of making you agree." Kelso jiggled the baby, and his minions stepped closer. The man with the tattoos pulled a knife from his waistband and tossed it casually end-over-end in his hand.

Delilah shook her head. "That won't be necessary. But before we head into any further discussion about this, would you at least give me a chance to feed the baby? She's hungry." She nodded toward the infant.

Rose rolled her head from side to side, her mouth searching for some source of food.

President Kelso ignored both Delilah's plea and the baby's obvious need. "I don't think so. Why would I go to the trouble of bringing her here if I'm just going to hand her back to you? No, no. Vice President Henderson, I think you understand I'm not that foolish of a man."

Delilah swallowed. "What, exactly, do you propose?"

Kelso gave a toothy grin. "It's quite simple. Little Rose will live with me for a time to ensure your undying loyalty to your future president. Don't worry. I'll hire the best nanny to take care of her, and I'll be sure to dote on her myself. In due time, when I'm completely sure you won't try to go against me again, I'll consider giving her back."

Vance knew he'd told her to agree to anything Kelso wanted, but this was going too far. "You can't seriously expect anyone to support you as Alpha over all shifters once they know you're holding a child hostage. Give her back now, and we'll do everything we can to help you on your political pathway." He felt sweat threaten to break out on his forehead at even the thought of not getting his daughter back. Vance listened for footsteps in the rest of the house, wondering if any other shifters were present. Had Max and Jack made it yet?

"Please," Kelso chuckled. "I could get away with murder

once they realize one of their own is about to become such a VIP. Bears, tigers, cougars, lions, wolves, they'll all come together under one flag and under me. I'll raise their ire and determination, and sweet little Rose here will melt their hearts."

Rose was fussing now. Her little pudgy cheeks had turned bright red, and a brilliant blue vein stood out in the center of her wrinkled forehead. She let out a cough of agitation followed by a howling wail, tongue vibrating and everything.

"She really is hungry," Delilah insisted over the noise. "You can't just let her cry like that."

The tall man folded his arms yet more protectively around the babe. "What sort of mental bond do the three of you have?" he challenged. "Are you provoking her into doing this?"

Vance smiled. There was a bond, but it wasn't anything like the telepathic link that Kelso was implying. Neither was it likely that such a tiny kitten could do anything to a grown man. "I don't think you can handle a child like this," he shouted over Rose's healthy howls. "She's quite a lot of work."

Kelso's confidence was breaking down. Vance could see the panic on his face even as he snarled. "I think I can handle a goddamn baby!" he screamed.

Any other baby, perhaps, but Rose seemed to have ideas of her own. She turned her head from side to side, looking desperately for the food that wasn't coming. Instinctively, she twisted toward the nearest warm body.

A second scream joined Rose's, but this one came from Kelso. He thrust the baby away from his body, revealing a ring of brilliant red against the starch white of his shirt. "She bit me! The little shit bit me!" In one last gesture of disgust and horror, he let go.

Vance could see it coming even as it happened. He shot off the couch and across the room, his boots sliding on the warped floor as he darted toward his adversary. His body fought to remain human. He would've had better traction and speed as a cougar, but Vance knew he needed his human hands more than anything as the bundle of blankets went tumbling toward the floor. More screams ripped through the air, and it was possible that one of them might have even been his. He slid to his knees in the dust just as Rose plopped gracefully into his arms. Vance looked down at her just in time to see a set of razor-sharp fangs retreat into her innocent gums.

That split-second had taken an eternity of slow motion, but the room suddenly burst into action around him. Delilah soared over his head in her full cougar form, using her natural jumping talent to send Kelso flying back through the kitchen door. The man with the tattoos shot forward. His knife flashed in the air, but his head snapped back with a perfect round hole between his eyes.

Vance didn't have time to look for the shooter. The

scarred man was coming after him. He was big and bulky, not the kind who looked quick on his feet, but he'd mastered his shifting techniques. In the time it took him to leave his post by the door and get to Vance, he'd melted down into a jaguar. His spots were brilliant against the dilapidated interior of the old house. His triangular nose wrinkled as he dove for Vance with his mouth open, his eyes flashing.

Pulling his legs underneath him, Vance shoved upward with all the force he could muster while still holding onto Rose. The big cat tumbled backward and into the banister, knocking its head violently against the old hardwood. It let out a pitiful yowl as it stumbled back toward the door.

In perfect timing, Jack burst through that very door. Vance stood, holding out his precious parcel. "Take her! Delilah's got Kelso in the next room." He shoved Rose at his comrade, hating to let her go but also knowing he couldn't leave it to anyone else to help his mate.

Someone or something was upstairs, and the old floors rumbled and dropped dust with the efforts of the fray. Vance hoped the right person was winning as he shot into the kitchen, his heart in a panic. Delilah was angry and emotional, and he worried a man such as Kelso would get the better of her. She'd been too confident when she'd torn apart Edira, and she'd also been lucky in that the woman hadn't been carrying any weapons.

He charged into the kitchen, finding a typical cat-and-dog fight before him where a kitchen table had once been. Kelso had morphed into his wolf form, a massive canine with fur so dark it was nearly black. Sharp white teeth were revealed as he curled his lips back, and the hair all along his spine and tail stood on end. He spun in slow circles around Delilah, who was still full-on cat. Her ears were pinned to her skull as she hissed at her opponent, followed by a pitchy growl of irritation. Blood soaked the pale gold fur of her face and chest, but Vance quickly realized that it wasn't hers. The damage was just difficult to see on the dark coat of the wolf.

Her back legs hunched and she leaped. Delilah and the wolf became a tangle of fur and blood and noise as they fought. Kelso had the advantage for a moment, his mouth closing around her shoulder as he shook his head vigorously in an effort to break her neck. But the she-cat used the momentum to leap up onto his back. She sank her claws into his body to brace herself as her jaws snapped on the back of his neck. The giant wolf let out a sharp yip of pain that made even the noise on the second floor stop for a moment. He reeled, the weight of the cougar still heavy on his back as his paws sought purchase and slipped on the old floor, and then he collapsed.

Delilah sat back, panting. Blood dripped from the tip of her tongue onto the floor and soaked into the wood. A thundering sound rumbled down the stairs, and Jack and Max joined them in the kitchen. "There was a guy waiting on the second floor, but I finished him," Max explained. "Looks like you've got everything taken care of?"

Vance took Rose out of Jack's arms and held her to his chest, and Delilah joined them. Every parent said they would kill for their children, but the two of them actually had. Vance was ready for all of this to be over with, but he knew he'd do it again and again if need be. "Yeah," he said as fatigue took over him. "I reckon we do."

10
———

Delilah's legs pumped, slamming down into the ground. Her lungs burned with the effort as she made her way down the trail, the trees flying by. She felt the wind in her hair and smiled as the back of the ranch came into view. It was a beautiful place, one of peace and solitude when she needed it to be and yet full of love and family when that was what she desired instead.

She slowed, walking now instead of running to give her muscles time to recover. She's started her run on all fours, exercising that most primal part of herself that she'd so rarely given a chance to come out and play in her past. Her time had been too devoted to her work for shifters and blending in with society, but out there, she could truly be herself. The cattle still sometimes spooked when they saw her dart past, and Mr. O'Rourke might've caught a glimpse of her sleek form from the back of his tractor, but she made sure she never shifted back to two legs until she hit the property line and turned back for home.

A figure strode slowly along the fence line near the barn, dust kicking up from his boots. He held a little girl on his hip, one who was just beginning to get light brown curls the same color as her father's hair that could be pulled up into the tiniest topknot. She kicked her pink cowgirl boots in the air as she watched her father scoop sweet feed out of a barrel and dump it into feed bowls for the horses.

"Aren't you two adorable," Delilah said as she walked up. Seeing Vance was exciting on its own these days. Going through everything they had made it easier for her human and cougar sides to reconcile. Even living at the ranch together had become bearable by simple virtue of a deep mutual respect for each other. It was more than that, though. No matter how cranky her inner big cat got, she loved him. "I didn't keep you waiting too long, did I?"

He smiled and made no move to pass off the little girl. "Rose and I were just getting the evening chores done. She insisted that we come feed the horses."

"Uh huh. And I see she's dressed for it, too." Delilah took in the baby Levi's and pink shirt with a horse on it. "I don't remember seeing that outfit anywhere."

"Caroline dropped it off for her the other day. She thought she could wear it for a little while after her bath. I'll have to make sure I send Caroline a picture of her in it.

She's already asked me twice." He leaned forward, bringing Rose closer to the fence where Cedar poked a curious nose over the top rail. He was a gentle giant, and he nuzzled her leg with his velvety lips while Rose squealed with delight.

As had become their nightly ritual as long as one of them wasn't called out of town for work, Delilah and Vance worked side by side to finish the chores. "You know, this reminds me a bit of that night we met," she said with a smile.

"Don't talk to me like that when I'm holding a baby," he warned her with a half-smile. "I can call Caroline and have her over here in half an hour if you want me to rumble you through that hay again." He planted a kiss on her lips, which made Rose squeal all over again.

"Oh, is that funny?" Delilah asked her daughter, amazed all over again at just how adorable this tiny creature was. She planted another kiss on Vance's lips just to hear that baby laughter. "I'll have to remember that."

"Yes, you will." Vance grabbed her by the hip with his free hand and pulled her close, kissing her more passionately than the peck on the lips that had delighted the little girl. His eyes were full and soft when they parted, and she understood his meaning without asking.

They turned to go in the house, Delilah smiling as she opened the back door to the kitchen. She continued to smile as she began preparing dinner and Vance took Rose into the living room. Their laughter and playtime was the most beautiful music she could ever imagine, and she hoped it would always be this way.

After everything that'd happened with the Austin conclave, Delilah knew she could no longer deny the part of her that wanted to be with Vance. He must've been feeling the same way, because on that first evening that the three of them were reunited, he asked her once again to move in with him. Delilah wasn't sure she could ever come to think of the ranch as home. It wasn't her own place where she made all the rules and decisions. It was further from the office, and they didn't always share the same taste in décor.

Vance, however, had come through like the sensitive gentleman he always was when he wasn't in fighting mode. He'd sat down and gone through long discussions of how the two of them could make their lives work together, and his focus was always on making sure everyone was happy. The part that surprised her the most was that they each wanted the same things. She and Vance both wanted time together as a family as well as time alone. She'd let herself be convinced right at first that he wanted to take up every second of her day for himself, but that wasn't the case at all. With his cousin Caroline as a nanny, they were able to create a balance between romantic dates, family time together, and evenings where they could attend to their own agendas. Delilah sometimes wondered if other couples were so lucky.

The chicken was ready, and she headed for the living room. Delilah paused in the doorway, leaning against it to watch. Vance had placed Rose on the little cushioned mat they used for tummy time. He was laying on the floor right in front of her, propped up on his elbows and flipping the pages of a board book. "Look at the little piggy. You see it right there? It's a pink piggy. You've got piggies, too!" He reached down and tweaked one of Rose's toes.

The result was yet another resounding round of laughter and squeals as he rolled around on the floor with his daughter, all sweetness and sunshine.

"I hate to interrupt, but dinner's ready."

"You hear that, cowgirl? The chuckwagon just pulled up." Vance scooped Rose up from the floor and headed into the kitchen, setting her down in her highchair as he went to the sink to wash his hands. "Is there anything going on tomorrow night?"

"I don't think so." She'd spent a lot of time down there in the last couple of months, and it was far more time than she'd like to be out of town. She always felt like she was missing out on something if she went for a day without seeing Rose.

"Good. My buddy Gabe that I was telling you about is coming back through town. I thought I'd take him out for a few rounds and catch up."

Delilah nodded as she pureed small amounts of the chicken, green beans, and mashed potatoes she'd just made so Rose could join them in their dinner and put them all on a little plastic plate with a unicorn design. "That shouldn't be a problem."

"You sure?" Vance looked up at her as he sat down with his own plate. "I know that's not the kind of thing all women approve of."

Warmth and happiness flowed through Delilah's body. She never had any reason to tell him no, but he always gave her ample chance. "I'm sure you're right, but I'm not every woman, and you are most definitely not every man. It's good timing, anyway. You can get your night out before I leave." The thought sobered her good mood.

"You okay?"

"Sure. I'm just tired of running down there all the time." Almost the entirety of the Austin conclave had been killed or arrested, thanks to President Kelso's fanatical hopes of domination. It was a sad day for the shifter residents of that area, not because they mourned their elected Alpha so much as they mourned the fact that he'd ever gotten into office in the first place. Delilah and the other members of the Dallas conclave had been working diligently to help their counterparts to the south. "The more work we do down there, the more corruption we find, even going back to the most recent election itself. I have to wonder just how far Kelso's madness reached."

Vance reached across the table and touched her hand. It was the lightest caress, not too much to make her feel suffocated or overwhelmed, but just enough to let her know he was there for her, no matter what. "You're doing a good thing," he reassured her. "Rose is going to grow up knowing that her mother stood up for what was right, and that she wouldn't tolerate anything less. The shifter citizens of Austin will be grateful to you, too."

"I hope you're right. It's been a bit of a mess down there. Mostly, we're just trying to make sure everyone is taken care of. We'd suggested a registry to them quite some time ago, back when one was started here, but of course they didn't bother. They, like most conclaves, have nothing set up for medical care. I'm starting to realize that Kelso didn't let us extradite Paul Grimes not because he was trying to protect him, but because he didn't really even know what was going on with the man."

"Don't take the burden too heavily on yourself. You're doing a good job."

A knock sounded on the door, startling them both. Usually, their excellent hearing told them as soon as a vehicle turned in the long driveway, but they'd been lost in their conversation.

"I'll get it." Vance went to the door, and a moment later, he returned with President Whiteside, and Delilah jumped to her feet.

"Sit down, my dear. I didn't mean to interrupt your supper." He waved Delilah back into her seat before bending down and touching his fingertip to Rose's nose.

"And I've got a present for you when you're done eating, my little sweet."

Rose responded with a potato-covered grin.

"Has she shown any other signs of shifting yet?"

It'd been quite the talk of the community once word got out that Rose's freshly shifted teeth had played an essential part in defeating President Kelso. "Not yet," Vance answered. "We think she was just so upset that she couldn't help it at the time. I'm sure we'll see more from her soon."

Delilah was always happy to see the man. They'd worked together for a long time, and she was already close to him even before everything went crazy. The laceration and surrounding bruise on his forehead was reduced to a thin white line to remind them of that horrible night. Still, it was unusual for him to stop by without calling first. "What brings you here, sir? I think I've got everything prepped for tomorrow morning's meeting."

Harris Whiteside sat down in the remaining chair and leaned forward with his elbows on the table. He looked tired, and his casual clothing made him look much older than usual. The lines in his face seemed a little deeper in the kitchen lighting. "Yes, I still plan to have a meeting in the morning. That's when everything will be official, but I wanted to tell you first. I won't be running for president again in the next election."

Though she wasn't completely surprised, Delilah's heart broke a bit for him. "You've been such a good leader, though. It would be a shame to lose you now that we've got so many things going for our territory."

"Exactly. Best to quit when I'm ahead." He waved off her next attempt at protesting. "I'm going soft, Delilah. I should've taken a harder stance with Kelso and his cohorts. It might've saved lives, and it certainly might've saved the two of you a lot of heartache. I was overthinking things instead of going with my gut. That's a sure sign that I'm ready for a rocking chair in a cabin instead of a leather chair in an office."

"I understand." It would be tough to see him go. He'd served more terms than anyone else in Dallas, and he deserved every election he won. "It's the end of an era."

"Yes," he said with a nod and a twinkle in his eye, "but it's also the beginning of a new one. It's up to the voters, ultimately, but I know who'd I'd like to nominate."

"Who?" Delilah asked eagerly. Several names ran through her mind.

Whiteside and Vance exchanged a knowing look over the table. "You, my dear," the president said with a laugh.

Her body was suddenly so heavy, she didn't know if she'd ever be able to get out of her chair again. "Me?"

"Who else?" Whiteside looked at her warmly as he put a hand on her shoulder. "Delilah, you stood up the way a leader needs to, and you defeated a very evil man. Then you came back and ran the conclave like you'd been doing it all your life while I recovered. Anyone else might've demanded a vacation after that, but not you. You're still working on both the local problems and those in Austin. I've heard nothing but good things about you, and trust me, I've heard plenty."

She flushed at the notion. Moving up to such a prestigious position was what she'd always dreamed of. Delilah didn't want it for the same reasons that Kelso did. She had no interest in power or control for their own sake, but for the purpose of helping all the shifters who needed it. To her, it was about service more than leadership. Even though she was already as close as she could possibly be in her current position as vice president, the leap seemed like a big one. "That's very flattering, but I don't know if I can do it."

"Yes, you can," Whiteside countered. "You practically do the job anyway, and I don't think you'll have any problem getting votes. You can be sure I'll do everything I can for your campaign."

They discussed the matter a little longer before Whiteside headed home. Rose had her bath and went off to bed, and Delilah and Vance were left alone for the rest of the evening.

"You're going to wear a hole in the floor if you keep pacing like that." Vance caught her by the waist and held her close.

"I can't help it," she sighed. "This whole idea of becoming president makes me nervous."

He pulled back enough to look into her eyes. "It's an excited kind of nervous, though, isn't it?"

Delilah smiled up at him. "You're not supposed to be able to read my mind unless we've shifted."

Vance lifted one shoulder. "Who needs rules? I never really followed them anyway. Besides, it doesn't take a mind reader. I just know you. This is what you want, and it's certainly what you deserve. But you're unsure about taking on a bigger role that might keep you away from Rose. It all sounds too good to be true, so you're afraid it isn't. But darlin', I think Whiteside is absolutely right. You're perfect for the job. You don't have to worry about anything here, because I'll take care of it. That's the thing, Delilah. You can have your peace and solitude when you need it, but you're never really alone." He took her hand in his and brought it to his mouth, kissing the back of it gently.

A thrill shot through her body even at such a small gesture. "And I don't think I want to be alone right now, either."

"You don't have to ask me twice." Vance gathered her in his arms, holding her easily as though she weighed nothing. He kissed her soundly on the lips, reminding her of just how much she meant to him. "Would you care to join me in my room, future Madame President?"

Delilah laughed as she put her arms around his neck. "I don't think I could refuse. I love you, you know."

"I know." He kissed her again, his tongue tracing along the lines of hers. "I love you, too."

He ascended the stairs quickly with her in his arms, his hands already roving over her body. By the time he snuck past the nursery and nudged the bedroom door open, she could feel his hardness throbbing against her hip through his jeans. Vance laid her on the bed as he continued his caresses, eagerly sweeping his palms over her body. "I love you for so many reasons," he moaned into her ear between kisses along her neck and jawline. "I love how smart you are, how stubborn you are, and what a good mother you are, but this body of yours... when I'm inside you, I just can't get enough."

The lamp in the corner had been left on, illuminating the hardwood paneling and the custom-made king-size bed. Delilah was spending more nights in there than in the room Vance had set up for her lately, and she knew for certain this would be another one. "You keep talking to me like that and I'll never leave."

"Good." Vance had moved down, and he pressed his lips against her navel as he stripped off her running pants and left a line of kisses down each leg before trailing his lips back up to capture her in his mouth. "That's exactly what I want. You. In any way. In every way. I just want *you*."

Delilah gasped, her body involuntarily writhing on the bed as he pleasured her. They were the only two people in the world at that moment, and every touch was like liquid warmth through her body. She wrapped her leg around his torso, closing her eyes against the dim light to concentrate on the way his tongue felt against her warm flesh. There were no other men like Vance. Delilah could draw so much comfort from the brush of his hand against her shoulder or the touch of his bare leg against hers in bed, yet it only took a look or a word to change the energy he injected into her. Delilah felt it now in the shivers and contractions he sent rippling through her, making her come to life in a way that was completely separate from her job in the conclave or as a leader.

Vance stood, the glow from the lamp illuminating his muscled body as he unbuttoned his shirt. Delilah put her hands behind her head and pulled at her lower lip, happy to watch the show as the light limned every hard line. She'd come to admire the strength in him, both physically and emotionally. "How long are you going to keep teasing me like this?" She hooked her heel around his leg and pulled.

He dropped to the bed, but he kept himself up on his arms, taunting her with the length of his body so close above her, yet not touching. "As long as I can," he replied as he stroked a finger from her jawline down her neck, across her shoulder, then down to skim the roundness of her breast and the inverse curve just before her waist, leaving a shiver of pleasure in his wake. "Never mind. I'm just teasing myself now." Vance plunged inside her, filling her, bringing with him the part of her that had been missing for so long.

Delilah let herself fall completely into the rhythm of their bodies, feeling the way her blood thrummed in her veins and inhaling the scent of soap and hay from his skin. He held her in his arms as he moved against her, but she knew now that he didn't hold her because he wanted to hold her back. He held her to love her, to support her, to lift her up to all that she could be.

Her breaths turned to gasps and then to cries of pleasure as he moved, the world tipping sideways and upside down as Delilah lost all sense of time and space in favor of the universe that expanded inside her body. She clung to him, her muscles tensing as she demanded more, his body giving and giving until she felt the tremble of their rapture synchronize and pull them that much closer together.

Falling back into the right dimension and her own body, Delilah reeled for a moment as Vance laid down beside her. He arranged the covers over them, always concerned she'd get cold, and wrapped his arm around her waist. "You all right?"

"Yes. God, yes." She still felt as though she couldn't catch her breath. He was good at doing that to her. "I think that was just what I needed, too."

"You're still worried about this whole presidency thing." It was a statement, not a question. He knew her now, and there was no point in trying to deny that.

"I'm sorry. It's hard not to think about." Her tryst with her mate had been a welcome respite from all the cares in the world, and many of them rested so squarely and heavily on her shoulders on a regular basis. She couldn't keep the world out forever, but it felt so good to have Vance at her back both literally and figuratively.

He nuzzled against her neck, his stubble scratching and tickling her until she melted into a fit of giggles. "You're still going to do it, aren't you?" he asked.

She moved her hand down to cover his where it rested on her stomach, their fingers intertwining. It'd been nothing short of flattering to hear President Whiteside recommend her for the job. She imagined the other current members would support the idea, and it was the chance of a lifetime. Delilah already had so much that she wanted and needed out of life. Her understanding and loving mate was at her side, and the sweet child they shared was the most wonderful thing in the world. Helping her fellow shifters and leading them into a new age of modern life was irresistible. Delilah tightened her grip on Vance. "Yeah. I am."

"Good." He dropped a kiss on her shoulder. "Now that I have the easy question out of the way, I have a harder one for you."

She smiled, thinking he was being facetious and was ready for another tumble. "Yeah?"

"Will you stay here with me? Not just tonight, but forever." Another kiss was a warm press on her skin.

They'd already acknowledged their love for each other. They knew they were meant to be together, and there was no way they could live apart. But she knew what he meant. He didn't want her down the hall in her own bedroom anymore. Vance wanted her there, at his side, in his bed.

Delilah turned, burrowing into his embrace. "Absolutely."

THE END

GABE

Gabe Vinson scanned the dusty parking lot just before he stepped into the bar. It was a force of habit that he doubted he'd ever be able to drop. His time with the Delta Force had kept him constantly vigilant. Sure, there didn't seem to be any threat from this place. Vance wouldn't have invited him there if that were the case. Gabe smiled, thinking of some of the times they'd shared before Gabe had moved on to Delta and reconsidered. *Or maybe he would have...*

He found his old friend at the bar and slid onto the stool next to him. He glanced at the chalkboard menu on the wall and the clean tables scattered around the place. "This isn't quite like the shit holes we used to frequent."

Vance laughed and took a sip of his beer. "Yeah, it's a little cleaner than those. And hey, you won't get any sand in your whiskey here." He gestured at the barkeeper to pour Gabe a drink. "How are you holding up?"

"Well enough," Gabe said with a sigh, scratching his fingers through the short beard he'd grown out ever since his medical discharge. "You know how it is. You think when you get out that everything will have stayed the same, but it's all different. All the girls you used to date have gotten married and had kids. Some of them even married your buddies, so they're not interested in going out, either. Your family wants you to come visit, but they don't know how to talk to you anymore. And even though they say they want to hear what you've been up to, you can only tell them so much." He nodded at the bartender for the shot of whiskey and took a sip, enjoying the burn.

"I'm sure it's even worse for you. The Delta Force doesn't fuck around with that sort of stuff," Vance agreed. "I'm mighty glad you made your way back around through Dallas, though. There's something I wanted to talk to you about. You said you were trying to figure out what to do with yourself now that you're out."

"Right." Gabe knew that Vance was a member of the Special Ops Shifter Force, a group of veteran soldiers with special skills on top of their ability to shift. It was supposed to be a secret, and it still was when it came to the human population, but the more work the Force did, the more word spread about them throughout the shifter community. Right now, they'd essentially achieved rumor status. It sounded like just the kind of work Gabe would enjoy, but it wasn't as though the Force just stuck a 'Now Hiring' sign in the window when they had a vacant spot.

Vance looked casually over his shoulder. The bar was loud, and no one had been rude enough to sit down right next to them. "Well, have you decided where you want to live?"

Gabe let out a snort of laughter. "One place is about as good as another to me as long as it's stateside. I came from a military family, so I've never been in one spot for very long."

"How do you feel about Los Angeles?"

"L.A.?" The grizzly tossed back the rest of his drink and let is swirl on his tongue as he thought about it. "I guess that would be all right. Just like any other city, right?"

The cowboy tipped his head from one side to the other. "Sort of. It's got a hell of a lot of people in it, and a decent percentage of them just happen to be shifters. There are more of them than the local conclave has been able to keep track of, actually, and it's come to light recently that some of them are forming gangs. It could be incredibly dangerous for shifters as a whole if this is allowed to get out of hand."

"What exactly do you want me to do about it?" Gabe had spent his entire military career trying to hide his true identity from anyone who was pure human, and the other soldier shifters he managed to find were few and far between. The idea of connecting with so many more people like himself was an intriguing one.

"Not just you, but a group. See, the SOS Force was started in Washington, D.C. by Dr. Drake Sheridan, a Special Forces Medical Sergeant. As the need for the Force expanded across the country, the Dallas unit was formed. After you came to see me on the ranch, I talked a bit with the guys in Dallas and with Drake himself. It seems that we may need to start up yet another unit, this time in L.A. We'll have to find all the right people to staff it, all shifters, all former Special Ops." Vance pointed at him with the mouth of his beer bottle, his eyes steady. "I've recommended you."

Gabe lifted his empty glass to get the bartender's attention. He watched the liquid swirl in the glass for a long minute as he thought. Gabe was the type of man who liked to take action. Not only did he not mind being busy, he lived for it. There was nothing worse than sitting around idly, and even in the Delta Force, he'd had his share of that. This could be one hell of an opportunity, and he didn't think he could dare pass it up. "You've got yourself a recruit, Vance."

"Hell, yeah!" Vance rang his beer against Gabe's glass. "We'll be working on a list of other potential members, and we'll get you set up with a headquarters building out there in L.A. Garrison, part of the D.C. unit, is great with construction, so you'll have everything you need."

Gabe smiled. When that mortar had blown him up and left his ribs peppered with shrapnel, he thought he'd lost everything. His job and the missions he'd worked so hard on for the U.S. Army had all gone down the drain and left him with no direction and no future.

But he was about to have it all back and more.

———

If you enjoyed this preview of *Secret Baby for the Soldier Bear*, book 1 in the Special Ops Shifters: L.A. Force series, the paperback is now available for sale on Amazon.

ALSO BY MEG RIPLEY
ALL AVAILABLE ON AMAZON

Shifter Nation Universe

Special Ops Shifters: L.A. Force Series

Book 1: Secret Baby For The Soldier Bear

Book 2: Saved By The Soldier Dragon

Book 3: Bonded To The Soldier Wolf

Book 4: Forbidden Mate For The Soldier Bear

Special Ops Shifters: Dallas Force Series

Book 1: Rescued By The Soldier Bear

Book 2: Protected By The Soldier Tiger

Book 3: Fated To The Soldier Fox

Book 4: Baby For The Soldier Cougar

Special Ops Shifters Series (original D.C. Force)

Book 1: Daddy Soldier Bear

Book 2: Fake Mate For The Soldier Lion

Book 3: Captured By The Soldier Wolf

Book 4: Christmas With The Soldier Dragon

Werebears of Acadia Series

Werebears of the Everglades Series

Werebears of Glacier Bay Series

Werebears of Big Bend Series

Dragons of Charok Universe

Daddy Dragon Guardians Series

Shifters Between Worlds Series

More Shifter Romances

Beverly Hills Dragons Series

Dragons of Sin City Series

Dragons of the Darkblood Secret Society Series

Packs of the Pacific Northwest Series

Forever Fated Mates Anthology

Shifter Daddies Anthology

Early Short Stories

Mated By The Dragon Boss

Claimed By The Werebears of Green Tree

Bearer of Secrets

Rogue Wolf

ABOUT THE AUTHOR

Meg Ripley is an author of steamy shifter romances. A Seattle native, Meg can often be found curled up in a local coffee house with her laptop.

Download Meg's entire *Caught Between Dragons* series when you sign up for her newsletter!

Sign up by visiting www.redlilypublishing.com or Meg's Facebook page:
https://www.facebook.com/authormegripley/

Printed by Amazon Italia Logistica S.r.l.
Torrazza Piemonte (TO), Italy

16363470R00394